Milly Johnson was born, raised and still lives in Barnsley, South Yorkshire. A *Sunday Times* bestseller, she is one of the Top 10 Female Fiction authors in the UK, and with millions of copies of her books sold across the world, Milly's star continues to rise. Milly was chosen as one of the authors for The Reading Agency's Quick Reads 2020 campaign. *My One True North* is her seventeenth novel.

Milly writes from the heart about what and where she knows and highlights the importance of community spirit. Her books champion women, their strength and resilience, and celebrate love, friendship and the possibility of second chances. She is an exceptional writer who puts her heart and soul into every book she writes and every character she creates.

Milly Johnson

My One True North

**SIMON &
SCHUSTER**

London · New York · Sydney · Toronto · New Delhi

A CBS COMPANY

First published in Great Britain by Simon & Schuster UK Ltd, 2020
A CBS COMPANY

Copyright © Millytheink Limited, 2020

The right of Milly Johnson to be identified as author
of this work has been asserted in accordance with the
Copyright, Designs and Patents Act, 1988.

1 3 5 7 9 10 8 6 4 2

Simon & Schuster UK Ltd
1st Floor
222 Gray's Inn Road
London WC1X 8HB

Simon & Schuster Australia, Sydney
Simon & Schuster India, New Delhi

www.simonandschuster.co.uk
www.simonandschuster.com.au
www.simonandschuster.co.in

A CIP catalogue record for this book
is available from the British Library

Hardback ISBN: 978-1-4711-7849-8
Trade Paperback ISBN: 978-1-4711-7850-4
eBook ISBN: 978-1-4711-7851-1
Audio ISBN: 978-1-4711-7881-8

Excerpt from 'Funeral Blues' by W.H. Auden, first published
in *The Year's Poetry* by The Bodley Head, 1938

The author and publishers have made all reasonable efforts to contact
copyright-holders for permission, and apologise for any omissions or errors in
the form of credits given. Corrections may be made to future printings.

This book is a work of fiction. Names, characters, places
and incidents are either a product of the author's imagination or are
used fictitiously. Any resemblance to actual people living or
dead, events or locales is entirely coincidental.

Typeset in the UK by M Rules
Printed and bound in Great Britain by CPI Group (UK) Ltd, Croydon, CR0 4YY

MIX
Paper from
responsible sources
FSC
www.fsc.org   FSC® C020471

For my dad.
For carrying a massive typewriter halfway through Leeds and all the way to Barnsley on the bus just because they were giving it away. He wanted his teenage daughter, who loved writing, to have it so she could start on her new bestseller. One of my most precious memories. Rest in peace, you darling, beloved, wonderful man. It's an honour to be your daughter.

Terence Hubbard 10.10.1933 − 6.12.2019

He was my north, my south, my east, my west

W.H. AUDEN

PROLOGUE

February

This, thought Pete Moore, was what most people presumed being a firefighter consisted of day in, day out. The high-octane thrill of hurtling towards a disaster to save lives, breathing apparatus and high-vis jacket at the ready, adrenaline thundering through one's veins, heart quickening more with every turn of the fire engine's wheels. They were wrong. But it was what they were trained for in case it was day in, day out. Tonight, it was the full fantasy adventure shebang: ambulances, paramedics, police deployed, both fire engines from their station plus two from the next nearest, sirens, blue lights. It was a bad one, Andy the gaffer warned them as the information fed through to the onboard computer. A ten-vehicle pile-up on a notorious blackspot stretch of a dual carriageway south of town. It was dark, it was February, black ice, sleet, cold, roadworks: all the ingredients present for a perfect recipe crash. Someone who set off for work that morning with a cheery 'See you later' would not be going home ever again. Pete used to chew on the emotional details of bad incidents, but somewhere along the line, he stopped. He didn't set out to mentally detach himself, it just happened. He did his job to the best of his ability and he was good at it: strong, fearless, insightful, tenacious; but he left it at the door with his boots.

He shouldn't have even been there that night. He was covering a couple of hours for Rav whose dad had had a fall. He should have been at home, shoes kicked off, fire on, dinner in the oven – whoever was first in made the evening meal was the unwritten rule, although he was a much better cook than his wife was and so he tended to do more than his fair share of that particular duty. He should have been looking out of the window at the sleet, grateful to be dry and indoors and intrigued about what the night would hold for him as he twisted the top off a bottle of red and poured out two glasses to let them breathe and air.

Looking back, he wasn't sure what would have been worse: waiting in the cosy warmth of the kitchen, getting slightly annoyed that the top of his shepherd's pie was over-brown, the peaks blackening, wondering where Tara was after she'd rung and asked him to go straight home after his shift because she had something she wanted to tell him; looking at the clock, getting anxious. Or being there in the thick of it all: the smoke, the bitter hard rain turning into snow, the lights, the noise, the chaos. Being part of the scene, seeing it all first hand. Registering the red car in the middle of all that crushed, mangled dark metal, like the one coloured frame in an otherwise black and white movie. Krish Khatri madly wrenching glass away, Sal crunching determinedly with the cutters, the paramedic pushing in through the driver's side window at a weird, uncomfortable angle in order to get to the driver.

Pete remembered screaming, *'Jesus Christ, it's Tara.'* He remembered big Andy Burlap's arms closing around him. He remembered holding his wife's tiny, beloved hand, chill to the touch, desperately trying to rub warmth into it, a warmth it could not sustain because Tara, who had set off for work that morning with a cheery, 'See you later', would not be going home ever again.

SOUTH

I quote my practised answer
My face a perfect mask
I'm doing good, I'm fine
How very kind of you to ask
I stumble and exist
And I pretend that things aren't hard
While my compass spins and spits
Behind a stoical façade
My life is plunging south
Yet I smile, make you believe
That I'm waving, and not drowning
In this lake of acid grief

LIFE GONE SOUTH
LINDA FLOWERS

Chapter 1

Late August

For a couple of hours every Wednesday evening, this lovely room was Molly Jones-Hoyland's kingdom. She'd originally planned to hold her Molly's Club sessions in her home, but then her friend Leni had suggested she use her teashop. After all, there was plenty of parking nearby, comfortable seating inside, and more than enough tea and cake to accompany the sympathy. Plus it had the atmosphere, for the teashop had a welcoming, soothing ambience perfectly suited to people who were feeling disorientated, adrift. Indeed, the little 'Teashop on the Corner' had drawn Molly in like a magnet years ago and she had found not only friendship there but a true purpose. Opening the door to it had heralded the opening of a door into another life, a bigger life than the one she had been living up to that point. There was magic within its walls, she was convinced of it. The teashop might have been a newly built property put up on the site of a demolished wire factory but she had long suspected that beneath it, ancient and benign ley lines ran, because there had to be some explanation why anyone who stepped inside felt instantly calmed, relaxed, at home.

Molly was in her mid-seventies but she still had a lot of energy for her pet project: to help people through grief, to see them through their loss, their anger, their bewilderment, help them to reach acceptance just by bringing them into a safe arena where they could talk, and share their experiences. She had no formal qualification in grief counselling, though she'd known much sadness and loss in her own life, but she had personally gained so much from friendship and, above all, kindness that she felt duty bound to pay it forward. It had healed her and given her hope when she had felt none, when on her horizon were only clouds and not a peep of sunshine. It had made her see herself – and made others see her – as a strong woman behind her gentle façade. Molly emanated a tranquillity that people responded to and they opened up like flowers to her, spread their leaves as if she were a welcome of warm rain.

There were never more than six 'guests', as she referred to them, in her sessions; she'd found that a small group worked best, five being the optimum number for some strange reason. If Molly could help people to locate the pin-prick of light in their black pit of despair, she knew she could show them that the sun still rose in the east and she could guide them towards the dawn of a new happier existence. Every life gone south could be fixed, every compass could be recalibrated to point upwards to a north of hope.

The teashop really was a special place. Here, Molly and her circle of friends – some young, some old and all ages in between – had had many a discussion over literary works, inspired by all the wonderful book-related goods that filled the cabinets around the room. She had learned as much as taught and it had given her jaded heart a new lease of life. One of her new-found friends was a retired surgeon, a widowed Sikh gentleman who had become as close to Molly as it was possible to be without overstepping the boundary into something closer still. Friendship was enough for both of them. In Molly's Wednesday night 'Molly's Club' sessions, Pavitar Singh acted as barista. He donated his time and services for the price of refreshment and considered himself more than reimbursed.

'I'm expecting new faces tonight, Pavitar. A Miss Laurie De Vere and a Mr Peter Moore,' Molly called to him. Their names had reflected them well, Molly thought when they had spoken on the phone. Laurie, gentle and cultured: Pete, solid and no nonsense. She was looking forward to helping them; they were so young to be going through what they were.

'Good, good,' said Pavitar, checking his watch. He knew as well as Molly that the new people were often late. They had to build up their confidence to walk through the door, but they usually did so eventually, give or take a couple of false starts. Ringing up Molly and asking if it was possible to join the group was the biggest hurdle.

Two places had come up recently: Maureen wasn't coming any more. She felt able to cope now and she didn't want to take up a space that someone else might need. Reginald, who had been coming for nine months, had cried and said he hadn't thought it would have been possible to feel as if he could carry on, but he could now and had taken flight into a new life – a different life – without his beloved wife. The light had come back to his horizon. He'd donated a hundred pounds for tea and cake for those who came after. That left Maurice, who had lived with and cared for his mother since he was a child, Yvonne, recently widowed and Sharon who had lost the dog she doted on: some people grieved as much, if not more, for animals they had loved and Molly saw nothing wrong in that. Pete and Laurie would join them: a young man who had tragically lost his wife in a car accident and a young woman who had lost her fiancé in similar circumstances.

The clock on the wall chimed seven and right on cue in walked Yvonne and Maurice together. Yvonne was surprisingly chipper considering she had only buried her husband two months ago. But then Molly knew that the outside didn't always match the inner.

'Hellooo,' said Yvonne, in a chirpy voice. 'I hope there's plenty of cake.'

'Plenty as always,' said Mr Singh, rubbing his hands together. 'What can I get for you, Yvonne?'

'Chocolate, always chocolate if available,' she replied.

'And tea for two?' Maurice turned to confirm that with Yvonne. Despite them both being in their fifties, Maurice had taken Yvonne firmly under his wing. It hadn't escaped Molly or Mr Singh how much his mood had brightened since Yvonne had joined them.

The doorbell tinkled again and in walked Sharon. She was a small, round woman in her early forties who wore her grief like a coat that weighed heavily on her shoulders.

'Hello Sharon, love,' said Molly. 'How are you doing?'

'Bit rough this week, Molly,' replied Sharon, her voice crumbling with emotion. 'Billy would have been eight.'

'Date anniversaries can be tough. You come and join the queue for cake,' said Maurice, beckoning her over.

'My husband would never let me eat cake,' said Yvonne. 'He said I'd get fat. If only he could see me now,' she added, as Mr Singh handed her a wedge of chocolate cake on a china plate. A fat Yvonne was difficult to imagine, everyone thought together. She was built like a bird which had fallen out of its nest before its feathers had had a chance to sprout. Her fragile bones would never have supported fat.

'My mother loved cake,' said Maurice. 'She'd have eaten a whole one at a sitting if I'd let her. "Sundays and birthdays, Mother," I used to tell her. Towards the end, the rules went out of the window though. She had coffee and walnut for breakfast on quite a few occasions.'

Molly checked the time again just as the café door opened a fraction and a sliver of nervous person appeared: a tall, slim woman with a long white-blonde plait resting on her shoulder and a sweet, heart-shaped face.

'Come in,' said Molly. 'Is it Laurie?' She darted over, hand extended to draw the young woman in. Laurie stepped into the shop now that she had been seen and couldn't exactly backtrack. She'd been sitting in her car for over ten minutes, building up to joining them. She never felt the slightest bit discomfited mixing with people, but this was different. Here she was expected to let people in, past the armour-plating that had been welding itself around her for six months, exposing her soft, vulnerable underbelly.

'Yes,' said Laurie, coughing away a croak.

'You must have cake, it's obligatory,' said Molly. She smiled and Laurie responded with a smile of her own.

'Okay, if I must, then I will. Thank you.'

'Well as soon as you're served, we'll make a start,' said Molly. It didn't look as if Peter Moore was going to make an appearance. Maybe next week, she thought with hope.

Outside the café, Pete told himself not to be so bloody stupid and just open the door. It felt like the equivalent of jumping into a swimming pool; the water was always lovely once you were in but taking that initial dive was sometimes hampered by a ridiculous negative anticipation. He ran into burning buildings for a living and yet he was standing outside a café geeing himself up to walk in and have a sodding cup of tea with a pensioner. He counted down from three, depressed the handle, pushed slightly and the cheery bell above his head announced his arrival in a way that said he couldn't possibly turn and head back to the car. His foot was already over the threshold when his eyes took in the company he was to keep for the next hour or so and his brain sighed. How the hell could this motley crew all sitting around eating cake and drinking tea even hope to help him to fit into the world again?

The *Daily Trumpet* was in court this week to witness Jason 'Juice' Hughes appearing before magistrates after pelting the mayor and lady mayoress with vegan sausage rolls on the steps of the town hall in protest at Brexit and Climate Change. Mr Juice asked it to be taken into consideration that he had not wanted to cause undue offence by lobbing meat-based products at the couple as he respected the mayor and mayoress were virgins.

Chapter 2

August, two weeks earlier

Laurie De Vere pulled up in her usual parking space at *Daily Trumpet* HQ. It said a lot that a visiting solicitor had her own allocated spot. Coming here was the highlight of the week for her. Much as she loved the daily grind as a general solicitor at Butler and Jubb Legal Associates, the job she did at the *Daily Trumpet* was more like playtime and the people who worked there like a dysfunctional family that both infuriated her and amused her in equal measures. Laurie had never had the desire to specialise in a particular branch of law; she considered herself a GP of the legal world. One minute she was sorting out Mrs X's divorce, the next helping Mr Y take Company Z to court for constructive dismissal, but if she was ever going to throw all her eggs in one judicial basket, she would have picked defamation, libel and slander, which sounded like a firm of solicitors in itself – and which was a subdivision of litigation developing at the rate of a Triffid in a growbag. Thanks to all the errors that appeared in the *Daily Trumpet,* people were always trying to sue it, hoping for a multi-million pound settlement but, maybe not surprisingly, settling instead for an afternoon tea for two or a pie and pea supper at a local hostelry. At the moment Laurie needed the jolly bunch of field reporters and office staff as much as they needed her. Her duty to the newspaper fuelled a joie de vivre that she always felt guilty for experiencing, as if she were benefitting from someone else's despair. And the editor of the *Daily Trumpet,* Alan Robertson, really did despair.

The hot summer sun was shining in the cloudless sky and yet it couldn't warm the chill Laurie felt in her heart which had been there for six solid months, like an emotional permafrost that stubbornly refused to melt. It had been frozen, dark February when Laurie's world had tipped on its axis and yet for weeks afterwards she had felt a spotlight as intense as this August sun above trained on her with unrelenting brightness, marking her as a creature to be skirted around, dashed away from because she represented an awkward encounter. However adept people thought they were with words, all of them dried up when they had, in their midst, someone recently bereaved. People had even avoided her rather than deliver a platitudinal, 'Sorry for your loss', or 'Sorry to hear your bad news'. Others flapped around in a pool of clichés hoping to net something that would give comfort, but there was none to be found. Even Alan Robertson, who usually had more wise words than a monastery full of Dalai Lamas – albeit mostly invective that he attributed to his great gran – hadn't even attempted to say anything profound to her at Alex's funeral. He had put his arms around her and that hug said more than anything words could have conveyed, especially as he wasn't at all an emotionally demonstrative man. She had taken much strength from the gesture; it had helped her get through a day that was saturated with sadness and one that she thought she might never properly recover from.

Laurie zapped her car shut and headed towards the front door underneath the letters that spelled 'DAILY RUMPET', because the T had long since dropped off as if falling in with the character of the place. Its frontage was crumbly and quaint, belying the chaos that went on within its walls. A chaos that had become incredibly profitable over the last few years, it had to be said.

The *Daily Trumpet* had started off as a barely breaking-even periodical pushed to the edge of bankruptcy by incompetence. Glaring editorial errors brought more complaints than the leanly manned postroom could manage. Either the reporters or printing presses must be possessed, deduced the executive management board – it turned out to be both. Then something very odd happened. The figures started to improve, as low troughs in the sales statistics began to invert to high spikes. The owner of the paper (the *Trumpet* being one of only a few privately owned newspapers in Britain) commissioned market research which revealed that people were buying the *Trumpet* for its hilarious blunders and ensuing apologies more than they were for the news. The money that it was forced to pay out in compensation became less than the gain in revenue. In short – it made good business sense for the *Daily Trumpet* to print crap.

That was not to say that the top brass was happy with this. Sir Basil Stamper, the owner, was initially mortified that his pride and joy had become a laughing-stock. Money was second to prestige in his world so out went all the inept equipment and personnel and he set on a proficient editor – Alan Robertson – who shared Sir Basil's vision to restore the newspaper to its glory days.

This caused the sales to dip again.

People complained that the *Trumpet* had become stale, uninteresting, unentertaining. Sir Basil realised that he had to sacrifice his integrity on the altar of cash because pride was one thing but he very much enjoyed living a privileged lifestyle and driving an Aston Martin. He tried to swallow it by forcing himself to accept that the *Trumpet* had acquired a singular reputation and he owed it to the public to pursue a new legacy. Alan Robertson was sent for 'retraining', at least that was the official line. He was actually given a month off to let the idiot deputy editor bring the paper down to its optimum shocking level. Alan was told to either permanently shove off or manage the beast without blunting its claws and teeth. He had rejoined the team hoping to limit some damage if nothing else, but he despaired continually of what he had been reduced to – the man had standards, after all. It was the journalistic equivalent of a virtuoso pianist being forced to tinkle the ivories on a priceless Steinway in the style of Les Dawson.

The façade of the *Daily 'Rumpet'* offices indicated it was no bigger than a large double-fronted shop, but it was labyrinthine inside. Once upon a time it had stood on its own at the edge of town, but a sprawling angular industrial estate had grown around it like the architectural version of Japanese knotweed. It remained the last bastion of ancient building among the new boys.

The sensor on the heavy front door registered Laurie's presence; it groaned open and she walked into the cool pool of the ground-floor reception. There was a small waiting area to the right and to the left was a long counter. An old lady with a dowager's hump was standing there dictating a classified ad to Mo, a woman who had been in charge of reception since God's dog was a pup and who, to extend the canine imagery, made Cerberus look tame.

'Do you want a box around it?' Mo was asking, slowly, enunciating each word at volume.

'No, I want it flat on the paper.'

Mo grabbed a sheet of paper and a pen and began to demonstrate what she meant, as patiently as she was able.

'Oh, I see. No, I don't want one of those,' said the old lady. 'What can you do to make it stand out, though?'

'Put lines around it.' Mo's exasperation was seeping through her words now.

'Yes, I'll have those. Four lines.'

'A box then,' said Mo. 'Great. Glad we got there in the end.' She gave Laurie the sort of smile that said, *I wish I could put this old bat in a box*, then pressed the button under the counter desk that released the lock on the door into the main building. 'Go up,' she said to her.

'Thank you, Mo.'

'Oy, does it cost more?' asked the old lady, tapping a gnarled finger on the paper.

'Yes.'

'I don't want it then.'

Laurie left them to it, walked through the door and along the passage. Up eight steps, turn right, down three steps, turn left, up a flight of twenty-two steps. Whichever architect had designed the building must have done so after a blow-out drinking session. The most that could be said about it was that visiting the editorial department was a great workout for the calves.

She entered the busy newsroom where immediately hands were raised to wave to her or smiles appeared on faces or welcoming nods animated heads. One of the reporters, Flo, was on a call and stuck up her thumb as a hello.

'I'm so sorry you've had that terrible experience, Mrs Hasselhoff ... sorry, Mrs Hashcroft.' She held the phone away from her ear and Laurie could hear Mrs Hashcroft screaming from Doncaster.

'Rest assured we will be in touch with our legal department as soon as humanly possible,' said Flo, replacing the phone to her ear. Her tone couldn't have been sweeter. 'Yes my name is Florence Carter and I'm a reporter. Goodbye Mrs Hassss ... shcro— oh, you've gone, have you? Stroppy tit.' She put down the phone, turned to Laurie and said, 'And that's another one for your five-foot-tall tower of complaints this week, Laurie. Go and bring Alan's blood pressure down, for heaven's sake, before I raise it even higher by adding to the pile. We got Mrs Hashcroft's copy wrong. We printed under their anniversary picture that it was their diamond wedding not their ruby and that she was married to David Hasselhoff not Dustin Hashcroft.' She sniffed. 'No pleasing some folk. She's attempting to sue us for a million pounds for hurt feelings. My guess is that she'll take a meal for two at the Royal in Dartley as fair recompense.' She grinned and Laurie grinned with her. The newsroom of the *Daily Trumpet* was a perfect tonic. At least it was for a visitor.

Alan's office was a glass pod in the far corner. He was on the phone when Laurie approached and he waved her to come in before she had the chance to knock. He was just finishing off a call to Sir Basil who governed them from his manor house in Penistone.

'Yep ... yep ... got that ... two hundred quid donation and free advertising for a month ... Yep ... yep ... Cheers, Sir Basil.' He put the phone down none too gently.

'God save me from that old fucker. Just because he owns the newspaper, he thinks he owns my soul as well. I'm surprised he hasn't demanded we're all branded "Property of Sir Basil Stamper" on our buttocks like cattle in cowboy films,' he said to Laurie. Alan wasn't one to mince his words. 'Boy, am I glad to see you. Has it only been a week since you were here last?'

'Exactly a week, Alan.'

'How come I've got another five hundred grey hairs, then?' he said in a voice that sounded as if it was fresh out of a cement mixer. 'Coffee?' He slotted a pod into his over-worked Nespresso machine, presuming that yes would be the answer.

'Bloody pile of complaints, never goes down. It's like a torment in a Greek tragedy,' he grumbled. 'Given the choice I'd have preferred to have my liver pecked out daily like Prometheus than have Sir Basil constantly kicking me in the bollocks. This week has been particularly a c— . . . taxing.' He twisted on his heel mid-sentence.

'Bad, eh?' asked Laurie.

'Like you wouldn't believe. Nobody can bloody proofread any more these days. I don't know which planet we get these knobheads from. They come to us armed with qualifications dropping out of their arses and not an atom of common sense. Not one. I mean . . .' He picked up a letter from the pile on his desk and read aloud. '"I was greatly offended by the story in last week's *Daily Trumpet* about my mother Mrs Doreen Pitt".'

Laurie's brain spun; trying to work out why Mrs Pitt's daughter was annoyed enough to send in a letter to the editor.

Alan now read from the newspaper clipping attached to the letter.

'"Mrs Doreen Pitt was awarded first prize in the WI croquet competition. The judge said that he took it into consideration that the woman had never been in trouble before and sentenced her to forty hours of community service." Clearly two stories have got mixed up there. Three if you count that she was actually the winner of a crochet competition. We issued an apology. Of course we did. To Mrs Doreen Titt. Apparently we are responsible for the flare-up of her acne.'

Laurie hooted. She couldn't help herself. At the same time she realised how alien it felt to laugh these days, to feel the stomach muscles work.

'The one I'm most worried about is the day in the life of the mayor where he insists on starting each day with a golden shower instead of a cold one, according to us. He's a nasty bleeder, this mayor, as well. And he's got about as much of a sense of humour as I have. Doesn't help that bloody Juice Hughes keeps chucking sausage rolls at him everywhere he goes. Oh yes, go on laugh, why don't you, young lady.'

'I'm sorry,' said Laurie. 'Thank you for this already, Alan. I haven't laughed like this in months.'

The phone rang. Alan snatched it up and the look on his face said it all. His eyes shuttered down as if he wanted to keep out the world. When he did speak, he was remarkably calm. Or spent, as he would have described it.

'He's a golfer isn't he? Suggest a donation to their retired old bastards fund, Flo, he'll take it. I know him. Pringle-wearing prat. Goodbye.'

Alan made a noise like a punctured balloon, before turning his attention back to the coffee machine. He put down a mug in front of Laurie.

'As my great gran, God rest her soul, used to say, "If you don't laugh in this shithole, you'd cry buckets,"' he said. 'Drink your coffee before we make a proper start. Here – posh treats. Fortnum and Mason hamper arrived for Sir Basil but they inadvertently left out the biscuits which arrived by separate carrier so I nabbed them. I'll deny all knowledge if asked. He's diabetic anyway. I'm saving him from himself.'

Laurie picked up the first foolscap file but her thoughts were lingering on what she had just said. *She hadn't laughed in months.* No, it was longer, much longer than that.

Chapter 3

There was a lot of time to think in this job, more than people would have realised. They presumed being a firefighter was continual stimulation and Pete Moore had seen a lot of people who joined up and couldn't hack the amount of tedium that far outweighed the gung-ho stuff. Luckily for him – although not so lucky for others – there had been a lot of call-outs recently. Vandals setting light to rubber tyres, malfunctioning alarms, wood fires; nothing too major, though. He was glad of the activity. It took his mind away from settling on thoughts he didn't want to have. Thoughts about how different his life was now to how it had been six months ago. Before his wife died.

A job came in to attend the children's playground in Edgefoot. It was still referred to as 'the playground' even though the council had grown sick of replacing the vandalised swings and called it a day. All that remained of it now were bare patches of grass where the spider's-web roundabout, climbing frame and slide once stood and a large rectangle of tarmac which still served as a basketball and football pitch. The demarcation painted lines had long gone, as had the slam-dunk hoops but the iron fence around it still remained. It would take colossal strength to bend the rails, but someone had managed it, which is why a fire engine had been deployed here. With his head stuck in between them was an infamous town drunk, Jason Hughes, better known as Juice because of his once bright-orange hair, as long gone as the swings.

'Now then, Juice,' said the gaffer Andy Burlap, 'how the heck did you get in this mess?'

'No idea,' said Juice. 'I just woke up like this.' There was a mug of milky tea in front of him, untouched. Apparently the woman who had phoned 999 had taken that and a round of toast over for him on a paper plate, but then she'd had to dash off to work.

Andy leaned over to assess how they were going to get Juice out of there. He coughed as his nose entered Juice's personal space. Weed, wee, alcohol, sweat and more layers of unpleasantness assaulted Andy's nasal receptors. He'd been at school with Juice; he'd been just an ordinary kid then. He was never going to be chief scientist at NASA but he should have achieved more in life than to become the town joke, the one who bought sausage rolls in the Pound Bakery just to break up and throw at policemen and dignitaries; who busked outside the market with a school recorder even though he couldn't play a note. In his head, Andy still saw the flame-haired kid in the too-big jumper and holey shoes whose mam was known to everyone as Dirty Di.

'The bars have been bent back in to make sure he doesn't get out,' said Andy to Pete. 'Britain's Strongest Man couldn't have done a better job.'

'Silly cow didn't put any sugar in that tea,' Juice said with a chuckle, still obviously drunk or high. 'And I hate milk. It gives me the shits.'

Pete noticed Juice's neck was red raw. He'd obviously been struggling to get out, even if he couldn't remember doing it.

'You've got yourself in a right pickle here, lad,' said Krish, who had come over from India in his teens but spoke 'Tyke' as well as any born-and-bred Yorkshireman. He shook his head, let drop a heavy sigh; his expression read, *what a waste*. Krish had saved Juice's life once when he'd decided to have a barbecue in the squat he used to stay in. The fire he caused hadn't killed him, nor had the carbon monoxide fumes. He had the luck of the devil, which was ironic considering the state of him.

A small amused crowd had gathered to watch the activities, including a smart young man taking photos on an iPad. Pete recognised him as a reporter from the *Daily Trumpet* who had turned up on his doorstep just after the accident. He'd got as far as 'I know this must be a difficult time but I'm Jordan from the *Daily Trumpet*, could you give us a few words . . .' before Pete's brother Griff had butted in and dealt with him, sternly but still politely. The kid was only doing his job after all, but on that occasion, he'd have to get his information from elsewhere.

'Are you all here?' said Juice. 'Full fire engine?'

'Yes, Juice, you've got all five of us,' said Sal.

Juice responded to the pitch of her voice. 'It's you – the woman fireman again. Fuck me, are you still with 'em?'

'Firefighter to you,' said Sal, with good humour. 'And yes I am.'

'Women firemen, whatever next?' he went on, ignoring her correction.

'You'd be grateful for me if I had to carry you out of a building next time you decide to have an indoor barbecue.'

'Oh I'm not doing that again,' said Juice, trying to shake his head. 'Burned all my bridges as well as my sausages. They won't let me back in there.'

Andy tried to spread the bars a little so that Juice could wiggle out but not even he and his mighty arm muscles could budge them. Then Pete took one rail while Andy concentrated all his strength on the other as Krish tried to gently manoeuvre Juice's head so that his large ears weren't impeding the process, but the bars remained stubbornly rigid.

'You must remember who put you here, Juice,' asked an exasperated Andy, gathering his breath.

'Can't remember. Likkle kids I think,' said Juice.

'Unless they were all on steroids, it wasn't kids,' replied Pete.

'Around here, they might be,' said Andy. He'd grown up on the large sprawling sink estate and knew anything was possible. The police once broke the neighbour's door down in the 1990s and took a five-foot live alligator away that was being kept as a pet in their bathroom.

'We'll have to chop,' Andy decided, walking to the vehicle to fetch the hydraulic cutters.

'I hope you don't mean my head,' said Juice with a snort of laughter. 'I could carry it under my arm like Anne Hathaway.' He started giggling to himself.

'Anne Boleyn, you mean,' said Pete.

'I used to know all the seven wives of Henry the eighth at one time,' said Juice with a thoughtful *hmm*. 'Anne Hath— ... Boleyn, Jane Seymour, Catherine Tarragon, Elizabeth somebody or other, Bloody Mary.' He ceased reciting as Andy knelt beside him.

'Now I need you to keep still, Juice. And preferably quiet.'

'There won't be sparks, will there? I don't want my hair set on fire,' said Juice, a note of fear in his voice. The state of him, and he was worried about damaging any of his hair, thought Pete.

'There's no sparks with these and hardly any noise, your mane is safe.'

There was barely enough of Juice's hair to set alight these days, just wisps of faded peach around the back. He'd tried to dye it blonde once at school, Andy remembered. Used household bleach and burned his scalp.

As the cutters pinched the metal, Juice farted.

'Oops, pardon.'

Jacko, who was supporting Juice's head, turned his own head away into clean air.

'What the hell have you been eating?' he asked.

'That's a combo of beer and fear,' said Juice.

The stench reached Andy and pushed him to make his snips faster. Within the minute, Pete and Krish were hefting Juice to his feet. He was surprisingly heavy considering his wiry build.

'Any chance of a lift back to town, lads? Oh, and lasses,' he added with a head-bob in Sal's direction.

Andy opened his mouth to reply but Juice flapped his hand as if flicking away the answer to come. 'I know, I know. You're not allowed. Insurance, health and safety and all that bollocks.'

'Sorry, Juice,' said Pete, clapping him on the shoulder. 'You all right?'

'More or less,' said Juice, rotating his neck. 'Probably need a bit of medicine now for the pain, if you know what I mean. Cheers, boys . . . and girl.'

He grinned and began to weave off, hands stuffed in his trouser pockets, in the direction of the main road where he would try to thumb a lift to one of the town pubs for his 'medicine'. His gait was jaunty, hopeful, devoid of cares. *He's happier than I am*, thought Pete. Maybe happier than he ever would be again.

Chapter 4

February, earlier that year

The last conversation Pete had with his wife was short, to the point. He picked up his mobile, alerted by Tara's assigned ringtone.

'Are you finishing on time tonight?' she said.

'No, I'll be a couple of hours late. Rav's dad's had a fall so I'm covering until he gets back from the hospital.'

'Well get home as soon as you can,' she said. 'I've got something I want to tell you.'

'What is it?'

'No. I want to tell you to your face.'

'Sounds intriguing.' He smiled. 'Where are you now?' He looked out of the window at the lumpen clouds, the heavy precipitation, hoped she wasn't too far away from home.

'On the M1, just coming back from my last appointment in Leeds.'

'Drive carefully in this, Tara.' Rush-hour traffic on a freezing February night with a sky full of sleet that would likely turn to snow at any minute. 'Don't take any chance—' Three curt beeps. The line had gone dead. The M1 had patches where the signal died. He contemplated ringing her back, but didn't want to distract her. She was a sensible driver, of course she'd take care.

An hour and a half later, he'd been checking the breathing apparatus when the fire station alarm had gone off, the persistent beep-beep calling Red Watch to arms.

'I hope this isn't another bleeding parrot stuck in a tree,' said Jacko, who'd spent two hours the previous day trying to coax an escaped African Grey down from a giant conifer.

It wasn't. It was a major road traffic collision on a dual carriageway. It was carnage. A lorry driver had skidded on the wet snow, crossed the central reservation and caused a ten-vehicle pile-up. And smack in the middle of all that bashed and mangled metal was a red car with a customised black stripe, just like the one Pete's wife drove. Because it was the one his wife drove.

It was weird the things a brain remembered. That day had started so normally and he could recall it all – even now – in glorious technicolour. Meeting Krish by the office door, who took the piss out of his new haircut: 'Bet that clogged up someone's Flymo.' He could remember Dave Prigmore nearly crying because he dropped his 'Mr Wonderful' mug and smashed it. He could remember Sal Thomas being giddy as a kipper because she'd won the lottery – well, one hundred and forty pounds. He could remember Jacko talking to a reporter at the *Daily Trumpet* who wanted to run a piece on him rescuing that parrot. But everything that happened after his eyes picked out that red car sat as a jumbled mess in his head and the events would not unpick themselves but stayed there, scratching against the inside of his skull like a big, knotted ball of barbed wire.

Three weeks later, Tara's funeral had been jointly arranged by her family and Pete, both carefully respectful of the other's wishes. Tara's dad owned twenty florist shops across Yorkshire and his youngest daughter's funeral was as flower-filled as her wedding had been; no expense spared for Bob Ollerton's girl. She rode to the church to be buried in a carriage with six white horses as she had ridden to it to be married two years previously. She would be interred wearing a white suit, white flowers studded in her long caramel hair; white lilies punching out heady perfume sat on top of her white coffin. The organist played 'All Things Bright and Beautiful' on both occasions and Tara's sisters each stood at the pulpit and gave readings. Her mother was a bastion of dignity, her father was an emotional wreck. At the funeral he sat holding his wife's hand and his son-in-law's, squeezing tight as if they kept him from falling into an abyss. People said it was the most beautiful funeral they had ever been to, which was a consolation to the family because they wanted to do her proud.

At the other side of Pete sat his twin brother Griff. There was only one man as good to have in a crisis and that was Pete himself.

The white coffin was lowered into the churchyard ground and dozens of pink roses were kissed and dropped in with her. Except for two red roses from Pete; one for his wife, one for his unborn child.

The pregnancy kit was still in Tara's handbag when her effects were returned to Pete. She had wanted him home that night to tell him to his face that she was pregnant.

Chapter 5

'Don't be late home, Laurie. There's something important I have to tell you.' The last words Alex had ever spoken to her, except he hadn't spoken them to her because her meeting at work had overrun and she'd heard them on her voicemail when she came out and switched her phone back on. She'd tried to ring back but annoyingly all the calls went to his voicemail. She'd rushed home then, as much as the weather would allow her to, to find that he wasn't even there and then she'd been a little cross.

Later she'd found out that he was going to cook dinner for them and she knew this because an M&S dine-in meal for two had been found in the passenger side footwell. Alex was smashed like an egg, but their romantic dinner à deux survived. No champagne though. She'd thought that strange when her brain was sifting through the details of the crash. He had a diamond solitaire ring in his pocket for her but no champagne and he was a champagne sort of guy.

He promised her once that she would never forget the date when he proposed, that he'd make it memorable so it was forever etched in her mind. Well, life had certainly taken that promise and given it a twist because just as he assured her, 6 February – the date of their supposed engagement – was certainly one unforgettable day.

When Alex's effects had been handed to her at the hospital, the engagement ring had been in his jacket pocket along with his phone and wallet and the receipt from M&S. They hadn't given her the shopping bag of food and afterwards she did wonder if the police had had a discussion about it, should they or shouldn't they? It was funny where the mind went after a catastrophic event, ruminating about policemen handing over chicken cooked in a lemon sauce, the profiteroles she loved and a bottle of Tempranillo; the stupid details it fixated on. The ring was platinum, from Van Cleef & Arpels in a heart-shaped box and had a simple but exquisite carat of square diamond set in the mount. Inside the band had been engraved in tiny letters 'Always on my mind', like the song. It must have cost him a small fortune – but it didn't fit. It was far too small, which she'd also found odd because Alex would have wanted to slip the ring on her finger, make a trumpeted moment of it. Alex always had been about the big showy gestures, always perfectly executed. Something else that didn't fit.

She'd tried to have the ring resized at three jewellers, but they said they couldn't do it, so she wore it on a chain around her neck. Anyway, she didn't want to put the ring on her own finger and declare herself the fiancée of a man who would never be able to make her his wife. Her hand strayed often to it, when she needed to feel close to him. *Always on my mind*. They were important words and they were for her, she knew that. They were why he'd come back to her three and a half years ago, because he couldn't forget her.

She hadn't been able to listen to the song since he died and it had haunted her: on the radio, on the TV, even blasting out of speakers on her first trip to the supermarket to buy food for one. She'd abandoned her full trolley and left the store barely able to see for the tears pumping from her eyes, almost too fast to clear. There had been frozen things in the trolley and she'd felt guilty enough never to return to that Tesco in case everyone pointed her out as the woman who ruined food. One more thing to fret about. A therapist would have unravelled her worries, airbrushed them into a smooth sheet of calm but therapy equalled weakness, unable to cope-ness. She didn't want to start talking about Alex's death to someone because she thought she might not be able to stop. She would vomit out all those stupid points plaguing her brain, like why the ring didn't fit and why there was red wine and not champagne in the M&S carrier bag and she would overrun on her fifty-minute session and not manage to spoon her broken liquid heart back into her chest in time to exit so the next screw-up could sit in her still-warm chair.

Alex's parents had started off helping Laurie organise his funeral and then completely took over, but she hadn't resisted his mother Meredith's insistence on her choice of reading, hymns, guests. Meredith had wanted Alex to be buried in his dark green Armani suit, the one he had worn to the engagement party of his sister Naomi and best friend Jefferson. Sharp white shirt, green tie, waistcoat. Laurie hadn't fought her on that, even though she thought the blue one suited him much more. Not that it mattered. Meredith and Brendan had insisted on paying for everything, refused to take a penny. It hadn't sat comfortably with Laurie who was determined to reimburse them somewhere along the line, when it felt right and proper. They'd chosen the best of everything for their only son, lots of it unnecessary. The only thing that Laurie contested was Meredith's decision to bury him next to her parents because that, she was adamant, he wouldn't have wanted.

They'd had a boozy discussion with friends over dinner a couple of years ago about burial versus cremation and Alex, albeit flippantly, had said that he wanted to be kept in an urn in his bedside cabinet. Less flippantly he was terrified of being buried alive. On the way home, he'd made Laurie promise that if anything happened to him, he was to be cremated. He'd then started choosing his funeral songs and Laurie told him to stop because he was being morbid. He'd been twenty-seven years old at the time. She laughed then and said that they'd pick up this discussion again when they were in their eighties.

It was the first time that Laurie had been witness to a Meredith that didn't get her own way and that one was very different from the twittery, frothy Meredith that was the norm. Luckily for Laurie, Alex had written a will and in it cited his command to be cremated and for those ashes to be entrusted to Laurie who would 'lay him to rest in the place she best saw fit'. She found out that he'd written it days after they'd had the dinner conversation. Meredith was forced to concede but she wasn't happy at all about it.

Laurie's mother had flown in from Spain the day before the funeral. Thankfully she had been alone and not with her dreadful present partner for whom Laurie had no tolerance. Her mother had a habit of picking affluent, grateful men with no personality and zero charm. She had been as much comfort to her daughter as she had been of use throughout

Laurie's formative years. Her visit to England was short and not sweet.

In his will, Alex left everything he had to Laurie, give or take a few disbursements: his collection of wristwatches to his father, the rather vague instruction 'anything his mother wanted' and his vast music and DVD collection to his best friend Jefferson. Laurie had always liked Jefferson until he turned up unannounced a few days after the funeral to collect what he'd been bequeathed, car full of packing boxes in preparation. After the shelves had been cleared, Jefferson asked for a coffee, which Laurie had duly made. Within the half hour, Laurie had flung her lukewarm drink in his face and told him never to come back. He had walked out then, silently and dripping. This, the man who was going to marry Alex's sister in November, and who had been his best friend since school, had just made a pass at her. And she'd been so wrong-footed by it that he'd more or less had to spell out what he wanted to happen between them before she'd reacted. The goalposts of normality in Laurie's life had been shifted so far they were off the pitch.

Chapter 6

Early August

Laurie felt the shift inside her appear out of nowhere as it usually did. A bout of panic that pounced on her, as if it had been waiting around a corner with malicious intent. There was no trigger, no pattern, it just happened. Alan was taking his umpteenth call of the day from Sir Basil about the quality of the paper the *Daily Trumpet* was printed on and if cost cuts could be made. It had no connection to the thoughts which rolled into her brain like a cold, dark fog. She had been surviving between such episodes, plastering on a smile over the cracks, convincing everyone she was fit to be back at work, of *course* she was. But she wasn't, not by a long chalk.

She felt the prickle of tears behind her eyes, as painful as if they were full of acid rather than salt. She tried to wipe them away secretly while Alan had his back turned to her, attempting to talk some sense into an old man who had more money than brain cells, but they started to drip out of her eyes as if the tail of one was attached to the head of another. She reached down and fumbled into her bag for a tissue, desperately, because she did not want to be seen as someone who wasn't coping. She'd hidden it successfully from everyone so far and didn't want her weakness showing. She'd get through it without having to go to a doctor for anti-depressants, or be referred to a shrink. She didn't want to turn into her mother who popped Prozac like Smarties and booked in for emergency crisis talks with a therapist if she broke a nail.

Alan turned, saw her trying to dry her eyes with a tissue that was more water than paper.

'I'll have to go, Sir Basil. There's a fire,' he said and put the phone down.

He crossed to the window that faced out into the main office, twisted the rod that shut the blinds which was a fierce indicator that he was not to be disturbed under any circumstances. Not even for the four-minute warning of a nuclear blast or an impromptu visit by the queen. No exceptions, message received and understood.

He then passed Laurie a box of 'man-sized' tissues.

'I still have boxes of these un-PC things,' he said. 'Blokes have much bigger noses than women anyway so I could never see what all the bloody fuss was about. World's gone chuffing mad.'

A small laugh escaped her, mingled in with the embarrassment of being so exposed.

'I'm so sorry,' she said, her throat dry.

Alan sat down heavily on his chair which creaked in protest.

'Ey Laurie, I've known for a while you weren't right, but it wasn't my place to say. I imagine you're sick of people asking you if you're okay, so I thought I'd go against the grain and not probe. Until I felt that I had to – like now.'

'I'm okay mainly,' said Laurie. 'Just every so often this happens. No idea why.'

'It happens because you came back to work too early and haven't given yourself enough time to grieve properly.' Alan stabbed his finger in the direction of his workforce. 'Even those idiots out there would have had enough perception to tell you that.'

'I couldn't just sit there and stare at four walls, Alan. But I don't fit in anywhere, I can't find the place where I used to be.'

'Because it's gone, lass,' said Alan, as softly as his gravelly tones could manage. 'You have to find a new place and that takes time. More than you think. Three steps forward, four steps backward mainly in the beginning. But there will come a point when you find you're one step in front and you don't slip back.'

He leaned towards her slightly before speaking again.

'This stays between you and me. I lost my first wife when I was twenty-one and she was nineteen. We'd only been married a few months when she was struck down with meningitis and it swept her away from me.'

Laurie gave a small gasp. 'I didn't know that.'

'No one does. Well, no one outside the inner circle. You never get over it. You just find somewhere to put it. A bit like learning how to walk differently in a shoe that rubs your heel when you've only got one pair.'

Laurie nodded, though she couldn't imagine the ache inside her ever subsiding to a degree where she wasn't constantly aware of it.

'My boss at the time sent me home when I turned up for work the next month looking like a bag of crap,' Alan went on. 'He told me not to rush trying to get over it and to seek help when I needed it instead of trying to be bloody brave. He was a man with vision who knew a broken mind needed as much care as a broken leg, and he was right, Laurie. Just because you can't see an injury, doesn't mean it isn't there.'

Alan shifted his chair so he could open his drawer and he pulled out a business card. It didn't have much on it, just the words 'Molly's Club', a local telephone number and the name Molly Jones-Hoyland.

'I've known this woman for years,' said Alan. 'I wanted to do a feature on what she does but she'd rather not and I respect that. It's for people who need some help getting over a grief hurdle. Chat, tea and buns, that sort of thing. It's free. She's a good woman. I wish she'd been doing then what she does now when I lost Pam.'

Laurie took the card. 'Thank you, Alan.'

'I only found out when I sought help myself just how much I needed it. It's not my call to lecture anyone, but Molly has been through a lot in her life and yet she's come up smiling. Jump in and let her work her magic.'

'I will,' said Laurie and she meant it. She knew she was stuck and needed help. And a recommendation from Alan was a proper accolade. She'd ring Molly Jones-Hoyland and hope she could fix her broken mind. Her broken life.

Chapter 7

Pete was with Krish in the fire station gym talking about Juice's rescue the previous day when they heard the alarm. They dumped the weights and moved quickly towards the fire engine, stripping off their sweat-damp T-shirts and grabbing the dry ones they'd left out in case of a situation like this. Andy was striding from the office, Sal close behind him. She jumped into the driver's side of the cab, Andy in the passenger side; the rest of them piled into the back, changing quickly into their fire kit.

'RTC, six vehicles reported,' said Andy, buckling up then checking the precise location of the incident they'd been called to on the MDT screen in front of him – the mobile data terminal. Their station was situated near to the motorway junction; the estimated time of arrival was ten minutes.

Sal sped down the hard shoulder, siren blaring. The traffic tailed back several miles already. The second engine was close behind, she could see it in her side mirror. In front of them smoke plumed upwards marking the site of the crash.

They were first on the scene, before the police, before the

ambulance which was more often than not the case. All three lanes of the M1 were blocked, vehicles – more than six – pointing in all directions like bumper cars, all battle-scarred somewhere from contact. Sal braked, Andy jumped out of the cab and directed Jacko, driving the second engine, to park across the carriageway, preventing unauthorised access. Andy's eyes worked quickly to assess the scene. White smoke from airbags was hanging in the air, mingling with black smoke pouring from a white van lying wounded on its side, tongues of flames seeking their freedom from under the crushed bonnet. A cluster of people were huddled behind the barrier on the hard shoulder but an elderly man was standing by an old red Fiat, talking to the driver through the smashed window.

The priority was getting that fire out; the smoke was acrid and the wind was hostile, blowing its load of carcinogens towards receptive lungs. Krish, already wearing his breathing apparatus, ran off the hose reel while Sal engaged the drive for the pump. The woman in the red car was visibly distressed, holding her neck; her car door was buckled beyond any chance of opening. Gaz escorted the old man to the sideline, noticing he had a nasty gash to his eyebrow that would need looking at; shock had probably stopped him from even registering he was injured.

'The woman in the Fiat's called Shirley,' the old man told them. 'She's hurt her neck.'

The ambulance had just pulled up and Andy went over to converse with them before jogging quickly back to the others.

'We'll have to take the roof off because we can't take the risk that she hasn't got a spinal injury,' he said to his team. They knew the drill. Krish disconnected the car battery,

Dave and Jacko fitted blocks under the car to stabilise it, take out the suspension. Sue was already in the back of the Fiat, holding Shirley's neck steady. Robbie and Deano were pulling out all the equipment they'd need. Andy set Pete on cutting; he should have her out pretty quickly. A more modern car wouldn't have crumpled as much and an airbag would have been deployed, but at least with these old vehicles, the metal gave so much more easily.

Pete released the cutting tool from the fire engine and walked towards the Fiat. Another waft of white smoke blew in his face and through the haze the red Fiat became another car, Tara's car. He saw it all again, as it was that day in February: Sal, crunching metal with the cutters, Krish ripping glass away from the windscreen, the paramedic working on Pete's trapped, unconscious wife trying to stem the blood – the *life* – gushing from her femoral artery. Every desperate beat her heart made doing its best to keep her alive but bringing her closer to death instead.

Pete lost purchase of the cutting tool, it dropped to the floor and he stumbled to the side, only managing to stop himself falling by a lucky placement of limbs. He heard Andy shout at Gaz to take over. It clicked Pete from the past into the here and now. 'I've got it,' he said, back to being Pete Moore, firefighter. But Pete Moore, grieving widower was sharing the same body and dangerously hampering his detachment. Andy stood him down.

'Can I have a word, Pete?' said Andy, when they were back at the station.

Pete had been expecting it of course.

'Shut the door behind you, lad.'

Pete did as he was told.

'Sit down,' said Andy. His voice was calm, avuncular. 'You all right?'

'Yes,' said Pete. 'I'm okay. I know what you're going to say and it won't happen again.'

Andy's head made a slow nod. 'We've seen much worse than we have today and we *will* see much worse than we have today. You know that.'

Pete opened his mouth to speak but Andy held up his hand to stop him.

'Let me finish. I did wonder if you'd returned to work too soon, but you fell back into it and did a good job, you always do, but there was something not *quite* right. We've all spotted it. I let it go, but I'm not sure I should have.'

We've all spotted it. That shocked Pete.

'I'm good, Andy. Please don't force me to take leave when I need this job more than I need to sit at home thinking.'

Andy sat back in his chair, studied the man in front of him, for whom he had the most tremendous respect. He could easily see Pete in his shoes, running teams in the not too distant future. He had no weak spots in the job: he was careful, methodical and fast-thinking, he was a splendid ambassador for them. The public liked him, his peers trusted him and new recruits looked up to him. But Andy had a duty of care to his whole team as well as to the individuals within it.

'I want you to be realistic, Pete, not brave.'

'I know,' answered Pete. 'I do, really. You have my word. I promise it was a one-off.'

'You can take time off for therapy, we'll sort it.'

'Thank you. I don't need it though, An—'

'I think you do. I want you to see someone. I don't want to force your hand on this, but . . .' The implication was that Andy *was* forcing his hand.

Pete rose from the chair. He was ashamed at his weaknesses being so obvious.

'Six weeks leave was way too short in my opinion after what you went through,' said Andy, as Pete opened the door to go. Pete didn't reply. Better to say nothing than to lie.

There was an odd atmosphere for the rest of the shift that everyone tried to play down. Pete could feel it as heavy as the smoke was at the scene and he was the white van aflame in the centre of the crash giving it out. It was understandable that there would be interest in how he handled the first major RTC. He'd scraped a pass, he reckoned, but it had been enough to unsettle everyone, to show them that the Pete Moore of six months ago was not the same one that stood in their midst now.

At the end of the shift Sal walked out to their cars with him.

'All right?' she asked.

'As I can be. Shit day and all that,' said Pete, attempting to smile. Hard though now he knew that everyone could see the cracks in him. 'I'm fine.'

'Yeah and I'm Taylor Swift. How long have we known each other?'

'Too bloody long,' said Pete.

Sal grinned. 'You know me well enough by now to be able to talk to me if you need to. In here ...' she poked herself in the chest '... I'm all sensitive woman, even if you look more feminine than I do.'

'I'm fine,' he repeated, but the words scraped their way out of his throat, as if they had been dragged out under duress, and he felt a slam of sadness hit him from left field. His vision blurred and he punched his fists into his eyes in an effort to grind the rising tears away. He turned from Sal in embarrassment.

'Jesus, where did that come from?' He didn't realise he'd spoken the words aloud until Sal answered him.

'Inside a wounded heart, Peter Moore, that's where they came from.'

'I'm good, I'm good,' said Pete – the flash flood gone as quickly as it had arrived. 'It's you and your silky woman voice that did that to me, nothing else,' he tried to joke, couldn't pull it off.

'Don't bawl me out, but take this,' said Sal, reaching into her jeans pocket and bringing out a business card.

'What is it?' He looked at the wording, 'Molly's Club' and under it the name Molly Jones-Hoyland. It meant nothing.

'Molly's Club?' he asked Sal.

'I've been carrying this around with me for weeks ready to give to you. I think today's the day.'

'Who is she?'

'She's a neighbour of my mum's. I've known her all my life and she's a really lovely person. She's retired, a pensioner and she runs a club where people in your shoes go and meet, talk.'

'People in my shoes? Fuck-ups you mean?'

'People who need help.'

'A counsellor?' Disdain leaked into his tone.

'A listener. She's good and I think you need her, Pete. Do yourself a favour and let her help to heal you.'

'So you think I need counselling as well as everyone else?' he asked. He respected Sal's opinion greatly as a mate as well as a workmate.

'Yep. I do. We need the old Pete back. This one looks

like Pete . . .' she flicked the back of her hand into his chest '. . . but it's been like waiting for thin ice to crack.'

He hadn't realised he'd done such a rubbish job of trying to show the world he could cope. That Sal had been carrying the card around with her for weeks to give to him was information he didn't want to acknowledge.

'Okay, I promise then, I'll ring her,' said Pete, slotting the card in his jeans pocket. 'For you.'

'No, Pete, for you,' said Sal, giving his shoulder a thump which spoke of more affection than any hug she could administer.

Chapter 8

28 August

'Peter, I presume, do come in,' said Molly. Her delight was evident, he'd made it, acknowledged the courage it had taken for him to open the door. 'Come and have a coffee and some cake and take a seat.'

Pete raised his hand. 'Hi' he said, reminding himself of a native American Indian in an old cowboy film saying, 'How'. He felt his heart beating a ridiculous tattoo in his chest. He knew it wasn't walking into a room full of people that was throwing his body into panic, it was because he didn't want to lay his suit of armour on the welcome mat, like a pair of shoes. Admitting he was one of them, needing help, jarred with his pride.

He didn't want a slice of cake, didn't think he had the saliva to help him swallow it as his mouth was as dry as powdered cement, but he took a slice, and a coffee, played the game. He sat next to the woman with the silver-blonde plait who looked more the same age as him than anyone else there.

'Welcome to our new people, Laurie and Pete,' said Molly, smiling, nodding to them each in turn and Pete realised the woman at his side must be a fellow newbie; maybe that's why he was drawn to sit beside her. 'Shall we make some introductions – who wants to start?'

'I will,' said Maurice, which heartened Molly. He really had come out of his shell since he'd been here. It was amazing how much of an effect kindness had on people, instilling them with confidence. Life hadn't been that kind to Maurice; neither had his mother whom he had cared for since he was old enough to unscrew the lid on a bottle of tablets, and yet he'd taken her passing very hard.

'My name's Maurice and I'm a bookkeeper. I don't mean that I keep books, basically I add things up.' He smiled, hoping his little joke impressed. Laurie smiled back encouragingly and Molly noted that. Her observational skills had sharpened with age, more so since she had decided to plough her energies into this little club. 'I lost my mum last year,' Maurice continued. 'She was an invalid and I can't remember a time before I was looking after her. She took advantage, I know that, but I did love her and I do miss her. I have all this life now, this freedom and I don't know what to do with it. So that's me in a nutshell.'

'I'll go next,' said the thin woman with springy copper hair. 'I'm Yvonne, housewife ... well house widow now, I suppose. I was married at sixteen and I lost my husband in June. The doctor thought it might be a good idea if I found a good counsellor because I can't grieve. I haven't cried once. I know it's not normal and I'm expecting it'll catch up with me and I'll fall to bits, so the sooner it happens the better. Okay?' She gave the newcomers a wide smile then gave Sharon a nudge. 'You next, love.'

'Well I'm Sharon and I'm a cleaner,' she began. 'My dog died, which I know isn't the same as losing a partner or a parent but I've never loved anyone the way I loved him. And I miss him so much.' She pulled a photo out of her bag of a black mongrel with soulful eyes. 'Billy. He was only seven. I know he's just a dog . . .'

Maurice made noises of protest. 'Nothing you love is ever "just a",' he said. 'I had a hamster when I was a boy. I cried for months when he died. And I was very attached to Mother's budgerigar Whistle, but sadly he passed the week after she did. I popped him in with Mum, I think she would have liked that.'

Laurie coughed, feeling obliged to leap in with her own contribution, become a fully paid-up member of them, even though the sessions were free. 'I've got a goldfish. My fiancé and I won him at a fair a few years ago and I think I'd be gutted if anything happened to him.'

'I've got a Siamese cat called Pong,' put in Pete, feeling the need to add himself to them all, in the way that people at charity auctions felt obliged to put in a low bid so they could relax for a while, knowing they'd done their bit. The name Pong made everyone laugh. 'I love him nearly as much as I love my twin brother, even if he's a taker rather than a giver. That's cats for you.'

Sharon felt heartened by that; she always worried that if anyone new came to the group they'd think she was a fraud for taking up the place of someone missing another human being, so it was nice that these younger people were both animal lovers. And Molly felt gladdened that the newbies had joined straight in with small gifts of themselves. She sensed a good, caring vibe from them. She was rarely wrong these days.

'I always think that animals give merely by being there,'

said Maurice. 'I'll be quite honest, I didn't get much affection from Hammy, my hamster, when I was a boy but just from giving it to him, I received a lot of comfort.' He dropped a heavy sigh. 'I was going through a patch at school where I was being bullied and playing with Hammy gave my head somewhere nice and simple to go.'

'That's a shame,' said Sharon. 'Bullies are awful. I once lamped a bully at my school. She didn't think I'd dare because I was littler than her, but she got a shock. And a bloody nose.'

Maurice and Yvonne chuckled.

'Good for you. Even worms turn,' said Maurice, adding quickly, 'Not that I'm saying you're a worm, Sharon. Far from it.'

'She never bothered me again. For a little worm, I had a temper when I'd reached the end of my limit.'

Molly herded the conversation away from worms and addressed the two newcomers. 'If you want to leave it a while before telling us your story, that's fine with us,' she said.

'I don't mind,' said Laurie, thinking that she ought to take Alan's advice and 'jump in', otherwise what was the point of being here. 'My name is Laurie, I'm a solicitor. I lost my fiancé a few months ago.' Her hand unconsciously strayed to the necklace she wore with the small ring threaded through it, seeking strength. 'I've been stuck, I can't seem to move forward. Alex died very suddenly and I haven't been able to clear the shock. I'm not close to my own family and I feel as if I don't want to burden my friends ...' She tailed off but saw people nodding as they listened, especially the man who had come in after her, the man with the shining grey eyes.

'I think it's better to talk to strangers sometimes,' said Yvonne. 'My daughter Lola idolised her dad, she thinks I'm heartless because I'm managing quite easily to get on with things. I think she wants me to dress in black, close the curtains and marinade in gloom like Des's mother did when his father died.'

'Grief affects everyone in different ways,' said Mr Singh from behind the counter. 'I was a surgeon, I saw a whole spectrum of reactions from indifference to heartbreak. But the person usually negotiates a grieving process. Sadness turns to anger, to disbelief, to depression – these are all natural ways of working towards acceptance. But not everyone travels that long, straight road.'

'I certainly haven't,' said Yvonne, with a hard note of laughter. 'I've had no anger or sadness anyway. It's just as if Des has popped out to the shops and he'll be back at any time. I get that ...' she patted her chest '... that anxiety in here while I'm waiting for him to turn up.' Then she mumbled something else under her breath but no one could quite catch what she said.

'Maybe the floodgates will open when it's your anniversary or his birthday, Yvonne,' suggested Sharon.

'It was his birthday last Thursday,' replied Yvonne. 'We took some flowers up to his grave because our daughter wanted to and I put on a sad face but in all honesty I couldn't wait to get home to watch *Columbo*. Now I've got the TV all to myself, it's marvellous.' And she grinned.

No one made shocked faces. It might have been odd, but even the newcomers felt as if they were in a space where they could say anything about their state without the fear of reproach, or judgement. They were all out of synch with 'normality', or 'cracked up' as Pete thought to himself.

He opened his mouth to speak then. 'And I'm Pete, I'm a fireman, well firefighter I'm supposed to say now. I lost my wife a few months ago too. She was pregnant with our first child so it was a double loss for me.' Little murmurs of sympathy rippled around the room. 'I'm lucky that I do have friends to talk to, good friends, and I lost my mum three years ago so my dad knows what I'm going through except ... except I just don't want to load them with my troubles. So I feel isolated.' He felt a croak claim his throat and took a quick slurp of coffee to wet it. 'And they'd be so gutted if they knew I felt like this because they'd want me to turn to them first. But here I am, in a room full of strangers.' He forced out a smile and it sat precariously on his lips.

'A stranger is just a friend you don't know yet,' said Maurice, sounding very sage-like without being in the slightest bit patronising because it was obvious his heart was in the right place.

'When are your hardest times?' asked Mr Singh from behind the counter, in between mouthfuls of red velvet cake.

Laurie and Pete both started to speak at the same time and Pete indicated with his hand that Laurie should go first.

'There's no pattern. I can be doing something as simple as ironing a skirt and memories will start to bombard me. I'd understand it more if there was some connection but it comes out of nowhere.'

'Same for me,' said Pete. 'I was fitting a smoke alarm the other day in a pensioner's house and I started thinking about our honeymoon in the Lakes. I've noticed it seems to happen most when I'm doing something mundane. When I have space in my head, thoughts of her jump in. So I try not to have space in my head and end up exhausting myself.'

'Do you cry?' Yvonne asked him.

'Yes, I do,' said Pete, surprising himself with the ease with which he admitted that. 'I can control it to an extent, but when I'm alone, I fold.'

'I wish I could let go,' said Yvonne. 'I have to play act the other way, to dab my eyes and put on a sad face in front of the family when I feel nothing. I wish onions weren't so smelly, I'd have slipped one in a hankie.'

'When did you go back to work, Pete?' asked Maurice.

'I only took six weeks off. I was climbing the walls. I thought it would be the best thing for me and it was . . . in a way. Then . . . something happened on duty recently and I realised that I needed . . . help before I cocked up big time and endangered people. I hadn't done quite as good a job as I thought I had about convincing everyone I was okay. This club came recommended to me by someone whose opinion I wouldn't discount lightly. I didn't want to sit in a counsellor's office and do that one-to-one thing on a fifty-minute timer, if you know what I mean.'

'I do,' said Laurie. 'I didn't really want to admit that I needed help either. I've always been so . . . together, so capable. But I had no time to adjust. One minute my life was fine, the next – everything had changed.' She smiled empathetically at Pete. It was so liberating to find like-minded people; she didn't feel as unhinged as she had only an hour ago.

'More coffee, anyone?' called Mr Singh and Sharon jumped up, taking Maurice's cup for a refill without him needing to ask. These small considerations were weighty for someone like Maurice who hadn't experienced many of them, Molly knew.

'I don't know what's worse, a lingering illness like my

mother had or being cut down – *whoosh* – like a plant,' said Maurice, with a chopping motion. 'I hated seeing her suffering but she had the chance to do all the things she'd wanted to do for ages, like go back to Morecambe where she met my dad and she'd always wanted to see the Eiffel tower so we took the Eurostar to Paris and went right to the top and had a glass of champagne. It was wonderful. Do you know, my mother never told me once that she loved me until two nights before she passed. She wasn't that sort of woman, one who did affection, but it's helped me a lot that she didn't leave me before doing that. I think it's all I ever wanted, to hear her say those three words.' His voice faltered and Yvonne leaned over and gave his arm a squeeze.

Laurie felt a hard lump of emotion clog up her throat. The poor man. She wouldn't have wanted to see Alex suffer but being taken so suddenly and violently had left so much undone and unsaid. Unlike Maurice she hadn't had the chance to say things she wanted to say. Or to ask the questions which now plagued both her waking hours and her dreams. Fate had stolen the time she needed to mend what was wrong. Now it would always be broken.

'Mother was in such pain at the end,' Maurice went on, shaking his head slowly from side to side. 'I wish I could have taken her to the vets and have her put down like you did with your Billy, Sharon. Just an injection and let her drift off into her forever sleep, save her all that distress. I thought about putting a cushion over her face one night. It would all have been done in a minute.' He held his hands up. 'Then I'd have had to end it myself because I couldn't live knowing I'd murdered my own mother. But I couldn't have left Whistle with no one to look after him—'

Fearing that he was getting himself in too dark a hole, Molly butted in.

'But, dear Maurice, you were a wonderful and dutiful son and could have done no more. And your mother is at peace now and it's time for you to live a life for yourself.' *Life is meant for living* was one of Molly's dear husband's phrases. He had made her promise to squeeze all the juice out of it – for both of them.

'I went to the pictures by myself on Saturday,' said Maurice. 'I wanted to see that new Star Wars film in 3D but I had no one to go with and so I said to myself "Maurice, go alone." So I did. And it wasn't half the ordeal I thought it would be.'

'I love the pictures,' said Yvonne. 'If I'd known, I'd have gone with you.'

'Next time then, Yvonne,' said Maurice.

'You're on. I mean it.'

Yvonne and Maurice were such very different people but Molly and Mr Singh had remarked how well they had connected. Yvonne came from a rough background and had struggled all her life, Maurice came from an aspiring middle-class mother who had plenty of money and pretensions but both were united in just wanting some gentle company, some affection. Molly suspected they'd both given out a lot of love and received little in return.

'Have you gone back to work, Laurie?' asked Sharon. Laurie was impressed that people here had taken care to remember her name as she was more often than not called Laura.

'Yes, I went back a few weeks after the funeral. I didn't know what else to do with myself.'

'Me too,' put in Pete. 'Exactly that.' He wagged an

emphatic finger and when Laurie turned to him, she noticed the dimple in his chin. Alex had once told her that when he was a young boy, he used to sit there poking his chin hoping to get a dimple in it like his father had. And Kirk Douglas. She switched off that thought, continued with her story. She could find connections with everything and everyone and Alex and her brain felt duty-bound to hunt for them.

'I do a lot of work with the *Daily Trumpet*. I'm their retained solicitor. Going to their offices every week is the best cheer-up. They should bottle it and dispense it as medicine.' But, like an over-prescribed antibiotic, even that was failing to work enough these days. 'It was the editor who recommended I come here.'

'Dear Alan,' said Molly. 'I know him well.'

'I love the *Daily Trumpet*,' said Mr Singh, chuckling in the background and clapping his hands together with glee.

'I imagine you need to have a lot of humour in your job too, Peter,' said Maurice. 'The same sort of humour that policemen have, to offset the darkness you must encounter.'

'There's a lot, yes, Maurice. And brilliant camaraderie. I'm lucky to work with a great set of people.'

'Not a lot of humour in bookkeeping, alas,' said Maurice. 'It's terribly boring, but it suits me well. I was never the most dynamic of people and I could work from home when Mother was particularly bad. Good pension. I could avail myself of it and take an early retirement but I see no reason to yet. I don't know what I'd do if I was ever made redundant.'

'What would you like to do, if you could do anything?' Laurie asked him and Molly marvelled at how well this group of people were all interacting. It wasn't always like this when new people joined. Sometimes it was like a pastry mix with too little water, the crumbs would not adhere together without a great deal of effort.

Maurice considered the question before delivering his answer. 'I suppose, I'd like to buy a house in France and run it as a gîte. Not a hotel, I'm not one for cooking more than I have to, but I'd give people who stayed there a basket of warm breads and spreads for their breakfast. I fell in love with France when I took Mother to Paris.'

'That sounds lovely,' said Yvonne. 'I've never been abroad.'

'What, never?' said Sharon.

'No. Des wasn't one for holidays. I used to take my daughter away for the day on the bus, you know, but Des didn't want to go with us ever. And so that was that.'

'You should book a holiday in Spain. Or a cruise,' said Sharon. 'I've always wanted to go on one of them big ships and dress up.'

'Me abroad, ha.' Yvonne laughed at the idea. 'I'd be like a duck out of water. I've never even been to London.'

That disclosure landed like a stone on still water sending ripples out to them all. It seemed to speak volumes about what Yvonne's life must have been like. A *little* life.

Mr Singh made more coffees and Pete, Maurice and Yvonne had a second piece of cake each. And when the session came to a natural close – over an hour and a half after it had started – Laurie couldn't believe where the time had gone.

Did she feel any better for Molly's Club, Laurie asked herself on the way back to her car. She couldn't tell. She certainly didn't feel any worse, considering the edgy matters they'd discussed like that meek bookkeeper contemplating murder. People hid so many secrets behind their innocuous façades.

She was just hunting in her bag for her car keys when she heard the firefighter call her from behind. He was holding something up in the air. Keys. How the hell did they slide out of her bag? She had never lost a bunch of keys in her whole life.

'I don't think you'll get far without these,' he said, striding quickly to her.

'Thank you,' she said. 'I have no idea how they fell out.'

'That your goldfish?' he asked, handing over the keyring with the padded goldfish on it.

'No, but it looks exactly like him,' said Laurie. She'd bought the keyring for Alex at Christmas. Now she used it, a stupid human thing to try and keep him close. 'Thank you.'

'What did you think about it? The meeting?'

Laurie pondered for a moment. 'It was . . .' What words could she use: *nice, odd*? Both fitted. She plumped for '. . . better than I expected. I thought I'd give it a go.'

'Me too,' said Pete.

'I wasn't expecting miracles,' said Laurie with a soft smile. 'But I didn't feel as uncomfortable as I thought I might.'

'Me too. Again,' said Pete with a small chuckle. 'There's a comfort to be had in being with people who are going through the same thing. And the cake was moreish. I didn't want any and I ended up having two big slabs.'

'See you again. Have a nice week,' said Laurie, not sure if she'd be back. Not sure if this really was for her.

'Have a good one yourself,' Pete replied. He didn't think he'd be back. Nice as it was sitting eating cake, he couldn't see it working enough to chase the blackness away.

Laurie got into her car and Pete got into his. On the

way home Pete thought about calling in to a shop to buy Pong some more cat food and Laurie thought about what she should buy for her boss's upcoming birthday. They did not think about each other at all.

Chapter 9

Laurie had nearly always arrived home before Alex, so she'd become used to walking into an empty house after work. Usually she'd change out of her suit, tidy anything that needed tidying, although not much ever did because both she and Alex were neat by nature. Then she'd feed Keith Richards the goldfish, who was still going strong after five years. Alex had won him at a fair on one of their first dates. They'd expected him to have died by the morning, but he was still there, in the pan they'd transferred him to from the small plastic bag. The week after, Keith was residing in a luxury BiOrb tank complete with plants, reef, lighting and furniture of interest to hide in and swim around. He'd overcome fin rot and white spot disease and – like his namesake – seemed indestructible. Alex had joked once, 'That bloody fish will outlive me.' *Joked*.

But coming home to an empty house since Alex had died was a totally different experience and she hated it, hated the realisation that the echoey hollowness would not be alleviated by another presence within a couple of hours max. The feeling was compounded by the fact that she'd always thought of this house as more Alex's than hers, even though she put down most of the deposit. He chose it, it was his vision to turn it into the perfect family home. And now he was gone and the house seemed far emptier than it had when he was alive but just not in it, as if his essence was bigger than the sum of his parts.

Laurie changed into her old comfortable tracksuit bottoms, adjusted the cushions on the sofa, gave the carpet a once over with the Dyson, dusted surfaces and the TV. She dropped fish flakes and some tiny defrosted shrimps into Keith Richards' tank and he appeared from his sea tree, catching one of the shrimps before it had a chance to fall far.

'Hi Keith. Sorry I've been a bit distant recently. But I've taken steps to make me better. I went to a group yesterday. Not quite sure if it's for me but it was interesting. Do I go again, what do you think?' Alex used to laugh at her talking to Keith when she fed him but he'd play along. Sometimes he'd hold his phone screen up to the side of the tank and ask Keith what he thought about a tweet or a news item and he would become a temporary ventriloquist and channel Keith's voice. 'Will Brexit affect my diet in any way before I answer your question?' Alex gave Keith the voice of Hugh Grant.

Tears suddenly blindsided her as she recalled them laughing hard at Keith's views. She and Alex had laughed a lot once. *When had they stopped?* She killed that maggot of a question by over-stamping it with a memory of Keith Richards having some choice words to say about Mick Jagger. Alex could be so funny. Charming, magnetic, the life and soul of a party – someone who dictated the mood of a room he walked into. Laurie felt a cool tear slip from the corner of her eye; she dashed it away, then her system went into mad recalibration. It was too easy to cave in and cry when she was away from people, however much she didn't want to. She'd climbed a few rungs out of her grief by going to that club and she needed to carry on climbing. Something strong in her core spoke to her with a kind voice. 'Come on, make tea, you need to eat.'

The kitchen was insanely huge. The whole house was ridiculous for two, never mind one. Half the cupboards were empty because they never had enough things to put in them. There were two double ovens and one had never been used, not even by the previous occupants who'd had the house built. Laurie opened up the massive American fridge where a pint of milk, a block of butter, some Laughing Cow cheese triangles and a bottle of white wine resided. She closed it, opened the freezer side, took out a frozen sweet and sour chicken meal for one which she didn't really want but there was hardly anything in the drawers. She forced herself to eat most days because she didn't want people commenting that she was losing weight and fussing around her, making a big thing of it.

She stabbed the plastic carton with a fork, put it in the microwave, set the timer then returned to the fridge, taking out the white wine and pouring herself a glass. The cold liquid slipped too easily down her throat. She'd drunk far too much over the past months, but she was on top of it now: one glass per alternate day tops as opposed to one bottle every evening and passing out on the sofa. She'd felt herself on a slippery slope until one night when she'd had a dream about Keith talking to her in Alex's Hugh Grant voice: *Come on now, enough girl*. It had felt spookily real, enough to make her take notice.

She nipped to the downstairs loo when the microwave beeped that the cooking time was up and they had now entered the two-minute standing period. The loo was next to Alex's office. She really did need to go in there and look for paperwork that she hadn't been able to find. There had been so much to sort out that she hadn't tackled yet: putting bills into her sole name and the MOT on Alex's sports car was due according to the note on the calendar on the kitchen wall. And upstairs his clothes still hung in his dressing room, rows of beautiful suits and shoes. She didn't know what to do with them. Getting rid of them would be like getting rid of him again, accepting that he wouldn't be coming back. She knew he wouldn't be, but she didn't want the message hammered into her brain with a ten-ton mallet.

She ate, finished and was about to look at some work files when the doorbell rang. She peeped through the spy hole and saw Meredith and Brendan Wilder – Alex's parents. She opened the door. They both looked older than the last time she had seen them, as if weeks had been years.

Meredith's arms opened as she walked over the threshold. She enclosed Laurie in a bony embrace, pulled her tight. She smelled of hairspray and an over-mist of Rive Gauche and as usual was rigged-out as if she was en route to a wedding where the dress code on the invitation stated smart-informal but she had ignored the second word. This time, a white dress and matching coat both crowded with brightly coloured flowers, plus low heels, a matching handbag, a Chanel palette of make-up and a perfect puff of blonde hair. The only things missing were a corsage and a fascinator.

Even in the eye of her grief, her grooming standards hadn't slipped, unlike Laurie's. Brendan followed in her fragrant wake. He was a bulky man, more old-fashioned and casual in his choice of attire: almost always muted shades of blue and relaxed fits but as pristine and pressed as his wife. Brendan, less effusive than Meredith, gave Laurie a small peck on the cheek as he passed her, as if politeness had forced him to concede to an awkward duty.

'Not disturbing you, are we?' said Meredith as Laurie ushered them in, asked them if they wanted something to drink. They both said that a tea would be lovely. As usual, whenever she walked through, Meredith would look up and around as if she were at a house-buying viewing. Laurie knew that Alex's parents believed Fairview had been an unnecessary luxury and that their son had been pressured into buying it by her, rather than the other way round.

'I have rung,' said Meredith, 'but no one answered so I left some messages.'

Laurie cast her eyes sidewards, saw the blinking red light on the house phone. She couldn't remember the last time she'd used it.

'I'm sorry,' she said. 'I never noticed.'

'We didn't want to harass you. We knew that you'd ring us if you wanted to talk to us, but when we didn't hear from you . . . we just thought we'd check in and make sure you were all right. We rang a few times over the last couple of weeks, didn't we Brendan?'

A scoop of guilt landed on Laurie's shoulder; she felt the weight of it as surely as if it were a cold blob of cement. She should have rung them to see if *they* were all right. There should have been more things on her to-do list than work, drink, sleep.

'I'm so sorry,' said Laurie again. 'I've been a bit all over the place. You have my mobile number, don't you?'

'Well, yes, we do but I didn't want to seem as if I was hounding you,' said Meredith. 'Plus I did think if you weren't answering the house phone, you wouldn't answer the mobile.'

'I would have. I wasn't avoiding you,' said Laurie with a watery apologetic smile.

'I'm not trying to say you were.' Meredith smiled back but there was a nip in her tone.

Meredith and Brendan sat down in the lounge while Laurie brewed some tea. Meredith didn't like to sit in the kitchen because she found the seats there uncomfortable. *Comfort often becomes a casualty of style*, she had remarked once. And if Meredith didn't like the seats, Brendan was expected not to like them either.

'How are you two doing?' Laurie called from the kitchen.

Brendan opened his mouth to reply but Meredith cut in. She didn't only wear the trousers in their relationship, but the shirt, Blue Harbour jacket and Panama hat. 'Not bad, considering. We're ploughing all our energies into the arrangements for Naomi and Jefferson's wedding.'

Naomi was Alex's younger sister by ten years. They hadn't been particularly close siblings. Naomi was a spoilt brat indulged child who had grown into a spoilt brat indulged adult. The last Laurie had heard about the wedding was that Naomi couldn't decide between arriving at the church in a Cinderella coach and horses or by helicopter. Meredith saw everything through the prism of her beloved children. Alex used to joke that Laurie, by association with him, was bathed in the same angelic light, but woe betide her should they ever split up. Laurie was an extension of Alex in

Meredith's eyes, and without him she was no longer an honorary member of the charmed family circle.

'Goodness, it's getting close now isn't it,' said Laurie, doing a quick calculation.

'Twelve weeks. It's costing us an arm and a leg,' said Brendan, the words riding on a long outward breath.

Laurie brought a tray of tea through, set it on the coffee table. Three delicate mugs from a set of four bought especially for Meredith's visits because she would only drink from fine bone china.

'Such a big house this,' said Meredith. 'I always wondered why you and Alex went for something this size.'

'Well, it was never meant to be just for us two,' Laurie answered that – again. 'Here, let me move that for you.' She lifted the *Daily Trumpet* file from the sofa so Brendan had more room to spread out.

'Back in the swing of work?' asked Brendan.

'Yes,' said Laurie. 'Back in the swing.'

'That's good,' remarked Meredith. 'We all have to earn a crust. It's what makes the world go round, after all.'

I thought that was love, Laurie didn't say.

Meredith reached for her mug as Brendan reached for his, as if they were synchronised. They both took a sip at exactly the same moment.

'Have you done anything with Alex's clothes yet?' asked Meredith.

'No, I haven't,' said Laurie. 'I should really but I'm not sure what to do with them. Do you ... is there anything you want of his? I know I have to ... do something with his suits but they're too expensive to give to a charity shop and so I ... so I haven't done anything. Yet. I should. I will.' Meredith always made her feel as if she were lacking in efficiency and needed jollying along. *Haven't you got that curtain rail fixed yet? Haven't you rung up about having your guttering cleared? Haven't you packed up my son's worldly possessions and given them to deserving people who might make use of them?*

'Someone in church told me about a place called Fashion . . . something or other UK,' said Meredith. 'They take the clothes and sell them on and the money all goes to charity but they deal with more quality goods. You can choose which charity the money goes to. The Air Ambulance would be a good one to pick.'

'That sounds an ideal solution,' said Laurie.

'I can come and help you pack them away if you want,' suggested Meredith. 'Unless your mother is coming back to help you. I wouldn't want to get in the way.'

'I don't think she has plans to come back for a long time,' said Laurie with certainty. Her mother had done her duty by flying in for the funeral on a haze of Chanel No. 5 complete with big hat and facial net and cried her way through three packets of tissues despite only meeting her prospective son-in-law a handful of times. 'Thank you for asking, but I'm fine doing it by myself.' She didn't want to risk blubbing in front of anyone, and she'd partly held off from tackling it because she knew that it would break her.

Meredith and Brendan both sipped their tea silently and elegantly as if they were at a garden party. The atmosphere seemed strange, charged with an odd energy, as if there was something they weren't saying running underneath the words they were.

'Is that still the same goldfish?' asked Brendan, as if scraping an invisible barrel of subjects for something to talk about.

'Yes, still same Keith. He's indestructible,' said Laurie.

'He landed on his feet here. Look at that tank, must have cost a small fortune,' said Meredith with a hint of disdain. 'All for a fish.'

'So, how are Naomi's wedding plans going?' asked Laurie. Meredith didn't do pets, she would never understand how anyone could have become attached to a goldfish and Laurie wasn't really in the mood for trying to convince her how that worked.

'Expensively, that's how they're going,' replied Brendan. 'Her dress cost fifteen thousand pounds.'

'She bought that herself,' added Meredith quickly, while grinning with pride. 'Like she says, you only get married once.' She took a throatful of tea before continuing. 'You can appreciate that we want to give our girl the day of her dreams.'

'Of course.' Laurie nodded. She could.

'She's our only child now.' Meredith sighed.

'She'll have the best day that money can buy,' confirmed Brendan.

More mention of money; Laurie picked up there was a theme running here.

'As Brendan says though, the best day will be expensive,' continued Meredith. A beat. 'So, do you think you'll be able to afford to stay in this house alone?'

'I expect so,' said Laurie, confused at the quick turn in the conversation. 'For now, I'll stay put until I decide what I want to do with it.'

'It's far too big for you to manage,' Meredith went on, sweeping critical eyes over the room as if seeing every mote of dust in glorious technicolour.

'I'm going to get a cleaner,' said Laurie.

'They're not cheap,' said Brendan, with a 'huh' of sarcasm.

'It's affordable and would be worth it,' said Laurie. They had a cleaner so she wasn't quite sure why she shouldn't. Another job she'd been meaning to get around to and hadn't.

'It's just ... that ... we could really do with our share of the money,' said Meredith. 'Not for us, we don't need it, of course we don't, but for Naomi.' Then she added, 'Alex's sister,' as if Laurie was in any doubt.

Laurie's head gave a slight wobble, as if she needed to shake it to rearrange Meredith's words into an order that made sense.

'I'm sorry, what?'

Meredith's brow crinkled. 'Oh dear ... there's no not-awkward way of putting this, Laurie, but it does need to be said. I think we've left it long enough.'

'What needs to be said?' asked Laurie, clearly confused.

Brendan made a strained noise, shifted in his seat as if feeling the growing discomfort of a pressure sore.

Meredith attempted to clarify and chose to do it in the manner of a patronising and overworked headmistress talking to an idiot child. 'The house is half Alex's, dear.'

Laurie's jaw tightened. Ah, now she saw. So that's what this visit was all about. Had they left her alone to come to this conclusion by herself and when she didn't, decided to chivvy it along into the open? She felt hurt that this had been the reason for their calling on her and that helped to shift the track of any potential response from emotional to rational. When she spoke it was as Laurie De Vere, solicitor, armed with more clear facts than muddying sentiment.

'I'm sorry, Meredith, but you're wrong. The house is all mine. When Alex and I took out the mortgage, we did it as what's called joint tenants, which means that if one of us were to die, the whole house would automatically be the property of the other. It works both ways: if I'd died first, then the house would have been all Alex's, not half my mother's.' Her unapologetic answer served to inflame Meredith, if the way she put her mug back on the coaster was anything to go by. Then she rose to her feet and stared down at Laurie, as if to intimidate her.

'So that's the way you're going to play it is it? Don't you think that Alex would want to see his sister have her dream wedding day and be set up for life? She's his family.' Meredith turned to her husband for backup. 'Brendan, say something. Don't leave it all to me.'

Brendan got up then, eyes cast downward, less comfortable with the confrontation but engaging nonetheless.

'You've inherited a lot of money from our son, Laurie. I know there was his life insurance and his pension, and the car insurance will pay out if it hasn't already. And you'll no doubt use that money for a life with another man . . .'

Laurie stood then; she wasn't going to be peered down on or spoken to like this. 'Whaaat? Brendan—'

But Brendan was determined to finish. 'It's what Alex would have wanted – to see his sister secure.'

How do you know that, Laurie wanted to retort. Alex wasn't fond of his sister at all. Naomi was eight when he left home for university and he never went back to live there. He found her empty-headed and selfish and told Laurie on more than one occasion that blood was their only tie. If she hadn't hooked up with his best friend, he wouldn't have had any interaction with her outside the obligatory family get togethers. Indeed, he couldn't understand what Jefferson saw in 'the vacuous brat' as he called her. He rolled his eyes a lot when he heard the latest news about the wedding from either his parents or Jefferson, who didn't seem to have much say in what was happening on his big day.

Laurie opened her mouth to quote Alex: that if Naomi wanted all the preposterous bells and pricey whistles then it was up to her to pay for them, not his parents, but Meredith rushed in to the space to take over where Brendan had left off, her voice becoming louder and yet more wavery with each word. A furious shake of her limbs accompanied her speech as if the effort of talking like this sent tremors through her sinews. It had all been building inside Meredith for a while, Laurie guessed. That's why they'd stayed away, stoking the fires of this passive aggression until it was finally ready to be unleashed.

'It's cruel that you're denying his only sister. We are all devastated by what has taken place and by rights – both moral and legal – you should see that it is only fair his family isn't left high and dry. You have benefitted far too much from his death.'

Laurie felt the first rumblings of her own anger building, an emotion which had filled her after the accident, packed her to the gills, only for it to ebb away violently, leaving her hollow, reeling. At least when she was angry, she had energy, she could function but when it moved out of her, it took her focus with it, left her wilted as if she had no bones to scaffold her. But now it was mounting again. When she answered, her voice was calm, totally at odds with what was happening within.

'You think I've benefitted from having my heart ripped out? Do you think I want to be here without him?'

'You're a young woman. We know it's unreasonable to expect you'll spend the rest of your life without someone else,' said Brendan, intimating that she had their grudging permission to move on, so long as she tipped up the money instead of spending it on holidays to the South of France with young gigolos.

'Meredith, Brendan, I haven't scooped out the contents of Alex's bank account. The money I have is what the insurance companies paid out on policies we set up to ensure each other's security. It means that I, as the woman he was going to marry, wouldn't have to worry about the mortgage and paying bills on top of the heartache of losing the love of my life, of having my future with him taken away from me.' She fixed Meredith with her soft, bright eyes. 'I can't imagine what it must be like losing a son but I know your heart must be breaking. Mine is too, I feel empty inside without him.' She took a deep breath. 'Alex and I were planning on giving Naomi a thousand pounds for a wedding present and I had every intention of honouring that. If you want it in advance, I can write you a cheque now, but I repeat our finances were jointly set up to pay for our security, not to blow on your daughter's extravagances.'

The last three words seemed to play over and over in the silence that ensued and became colder and more insulting with each echo. From the slapped look on her once future in-laws' faces, Laurie knew she had stepped over an invisible line. Meredith's neck was blotchy with rage and her mouth ironed flat into a grim line.

'Yes, I'll take the cheque now,' she said, words ground out between her teeth.

Laurie crossed to the drawer where she kept, among other things, a cheque book and card for an account with no money in it, a cancelled passport – because she'd lost it and then found it after it had been replaced, a purse with a hundred pounds in it and a fake Rolex in a fake Rolex box bought from a Turkish bazaar. Her 'stupid drawer' as Alex called it: her attempt at foiling any burglars who might be satisfied enough with the contents to cut and run rather than ransack the house in search of further treasures. She felt Meredith's eyes like knives in her back as she opened it.

Laurie made a mental note to transfer some money to cover the sum and avoid bouncing a cheque on them. It was the only account she had a cheque book for and she couldn't remember when she'd used it last. She wrote it, ripped it from the book and held it out. No, she'd make them come over for it, she wouldn't deliver it as well.

With little compunction, Meredith did just that – marched over, snatched the cheque, spat out a *thank you* and, with Brendan close behind, she strode out of the house she thought of as her son's, where Laurie now resided as an illegal squatter. Until the front door slammed, Laurie had no idea how much her heart was racing, whatever her outward composure may have conveyed. She sank onto the arm of the sofa and tried to fathom what had just happened. Well, she wouldn't be going to Naomi's wedding, that was for sure. That let her off the hook, seeing as she wouldn't have felt comfortable watching the groom vow to love and cherish Alex's sister, etc., knowing what he'd said he wanted to do to his fiancée. She felt gloom envelop her like an uncomfortably heavy garment. There would be no coming back from this, which was beyond sad because she had liked Meredith and Brendan. They had welcomed her into their home, given her a template for proper close family life; she'd had barbecues in their garden, she'd loved sourcing unusual presents for them at Christmas and birthdays and never minded when they popped round. She'd anticipated the joy they'd feel when she had a baby, knowing they'd be hands-on grandparents – all now dashed against the rock of cold hard cash. She had more money than she knew what to do with, it was true – and much more to come from the car insurance settlement – but it was all sitting in an account because she didn't even want to think about it yet. Money she had in place of the love of her life.

She'd lost Alex's whole family now, not just him. Death really was the gift that kept on giving.

The *Daily Trumpet* would like to apologise for a feature that appeared in last Friday's edition. Miriam Pearson has been appointed as the council's new head of Public Relations not 'Pubic' Relations, as reported. The wording underneath the photograph should have read 'Miriam Pearson pictured with Will White, CEO of Private Parks' and not Private Parts. Private Parks is an exclusive valet-parking service what have just secured a contract with the hotelier chain Forest Hotels. We apologise for this error and any distress caused.

Chapter 10

Laurie reached into her bag for her phone, pulled up her best friend's number, rang it. Bella answered after two rings.

'Hiya.'

'Can you talk?'

'Yep. I've got you on speaker in the car.'

Laurie took a deep breath. 'Sorry, I had to speak to someone but I don't want to distract you.'

'Distract away. I'm crawling in rush-hour traffic, although I use the term "rush" loosely.'

Laurie launched then into a muddled, disconnected story which made little sense. Bella cut in.

'Laurie, put the kettle on. I'll be at yours in fifteen minutes tops. I was on the way to the supermarket but I'll make a diversion.'

It was on the tip of Laurie's tongue to protest: *No, don't let me put you to any trouble* but she didn't. 'Tea or coffee?' was what she said.

The only good thing to come out of the past six months was that she and Bella had been reunited after drifting apart. She had no idea why that had happened, though she knew it had originated on Bella's side and coincided with Stu, Bella's present partner, entering her life. No other man had ever managed to put a wedge between them, but Stu, it seemed, had achieved it somehow. And yet he'd always appeared so affable when they met.

It started in small ways: Bella's phone going straight to voicemail, but she didn't return any calls. Bella's diary being too full to squeeze in a cinema trip or meeting for a meal. Then contact tailed off to virtually nothing except the odd text. Variations on *Sorry not ignoring you just busy.* For the first time in eighteen years, they hadn't even exchanged Christmas presents and that said it all.

Then Alex had died and Bella had drifted so far off the radar by then that Laurie hadn't even rung her to let her know. But she'd heard somehow and turned up on the doorstep with tear-filled eyes and a bag of shopping – just like the Bella of yore, picking up where they left off, sort of. It could never quite be the same because they'd broken up over something unsaid which had cleaved a scar in the flowery field of their friendship. However much the grass grew back over it, the scar remained underneath.

Bella knocked once and breezed in.

'In here,' called Laurie from the kitchen.

'Okay, what's up? I couldn't work out what you meant, it was all jumbled,' said Bella. She sat on one of the six chrome bar chairs that stood around the island, the ones that Meredith wouldn't deign to perch on. 'Now, tell me again, Brendan and Meredith what?'

Laurie lifted up the cafetière and poured. 'They came round,' she began. She noticed her hand was shaking. 'It was awful. They more or less accused me of stealing Alex's money.'

'Put the jug down, I'll pour the coffees out. You look freaked. What do you mean "stealing"?'

Laurie did as she was told, let Bella take over.

'Stealing monies that the insurances paid out,' Laurie explained.

Bella's face crinkled into a mask of incredulity. 'What?'

'They think I should hand over a load of cash to Naomi.'

Bella put the cafetière down with an unconscious slam. 'Why?'

'Because I'm benefitting from his death and I'm not family.'

'Benefitting? Odd word for it. Cheeky fuckers.'

'I tried to explain to them but they've obviously been chewing this over for some time. They want me to sell up.'

Bella's jaw dropped. 'They actually said that?'

'The inference was clear enough, I thought. Then hand over half the money to them. They need it to finance Naomi's wedding and her future. It's what Alex would have wanted, they said.'

'Not if he'd found out the truth about his best mate's thoughts towards you, he wouldn't. Did you tell them about their soon to be new son-in-law's shag-banter?'

Despite herself, Laurie laughed. Bella always had called a spade a bastard shovel.

'No, I didn't, but I expect that the truth will out. Lies never like to be underground for long, do they?'

'Got any biscuits?'

Laurie slid the biscuit tin towards her.

The tin had stood empty for months but she'd remembered to refill it at the weekend. She didn't eat them herself but Alex had mainlined biscuits: Oreos, Nice, Malted Milk mostly; she couldn't bear to buy any of those.

Bella unwrapped a Twix finger and devoured half in one bite.

'I'm starving,' she explained. 'Haven't had time for lunch today.'

'Let me make you a sandwich. I've got cheese or—'

'No, Stu's doing one of his pot-roasts. This'll do nicely.' Bella batted the offer away. 'I tell you, Laurie, the manager of the Golden Oak is a complete tosser. Couldn't sort a staff rota out if his life depended on it.'

Bella was the HR executive manager for a chain of hotels and seemingly spent her life zipping between them sorting out problems. 'Pay peanuts and you get monkeys' was Forest Hotels' motto. Luckily they didn't pay her peanuts. She was their keystone, but she earned every penny of her high five-figure salary.

'I haven't known whether to say anything to Naomi about you-know-what,' said Laurie. 'Half of me says I should but the much bigger half tells me to stay out of it.'

'Listen to the bigger half. No way should you say anything,' said Bella, spraying biscuit crumbs on the table. 'No way at all.' She swallowed. 'You'll be labelled the bad guy, not him. Let's just hope that it was a miscalculated blip on his part, even though we know that it's not because men of quality don't make blips like that.'

'He had just lost his best friend,' said Laurie. 'I keep wondering if it was a misguided way of . . . staying close to him.'

'By asking you for a shag?' Bella pulled a face. 'Do you *really* believe that, Laurie?'

Laurie shook her head slowly from side to side.

'Not really.'

'Stay clear of the lot of them. Sounds like now you have the perfect excuse to. I always wondered if Alex's parents were as nicey-nicey as they seemed to be. There was just something about them that never quite rang true. They made the Brady Bunch look like the Mansons. No one is that wholesome.'

Laurie shivered, feeling suddenly as cold as if a blanket had been ripped from her shoulders, which it had in a way.

'I feel rocked.'

'They aren't worth feeling rocked about, Laurie. It's disgusting. In fact it's getting more horrible the more I think about it. Put them out of your mind and sod Princess Naomi.' Bella's voice softened then. 'Do you want me to come and help you with Alex's things? I know you're dreading it.'

'No, I'll manage,' said Laurie.

'I'm off tomorrow, I don't mind breaking the back of the work for you, sort stuff into piles . . .'

'Thanks, but I'm okay.'

Bella had known Laurie long enough to realise when she really meant no and wasn't just being polite.

'If you change your mind, you know where I am,' she said, sneaking another biscuit out of the jar.

'I didn't tell them this, but Alex didn't have any money in his account, Bella,' blurted out Laurie. 'I don't know where it went. I mean he put money in our joint account for the bills every month, but there was none in his own.'

Bella stopped chewing for a long second as if she couldn't think and eat at the same time, then carried on.

'Maybe he transferred it to an ISA or something. He was careful with money wasn't he, so the likelihood is that he didn't put it all on a horse.'

'He wouldn't even do the lottery so I know it's not gambling. No doubt I'll find out what he did with it when I go through the files in his office, because he was a stickler for paperwork. Always paper; even when he got insurance documents sent by email, he ran them off so he had paper copies. But for there to be not a single penny in his account at all . . .' Her words trailed off. Bella noticed the worry lines that had appeared on Laurie's forehead.

'I'm sure there's a very simple explanation.'

'I'm sure too,' said Laurie with a nod. But she wasn't. Not really.

Chapter 11

His work shift finished for the day, Pete walked into the house he used to call home when he shared it with Tara and still, after six months, it felt noticeably different to all the times he'd walked into the house when Tara was alive but not in there. His dad's neighbour, trying to be helpful, had said that Tara 'would still be around', hoping to give him comfort. But he'd never felt that. She had gone finally and forever, however much he had tried to convince himself she was just at the shops or at work. Sometimes it felt as if she had never even been there at all.

There were just his clothes in the wardrobe now, just his toiletries in the bathroom. He had taken the bulk of Tara's things around to Bob and Pam Ollerton's house for her sisters. Tara had been a shopaholic and had lots of beautiful clothes, jewellery and shoes, bags, boxes of unopened high-end toiletries and her family had been touched at the gesture. Pete thought it was right his wife's possessions went to people she loved, to use, wear, treasure, rather than strangers to whom they would mean much less.

Outside the front door was a skip. Pete had started to strip the house because he couldn't bear to live there any more and wanted to move. First step, decluttering; second, the For Sale sign. He didn't want to carry on trying to convince himself that Tara was 'out' and would be back soon.

He'd missed calls on the home phone because there was a red spot of light flashing. He pressed the button and heard an automated voice saying, 'You have three messages. Message one.' 'Pete, it's your dad. Just ringing in to see how you are lad. Give me a call when you've time.' He was just about to pick up the receiver when message two began. 'Pete, it's Bob. Ollerton. Pam and I are hoping you're okay. Don't be a stranger. You come and see us whenever you want, you know.' Message three was someone with a foreign accent telling him that he needed to stump up some cash as his internet security had been compromised. He'd ring his father and father-in-law after he'd eaten, he decided. He didn't even know if Bob was officially his father-in-law any more.

Pong, Pete's old Siamese cat, padded down the stairs making disgruntled and off-the-scale miaow sounds, Siamese cat language for 'where the hell have you been?' He spent the hours when Pete was at work sleeping on his bed, where he hadn't been allowed to sleep when Tara was alive because she said it was unhygienic. He occasionally ventured outside on warm days to sunbathe on the decking and wee on plants, but he was primarily an indoor cat. He wandered over to Pete and sat squarely in front of him, waiting to be picked up and worshipped. Pong had been his cat long before Tara had burst into his life. She hadn't really seen the point in having a cat as a pet, a statement which had made Pete laugh because he could see she had a valid argument in a way. Pong didn't give a lot back in return for free board and lodgings and when he sat on Pete's lap it was so that he could be stroked, not to give comfort. Pong had never really acknowledged Tara's presence, but he did allow her to feed him and pet him when she felt inclined to. Then Tara had died and Pong had made up for every point of his previous selfishness by just being there, a presence that saved the house from being a soulless vacuum.

Pete fed Pong, then showered, put on his tracksuit bottoms and T-shirt and looked in the fridge for something to eat. There was a lasagne in there, but he didn't feel like it – for more than one reason. Tara had hated cooking, although she was a dab hand at putting a pre-cooked meal in the oven, but he loved bustling around the kitchen, experimenting with spices and putting his own twist on established recipes and sometimes (when he was alone) even pretended he was a TV chef being filmed while delivering a commentary, but he'd lost his appetite for it all since he became a widower. *Widower*: a word he had always associated with someone much older than thirty-two. He closed the fridge, opened the larder. He was deciding between a Pot Noodle and a tin of soup when the doorbell rang. He closed his eyes briefly, an unconscious gesture of not wanting to engage. He just wanted a quiet night in with the TV for company, Pong on his lap and a possible hunt through Rightmove for a flat for one, a place that fitted snugly around him and his cat, that didn't leave lonely spaces. Then he heard the door open and a gruff male voice shouted.

'It's us, you in? Get the kettle on.'

Pete's mood automatically swooped upwards like a fairground ride as his brother entered the kitchen, greeted him briefly in the way they'd done since they were kids, half-handshake, half-hug, right shoulders bouncing. Once upon a time they were mirror images of each other but these days, not quite so. Griff 'The Griffalo' had abandoned the razor and embraced his hirsuteness. He was also much more muscular than Pete. He weight-lifted for fun, having caught the gym bug in his teens. He'd run his own gym since he was twenty and when a personal trainer called Lucy who used to be in their class at school had arrived for a job interview, he'd given her the job and then made her his wife. She followed Griff into the kitchen and always looked tiny when placed next to him. She was petite and trim with dark rock-chick choppy hair and the prettiest smile on the planet.

'Hello, Lucy,' said Pete, giving her a full hug, no bouncy shoulder action.

'Hello, darling,' she replied. 'How are you? Hello, Pong,' she added when the cat started rubbing against her leg the way he never did to Tara.

'Not bad,' Pete answered her. Standard answer to a question asked too often but always kindly meant, he knew that. 'So coffee for three then, is it? Sit yourselves down.'

'Not interrupting you are we?' asked Lucy. 'We were just passing en route to the supermarket and saw you were home.'

'You have eternal permission to interrupt me, Lucy,' said Pete, meaning it. Lucy was as close to him as his brother was. He could never tire of their company.

'So, what's happening?' said Griff, scraping the chair back from the kitchen table. He was incapable of doing things quietly, always had been. The much noisier of the two, bigger, louder, stronger. Everything '-er'.

'Not much,' said Pete, pulling three mugs out of the cupboard. One said 'Pete – My One and Only Valentine' on it. Something flicked his heart, like an elastic band pinging against thin skin.

'Any funny work stories?' asked Griff.

'Not really.'

'Juice not got his head stuck again?' Everyone in the town knew Juice.

'Not that I know of.'

'I heard he was in the *Trumpet* for pelting the mayor with sausage rolls.'

'Yep. A protest about Brexit, apparently.' Pete pulled a 'WTF?' face.

'Pass the biscuits while you relate said tale,' said Griff.

'I'll get them.' Lucy reached for the red tin that looked like a dustbin.

'Nothing much more to tell. He asked the magistrate to take into consideration that they were veggie sausage rolls as the mayor and his missus are vegans. It wasn't exactly a valid defence.'

'Poor Juice,' said Lucy, who recognised that there was a lost soul inside the laughing-stock he had become.

'I still have no idea how he got his head in those bars in the playground. Not even you could have bent them,' said Pete.

Griff beamed, lifted his arms into a pose, kissed his guns.

'Oh, please,' said Lucy with a tut.

'But you're okay, yeah?' said Griff. Concern always there, threaded through his frivolity.

'Okay as can be,' came the reply as Pete stirred milk into the cups. He contemplated telling his brother about the meeting at the teashop he'd been to yesterday then thought better of it, especially as he wouldn't be going again.

'Any *visitors* recently?' asked Griff. The word had a weight to it which Pete understood immediately and he gave his brother a glare of disapproval.

'Sorry. Didn't mean to ask that,' said Griff, drawing even more attention to what he shouldn't have said.

Lucy jumped straight on it. 'What's this?'

Pete brought all three mugs across together. He sat down then, opposite his brother.

'Well?' Lucy prompted. 'Don't you two dare keep secrets from me.'

'Ria,' said Griff, as if that explained everything. It didn't.

'What do you mean "Ria"? Do you mean Tara's sister? That Ria? What about her?'

'I've told you, haven't I?' said Griff.

'Obviously not, or I'd know what you were talking about, you numpty,' Lucy replied.

'It's probably nothing,' said Pete.

'It's not nothing,' said Griff.

'Will one of you please tell me what is going on?' Lucy growled.

'Ria's been bringing Pete food parcels,' said Griff, stroking Pong, who had leapt upon the table now, sitting between his human aunt and uncle like a porcelain ornament.

'And?' The tilt of Lucy's eyebrows implied that she needed more info to assess what that meant.

'I'm not ungrateful, Luce,' said Pete. 'But . . .' he scratched his head. 'I might be wrong . . .'

'You know you aren't,' said Griff.

'I'm presuming you don't mean the problem is the food,' said Lucy.

'It's just a feeling. I don't want you thinking I'm a prick,' replied Pete.

'I do that anyway,' said Lucy. 'Go on, tell me what you mean.'

Pete gave a resigned sigh before opening up the fridge,

returning seconds later with a foil container. He ripped off the top and put it on the table.

'Is that a heart?' said Griff, peering at the sprinkle of herbs on the top of the lasagne.

'It's not an ink-blot test,' said Lucy. She looked again. 'Actually, you might be right, Griff. So what's it all about then?'

'About three months ago, Ria called in to see how I was,' said Pete, putting the container back in the fridge. 'I hadn't seen her since the funeral. I opened the door and nearly dropped. She had one of Tara's dresses on. And she was wearing Tara's perfume. I took Tara's stuff around to her parents' house for Ria and Alana, so her turning up like that wasn't too left field, even if it did give me a bit of a shock.'

'Okay,' said Lucy, in a tone that suggested she was processing all the information.

'It's only a feeling,' Pete went on. Then he buried his head in his hands. 'God, Luce, I really hope I'm wrong but I wonder if . . . I think Ria is . . . trying to get close to me. She's been five times since, always with food, which is really nice of her, but . . .' He made a sound of exasperation. 'I know what you're going to say—'

'No you don't,' said Lucy, cutting him off. 'She's becoming "sticky", is that what you mean?'

Pete's head snapped up. He had expected Lucy, who was the epitome of common sense, to tell him his perspective was well off and not to be so stupid or ungrateful.

'Yes,' he said. 'That's exactly it.'

'Pretend you aren't in,' said Griff.

'I don't want to sit here hiding though, Griff,' said Pete. 'On Tuesday she was parked outside waiting for me to get home from work at half-eight in the morning. She was just passing on her way in to the salon, she said. She must have my shift patterns written down. She stayed nearly an hour and in the end I had to tell her I needed to get to bed because I'd had a hard night and was knackered.'

'She didn't offer to join you?' said Griff.

Lucy smacked his arm. 'That really isn't helpful, Griff,' she admonished him.

'It was awkward as hell. Do I tell her not to come round? That would be rude, wouldn't it? I've possibly got all this wrong.'

'And you possibly haven't,' said Lucy. 'I think you may have to . . . not be so nice, Pete, if this isn't helping you. It might be that she feels close to you because you were close to her sister, but then again, maybe it's more and I'm pre-suming you don't want that.'

'No I don't,' said Pete vehemently. 'It would be like you and me getting together.'

'Oh, cheers,' said Lucy.

'You know what I mean.'

Lucy's hand cupped over Pete's.

'Yes of course I do. You have your own grief to deal with, Pete. You aren't a plaster for anyone else's.'

He looked down at Lucy's hand and inadvertently com-pared it to Tara's. His wife had tiny hands that she hated, so she always tried to make her fingers look longer with ridiculous-length nails.

'Has Alana been to see you?' asked Lucy, about Tara's eldest sister.

'Yes, a couple of times. And I didn't feel awkward at all. She stayed for a coffee the first time, dropped off some photos she had of Tara the second time and invited me to go and see her and Rick whenever I wanted. And that was that.'

'Nothing "sticky",' said Griff.

'Not at all.'

'Then be careful,' said Lucy. 'Maybe you have to be cruel to be kind. In a small measure. Though I can't imagine you being in the slightest bit cruel.'

Her hand left Pete's and he felt his skin chill. He missed someone touching him. Then again, he had begun to miss that long before Tara had died.

'Change the subject. Brighten my day up, tell me how the tests are going,' said Pete.

Lucy and Griff shifted in their seats, a synchronised movement.

'Nothing to brighten up the day there, I'm afraid,' said Lucy. 'We're just waiting to do more and then we have to wait for yet more results.' She wasn't on solid ground talking to Pete about babies.

'Don't keep me out of the details,' said Pete, as if sensing this. 'You telling me that I'm going to be an uncle would be the best news.'

'You'll be the first to know,' said Griff and made a small growl of frustration in his throat. 'I sometimes wonder if they know what they're doing in that hospital, though. Loo still in the same place, is it?'

'Last time I looked, it was.'

Griff left his seat, walked out of the kitchen door. There was something his brother wasn't telling him, thought Pete. He didn't press it because there was plenty he wasn't telling his brother either.

'I mean it, Luce, I don't want you to keep me out of the loop because of what happened to me,' Pete said, when he heard the door of the downstairs loo shut.

'We're trying not to get screwed up about it all the way

some people do. If we can't have kids, we can't – it's not a right. I know it's me that's the problem. My sisters have got six between them and my brother's on to number four. I just know.'

'You could try and adopt if the worst comes to the worst.'

'I think we would. Nigel will make a lovely grandad, we can't deny him that role,' said Lucy, pushing out a smile.

Pete nodded. His dad would, she was right about that. He wasn't so sure about his new partner Cora being a grandma, but she might surprise them all. Maybe a step-grandmother status might soften her or unpucker her face, as Griff so delicately put it.

'He worries about you, your dad,' said Lucy. 'I'm telling tales but I overheard him talking to Griff about you last week. He's torn between not wanting to be a helicopter parent and being concerned about you.'

'I'll go see him on my next day off,' said Pete. He hadn't seen his dad for a month, which was possibly the longest period apart they'd ever had. 'I'll be honest, Lucy, things that seemed so effortless before take stupid amounts of energy these days. And I include in that going to see my dad, which makes me sound like the totally shit son I am.'

'Don't be ridiculous. You've had more than enough on your plate, but I know he'd be glad to see you. I also know that it's not as easy as it used to be to call on him now that Cora is on the scene. She doesn't exactly roll out the red carpet, does she?'

Griff returned, fingers crossed like a crucifix.

'Did I hear you mention *Elsa*'s name?' he asked and started to trill a very bad rendition of 'Let it Go' from *Frozen*.

'Griff, behave yourself,' said Lucy.

'Frigid old bat, I can't stand—'

'Griff. Shut up.'

Griff threw his hands up in surrender. 'The boss has spoken, so shut up I will. We're going to the supermarket, if you want to tag along. We can shop for beans together. How exciting is that?'

'Thanks, but I'm washing my hair,' replied Pete.

Lucy drained her cup and took it over to the sink to swill.

'I suppose we'd better shoot. Anything we can pick up for you and drop off?'

'Want another lasagne?' asked Griff.

'Funny.'

Lucy leaned over Pete and gave him a kiss.

'Don't get up. Come and see us whenever you want,' she said.

'I will.'

'Don't make us come and fetch you,' said Griff, thumping his brother on the arm.

'Don't nag him,' said Lucy, 'let me do that.' She wagged her finger at Pete. 'Remember what I said, don't be a stranger.'

'I totally promise.'

Pete picked up his mug and looked at the writing on it again. Tara had bought it for him the month after they had married, two years ago. When everything had been all right and life was about looking forward, planning, counting his blessings. When love had been two-way traffic.

Chapter 12

31 August

Pete arranged to meet his father at the weekend for a game of snooker. Ordinarily they would have met at the club, but Nigel's car had flashed up a warning light and so he asked his son if he wouldn't mind picking him up. No problem, Pete had said, feeling a knot of dread land with a resounding thud in his stomach at the thought.

Pete knocked on the door of the house he was brought up in and waited. It was a substantial, solid 1930s detached property in a street filled with the same. There was a warm, community feel to Northwood Avenue because most of its residents had been there for many years, some second-generation dwellers. It had been a wonderful house to be brought up in because the architect understood the importance of space and light, and gardens large enough for families to play in and enjoy while not being such a ridiculous size that maintaining them was a chore too far. Long after Pete had moved out of it, he still considered this house his home and breezed into it whenever he visited, put on the kettle to make a cuppa for his mum, plonked himself on the sofa to watch a match with his dad. His parents had told both of their sons that for as long as they were living there, it would always be their home. But all that changed when Cora had moved in the previous year. It was her home now, no longer theirs at all, something she had made very clear without needing to say a word. Pete respected this, of course, but it still felt weird to be treated as a stranger to a house he knew as well as if it were an old friend.

Through the glass panel in the door, Pete saw the fuzzy image of Cora walking down the hallway and he braced himself for her greeting, which, if she adhered to form, would be anything but welcoming. The more he knew her, the less he knew her, as if she had placed an impenetrable barrier around herself. He was happy that his dad had found someone else for love and companionship, but − and he knew that Griff felt exactly the same − he wouldn't have thought their father would have chosen someone like Cora. She was so different from their mother Julie-Anne, who had been warm and effusive. At her funeral Nigel had used the word *apricity* in conjunction with her, a word Pete had never heard before that day or since but it summed his mum up perfectly: 'The feeling of sun on your face on a winter's morning. That was Julie-Anne,' Nigel said. 'She brought sunshine to my every season.' Cora was the opposite. An aura reader wouldn't have been able to see any colours hanging around her for the polar blizzard.

Julie-Anne had been dead just over a year and a half when he'd met the sixty-two-year-old widow Cora at a St John's Ambulance first-aid course. Six months later she had moved in. Their dad seemed happy, told them all the platitudes: that Cora was quiet, different when they were alone, but somehow, Pete struggled to believe it. She had not said one thing to him, even when he was in the midst of his grief, that made him think a heart beat inside the woman.

Cora opened the door. She always kept it locked when she was in residence, probably to prohibit Nigel's family members from automatic admittance. She was an elegant woman of average height with soft curves and a flawless complexion but would have been infinitely more attractive had she not exuded such a froideur. She had one set to her face and it didn't feature even the hint of a smile. Still Pete was never less than polite, even if he had given up hope of ever breaking through her hard shell. He didn't think there would be anything to find inside even if he did.

'Hello, Cora,' he said, forcing out a smile of his own. 'Dad ready?'

She didn't answer, just moved aside to allow him to enter. She jabbed a finger towards the conservatory but turned left into the lounge herself, pulling the door to behind her.

'Hello lad,' said Nigel, who was sitting at a small table looking at a manual. Nigel had a ready, cheerful air like his sons. They had inherited their mother's gentle manner and soft, grey eyes but everything else from their father: thick dark hair, height, big shoulders, strong physique and a slightly larger than average nose that was nevertheless a perfect fit for their faces. 'Car needs a software update apparently. I was trying to see if I could do it myself.'

'Dad, just take it to the garage.' said Pete.

'It's booked in for Monday. Software update, I ask you.' He made a *pah* sound. 'Too much technology. Same with TVs. They used to last forever, but these days after three years you have to buy a new one because nothing is compatible with these *smart* contraptions.' He slammed the manual shut, put it back inside the plastic case and then into a drawer behind him. Nigel had instilled in his sons the need for order from an early age. He kept manuals, receipts and guarantees so that if he ever needed them, he could lay his hands immediately on them. 'Just give me a minute to get my cue,' he said.

Pete sat down on one of the two sofas in the large space. His mother had always wanted a conservatory and the builders had been putting the finishing touches to it when she died. She'd never had the chance to sit in it and read while Nigel played snooker in it as they'd planned. Then Cora had moved in and the conservatory became her 'parlour' as she called it. She entertained friends from her ladies' club here, got out the best china and homemade cake for them.

'Here I am,' said Nigel, threading his arms into his jacket. 'I'll just say goodbye to Cora. She's watching a box set about the queen.' He pulled a face then walked down the hallway, bobbed his head into the lounge. Pete heard Cora say, in a voice meant to be overheard, that Nigel was not to be late home as Francis and Lesley were coming for tea. Francis was Cora's older brother, Lesley his wife. Both shared an equal disposition to being miserable twats.

The snooker club was Nigel Moore's happy place. Concentrating on potting coloured balls into holes had helped him rejoin the human race when Pete and Griff's mum – his wife of thirty-five years – had died. That was why Nigel was so worried about his son because he knew what a dark place he'd been to when Julie-Anne left him. He also knew that his son needed some time alone to grieve in peace and wrestle with a whole host of unreasonable feelings of guilt that he hadn't been a good-enough husband to his wife or told her enough that he loved her – and, in

Nigel's case, that he'd not gone with her to the supermarket that day as he usually did, and hadn't been with her when she collapsed from a massive heart attack and never got up again.

As they parked outside the club Pete said, 'Sorry I've not been in touch before, I—'

Nigel cut Pete off. 'You don't need to explain, lad. I know how it is. I wanted to give you some space but I'm glad you rang me, I really am. Now, let me whip your arse with my super cue.'

'You wish.'

Nigel paid for two hours play at the reception desk, batting back his son's insistence on paying.

'I'll get the drinks in which is more expensive, shall I? Yes, I know your game,' said Pete with mock annoyance.

'If you insist. I'll set up, you go and spend your wage on treating your old dad to a pint of John Smith's,' said Nigel with a chuckle.

'Heads or tails?' asked Nigel when Pete returned.

'Heads,' called Pete. 'I'm not getting caught out on that double-headed coin you used to carry around when we were kids.'

Pete had no doubt that he still had it, along with the distorted penny that he pretended to stretch and a selection of other pocket magic detritus he carried around with him whenever he suspected there would be children who might need entertaining. Nigel Moore was a man waiting for a whole new generation of Moore children to convince he was a wizard. All hopes were now on Griff and Lucy producing the first of them. After years of trying naturally without even a sniff of success, they had got to the point where medical intervention had had to be sought.

'Tails,' said Nigel, removing his hand to prove how the coin had fallen. 'I'll break.'

He chalked the tip of his cue. Pete had bought it for him last year as his sixty-fourth birthday present and it had been made to the same weight, length, tip size and balance point stats as his hero Ronnie O'Sullivan's cue. Plus it had a plaque bearing his initials.

'Have you seen anything of Tara's family recently?' asked Nigel, thudding the white into the bottom cushion. It rebounded into the triangle of red balls and fluked one into the middle pocket.

'You jammy git.'

'Skill, lad, not luck,' said Nigel, strutting around the table like a peacock.

Pete answered the question then. 'I haven't seen her parents, but I've spoken to them on the phone. Her sister Ria's been round a few times and brought over things to eat.'

'That's kind of her,' said Nigel. 'Your auntie Sue did the same for me when your mother passed away. I hope Ria's cooking is better. Your auntie Sue nearly made me fill my burial plot a bit sooner than I'd planned for.'

Pete smiled at that. His auntie Sue was as loud and brash as his mother was quiet and refined, but her heart was totally in the right place. 'Yes, it's all good stuff.' *Perfect in fact*, Pete thought to himself. Designer cuisine.

'Way to a man's heart is through his stom—' Then Nigel cringed. 'Ignore that. I don't even know why I said it, it was crass. As if it would even cross your mind . . . with Tara's sister. Sorry.'

'It's okay Dad. Don't worry about it.'

Nigel lined up to sink the pink ball.

'I'll be honest, and I've never told anyone this before, but when Sue used to come round, I started to see her in a romantic light. I never did anything about it obviously because I knew I was doolally tap up here—' he poked himself in the temple '—plus your mother would have sent down a thunderbolt for making a move on her sister. I knew Sue was just being kind, no more than that. Grief connected us, that's all it was. I came to my senses and no one was any the wiser . . . Bingo.' The pink hit the pocket.

'You never told me that before,' said Pete. 'Not sure I want to think about you and Auntie Sue.' Auntie Sue was only slightly less hairy than Griff.

'I know you've gone back to work and are craving normality, but be warned, son, it takes your brain a bit of time to catch up with everything that's happened. You get so good at saying you're fine, trying to make people not feel awkward when they ask if you're coping that no one realises if you're struggling. You end up believing your own lies. Everything gets distorted. It's only been six months for you. It helped me to finally admit that I wasn't as all right as I was telling everyone I was. Even to you and Griff.'

Words of wisdom indeed. Maybe he was seeing Ria in a light that she didn't deserve to be lit with. His thinking processes outside work were off-kilter, he knew that. He just hoped they weren't so skew-whiff that he ended up feeling lonely enough to settle for the companionship of a cold fish like Cora Caldwell. Griff and Lucy referred to her mostly as Elsa, after the *Frozen* character, and not because she was beautiful and misunderstood.

'Hurry up and miss a ball, I'm getting bored,' said Pete as Nigel potted another red and a blue.

'Work gone all right this week?'

'Yeah.'

'I'm glad. There, I've missed. I did it deliberately for you, because that's the sort of dad I am.'

''Course you did,' said Pete, getting in position to pot the red his father had just missed, which was tantalisingly near the top pocket.

'Rescued any cats from trees this week?'

'I wish I had a pound for every time you've asked me that, Dad. No. I've fitted ten smoke alarms and rescued a lad's arm from a chocolate vending machine in the gym. A boy called – I kid you not – Tommy Cruise.'

Nigel clicked his fingers. 'Oh, I knew there was something I meant to tell you and you've just reminded me. I've booked a holiday. It's not until next year though. I'm going on a cruise.'

'Well, you're getting to the age when cruises are starting to look attractive, Dad.' Pete nudged the red into the pocket and fist-pumped.

'Cheeky,' said Nigel.

'Where are you going and when?'

'Norway. Next Feb.'

Pete gave his father a look. 'Are you daft? It'll be freezing.'

'That's the idea,' replied Nigel. 'Your mother always wanted to go and see the Northern Lights, so I'm going for her.'

'But taking Cora.' It came out harder than he'd meant it to.

'Yes, well . . . I can't take your mum, can I?'

Pete aimed for the brown but his concentration had gone. He sank the white instead. The mood had darkened slightly. The mere mention of Cora had a tendency to do that.

'Are you happy with Cora, Dad?' The question was out before he had a chance to think about asking it.

'We get on well, if that's what you mean,' said Nigel. 'I know she isn't everyone's cup of tea. She's very different to your mother.'

Pete wrestled against making any further comment. It wasn't his business and he shouldn't have raised the matter. Who knew what happened behind closed doors? Maybe Cora revealed a warm and friendly alter ego to his dad.

'Well, I hope you have a nice time,' he said.

'Cora's not keen if I'm honest. I booked it as a surprise and I was a bit disappointed by her response. She wanted the Bahamas.'

'Oh? I thought she'd be—' *at home with all that ice* '—thrilled.'

'She'll come round. And if she doesn't, I'll change it for warmer climes.' Nigel sighed. 'No, it won't be the same as going with your mother, I'll give you that. She'd have started packing for it already.' He smiled, then as quickly as the smile spread, it contracted, fell from his lips. 'I miss her like hell, Pete. We both made a pact that if either of us was to go, the other should find someone else to love but it's not the same. It could never be the same.'

Nigel's blue eyes clouded. Julie-Anne used to say he had eyes like a doll – beautiful, bright, fringed with thick black eyelashes, which he still had. It had been his eyes that she had fallen in love with first, she'd always told everyone.

'Does Cora love you back though, Dad?'

'In her own way,' said Nigel with a sniff as he leaned over the table and took aim. 'I'm sure she does.'

Pete dropped his dad off at his home afterwards so he could spend the evening with Francis and Lesley which, said Nigel, was sitting on the list of 'things to look forward to' alongside an enlarged prostate examination. Nigel turned and waved to him before going inside and Pete imagined his mother rushing out, ordering him to park up and have a cup of tea with her. He'd end up staying for a meal because she'd insist. She was a wonderful cook, not a fancy one but everything she made was always so tasty and colourful. Greens with everything. Pete coughed away a ball of emotion that rose to his throat. He'd always wanted with Tara what his dad had with his mum and they would have had it, given the time. A house so full of love it rushed out at you when you opened the front door. He'd have made it happen. He would have found the love she lost for him and put it back in her heart where it belonged.

Chapter 13

Laurie had decided to bite the bullet and clear out Alex's things that weekend instead of procrastinating any longer. Common sense told her that it might make her move on more than she had done because, in her weak moments – and there had been many of those – the sight of his gorgeous suits, his ties, even his balled socks brought tears tumbling from a never-ending well within her. His jumpers sat patiently on the shelves like faithful dogs, waiting for their master to return, choose, wear. She would press her face into the wool, breathing in the faded scent, wishing him back there beside her with every ounce of her will, begging to feel the slightest touch of him through the membrane that separated the living from the dead. He would have tried to give her something, anything – however small – to convince her that she meant something to him, she knew, if there was an afterlife. Whether with love – or guilt.

Residing in this nebulous present full of undealt-with duties was a false sanctuary and practical everyday life was knocking at the door. Alex's possessions were now doing more harm than good to her. Letting them go would not mean she was expunging him from her heart, but she had to start getting through whole days without crying. And she also needed to make sure that Alex's financial situation was in order, that there were no outstanding debts or liabilities. She had to find out where the money in Alex's account had gone, even if she didn't want to. She needed to know that there were simple explanations for the things which were worrying her brain – awake and asleep. She needed to know that what was wrong between her and Alex could have healed with work and time. That *she* could have healed them.

She had taken some empty storage boxes from work. Not bin-liners; putting Alex's things in those wouldn't have felt right. She started with his wardrobe and took a deep fortifying breath as she reached for the first hanger. Alex spent a lot of money on clothes. Each piece had a memory woven into the threads for Laurie. This black suit, for instance, was one he had worn at his uncle's funeral. He'd said, under his breath, to her in church that as long as he was going to other people's funerals and they weren't coming to his, it was okay. In other people's wardrobes were now outfits that they had worn to Alex's funeral and they'd have that memory attached to them, and so it went on – a chain of sadness. She blinked rising tears away, knowing that she had a lot of work ahead of her and needed to be stronger than this. Maybe she should have asked Bella to help because she didn't cry in front of other people, she had control over herself then – mostly – but alone, with licence to let go, she liquefied.

She willed some steel into her spine, checked the suit pockets before folding it up, recording the size and a brief description for the charity people in a notebook. She'd arranged with Fashion Aid UK to collect the clothes from her on Tuesday. She'd searched for their website so she wouldn't have to ring Meredith for details. How had it come to this, that she was cut adrift from the only proper family she'd known?

The blue suit was her favourite, the one that Alex had planned to wear to Naomi and Jefferson's engagement party before he'd splashed out on the green Armani one. Meredith and Brendan had paid for a three-course meal for forty people at the high-falutin Woolbury Hall. It was grander than some wedding receptions. There had been a misprint on the menu worthy of a *Daily Trumpet* entry: 'Fish of the Day – Pan-fried Crap with seasonal vegetables'. Meredith had been furious and her complaint had led to ten per cent off the bill. Alex had been the one to first spot it and comment; probably the only person in the party who dared. He'd eventually made his mother laugh about it too; then because she had, everyone else had papal dispensation to join in with the hilarity.

Alex had Meredith wrapped around his finger, but then, Alex had everyone wrapped around his finger. He was charm personified, handsome, magnetic, killer smile, intense blue eyes that made you feel you were the only person in the world and he had hooked Laurie within an hour of meeting her. She recalled his opening line: '*Hi, I'm Mr Right, someone said you were looking for me.*' A hiccup of laughter brought tears with it, as if the two could not be separated. How could all that life and energy disappear from the planet in less than two hours from his last phone call to her? If she'd picked up, would that have somehow changed fate? If she'd kept him talking for only five minutes, he might have missed being in the crash. She felt a weight of sadness begin to settle inside her like fast-setting concrete and gave herself a shake to dispel it.

She packed up two boxes of suits and one of shirts and jumpers, including the blue cashmere one she had bought him for Christmas. She lifted it to her nose, hoping to breathe him in but it smelled only of newness because he hadn't worn it. Twenty pairs of shoes, sixteen pairs of trainers, some still brand new in their boxes. The male Imelda Marcos, someone once called him – she couldn't remember who, possibly Jefferson. She couldn't see the green Adidas trainers she had bought him for his birthday in November though. His light grey suit was missing too and the Zili jeans that he'd paid a ridiculous amount of money for but they'd been his favourite pair. Maybe he gave them away. *Maybe he didn't,* said a thought that slid into her brain like a poisonous eel.

She did put all his underwear in a black bag to throw away because she couldn't bear the idea of someone else wearing it, even if most of it looked brand new. She smiled as she pulled his bright pink swimming shorts from the drawer. He'd bought them for their first holiday together. She thought of watching his tall, toned body walking from the Greek bar towards her with two cocktails in his hands and she thought, *That man is all mine* with a quiver of proud delight. His walk drew eyes, his *strut*, oozing confidence and ego out of every pore. As a man he was beautiful. Their kids would have been gorgeous.

He had a drawer full of cufflinks, he loved them, collected them like a stylish magpie. Laurie had bought him lots of them: the monogrammed ones, the Superman pair, the football ones but not these red hearts enclosed in jewel-encrusted orbs, easily recognisable as from Vivienne Westwood. She'd never seen him wear these and wondered where they'd come from as he wasn't a lover of 'bling'. She closed the lid on the box of ties and cufflinks, even though she wanted to put everything back where it was, keep him there with her in some form – any form. She hadn't realised this process would be so tough. She stuffed some of her own clothes in his wardrobe, so it didn't look so empty, just grabbed the hangers and hung them up quickly. She'd organise them properly later, but that would do for now. Anything to fill the space that screamed at her that Alex was not coming back.

Alex's bedside cabinet contained hardly anything. He had asked her when she bought one for each of them: what on earth was he supposed to put in it? Maybe it would be more useful when he was older, then he could soak his teeth in a glass and keep them there with his incontinence pads, he'd said and guffawed with laughter at the idea. There was a spare phone charger, a pen, a Jack Reacher book, a pack of chewing gum, a receipt for a coffee from Starbucks, an old appointment card for an eye test, an almost depleted can of anti-perspirant. She pressed the top, and moved forward into the scent. It smelled of Alex when he walked in from the gym, showered, clean, fresh, his messy mid-brown hair still wet.

Laurie struggled downstairs with the boxes, piling them in the hallway, then decided that she should break for something to eat before tackling Alex's office as she was starting to feel slightly shaky. 'Sugar shakes' Bella called them. A quick cheese sandwich took them away, but she was champing at the bit now to tackle the office. Clutter-clearing was energising and she liked that hit of positivity that it had started to give her.

She pushed open Alex's office door, saw dust motes floating in the air, lit up by sunshine which was pouring through the large picture windows. Alex's study was, she thought, the loveliest room in the house. It was more like a barrister's office, with its dark wooden panelling and its air of dignified calm: an oasis of pseudo-old in an ultra-modern house. It was an outrageously sized office really, but then the whole house had been an outlandish investment. The mortgage was a fortune, what had they been thinking? Well, she knew the answer to that. At the time, she hadn't been thinking, she'd been too busy feeling. The house was Alex's idea, to repair them, to glue them back together again with Fairview's many rooms and surfeit of glass that let the sun find them in every place it searched.

The office shelves were mostly lined with faux book panels as Alex didn't really have that much to put on them. There were a couple of files full of scribbles, notes and workings-out which she'd dispose of in the garden incinerator so she made a 'burn' pile in the corner. She filled a box with textbooks and manuals. Alex's accounting, economics and business banking books looked dreadfully boring, but then he'd said that about her law books.

He loved numbers, loved deal-breaking, so becoming a financial advisor was the perfect job for him, and he was bloody good at it. He'd been planning to strike out on his own for a year or so now, but Gold Financier Services in Sheffield, who employed him, upped his salary to keep him sweet. He would have made the leap, she was sure of it. He had more and more private clients whom he went out to visit in the evenings and at weekends, or spoke to from the phone in this office. But she understood the ethics of putting in extra hours long after the day job had ended; neither of them had been nine-to-five people. His long working hours weren't the reason why she had felt him slipping away from her.

She cleared out his stationery drawer which was surprisingly untidy for him: a stray of paperclips, pens and pencils, loose staples among other office detritus. A pencil sharpener and an unused rubber in the shape of a goldfish which she slipped in her pocket to keep – something else she had bought for him. The right-hand cupboard in his desk was filled with printer inks – both spent in a recycling bag and new – and A4 paper. Alex must have been storing it up for a nuclear winter as there were reams and reams of it.

The cupboard on the left didn't open. She presumed the wood had swelled so she tugged the handle as much as she dared before it came off, then she realised it was locked. Alex's bunch of keys still hung on the hook by the door, minus the goldfish keyring that she now used. They'd been in the bag of effects which she'd been given at the hospital, though she hadn't a clue then what two of the keys were for: one tiny, the other with a long shaft and a pronounced bit – an old-fashioned key, the metal rusting in places. The small key worked in the desk lock, at least it did when impatience lent weight to her hand.

The hanging files inside were mostly empty except for an A4 pad with some more figures, more workings-out. There was a folder full of receipts and bills stretching back three years at least: the TV licence, his passport and, clipped together, MOT certificates and other paperwork pertaining to his car. This was what she needed. She'd decided to sell Alex's pride and joy, his red MR2. She didn't like to drive it, having outgrown gears a couple of years ago, but also she'd never been that keen on being a passenger in it either as Alex was overtaken by a boy-racer spirit as soon as he sat in it and always drove it too fast.

The only other file present was labelled 'personal

finances'. Laurie opened it and found an old building society passbook for an account which had been closed and the balance of six thousand and twenty pounds withdrawn in cash in January. There were all Alex's Visa bills going back for three years. She flicked briefly through the ones at the top of the pile, registered Zorba's on there: the Greek restaurant where they'd gone with Jefferson and Naomi last October, and The Southlea Hotel, where they'd stayed early last November in Whitby with Meredith and Brendan for the night. He'd spent a lot of money at Bird and Bryant, the menswear shop in Leeds which he favoured. His balance was cleared every month.

There was an ordered file of his bank statements but the dates stopped after last August. It was odd because Alex usually kept paperwork far longer than he needed to, he had a thing about keeping records, and this account was active until he died; it was the one his salary was paid into by BACS. So where were the rest of the statements? Even if the bank had gone paperless, he would have run them off and kept them here because that's what Alex did. She looked again, but they weren't there.

At the bottom of the drawer was a travel brochure for 'Figurehead Winter Cruises' which surprised her because Alex wasn't the cruising type. He'd laughed at her when she'd suggested they go on a cruise to see the Northern Lights, something she had always wanted to do; said that she had more chance of flying to the moon without a rocket than getting him on a ship. Meredith and Brendan liked cruising. They'd clocked up quite a lot of them. That put Alex off for a start, the prospect of ending up trapped for a fortnight with people like his parents in full-showing-off mode, telling all and sundry how big their suite was and that this was their zillionth time on board and they were now on the titanium tier, or whatever it was that enabled them to have dinner with the captain and fifteen per cent off purchases in the shops. She flicked through it and stopped when she noticed the names 'Mr and Mrs Wilder' scribbled on the top of a page for a cruise the following year. Alex's handwriting. A Valentine's cruise; the ship would moor in Alta on 14 February to 'Hunt for the Northern Lights'.

He'd been planning to take her on one as his wife. Or maybe he was planning for them to get married on board. Why else would he have kept the brochure in a locked drawer? Joy and sadness came at her in an equal rush. And relief, no more than a breath behind them.

Daily Trumpet Meet-Ups

Women seeking Men

Mary, 63, slightly overweight, non-smoker, seeks cuddly man to shave the enjoyable things in life.

Sandra, 58, not fussy but WLTM man between 6ft and 6ft 5, blonde or fair hair, arm tattoos only and piercings in ears only (one per ear). No facial hair, or groomed eyebrows, to weigh no more than fifteen stone. Other than that anything goes. Call me.

Iris, 67, single and sad after losing husband of forty years. Life is so lovely without him, looking for man to fill the hole he no longer occupies.

Denise, 41, medium build and height, likes walks along the beach, meals out, and the occasional drunk to round off a perfect evening.

Men Seeking Women

Barry, 44, not great looking, not rich, not got a posh car or high-flying job but I am a hug-loving, genital giant.

Trucker Dan, 55, fed-up of time-wasters, big-hearted, looking for his foul mate.

Steve, 65, looking for new lady to treat, take out for meals, buy flowers for. Solvent thanks to a thirty-year successful widow-cleaning business.

Dermot, 47, seeks flirty and dirty lady for sexy times and no strings fun. Tall, dank and handsome, one hair and teeth.

Chapter 14

4 September

Pete was glad to get back to work after his days off. When Tara was alive, he always enjoyed the time at home pottering about in the garden, mending things, building, painting. Subconsciously, he realised he was nest-building for the family they'd planned on having. When they first met, she'd wanted to get pregnant straight away and it had been him who'd talked her into having some time to themselves as newly-weds. As if the idea was perched on a see-saw, the more he softened to it, the more she suggested they wait. Until she'd climbed up a few more rungs of her career ladder, she said; until they were older, until they could afford it. The excuses mutated and grew and she kept taking the pill. He hadn't the energy or inclination for doing anything in the house now other than sleeping and eating in it. What was the point? The sooner he and Pong moved, the better.

He was making himself a cup of tea in the kitchen at the end of his shift, lost in thoughts of what area of town he would like to move to, when he felt a poke in the back.

'Oh go on then, if you're asking,' said Sal.

'You've got great timing.' Pete grinned, reaching for her 'World's Best Auntie' mug from the shelf and another teabag.

'Two sugars and don't stir it. I like that hit of sweetness at the end,' she instructed.

'You'll get what you're given.'

'How come you're hanging about here and not going ho— ... forget that.' Sal growled at her clumsiness. 'Stupid twat.'

'Me or you?' said Pete, bringing the two mugs over to the table where Sal was now sitting.

'Me. On this occasion.'

Pete sat down. 'Don't worry, Sal. The last thing I want is for you all to filter everything that comes out of your mouths.'

He'd said much the same to Andy that morning after he'd apologised for telling them how the builders doing his extension had turned the house into a car crash.

'It's amazing how many things you say without really thinking about them,' said Sal. 'Like Andy this morning. He felt shit about the builders' clanger.'

'I don't want to impact on everyone's mood. I feel bad that people have been pussyfooting around me for so long.'

Sal sighed. 'We're mates just looking out for each other, who care about you.'

And they were and he considered Sal the closest of them here. He'd been unsure about what to think of her when she transferred from Doncaster and joined Red Watch five years ago. First impressions were that she was overly blunt, aggressive. Later he realised that she was not only finding her feet in a new station but sailing herself out into the community as a lesbian after leaving her marriage. She'd had a lot of adjusting to do in and out of the job. She was, it had to be said, a damned good fire-fighter, strong, able, a proper team member and under all that bulk and bluster, there was a gentle, kind soul who was a bloody loyal friend.

'Had any more thoughts about going to one of Molly's meetings?' asked Sal.

'I went last week,' said Pete.

'Good,' said Sal.

'Not sure if it's for me if I'm honest.'

'Maybe you should have given it a bit longer than a week, Pete.' Sal's tone was iron fist in velvet glove.

'Well, I've missed the meeting this week anyway.' He looked up at the clock. It would be in full swing now.

'There's always next.'

Pete changed the subject. 'Anyhow, how come you aren't getting straight off? Excuse the pun.'

'Ha, funny. I'm picking someone up and she doesn't finish work until eight.'

'Oh yes?' said Pete. He raised his eyebrows to an interested height.

'Yep. Two months in and going well.' Sal clicked her tongue and winked.

'You never told me.'

'I didn't want to say anything until I was certain myself. After all the duff dates I've been on that came to bugger all. Her name's Natasha.'

Sal reached into her back pocket, brought out her phone, scrolled down some photos and showed the screen to Pete. Natasha was a very pretty redhead with sparkling eyes and a curvy figure. 'Lovely, isn't she?'

'You pulled *her*?' exclaimed Pete, feigning shock.

'I did and what's more she thinks I'm wonderful.'

'True, you are,' said Pete. 'Where did you meet?'

'Online. Yorkshire Pink Ladies. She was like me. Ready to pack in online dating as a bad job because, also like me, she's had a load of nutters contacting her.'

'I didn't know you did online dating,' said Pete.

'No one did. I don't tell people my business.'

'You usually tell me though.'

'You had other things on your mind, kiddo.'

That, of course, would explain why Pete had been out of the loop as far as Sal's love-life went.

'I did think that these days online dating was safer and attracted a saner set of people than it used to do in the old days,' Sal continued, 'but that's not how it worked out for me. I met a proper psycho about three months back.'

Pete waited for more detail and when it wasn't forthcoming, he urged her on. 'Well? You can't just leave me on tenterhooks like that.'

'We had a nice enough first date but no sparks – on either side, I thought. Went our separate ways, then two days later I got a text message saying something on the lines of *I thought you would have called*. So I replied that I assumed it was a no-go but good luck, tried to be polite. Then this. I kept it just in case she tried to murder me.' Sal again reached for her phone, went into her messages and showed Pete a very long, sweary and abusive text which crossed the borders of angry and deranged and had set up camp in loony land.

'Blimey,' said Pete. 'Have you blocked her?'

'I did. Then I got messages from another number, which I also blocked. Then another. I think she's gone out and bought a load of burner phones. I don't mind telling you, it got scary.'

'Please tell me she doesn't know where you live.'

'No. Nor what I do for a living and I gave a false surname. I know that sounds a bit dodgy but she's not the first nutter I've had, so I played safe. One woman was a bloke in a wig. Tried to tell me he was pre-op, but he wasn't – he was a bloke in a wig. Anyway . . .' Sal shuddered then waved away that story for another time. '. . . I was about to cancel the membership when I did one last sweep and saw Natasha's pic and profile. Her biog made me laugh so I thought to myself, *one final shot, girl*. And we hit it off from the moment we met. No agenda, no skeletons, no cock. Well I'm presuming so, we haven't exactly done the deed yet.'

Pete laughed. Sal wasn't one for mincing her words.

'I'm trying to take it slow but we like all the same stuff, want the same things, so it's a bit like holding on to a racehorse with a length of cotton. I think she's perfect, if I'm honest.'

'Maybe a fast pace is the right pace for you,' said Pete. He and Tara had slept together on the first night they met. He'd never done that before with anyone, but she was a grab-and-take woman. A tornado.

'Never thought of it that way,' said Sal after mulling over that mini philosophy. 'Maybe you're right. But I warn you, Pete, when you're ready to start dating again, you be careful. There are a lot of damaged souls out there. Love can make people fly or totally bollocks them up. Luckily for me, at the moment, it's bloody brilliant.'

'So I suppose my hope of you turning back to men is fading fast,' said Pete with a grin.

'I wouldn't turn back. Not even for you, and that's saying something, you gorgeous piece of beefcake,' said Sal.

*

He turned down the offer to share a Chinese meal with Sal and Natasha. He envied them because he wished he were going home to someone who lit up the house with her presence and who'd give his shoulders a rub, try and get rid of all the knots in them that Madam Tension had screwed in there. His muscles were like his head, all congested with crap: sadness, loneliness, guilt all vying for supremacy and he didn't want to pour cold water on his friend's fledgling happiness with his air of malaise. He set off for home with the intention of having a shower, finding a box set that he hadn't yet seen until he felt weary enough to go to bed and seek oblivion. But when he pulled around the corner to his house, his heart sank because parked in front of it was the familiar sight of a blue Golf. Ria Ollerton was waiting for him. She sprang out of the car with a paper bag when he swung into the drive, a smile expanding her surgically enhanced lips to maximum curve.

'Thought I'd call in and see how you were,' she greeted him as he zapped his car lock. She moved in for a peck on the cheek, a hug, holding on to him a beat longer than he'd anticipated, leading to an awkward moment where he moved back but she was still hanging on. Tara's perfume filled his nose and he breathed it in and remembered the layers of scent on his wife's body: the soap, the lotion, the perfume, *her.*

'So how are you then?' she asked without giving him enough time to answer. 'I'm not disturbing you, am I? I was passing. Late night for me as we've had a facial party at the salon. Just tell me to go if you're busy.' Nervous gabbling. She never used to be nervous around him, but the dynamics had changed between them since Tara's death.

'Come in,' he said because he was too polite to say otherwise. 'Do you want a coffee?'

'If that's okay with you. I know you'll just have finished work too so I won't keep you long.'

'It's fine,' he said and secretly cursed himself for being brought up too well by a mother who was incapable of making a guest in her house feel unwelcome. She'd invite Jack the Ripper in and get out the Madeira cake, his dad once said.

At the sound of the key in the door, Pong ran downstairs from the bedroom miaowing wildly and Pete picked him up, gave him a head rub and set him back down again.

Ria followed Pete into the kitchen and Pong followed them both with his majestic tread that made him appear as if he was walking on air.

Pete pulled two mugs out of the cupboard and filled up the kettle and while it was boiling he tipped a pouch of food into Pong's bowl which the Siamese tore into as if he hadn't been fed for a week. Pete hoped Ria wouldn't draw out the visit until it became uncomfortable because he didn't want to entertain or talk, just to let his brain power down so he could rest properly. It was exhausting trying to pretend to the rest of the world he was on an upward trajectory when he knew his inner satnav was dragging him further south. He hated being alone, lonely but he wasn't the type to bung up the hole in his life with the wrong size plug.

'I bought us a couple of pastries from the French patisserie that's around the corner from where I work. I'll probably put on a stone, but I don't care,' said Ria, who wouldn't put on a stone if she mainlined lard twenty-four seven for a fortnight.

'You fill your boots,' said Pete. He could see Ria reflected in the glossy cupboard door as he waited for the kettle and she appeared to be dabbing her face. It registered but he thought no more about it until he brought the mugs over to the kitchen table to find Ria mid-munch with a flake of pastry stuck on her cheek – there by design, not accident. The modern-day equivalent of a handkerchief artfully dropped to hook attention.

Ria slid the second pastry across the table towards Pete. 'Nice but messy. Have barely had time to draw breath today. I was starting to get that shaky feeling you get when you haven't eaten. Sugar shakes, I think they're called.' She grinned and took another bite of the bun, or rather a delicate nibble with her neat, perfect teeth. She chuckled as a flurry of small flakes scattered over the table but that big flake adhered resolutely to her skin.

Now there was a quandary – should he tell her about it or pretend he hadn't seen it? He didn't need these sorts of dilemmas: tiny ones that still carried too much weight.

'Come on, eat up,' she urged, her voice gentle and serious now. Her large Bambi brown eyes holding him in their firm embrace. She tapped the bag that the pastry sat on, reminding him of its presence.

'I'll have it later if that's okay. I ate something at work and I'm full.'

'Oh . . .' a note of disappointment before a quick recovery '. . . of course. Throw it away if you like.'

'No, I won't do that.' He would. He'd never liked flaky pastry. For some unknown reason it annoyed him. Tara had found that freaky-odd and was convinced there was something in his childhood that had made him like that, but there wasn't. No abuse centred around puff pastry, though Griff had once chased him around the garden pretending to shoot him with a vanilla slice.

'So how are you?' Ria asked again, patting her lips with

her fingertips. Her hands were like Tara's, small with impossibly long nails that never featured a chip from the varnish. 'Sorry, just asked you that. I mean, how are you *really*.'

'I'm getting on with things. I have no choice,' he said, his tone more clipped than he intended. He batted the question back over the net. 'How are you? How are Bob and Pam, and Alana?'

Ria sighed. 'Don't think Mum and Dad will ever be the same again. Alana's a closed book, always has been. She's on holiday in Spain with Rick at the moment and the pics on Instagram report she's having a good time.' She gave a little huff, then a sniff. 'I miss Tara so much. I've been to see a therapist.' She fumbled in her bag and brought out a business card. 'She's very good if you need someone to help you over a hurdle.' She slid it across to him, in much the same way as she had slid the pastry.

'Thanks, but I don't need anyone.'

'Pete, I didn't realise I needed someone to talk to as much as I did, until I saw her. She's called Jackie Crawford and she's really helped me.' Her voice dropped in volume. 'You could always talk to me, of course. I won't tell you to pack all your troubles away after fifty minutes.'

'I'm good. Really,' said Pete. Now it was his turn to lie because he did need some help. Griff would have been first call but he had his own stuff going on. His dad would have been gutted to find that his son wouldn't talk to him, but Pete didn't want to open up Nigel's old wounds when he was in a new life with Cora. He knew that Sal would have listened, but she was in a great place with a new girlfriend and he didn't want to bring anyone's mood down. Nor did he want to sit in a chair opposite a counsellor on a one-to-one basis, open up the floodgates for fifty minutes and then have to pack it all back up inside him until the following week. Ria Ollerton might have listened to him droning on about his miserable state but he didn't want to let her in any more than she was. There was no one he could open up to. Or maybe there was. Perhaps Sal was right in that he should give the group in the teashop another shot.

'Are you getting out, you know, socialising?' asked Ria, still wearing that pastry flake that Pete tried to ignore. 'Going out for meals, to the pictures, that sort of thing? Isolating youself socially is the worst thing you can do, Jackie says. Misplaced guilt can make you believe that you don't deserve to enjoy yourself any more.'

'I know. I had this conversation with my father when Mum died,' said Pete.

'Yes of course, I'm sorry, I forgot.'

It was so much easier to give advice than to take it. That's one thing he realised. He remembered his dad being crippled with guilt that he'd asked another woman out for dinner and Pete had told him that it was the right thing to do because he had to carry on living, not just existing. If only he'd known he was having dinner with Cora, he might not have been so encouraging.

'There are loads of good films on at the cinema at the moment. I miss going there, you know, since Josh and I split up.'

'I've never been one for the cinema,' Pete said, another lie. They were being pulled from him like tissues from a box. He did like a night out at the cinema; Tara wasn't keen so they didn't go.

That damned flake of pastry was still welded onto Ria's face, waiting for him to lean across romantically and stroke it away, he guessed.

'You might want to just wipe there,' he said, jabbing his finger into his own cheek, mirroring the place.

'Oh.' Her finger tips fell straight on it and it dropped. He saw the beginnings of a blush suffuse her skin, her plan thwarted.

Pete yawned, apologised. 'Sorry, it's been a long day. I'm ready for bed.'

Probably the wrong thing to say, said a voice inside him.

'I'll go,' Ria said without moving.

Pong picked that moment to jump onto the table and Ria made an instinctive comic 'Eek' sound, raising jazz hands of horror. She recalibrated, gave a forced chuckle.

'Pong, you silly thing, you scared me.' With the exception of Tara's sister Alana, the Ollerton family weren't cat people. She'd always made a tremendous fuss of Pong whenever she came round.

Pete stood to lift Pong off the table, transmitting a grateful telepathic 'nice timing' message to the Siamese. He didn't sit down again, steeled himself to be as dismissive as it was within his remit to be.

'Well, thanks for stopping by anyway, Ria. You really don't need to bring me food. I've got a freezer full of it and I tend to eat at work. It's sweet of you, but don't trouble yourself.'

He smiled then, to soften the words, afraid they had come out as too sharp. Ria was still seated. She was determined to make him work for her exit.

'I'm sorry if I've acted out of turn . . .'

'No, don't apologise, really.' He started to walk out of the kitchen towards the front door, making it impossible now for her to stay longer without entering ridiculous territory. She got up, followed him slowly as if giving him the opportunity to change his mind and ask her to watch a film with him, settle down with a bottle of wine, stay.

'Well, see you soon I hope,' said Ria. Her arms opened, she craned her neck to kiss his cheek, caught him half on the mouth. She laughed, apologised again. Her perfume enveloped him and evoked the essence of his wife, his child, his life with them wiped out by some bastard who thought it was okay to text while driving an articulated lorry in wet snow.

He closed the front door as soon as she had climbed into her car and he had given her one dutiful wave; she blew a kiss to him through the glass. He usually felt obliged to stand there until she had started driving off, but not tonight. He just wanted to sleep, shut out the world including this house with all the memories of his wife dyed into it like watermarks. And the flipside of the memory coin – visuals of what had been to come: him picking up a gurgling baby, a Christmas tree in the corner with stacks of presents under- neath. It suddenly became all too much for his head, set off by that damned perfume. He felt a tear pop out, slide down his cheek and dashed it away with the back of his hand, but let the others that came after fall. He wished they would dissolve him away like acid.

Upstairs, he took off his jeans and checked the pockets before putting them in the wash basket and found the card that Sal had given him, with Molly's name and number on it. He thought he'd thrown it away.

He'd go again, he decided, attempt to fit in with the mad menagerie of people who talked over tea and ate cake. He had no other option.

Chapter 15

Laurie drove home from work and thought that even if she changed her mind, she wouldn't be able to get to the teashop for her second session. Everyone would be eating, drinking, talking now. The man in the frumpy tank top and the little red-haired woman who looked like a bird, and the fireman who was a first-timer last week just like she was. Then her attention was hijacked by the sight of a black beetle-shiny Lexus with a personalised number plate parked up just before her drive, unmistakably Alex's parents' car. For a split second her spirits reacted as they used to, an urge to speed up so she could invite them in, put on the kettle. But then it twisted to an anxiety, a downward drag because of the souring between them and she wondered what they could possibly want.

She was slowing down to turn when Meredith strode out of her drive and went straight into the passenger side of the vehicle, eyes at pains to avoid Laurie. The Lexus sped off immediately, before Meredith could have had a chance to fasten her seat belt, which indicated how little the Wilders wanted a confrontation. They shouldn't be at war with each other, really they shouldn't, thought Laurie with an inward sigh. They were all grieving and it felt as if Laurie were doubly grieving because she had lost the whole of the Wilder clan. They had been pulled out of her life like a bee-sting and taken a big chunk of her heart with them. Yes, Naomi could be wilful, Meredith was too used to getting her own way and Brendan wasn't exactly a bon viveur – but they were part of Alex and she had loved them, loved being in the embrace of his family.

Maybe she should sell up and give them some of the money, if it meant keeping them. The thought was opened up and shut down immediately by another which was standing in her head with arms crossed asking if she was joking. The Wilders weren't hovering on the breadline by any stretch. They had a cottage in France and bought a new top-of-the-range car every year. They were always bragging about how well off they were. The greed was theirs, not hers. But this battle wasn't about money, it was about control.

Laurie stepped into the house to find some envelopes on the doormat bound together by an elastic band. She picked them up to see that they had all been sent to Alex Wilder at his parents' address. She kicked off her shoes and padded across to the kitchen island to sit down and read what they were. They had been slit open already and were all bank statements. She arranged them in order: September, October, November, December – two months before he died. All of them showed his salary from Gold Financier Services Ltd going in on the seventeenth of each month, on the nineteenth a transfer into their joint bank account for the household bills, then around the twentieth a direct debit to Barclaycard to cover his Visa bill. On the first of every month, the balance was reduced to nil as whatever remained in the account was drawn out in cash from a Southyork Bank branch in Sheffield. At the top of the December statement, a message emblazoned across the top: 'We're going paperless in April'. The Southyork Bank were, it seems, way behind every other financial establishment in Britain on that.

Where was January's statement?

Laurie stared at the sheets of paper and questions bombed her brain from everywhere. Alex rarely carried cash on him so what had he been using it for? Why had the statements been going to his parents' house? Why was he using his Visa and not his debit card? *That's not what he did.*

She went to the bag in the kitchen, destined for the garden incinerator, and took out the wad of Alex's Visa statements, laid them on the island and scrutinised them this time, ensuring her brain processed each entry. The spending on his Visa had increased hugely from last September; it appeared he had started loading everything onto it. Then she spotted a thousand pounds cash advance in January. Why on earth would he take out a cash advance on a Visa? That was a huge no-no in his book because he hated paying interest. Laurie pulled out her phone, checked the date. Alex had been on a four-day course in Edinburgh then. Why would he need a thousand pounds cash?

She felt something akin to the dreaded sugar shakes claiming her body; a panic. She leapt to an obvious conclusion, then as soon as it had its foot in the door of her head, she tried to shut it out again. He hadn't had an affair, she would know it. Her senses would have risen to meet the threat. Because that's what had happened last time.

Laurie had been going out with Alex for just over a year when she felt the change between them, subtle as the first autumn morning following summer, a portentous chill. For the past months, they had started talking about moving in together, settling down, the subject of a future family easing into their conversations, then that strange reverse thrust. At first, she had thought a fear of commitment was dragging his collar back, even though he had driven the pace. He stopped answering his phone, took an age to ring her back when she left messages. Suddenly he couldn't stay over at her small flat as often, citing excuses such as he had an early start in the morning or was tired, even though that hadn't bothered him before. She'd offered to stay at his instead but he put her off: the place was a mess, he wanted to cram in some work before bed. She knew he was hiding something. She knew he was hiding *someone*. A period of temporary madness happened where outwardly she tried to stay calm but inwardly she was a torrent of worry, stress and suspicion.

Then they were in his car one day and he pulled in at a garage to fill up with diesel. While he was paying for it, she had no idea what had made her do it but she opened up the glove compartment and a receipt had tumbled out. A hotel bill. A suite and dinner for two. It had to be a woman because the bill was itemised and the drinks were definitely female: a champagne cocktail, a Cosmopolitan. The date she recognised immediately because it was her mother's birthday. That night Alex had cancelled a trip to the theatre with her, saying he hadn't felt well, blamed it on something he'd eaten. She'd guessed it had been a lie then; now she was sure of it.

No, she wouldn't be treated like this, she'd decided. She got out of the car, slammed the door, began to walk, taking the first turning right down a path into a housing estate. She refused to cry even though her heart was cracking inside her chest. Anger, she knew because she had been here before with a past love rat, was an excellent driver-away of tears and so she focused on stoking it up, allowing it to burn up every other emotion that tried to get a look in. She rang for a taxi to take her home, expecting to find Alex there on her doorstep, waiting for her with a throat full of explanations but he wasn't. And so that, as far as she was concerned, was that.

Bella came round and together they tried to 'wash that man right out of her hair' with wine shampoo, but once the anger had subsided, the sadness moved in. She'd really thought Alex was *the one*. He ticked all her boxes and she'd ticked his, or so he'd told her. No one but Bella knew that her perfectly functioning façade disguised an inner devastation. She'd always been so good at hiding behind a mask of stoicism.

Then a few weeks after, Alex had turned up at her flat. He looked terrible, drawn, pale, he'd lost weight. She'd thought he must be ill, or he'd had some devastating family news, otherwise she might not have let him in.

He wouldn't sit down; he told her that he'd acted like a complete dickhead and he had no excuses for it. If it was of any consolation, he felt as if he'd thrown away the best thing ever to come into his life and he wanted her to know that. He didn't expect her to forgive him or take him back.

She did both. With hindsight she knew that she was stupidly grateful that he'd come back, that he'd rejected the other woman for her, that she – Laurie – had won. Alex pushed to get engaged the following year but she was still smarting from that affair, still not on solid ground. She may have forgiven, but forgetting was a different matter. Then Fairview came on the market. A couple divorcing acrimoniously wanted a quick and easy sell. Laurie should never have agreed to go and accompany Alex to the viewing because he forced her to see it through his eyes. The his and hers offices, the garden, the parking space for eight cars at least, the potential to be their forever house, their family home. But Alex couldn't afford it by himself. Another buyer was interested, they needed to act quickly or they'd miss it. So they bought it together and they began to build a future in it. Alex had never given her reason to think he would cheat on her a second time. 'It's you I want,' he told her over and over until, eventually, she believed it.

He wouldn't have done that to you again.

Laurie looked at the bank statements in her hand. They represented either the end of a puzzle or the start of it. The account had been closed, she could throw them away, forget that things didn't quite add up. Did she really need to poke around and possibly end up throwing a mortar into a happy past?

Alex was dead, she should let him and their life together lie softly in the grave. A completed episode that ended with love. They were going to be married, go on a trip to see the Northern Lights, that's all she needed to know.

But she wasn't the 'all she needed to know' type.

She had to find help from somewhere, direction, guidance. An idea dropped into her mind, a mad impulsive one that everyone she knew would disapprove of. It wouldn't stop her. She reached for her phone, googled some names, found the one she recognised, rang. The woman was booked up for weeks but there was a free slot on Saturday morning, for a price. Money talked with a very loud voice – and at least she had plenty of that.

The *Daily Trumpet* would like to apologise to the mayor of Barnsley Mr Philip Smart for wording which appeared alongside the report of his elder son's wedding recently. It should have read 'The groomsmen all wore white roses in their button-holes', not bottom-holes. A donation has been made to the Mayor's charity, which this year is in support of the older members of the community, Ale UK.

Chapter 16

6 September

Two days later, Laurie arranged to meet Bella at an Italian restaurant after work for a teatime special. She arrived early but Bella was earlier still, as her Audi TT was already in the car park and looking sparkling as if it had just been through the car wash. That reminded her that she needed to give Alex's MR2 a valet tomorrow as someone was coming to look at it with a view to buying it on Sunday. Within an hour of the advertisement going up on the 'Quality Cars of Yorkshire' site yesterday, she'd had a phone call from a local man asking if he could come and see it as soon as possible. He explained the speed of his response, that he'd had an alert emailed to him because he'd been waiting for this car model to turn up for years and *please* would she give him first refusal on it. He wanted to come over there and then, but she'd fibbed slightly and said that she was working away until Saturday night. The car needed cleaning before anyone viewed it and she'd rather have someone with her – Bella, or a neighbour if she wasn't available. She hadn't been that keen on having people over to the house, but she knew that a private sale was her best option. Garages would offer her peanuts and she didn't want to give Alex's baby away for nothing. And luckily, when Laurie rang her to check, Bella was free.

Bella was watching the door for her arrival and waved her over. There were two glasses of rosé already on the table.

'I got here early,' she said. 'I presumed you'd fancy a glass.'

'I do,' said Laurie. She sat down and opened her mouth to ask how Bella was.

'Choose food first, talk afterwards,' said Bella. 'The waiter's already been round twice to ask if I'm ready to order and twice I've told him I'm not a sad fart eating by myself but am waiting for a friend, or words to that effect.'

It wasn't a hard choice. Laurie loved their cannelloni here. They ordered an antipasto platter to share and pick at, just as they always used to. Before whatever it was had pulled a cloud over their friendship.

'What a frigging week,' said Bella, picking up her glass. 'I wish I weren't driving. I could sink a few of these. I can't tell you how abjectly stupid some so-called graduates are. Ask them to build a nuclear warhead and it'd be done. Ask them to reserve Mr and Mrs Smethurst a room with a bath not a shower and they'll cock it up.' She made a growling sound. 'Dealing with a double-booked wedding room today was not fun either.'

Laurie pulled an *ouch* face.

'How on earth did you sort that out?'

'Offered one of the couples an alternative venue. The joy of having a chain of hotels is that you can do that. They've now been upgraded to the Wentworth Room at Beechwood Hall and we've thrown the starters in and given them the honeymoon suite free of charge. And upgraded the Prosecco to champagne.'

'So no profit on that one then, I presume?'

'There's always profit on a wedding that size,' said Bella. 'And the champagne isn't exactly Krug. Everyone's happy, including the newbie graduate who thought she'd be kicked out on her arse but has managed to both keep her job and learned a valuable lesson about paying attention to detail. Anyway that's enough me, me, me, how are you, you, you? You okay?' Her voice suddenly faded as she remembered her friend might not want to talk about other people's weddings.

Laurie wondered where to start but decided to just jump straight in.

'I had visitors on Wednesday. Meredith and Brendan.'

Bella looked very interested and primed to be cross. 'Oh? And what did they want this time?'

'We didn't actually speak. Meredith was posting some things through my letter box and when they saw my car they sped off.'

Bella mumbled something nasty under her breath before asking, 'What sort of things? Bombs?'

Bombs. Yes, quite possibly, Laurie didn't say.

'Bank statements. I cleared out Alex's office at the weekend and found bank statements up to August but none more recent than that. The bank statements Meredith posted through my door were ones that came after those.'

Bella's brow creased. 'Why were they going to his parents' house?'

'I have no idea.'

Laurie reached into her bag and pulled the statements out to show her. Both she and Bella were aware of the slight shake in her hands as she handed them across the table.

'Look. Alex was taking all the cash out of his account every month to reduce it to a nil balance. He only started doing that in September, when he had his statements sent to Meredith's.'

'I hear that more people are using cash again these days,' said Bella, comparing the spending patterns on the statements.

'Not Alex. I've hardly ever seen him use cash. He was always scrabbling around for it. And he stopped using his debit card and started putting everything on his Visa – and he did have a debit card. Don't you think that's odd?'

Bella shook her head slowly from side to side. 'I don't know. Stu likes to load up his Visa and then clear it every month. I pay for everything with my debit card although I used to be a strictly cash person; we're all different.' She handed the papers back. 'What are you looking for here?'

Laurie took a deep breath in. She hardly dared say it because sharing it made it a real concern, not a stupid one born from an overactive imagination.

'Why would you deal with only cash, isn't it obvious?'

'Because you want to?' Bella answered.

'Because you can't trace it. Because it wouldn't show up on any paperwork that *I* might see. Bella, I wonder if . . . I'm worried that . . . Was Alex having an affair, do you think?'

Bella's hand stilled on the piece of complimentary bread she was about to lift up to her lips. It was a second at most but Laurie registered it, and the succession of blinks Bella's eyelids made in that time. She attributed little to it consciously, but her unconscious stored the movie byte of it.

'Don't be so bloody daft,' said Bella then. 'How can it even cross your mind? The man was on his way home to ask you to marry him when he— Oh, Laurie, you really can't think like this. What are you trying to do to yourself?'

Laurie felt tears rise to her eyes and coughed to sink them back down again.

'I can't make head or tail of it and that's the answer my brain keeps leaping to.'

'Well it can't be that can it?' Bella's voice hardened. 'Alex loved you and you would have known. Women always know, even if they pretend not to. Your spidey senses would have picked up something and they didn't, did they?'

They did. Something was wrong. I do know it.

'Or maybe, because he was careless the last time he had an affair, he'd learned to be more careful.'

'Or maybe you're talking crap. You got over all that and he never did it again.' Bella smiled sympathetically. 'Alex really loved you, Laurie. Everyone knows that. Don't let a load of silly conjecture spoil lovely memories. Have you thought that a little part of you never quite got over what happened and is always on the lookout for anything out of the ordinary, getting it all out of perspective?'

'Yes I have thought—'

'Maybe there was something he wanted to hide from you in a good way. Maybe it was to do with a surprise wedding ...' she leaned forward, pleaded with her friend to be sensible: '... Laurie, this is the man who died with an engagement ring in his pocket for you. You didn't have a clue he was going to propose, did you? You know he was big on surprises.'

'Why that date though, Bells?'

'Why not?' Bella came straight back at her. 'He wouldn't have done it on Valentine's Day, far too obvious and overdone. You wouldn't have expected it, that's why. He was going to make it a special date for every year going forward.'

Bella could be right, everything she said made sense. But still ... in the core of her, all these little anomalies added substance to her intuition that something had been wrong with them before he died.

'I need answers,' said Laurie, 'and if I can't get them one way, I'll get them another.'

Bella gave a nervous gulp. 'Please don't tell me you're thinking what I think you're thinking.'

'I don't know what you're thinking,' replied Laurie.

Bella was reticent to speak in case Laurie wasn't thinking that at all and she was about to plant a daft idea in her head.

'If you mean asking Meredith why my fiancé had his bank statements delivered to her home, no – not yet,' said Laurie. 'But if you mean consulting a psychic then you might be right.' As soon as the words were out, she wished she could have dragged them back into her mouth and swallowed them.

'Oh no, Laurie, please,' implored Bella. 'That's just bonkers.'

'You went to see one,' Laurie threw back defensively.

'And it was an expensive mistake.'

'You liar, you said she was really good.'

'I went for amusement purposes, not for anything important. She won't give you what you're looking for. She could end up generating more false leads than true answers. Please promise me you won't.'

'Okay, I won't then,' said Laurie, hoping Bella wouldn't ask her to swear because she was booked in for ten a.m. tomorrow.

The waiter picked that moment to arrive with the antipasto platter.

'Good,' said Bella. 'Now eat, and stop being a dick.'

Laurie reached for a cocktail stick to spear an olive and Bella pushed out a smile and hoped that Laurie wouldn't join up the dots, that Alex's bank statements going to his parents' house coincided with when she began her slow and painful extraction from her friend's life.

EAST

The sun rises in the east
Chasing the shadows
Bringing day to night
Light to dark
Always it rises

THE RISING SUN
ANON

Winners of the St Jude's WI wine-making competition, as judged by Florence Carter of the *Daily Trumpet*, were as follows.

1st Mrs Marjory Isherwood: (full-bodied and nutty)

2nd Miss Delia Scrimshaw: (mature and fruity)

3rd Mrs Nancy Sutton: (big, beefy and fleshy)

Mrs Sandra Timms: (tart, but should improve if laid down for a month) was awarded the runner's up rosette.

Chapter 17

7 September

Laurie lifted her fist to knock on the cyclamen-pink front door and then pulled it back quickly before it connected. This really was a bit drastic and desperate, she knew, driving all the way over to Leeds to visit a psychic, especially as she would be paying a hundred and fifty pounds to jump the queue. She rapped quickly before she had the chance to think about it, reason herself out of it. Within the minute the door was answered by a small, wide woman wearing a floaty kaftan, as pink as her door, her lipstick and her eyeshadow.

'Come in, lovey,' said Pat Morrison, psychic extraordinaire. 'Take a seat in here for five minutes while I finish with my client.' She led Laurie into a cosy sitting room that smelled strongly of strawberries. The room had pink walls and a pink suite and was the lounge equivalent of a womb.

'Now, just hold this until I come in and fetch you,' said Pat, placing a small but weighty crystal ball into Laurie's hand. 'And also' – she put a tub of objects down on the coffee table in front of Laurie – 'pick something out of here. The item that draws itself to you the most. Okay, lovey?' She looked nothing like Vera Duckworth but sounded exactly like her, it was most odd.

Pat left Laurie alone then. Laurie tried not to listen to the muted voices filtering through the wall and concentrated on infusing the ball with her energies. With her right hand, she rifled through the motley selection of things in the tub: a lipstick, a brooch with the word 'Mother' on it, a baby's bootee, a golf tee, a spent match, a pen, a condom in a packet, a menu . . . For some reason, Laurie was most drawn to the spent match so that's what she went with. Too many of the items gave telling clues; she'd make Pat Morrison work to find out why she was here. She wondered if the psychic would deduce from her choice that she felt redundant, which wouldn't be correct. Then she'd know that Pat Morrison was a fake.

It was nearer ten minutes when Laurie heard a door being opened, voices in the hallway: 'Thank you, thank you so much, Mrs Morrison,' from a man, one who sounded reassured. 'Bye, lovey. You take care now,' from Pat. The front door opened and closed and then Pat came into the womb-room.

'Ready for you, now, lovey,' said Pat. 'Bring your object of choice and the crystal and come with me, please, then we can get started.'

Laurie jumped to her feet. She was a mix of curiosity, apprehension and excitement as she moved into a large sitting room, also pink, which didn't surprise her at all. The air was thick with a pleasant scent of cherries drifting from a lit trio of pink candles on the table between Pat's squashy armchair and Laurie's sofa.

Pat smiled and held out her hand for the crystal ball. Laurie was temporarily fascinated by the length of her nails (pink, of course). She could have picked up a small child in them and carried it off.

'The way I work is that I feel your energy, which you have sunk into this crystal ball by holding it, lovey,' said Pat. 'It acts like a magnet, drawing your essence in.' She placed her other hand over it so it was completely covered, took a deep breath and closed her eyes.

Pat Morrison had been a psychic for a year. She'd been advertising herself and working as one for many years, but really she'd been expertly insightful, gifted at reading people – she was her master-con-man father's daughter. Then Pat had an unfortunate accident at the coming-out-of-jail party of her nephew, when she tripped on the dance floor doing the *Birdie Song* and banged her head hard enough to knock her out for a few minutes. From that moment on, Pat had never been quite the same. She hadn't lost any of her intuitive abilities, in fact they had been added to. Now when she was *reading* people, pictures came into her head that were unbidden and unexplained. And they were right on the money. It was as if that bonk had unlocked a room in her brain where second sight really was alive and kicking. In conjunction with her mastery of body language, Pat's predictions were more attuned with every passing day. So her prices went up. Ironically, she couldn't have foreseen that spot of luck.

'I'm seeing loss,' said Pat eventually, opening her eyes. That information came from the old steady reliable place in her head. It covered a multitude of scenarios. Rarely did people come to see her when all in their gardens was lovely.

The sceptical part of Laurie was prepared to give away as

little as possible by way of facial expressions or spoken word. She forced herself to stay blank, still.

'You're searching for answers,' said Pat, aware that this piece of information had come from the new, strange place. She felt that through the crystal: a restlessness born from looking for something that refused to be found. An image appeared, sharpening like a developing photograph.

'A maze,' she said. 'You've come to a dead end on what you're looking for, lovey, so you need to try a different way. The answer is there in the middle' – she drew a circle in the air with her nail, stabbed the centre of it – '... it's right there. I can see it but it's all wrapped up in fog' – Laurie made a small involuntary noise in her throat – 'so I don't know what it is.' Pat squeezed the ball again. Sadness, she could both feel it and see it etched into the woman's skin around the eyes.

'Someone you love has left you ...' Pat felt the warmth from the crystal. Since the accident she had realised that the ball felt cooler when someone's heart was smashed by a living soul, death brought a heat. '... Left you permanently. Someone you love died.' Another image, lit for a second as if by the flashbulb of a camera. 'I'm seeing a crowd, noise, sirens, blue lights. I'm seeing ...' It was too ridiculous to say, but all the same she would. She shook her head, grimaced. 'Sorry if this sounds odd, lovey, but I'm seeing a carrier bag full of food.'

Laurie's hand shot up to her mouth and she gasped. She couldn't help it.

Bloody hell, thought Pat. She wished she'd had that bang on the head years ago.

'He was going to tell me something on the night he died, but I don't know what it was. I hope I do, but ...' Laurie began, then realised she was giving up clues. She was, and

Pat leapt on the word 'hope' that stood out from her sentence as if painted with a massive highlighter pen.

'You're right, he was going to tell you something, lovey,' said Pat and smiled. She concentrated, wasn't sure if those church bells came from her perception or the magic brain room. 'I can see a ring. I can see a wedding . . .'

She noticed the corners of Laurie's mouth twitch up. Yep – spot on with that one.

'And a birthday,' said Pat. 'Did he pass on your birthday?'

'No,' said Laurie.

'Could be a few days either side,' Pat tried.

'No, the closest birthday would be his dad's and that was the month before.'

'Oh, that's odd,' said Pat. She could sense a birthday, clear as day and it was significant. 'His?'

'No.'

'Well I'm seeing a birthday very strongly and change centred around it,' said Pat. The feeling was undeniable and even though the woman in front of her was saying no, this birthday was coming through loud and clear. Many people left her house though and their minds began to spin on what they'd been told and what it could mean, working overtime to find the connection so she wasn't too worried.

'Where do I look for . . . answers?' asked Laurie.

Pat pressed the crystal, felt the hint of a thrum, an energy. She had no idea how she knew what it meant, she just did.

'Someone you know well. She doesn't want to talk to you though.'

Meredith.

'You used to be very close and then you weren't,' continued Pat. 'Does that make any sense?'

'Yes,' said Laurie with a sigh. 'Perfect sense.'

Pat was certain that it was a woman deliberately with-holding info. She recognised that sort of sigh. Women could often cause far more damage to another woman than a man could.

'She will tell you the truth . . . eventually,' said Pat. She made a small exclamation as the ball in her hand suddenly lost all its heat. 'Cold. Why am I feeling cold? Somewhere cold. Does that mean anything to you? Extreme cold . . .' the ball felt cold but clammy '. . . Is it snow? Were you planning to go on holiday – skiing, maybe?'

The Northern Lights. It had to be. There couldn't be many places colder than three hundred and fifty-plus kilometres north of the Arctic Circle in February.

'I'm seeing . . .' Pat continued but the image was fading fast. 'No, I've lost it. My head was full of colours, changing like one of them kaleidoscopes. I don't know what that means.'

But Laurie did. It had to be the Northern Lights.

There was nothing left of Laurie in the ball now for Pat to read. That was the trouble with crystals, they held a lot but not for a long time. She flicked her eyes to the clock. Her readings were mostly short, quick-fix plasters on hearts. She rather liked this new way of working though, feeling instead of computing.

'Right, let's look at your object, lovey. Oh, a spent match.' No one ever picked that one. So much simpler when they picked the bootee or the mother brooch. Pat chuckled. 'The obvious conclusion would be to say that you feel done with, useless, as spent as the match but . . .' she left a hanging pause '. . . in much the same way as the death card in Tarot isn't to be taken literally, the meaning of the spent match is likewise misleading.'

Pat knew from the quick rise and fall of Laurie's eyebrows that she was impressed. She took the match from Laurie's hand, closed her fingers around it.

'I see flames,' said Pat, almost embarrassed at having said the obvious. 'Which you might think I would, but it's not fire, it's life, it's warmth, passion. I see an image of true love. I see cold and I see fire very clearly together in your future.' Pat put down the match, threaded her hands together. 'You're going to meet your soulmate. He's very close. Is there someone in your life already that you feel a connection to that could grow?'

Laurie didn't even have to think about that. The men she was closest to were Alan at the *Daily Trumpet*, who was very married and Richard, the conveyancing solicitor, who was as gay as a box of yellow dusters.

'I can't think of anyone,' she answered.

'He's close, very close, no doubt about that, lovey. Oh he's a nice man, a perfect match – excuse the pun. I feel—' Pat smiled '—happy.'

Pat dropped a deep, slow nod; the full stop on their session. 'That will be one hundred and fifty pounds please.'

No wonder she felt happy, thought Laurie.

At the front door, Pat had an unexpected rush of emotion wash over her. She always tried to leave people with hope or comfort and that had been so much easier to do when she was just spinning them a load of crap. As soon as her new gift came into play, that didn't always happen and, in this case, she'd probably left this young woman with more questions than she had given answers.

'Seek help, lovey,' she blurted out. From the heart this, not from any secret room in her head.

'What?'

'Someone you . . . like, respect, has suggested you find someone to talk to.' A fair assumption. Everybody and their aunt had a therapist these days. And a bereaved woman must have been told by a friend somewhere along the line to find a good grief counsellor. 'You must do that, lovey. It will work for you so you must stick at it.' She emphasised the musts. 'This time,' she added, although she didn't really understand why the codicil.

'Thank you, Mrs Morrison.'

Laurie's head had plenty to chew on as she drove back home. She wasn't sure if what she had learned today made her feel better or worse. Maybe she should have left well alone as Bella told her to, but then again she couldn't. She would be stuck in this quagmire of confusion until she found out why Alex had those statements sent to his mother, what he was doing with his money, because nothing had yet come to light. What had he been hiding? *Seek help. You must stick at it. This time.* It could only mean rejoin Molly's group. Maybe, if Molly helped her galvanise her thoughts into some order, she would figure things out for herself and not need to confront Meredith. She'd do it.

Pat Morrison closed the door on her client but her brow was furrowed. These days she had much more of a conscience than she used to have and blamed the bump on the head for that too. It was an unnecessary complication in her life but she'd been forced to accept it as the price for her new-found gift. Sometimes what she experienced could totally freak her out. Like then. She had heard the words 'this time' as if they had been whispered in her ear, like a prompt. A man's voice, she thought.

The spirits, she had come to realise, worked in enigmas

and cryptic messages. Even the ones from Yorkshire. Death, it appeared, made even them leave their penchant for straight-talking outside the pearly gates along with their pit boots. How disappointing.

Chapter 18

8 September

Griff and Lucy lived in a new-build house on an estate in the village of Dodley. Lucy had been seduced into buying it by the lovely long garden, Griff by the proximity to the two-time British welterweight boxing champion Tommy 'TNT' Tanner. He lived next door with his wife and son and was in training for his next shot at defending the title. If he won this time, he'd keep the belt forever. The neighbours had got to be friendly over both boxing and baby talk. Lucy and Griff had babysat for them. As Lucy held the little boy, she imagined the time when this would be her own baby snuggling into her shoulder. She wondered if it would ever happen because things weren't looking great and she was reluctant to go down the IVF route after witnessing what one of their staff and her husband had gone through with it. Five unsuccessful rounds had put such a strain on their finances and their marriage that it had ended, and they'd been a rock-solid couple.

Lucy was beginning to think there was a rogue gene in her

family doing mischief and if that was the case, she had prepared herself for the possibility of not being able to carry a
baby even though she craved for it to happen. She didn't want
to ever risk losing Griff and she wouldn't have to if she made
sure that they kept the core of their marriage strong and sensible. They could adopt, they could have a child that way. The
baby would fold into their family, become their own. Who
cared if their blood was different? What did it matter if he or
she grew in her heart not her belly? But how she wished she
could feel the swell of a child growing inside her.

Now Lucy pretended to be exasperated by her husband
pacing around the kitchen looking at the clock.

'Where is he?' said Griff. 'Doesn't he know how important this is?'

'He's four minutes late,' said Lucy. 'Chill your stupid
man beans.'

'Chill your stupid man beans? What sort of an expression is that?'

Lucy laughed. 'You wouldn't be this excited if he was
taxi-ing you to meet Nigella Lawson.'

'I woul— no, scrap that, you're right, Luce.'

'You've waited this long, a few more minutes won't
kill you.'

A knock, the door opening, a cheery familiar voice.
'Hello, hello. Sorry I'm slightly late.' Pete knew his twin
would be most likely bouncing around the room like a wild
ping-pong ball.

'Four minutes twenty-seven seconds. You do realise what
that's done to my blood pressure?' said Griff.

'He's hardly slept,' said Lucy. 'Want a coffee, darling?'

'No he bloody doesn't want a coffee.' Griff answered for
him. 'Let's get gone.'

Pete crossed the room to give Lucy a swift peck on the cheek.

'I do hope it's what it says on the description or I don't think I can live with the fallout,' she said.

'You and me both,' said Pete, grinning.

'All this over a car,' said Lucy, tutting and rolling her eyes.

'*A car?* Er, excuse me . . . Do *not* reduce an MR2 with less than twenty thousand miles on the clock to the mere words *a car.*'

'Oh just give me a kiss and bugger off,' said Lucy.

She's always smiling, thought Pete as they walked out. *You don't know the half of it*, Lucy would have said if she could have heard that thought.

'Two owners from new but the first one never drove it, apparently. I couldn't believe it when I got the alert on my phone. It was like Santa Claus himself had emailed me. It sounds too good to be true,' said Griff, strapping himself into Pete's car.

'It probably is then.'

'Aw, don't say that.' Griff's bottom lip curled over and Pete laughed. His brother had been on the hunt for a MK1 MR2 for a long time. It had to be 1985, the year of their birth, when the first of them were sold in the UK. And it had to be free of rust, which was a total killer in those cars. So far all the 'perfect examples' he'd been to see hadn't been at all. Too many miles on the clock, badly aligned panel gaps telling of crash damage, unreported knocks, leaky seals. Griff knew every pitfall to look out for.

'What's the story why they're selling it then?' asked Pete, taking directions from the satnav to turn left and head off towards the village of Oxworth.

'Owner died, apparently. It was his pride and joy and his missus doesn't like to drive it.'

'I bet it's due its MOT and she's getting rid because she knows it's going to fall apart on the ramp.'

'It is due its MOT actually.'

'Told you.'

'Pete, shut the fuck up.'

The satnav led them down a lane of very choice houses that didn't have numbers on them but only names: Wind Ridge, The Elms, Gardenia House.

'Fairview, that's the one,' said Griff.

'I can read, you know,' said Pete, turning up the drive where the red MR2 was parked in front of a large house that seemed to be constructed of more glass than brick.

'Now look at that,' said Griff, in the same tone that a serial dieter might use for a giant chocolate eclair.

Pete parked up at the side of a treble garage. Two women came out of the house and he recognised one of them immediately because he'd last seen her eleven days ago. The woman he'd sat next to at Molly's Club – the solicitor. What were the chances of that?

'Hello again,' he said, getting out of his car, wishing he could remember what her name was.

'You know each other?' said Griff.

'Well, we met once at a ... function,' Pete said to him. Laurie overheard, took her cue from that. He'd avoided the specifics so she would too.

'Hello,' she called back.

'This is Griff, my twin brother,' said Pete and Laurie held out her hand. Both men were the same height, same twinkly eyes. Griff was wider with much more hair though.

'This is my friend Bella,' Laurie introduced her.

'I'm the muscle in case of trouble; I have a black belt in karate,' Bella said and was impressed that neither of the men made any disparaging remarks about her being short and slender or red-haired. They just smiled and looked remarkably similar when they did so, both women thought.

'Well, here's the car,' said Laurie. 'I pulled it out of the garage so you could have a good look at it in the sunlight. My partner loved it so I thought it was time to let it go to someone else who would love it too. All the service history is here . . .' Laurie opened up the passenger door and took out a file. 'He was fastidious over paperwork so everything is complete. The MOT is due next week. Under normal circumstances . . . er . . .' Her words dried up.

Bella jumped in. 'Laurie's partner died. She's had a lot on her plate.'

'I'm really sorry to hear about that,' said Griff.

Laurie gave a small nod of acknowledgement, handed over a key. 'You'll want to take it for a drive, I presume.'

'You all right with that?' asked Bella and Griff at the same time, the former with caution, the latter with delight.

Laurie smiled. 'Yes, I'm perfectly all right with that.'

'Oh boy,' said Griff, rubbing his hands together, his whole persona oozing glee as his eyes roved over the car. 'I think I've just found my soulmate. Come on, Pete.'

Pete, that was his name. Laurie had forgotten it and was grateful for the reminder.

'Are you sure they aren't going to just drive away and you'll never see them again?' said Bella, watching Griff set off with his brother in the passenger seat. 'I thought I was supposed to be here to prevent this sort of thing happening.'

'The less hairy brother is a fireman,' explained Laurie. 'I

met him at a counselling group I joined a couple of
weeks ago.'

'Whoa – back that truck up. You never told me this.'
Bella struck a pose of outrage, hands on hips, body
twisted, a flick of her long flame-red hair.

'I only went once, I wasn't sure about going back, but
on second thoughts, I think it might be helpful. Pete – the
fireman – lost his wife and their unborn baby earlier
this year.'

'Oh shit,' said Bella, dropping her arms back to
her sides.

'Quite honestly, even if they do run off with the car, I
don't think I'd lose any sleep. I was always terrified that
Alex would crash in it. Ironic, eh, that what he actually
dies in is a car that has a million safety features.'

Bella didn't say that Alex's car was still no match for an
overladen lorry being driven too fast on a notorious black
spot in the snow by a dickhead driver who was texting his
wife to say he'd be late home. He was very late home as
it happens, but he didn't die, not like the six people he
killed that night. He was out on bail, awaiting a trial that
would take place next March, walking around, living.

'Are you sure this Pete bloke checks out and that he's
not some charlatan joining groups to try and cop off with
vulnerable women?' asked Bella. 'I mean, it's a bit odd that
he turns up on your doorstep after "coincidentally" meeting you at a counselling group.' She took her phone out
of her back pocket and started tapping on it.

'What are you doing?'

'I'm looking him up. Pete . . . what's his surname?'

'Well the guy driving is Griff Moore so I'm presuming
he's got the same one.'

Bella fell silent for a few moments while she checked. 'Here we go, lots and lots of Pete Moores – great. Let's try a filter, South Yorkshire and fire. Oh, okay.' Her tone changed, softened. She held up a picture of Pete with a group of schoolchildren. '"Firefighter Pete Moore with the prize winners of the Art in Action competition", it says. When did his wife die?'

'No idea.'

'The article was published in January, so I'm presuming it was after this photo was taken.'

Eight months ago. Laurie looked at his picture, at his wide beam of a smile and thought, *that man had no idea what was around the corner for him.* Eight months ago she'd been looking at brochures for summer houses and holidays and finding that her eyes seemed more and more drawn to articles about motherhood. She shouldn't have put it off. She should have trusted that Alex was all hers and not let stupid doubts with long tails from the past stain their present. She would have had something of his to love, to make life bearable and give it purpose. Meredith and Brendan would have been able to keep a part of their son, heal the pain in their broken hearts. Eight months seemed a lifetime ago.

'He looks nice,' said Bella, interrupting her thoughts. 'That Pete.'

'Yes,' agreed Laurie, though she hadn't thought about him. Bank statements were taking up all her available grey cell space.

'Watch yourself though,' said Bella. 'He's vulnerable, you're vulnerable . . .'

Laurie laughed. 'I can assure you another relationship is the last thing on my mind.'

Since Bella had come back into her life, she'd been overly

protective, bordering on pitbull. She'd got even worse recently.

Twenty minutes later, just as Bella was becoming twitchy, Laurie heard the MR2 return. Through the window she could see Pete and Griff hop out and then proceed to give the car a very thorough once over: bending underneath, lifting the bonnet, feeling around the metal.

'I'll leave them to come in and tell me they're done,' said Laurie. 'They won't want me hovering over their shoulders.'

'At least they came back, I was beginning to doubt they would,' said Bella. 'Don't let them knock the price down. Stu says that you're offering it for a steal more than a quick sale. It's a bargain and they'll know that.'

Laurie liked Stu and she thought he'd liked her but she'd always presumed that he had something to do with why Bella went cold on her. They'd never had the conversation about why it had happened but she edged closer to opening up the dialogue every time she and Bella were together.

'They're walking towards the house,' said Bella, jumping back from the window so they wouldn't see her spying on them. 'Remember what I said, do not drop the price.'

Laurie opened the door and invited the two men inside.

'I'm having it,' said a delighted Griff before his second foot had cleared the threshold. 'It's exactly as you said it was.'

'I'm so pleased,' said Laurie. One less thing to think about.

'I can transfer the cash now, fill in the paperwork and take it off your hands straight away if that's convenient,' Griff went on.

'Good price, isn't it?' put in Bella, a hint of steel in her voice.

'Totally fair,' Griff replied.

'Fabulous,' said Laurie, throwing Bella a look.

'You've made him a very happy man,' said Pete. 'Just look at him.'

'Anyone like a coffee?' asked Bella, polite now that they weren't going to try and get one over on her friend.

'Not for me, thanks,' said Pete. 'I'm on nights and I'm going from here and straight to bed.'

'Not for me either thank you, I want to get back home and show my missus her love rival as soon as possible,' said Griff, with a beaming grin that would have put the Cheshire Cat to shame. 'I've been waiting for this car to turn up in my life for years. I promised her if I ever found it, I'd take her out for the poshest meal in town.'

'Sedgewick's fish and chip restaurant,' said Pete to the two women and winked.

'Nothing wrong with Sedgewick's,' said Laurie, turning to Bella. 'We used to go there a lot, didn't we?'

'Yeah, in the days when we could eat what we wanted without having to worry about calories,' Bella answered.

It took little over ten minutes for the monies to be arranged and the paperwork to be done. Griff was like an impatient child in his eagerness to be off. 'I can't believe I own the car of my dreams,' he said when the sale had been completed. 'Thank you so much,' and he shook Laurie's hand gratefully. 'And may I say, you've got a beautiful house.'

She contemplated asking if he wanted to buy that too.

'Thank you,' said Laurie. 'Well, I hope you enjoy your car.'

'I will. My *God* will I.'

'See you ... Wednesday?' Pete asked, hanging back slightly as his brother more or less skipped down the drive to his new car.

'Yes, I'll be there. Was anything said about me not being there last week?'

Pete's features arranged into a pained expression. 'Actually, I didn't go myself. Chickened out. Stupid of me.'

Laurie smiled. 'Oh goodness, I did that too. But I will be there this Wednesday.'

'Bye then.'

'Bye.'

She waved as he got into his car and he gave a cheerful pip on the horn as he headed down to the road.

'I'm having another coffee, that okay?' Bella called from inside the house.

'Of course. Make one for me too,' said Laurie, closing the door and heading towards the kitchen. It was good that Bella wasn't in a rush to be off; it would give them a chance to chat. Laurie swallowed, her mouth was dry with anxiety even though she knew she shouldn't feel like that with some-one she had known since school but she did. They were close again now, but something still stood between them and, as with Alex's effects, the time to deal with it was long overdue.

'He was right, that hairy brother; you do have a beautiful house,' Bella said as the kettle reached boiling point and clicked off.

Laurie looked around, seeing the kitchen and through to the lounge with someone else's eyes. It was stylish and beau-tiful and would sit happily on the pages of one of those 'Homes' glossy magazines. But had it ever felt like a proper home to her? No. Alex liked stylish furniture, she went for cosier fittings – she bent to his preferences. Children would have warmed it, made it more of a home than a house.

'I'm thinking about selling it and moving to somewhere smaller,' said Laurie.

Bella dropped a mug onto the work surface, luckily before any boiling water had entered it.

'Please tell me that you aren't doing that to give Meredith and Brendan a cut.'

'It crossed my mind.'

'*You what?*'

'Just some of it. As a peace offering.'

Bella opened her mouth to speak then shut it again. She had a quiet word with herself not to shout as she poured.

'Laurie, you don't owe them anything. Especially not after how they've treated you.' She brought the mugs over to the island, set them down then realisation dawned and showed on her face. 'Oh. My. God. Please don't tell me you thought of this just so you could ask Meredith about Alex's bank statements.'

'I can't lie and say that I didn't factor that into the equation.'

'No, Laurie, no,' snapped Bella. 'Let it go, stop worrying about it. I don't want to see you tearing yourself up or giving away money you're going to need for the future. Do you think your mother would have asked for half the house if the situation had been reversed? I mean we both know what your mother's like but not even she would stoop so low.'

'Thank you, you're a good friend. The best.' Laurie's question for Bella was settling in position on the starting blocks.

'Well, I'm trying to be. You certainly need one to look out for you, giving money away like it's paper.'

'I inherited a lot from Alex's insurances.'

'Yes, *you* did, because he wrote a will to make sure you did. What's the point of a bloody will if you can't exercise your own will, there's a clue in the name.' Bella pushed her wild red hair back from her exasperation-flushed face.

'What I also didn't tell you was that I went to see Pat Morrison yesterday.'

Bella's mouth formed a long 'O' of annoyance. 'You did? Even though I told—'

'—me to forget that idea. I know, but I'd already booked it. And I'm glad I went.'

'You really are a loose cannon, Laurie De Vere.' Bella threw her hands up in resignation. 'Come on then, what did she say?'

'She was spot on. She saw me finding happiness eventually.'

Bella didn't look convinced. 'Well, she was hardly going to say you'll have a miserable life, was she? You pay the money to hear you're going to be happy ever after.'

'She also said that I had a maze to get through to find answers. That a woman was withholding information from me.'

'Well, maybe she's said that to lure you back to cough up for more clues.'

'She knew that Alex was going to propose because she saw the ring. She also saw a holiday in the snow and strange lights, which has to be the Northern Lights. And this woman not telling me things, well that's got to be Meredith. Unless there's something you aren't telling me,' dared Laurie, watching for Bella's reaction.

'I'm keeping less things from you than you have from me, if we're judging ourselves on all today's disclosures,' said Bella. 'You're like International Secrets Woman.'

'Why did you and I have months where we didn't speak?'

There, it was out. The words hung in the air with a long echo, like a huge, resonant bell.

Bella was wrong-footed by the question. She opened her mouth to answer, but the words slid back down her throat.

'I'd like you to tell me now why you cut me off,' said Laurie, her calm voice belying the rapid thump-thump of the heart inside her chest wall. 'It doesn't matter what it was but too many things are weighing me down and I'd rather know the truth. Was it Stu? If not, what was it, Bells?'

Bella gave a sigh of resignation. 'Okay, I'll tell you but only if you promise to put out of your head any stupid ideas about trying to bribe Meredith for answers with your money.'

'All right.' She swerved the promise part.

'It was something that happened at Bertie and Anna's wedding,' Bella began.

Anna was an old school friend. They'd all drunk too much at the reception. The groom spent most of his wedding night face-planted in a flower bed in the hotel garden until Security found him and took him up to the bridal suite.

'What happened?' asked Laurie. She certainly couldn't bring anything to mind that might explain a falling out of that magnitude.

'I just didn't like how Alex spoke to you. I can't remember what he said exactly, but I thought his manner was off and I had a quiet word with him about it and he flew at me, more or less told me to butt out of your life. He said that you were fed up with me always moaning to you about work and men and that I was needy. That was it. That was all. I was hurt and annoyed and embarrassed and everything would have been fine in the morning but I made the mistake of telling Stu. He was going to say something to Alex but I persuaded him not to. But he didn't want to socialise with him any more after that and it made it awkward. So I thought I'd let things cool off and . . . well, the gap between us just got wider and wider.'

'I never said anything to Alex *ever* about me being fed up with you, because I wasn't. Why would he say that? It's a total lie,' said Laurie, completely befuddled by Bella's revelation.

'Well, we were both a bit pissed and that's probably why it got out of hand, but at the time I was miffed and I believed him. And yes, I should have said something to you about it and blown it out of the water, but it didn't happen. My fault entirely – I am not blaming you in any way.'

'That's all it was?'

'That's all it was. And I'm sorry. I wanted to pick up the phone to you so many times and just make this stupid thing between us go away but . . . oh, I don't know.'

You don't need her in your life. Just let her go. She's hardly a friend if she can cut you loose like that, Alex had said to her more than once when she asked his opinion about it all. He was certainly more encouraging about forgetting Bella and moving on than instigating a repair job in their gone-sour friendship. *I've never really been that keen on her, if I'm honest. She uses you as a sounding board and to patch her up when she's had yet another disastrous relationship. And now she's got Stu and she's dropped you. Coincidence? I don't think so.*

Bella had always been sensitive, as much for others as for herself. The feisty red-haired persona was a front. She and Alex had got on famously until he'd had his affair. Then she'd urged Laurie not to take him back, she said that if he'd done it once, he would do it again. But when Laurie had, Bella had put her own feelings on one side and sat on her own animosity towards him. Alex had shocked Laurie when he'd said that he didn't think she was that good a friend, because she'd always thought he liked Bella enormously.

'So that's another thing you can stop worrying about,'

said Bella. 'If I'd known it was on your mind this much, I'd have told you before. I'm sorry. Now can we put it to bed?'

'We can,' said Laurie. She must have got it all mixed up though because she was sure the breakdown came long after Anna's wedding.

Bella finished her coffee and said she'd better get off home. In her car she breathed a long drawn-out sigh of relief as if she'd had a tight band around her chest that had suddenly snapped. Pat Morrison had come so close to the bone there she'd hacked off some of the marrow. It wasn't Meredith keeping secrets, it was her. And what she'd just told her friend about Alex wasn't the whole truth, but it was the only truth she was going to part with. For Laurie's sake.

There was an unfortunate mistake in an advert that appeared in the 'Little Darlings' section of the *Daily Trumpet* last weekend, namely: 'Photographer Malcolm Robson will shoot your children in your home'. Mr Robson wants us to make it clear that he is only prepared to shoot children in his studio.

Chapter 19

10 September

'I despair, I fu— bloody despair,' said Alan Robertson at their weekly Tuesday meeting. He picked up the well-creased copy of the *Daily Trumpet* from his desk and began to read.

'*"Confidential information recently came to light that directors of the business had been syphoning money from the coffers for years. The source, Derek Eastman, has asked to remain anonymous for obvious reasons."* I ask you. What pillock deputy editor lets that through? I can't take any time off ever because this happens when I do and it's my chuffing head that's on the block. I'm going to resign, I really am. It's the only way I'll get any sleep. Sir Basil isn't paying me enough to manage that shower of shit, excuse language, Laurie. I've forgotten how to say a sentence without using an expletive. Swearing has become part of my DNA thanks to those . . . those . . . Why is there a finite selection of profanities in the British language? The one I want to use hasn't been invented because there isn't one strong enough. The Italians would have a word for it, I bet.'

Laurie smothered a laugh. It was always a pick-me-up coming to *Daily Trumpet* HQ but ever since Meredith had posted the bank statements through the front door, the trials and tribulations of 'anonymous Derek Eastman' et al. were an even more welcome diversion from darker thoughts which were stuck in her brain like teazels resolutely tangled in an Afghan Hound's coat.

Alan's phone rang and he snatched it up.

'You're joking?' he said, after listening to the caller for a few seconds. 'That's the best news I've had all day. There is a god.' He put the phone down, none too gently. He was too used to slamming it back on the cradle to tone down his style to respect his visitors' sensitivities.

'As luck would have it, Derek's dead,' Alan said to her.

'Oh no.'

'Very lucky for us,' said Alan. 'Not for poor Derek, obviously. I think we'll blame it on a misprint. No need for any action on that one. Which concludes our business for today, thank you very much, unless you feel like picking me out some less ugly kids than the rest for the Bonny Babies competition.'

'Thanks, but no thanks, Alan.'

Laurie stretched a crick out of her neck. She'd slept at a funny angle and woken in pain. The wonder was that she'd been sleeping at all. Questions were tumbling around in her head like a washing machine with no off button. When she slipped from consciousness at night, she was dreaming about Alex and Meredith and mysterious secrets and mazes and they had worked in conjunction to plough to the surface lots of emotions she had done her best to bury over the years. Feelings spun from his affair with the woman he had never named: soul-crippling betrayal and the cold, lonely hinterland of rejection.

'You okay there? I can recommend a good chiropractor if you need one. Sometimes I think someone has taken off my head and poured a box of Cornflakes down my neck. Crunch, crunch, crunch when I swivel it. He transforms my spine to a velvet ribbon. He's Russian. They don't muck about applying pressure.'

'I'm fine, Alan, thank you. I just had a bad night's sleep, that's all.'

'Okay then. I'll see you next Tuesday,' said Alan. 'Bet you can't wait.'

'I can't,' smiled Laurie. 'This is the highlight of my week.'

Alan opened the door. 'Then I feel sorry for you. Tell you what, let me see you out. I need some fresh air. It's filled with poison in here. From all those cocks out there. Yes, you can look, I'm talking about you, not to you.'

Those in the newsroom bowed their heads, smothering snorts and giggles.

'You love working here really,' said Laurie, when they were in the corridor.

'This job makes purgatory look like a frigging picnic in the park. I would love to know what I did in a past life to merit this torture. I must have buggered a nun,' said Alan. 'It's only bearable because every day is a day nearer to me leaving this devil's arsehole and jetting off to the sun.' His voice softened. 'How are you doing, anyway?'

'Oh, you know, curate's egg,' said Laurie, which was a lie because at the moment, her curate's egg was all bad. She felt back at square one after Meredith had brought those bank statements. She might as well have posted a grenade through her door.

'Molly will help you, on that I have no doubt. Have you been to see her yet?'

'I did go . . . once. A fortnight ago.'

'And?'

'I thought I'd made a mistake so I missed last week—'

'Ah.'

'Let me finish. I think the mistake was in *not* going back so I'll be there tomorrow, eating cake again and spilling my soul.'

'Good girl. You're doing the right thing.'

Am I? thought Laurie. But she would go because the psychic had told her she must. *It will work for you so you must stick at it. This time.* As if she realised she'd had a false start. Knew she had.

Chapter 20

11 September

'Ah, Peter, do come in,' said Molly, genuinely delighted to see him, though she'd had a feeling somehow that he would be back among them. He and Laurie both. 'You're the first to arrive.' Her eyes went from his face to the bunch of flowers he was carrying in one hand.

'I know. I came extra early to explain about last week,' said Pete.

'You don't have to.'

'These are for you, to apologise,' he said, holding the flowers out towards her. 'I'm not the messing around type usually.'

Molly chuckled. 'Oh bless you, that really isn't necessary at all. But thank you, I shan't refuse them as I do love flowers. It wasn't the first time and it certainly won't be the last that someone decides not to come again. Talking things through this way isn't for everyone. But more often than not, some—'

Molly's words were cut off as the doorbell gave a merry

jangle and in walked Laurie, wearing roughly the same sheepish expression as Pete had.

'Oh, I was hoping I'd be here before anyone else,' she said. She was carrying a gold ballotine of chocolates with a pink ribbon tied around it. 'Molly, I'm so sorry about last week. These are handmade truffles—'

Molly shushed her with a flappy hand gesture. 'Take a seat, dear Laurie and think no more about it. Actually don't take a seat, have first choice of the cakes. There are only three slices of the passion fruit left and I think Mr Singh has his eye on one of them. You really didn't have to bring chocolates. My, it's like Christmas. But I never look a gift horse in the mouth, so thank you. Both.'

Right on cue, Pavitar Singh emerged from the back room tying up his apron, which featured the wording *Old Doctors Never Die, they Simply Lose their Patience* and Molly crossed his path as she took the chocolates and flowers into the back room.

'I think you beat me with the handmade truffles,' said Pete to Laurie in a low, conspiratorial voice.

'It's a very small box, a gesture,' said Laurie, playing down her gift. 'There will probably be about two in it when Molly opens it up.'

'She can't eat flowers though.'

'Chocolates don't look so good in a vase.'

They both smiled at each other. They both thought what nice smiles the other had.

The doorbell rang and in walked Sharon. She looked delighted to see them.

'Oh, how lovely that you came back. We all hoped you would.'

Maurice greeted them with much the same expression

when he entered not long afterwards. 'Splendid,' he said, making a point of shaking both Pete and Laurie by the hand. 'You've done the right thing, not giving up too soon. You'll see.'

'Without wishing to draw attention to you too much,' said Molly to Pete and Laurie, when they were all present and settled with tea and cake, 'may I use the example of you missing last week's session to illustrate a point. Grief is often a dance of two steps forward and three steps back. Sometimes, when you feel as if you make some headway and you take four steps forwards, guess what happens?'

'Ten steps backwards,' answered Sharon with a grimace. 'Been there, done that, got the T-shirt.'

'It's like swimming in the sea, isn't it?' put in Maurice. 'Just when you get used to the warm waters, there can be a sudden cold swirl that hits you for six and you have no idea where it's come from. Especially the sea in Morecambe.'

'Perfectly put, Maurice. Grief is very complicated,' said Molly. 'Your mind and your body are attempting to process what has happened to you and none of it fits into a grid or a timetable. But structure in your life can help enormously. Having things in your diary to look forward to, to plough your energies into rather than just reliving your moments of sadness. This is a game of small steps, not giant leaps. I remember when my husband died, I felt as if nothing around me was real for a while. Somewhere between this world and a dream. And not a nice dream at that. Thanks to people like Pavitar' – Molly motioned towards him – 'who decided that a morning walk would be beneficial, and a theatre or cinema trip once a week and friends who laid down stepping stones for me, I found that a pleasurable routine helped me enormously. Not just the daily grind of meeting our basic needs; that is existing – not living. Grief can be a stubborn shellfish to dislodge.'

'Like a barnacle,' said Maurice. 'They might not cause harm per se to ships but they do hinder their movement in the sea.'

'Just like a barnacle,' said Molly with a warm Molly smile in his direction.

Maurice beamed at everyone as if he was five and teacher had just commended him in front of the whole class. He couldn't have looked more chuffed if Molly had presented him with a gold star to stick in a notepad.

'I feel the opposite,' piped up Yvonne. 'I feel as if I've been in a bad dream for years and have just woken up to find out that everything's more than all right.'

'Shock,' said Sharon. 'Like Molly says, you're all over the pigging place.'

Yvonne didn't look that convinced.

'I used to work with a woman who turned to a very strange quarter for help after her husband passed,' said Maurice, shaking his head. 'She was always a twinset and pearls type but suddenly she started wearing those hippy dresses and flower garlands in her hair and glitter on her face and believed she could see gnomes and pixies and little folk in the woods. She'd lie in meadows and paddle in streams in attempts to absorb their energy.'

'Eh?' asked Sharon. 'Little folk as in Enid Blyton books?'

'Precisely. "Guardians of nature" she called them. She even met up with a much younger man on the internet who'd had his ears and nose altered so he looked like a pixie. And I do recall she changed her name by deed poll to Littleseed Thistledown.'

'Sounds like she's away with the fairies to me,' Pete said with a grumble of disbelief.

There was a tumbleweed few moments of silence in which Pete wished he'd kept his mouth shut and then everyone erupted into a burst of self-feeding laughter. They couldn't stop. Maurice especially, there were tears racing down his cheeks by the time he got hold of himself. Even Mr Singh behind the counter was wiping his eyes with a tea towel. Attempting to bring them to order, Molly said, 'Well, it's horses for courses. Whatever works.'

'It worked very well for Pauli— ... er, Littleseed,' said Maurice, after blowing his nose on a very large handkerchief embroidered with his initials. 'I have to say, I scoffed a little less when I bumped into her and her purple hair in the Co-op last year. She looked rejuvenated and not at all concerned about the attention her wings were drawing.'

Laurie was consumed by a fresh wave of hilarity. She hadn't bargained on laughing like this at a group to help negotiate a passage through the grief process. She set everyone else off and they swam happily around in a communal pool of mirth for a while, exercising laughter muscles that most of them hadn't used so much in a long time.

The rest of the meeting had both feet planted firmly in rather more gravitas, but still humour danced around them all with light fairy footsteps. There were ways to discuss what they were trying to traverse without being bogged down by concrete blocks of gloom. They talked about the small kindnesses they had received from people which meant so much more than intended and what they all had done with the deceased's belongings. Sharon hadn't managed to throw out Billy's toys or bed yet because she wasn't ready to let them go, but if she ever did get another dog, she'd buy him new things, she said. They reflected on how hard it was to part with their loved ones' effects, as if objects had been bound to them with emotions, as if disposing of them was somehow symbolic of disposing of their loved ones and so guilt kept them from doing it. Pete told them that his wife's sisters had taken a lot of her things to use and everyone agreed that was a smashing solution. Laurie didn't say that her fiancé's best friend had taken his entertainment collection and used the opportunity to try and take her too. At least she didn't on this occasion.

Laurie left the meeting feeling glad she had rejoined the little fold of seven. Pat Morrison had been right on that, which lent a credibility to everything else she had said. She felt someone at her shoulder as she neared her car and turned round to find Pete.

'Think you'll be back next week?' he asked.

'Definitely. Especially if you're going to give out lines like the fairy one.'

She chuckled, a sweet airy sound like the bell above the teashop door, Pete thought. A laugh that would have suited a fairy.

He shook his head. 'I really shouldn't have said that.'

'Oh you should, you so should.'

'Making fun of the woman like that was bad form. Who am I to cast scorn on anything that works for someone in the same situation as we are?'

It was obvious he felt genuinely bad about it, which endeared him to Laurie. What would he have made of the news that her direction in life was presently being dictated by vibes she'd implanted in a crystal ball and a spent match, she wondered.

'I'm sure that you're just one of many sceptics, but if the lady is going into supermarkets wearing a large pair of wings, then she must have developed a wonderful resilience,' replied Laurie, taking her goldfish of keys out of her bag.

'She must indeed,' said Pete. 'It's obviously good for her mental elf.' He immediately apologised, even though Laurie burst into a fresh peal of laughter. 'Sorry, sorry, I couldn't resist.'

'Will you be back next week?' said Laurie, recovering.

'I will,' came the reply. 'I'll take any help on offer. I might even—' he cut off his words. 'No, I can't say that.'

'Have your ears fashioned into points?' Laurie supplied.

'Oh, don't. I've infected you,' said Pete.

'You have a good week,' said Laurie, zapping her car open. 'Hope you get gnome safely.'

'Stop now,' said Pete. 'We're like naughty kids.' He smiled at her. 'Hope you get *home* safely too.'

He gave her a quick wave when she set off and thought, as he followed her out of the car park, that it was people who formed the guide rope out of grief. The company of those with generous hearts, like Molly and Mr Singh who led where they had once followed, because they could. There was real magic in kindness.

The *Daily Trumpet* apologises unreservedly to Mrs Amy Cliteroe after police were called to her house on Tuesday after we wrongly printed that she had a bright red Vulva for sale and not a bright red Volvo. The Vulva was said to have had four owners from new, a snug interior and was a real head-turner when out on the street.

Chapter 21

17 September

'I'm thinking about having you in two days a week,' said Alan Robertson the following Tuesday. 'Have you seen the size of the backlog? It's like bleeding Everest. Luckily nothing about the mayor, so that's on our side at least. He has threatened us with legal action if we' – Alan drew two little wiggles in the air – '"target" him again. But as my old great gran, God rest her sweet soul, used to say: "He can fuck right off".'

Alan's great gran, if he was to be believed, said that phrase quite often about a lot of folks.

He put a coffee down on the table in front of Laurie and slid over a tin of biscuits.

'We finished the Fortnum and Mason ones, these are Fox's best,' he said. 'You should take a handful. You're looking a bit thin, missy.' There was concern in his voice. He liked Laurie a lot and he knew how grief could strip away an appetite and the sense to look after yourself because he'd been there. 'How are things?' He gave the final word a weight of its own.

Laurie lifted a jam and cream ring from the tin.

'Your friend Molly is wonderful,' said Laurie, presuming he was angling for an update on how 'things' were going with her. 'I have my third session tomorrow. I'm quite looking forward to it.'

'I'm glad,' said Alan. 'What do you talk about? I might have another go at persuading her to do a feature.'

'Well . . .' Laurie gave a small laugh, '. . . past subjects include: feeling guilty that you haven't murdered your mother with a cushion, how you can't stop eating cake and smiling because your husband has passed away and the healing power of fairies.'

Alan raised a brace of shaggy eyebrows. 'I might not, then,' he decided.

'I'm being slightly facetious. In context, everything we talked about was pretty heartfelt stuff, which is the point of it all I suppose. No one felt any awkwardness about contributing experiences which outside the group might sound a bit weird.'

'Yep,' said Alan, scooping up a handful of biscuits like a claw in an arcade game. 'I can see how wanting to smother your mother should be kept within a circle of confidantes.'

'What's Molly's story?' asked Laurie.

Alan scratched his head with the hand not holding a clutch of Viennese fingers.

'Molly was a vulnerable soul when she fell in love with a man called Harvey Hoyland. It didn't work out and he left her. A few years ago, he turned up on her doorstep hoping to make amends with her because he was a very poorly man and he'd never stopped loving her.'

'Then Harvey died?'

'He did,' said Alan. 'But he died in the arms of the woman he adored. True love always finds its way home, with or without a compass, my great gran used to say. It took Molly a long time to get over Harvey, and she didn't want to waste what she'd learned on the way to acceptance, which is why she set up her club. You won't find many people who know more about love and loss than she does.'

'Is she now with the Sikh gentleman – Mr Singh?'

'Pavitar Singh? No, they're just friends. Pavitar's a widower, Molly's a widow so the pair of them go on holiday and out for meals together. *Friends without benefits,* I suppose is what you'd call it these days. Just *friends* is what old bastards like me would say.'

'That's sweet.' Laurie smiled.

'Molly's sister is a case. Margaret sees dead people.' Alan leaned in close as he imparted this nugget in case he was overheard. 'She was a matron in hospitals and when anyone was near the end of their life, she'd find relatives sitting by the patient's bedside that no one else could see. If you knew Margaret, you'd think she was the last person on the planet to entertain such nonsense.'

'You've never run a story on that, then?' asked Laurie after a long whistle of astonishment.

'Margaret would kill me if I did. And I'd rather the mayor came after me with a cohort of armed Spartans than cross Margaret Brandywine, trust me. I just threw that into our conversation because I trust you to keep it to yourself. I'm glad you've taken the plunge and gone to the group, I really am, Laurie.'

'So you think some proper psychics do exist? That they're not all charlatans?' Laurie asked as something inside her reared its head, keen for acceptance.

'If Margaret Brandywine is anything to go by, yes. Even a hard-bitten old git like me would believe there's something in all that supernatural bollocks,' said Alan.

That would do nicely as a commendation, thought Laurie.

Chapter 22

18 September

When Pete pulled up in Spring Hill Square car park the next evening, Laurie's white Mercedes was already there and he felt quite gladdened by the sight. Maybe because they were both newbies, he reckoned. He didn't put it down to anything more than someone his own age, going through similar things at the same time.

He walked in on a full house laughing.

'Ah come in, Peter,' said Mr Singh, wafting his hand in the air at him as if conducting an orchestra.

'What's going on?' said Pete, his own smile appearing, brought to the fore by the merry atmosphere.

'We were just having a conversation about people taking advantage of the recently bereaved,' Mr Singh replied, before blowing his nose on his handkerchief.

'Well that sounds like dark humour,' said Pete.

'Have some coffee and cake, Peter,' said Molly.

'I'll have a bog-standard filter white coffee please and whatever that cake is there with the chocolate buttons on it.'

'Coming right up, sir,' said Mr Singh.

Pete said hello to everyone and then sat next to Laurie when Mr Singh had served him. He noticed that Maurice was looking particularly bright this week with a red and green checked waistcoat. Yvonne's hair was in soft curls rather than hard springs and Sharon had lost that air of melancholy that hung around her like a mist. Laurie greeted him with a warm smile but she looked tired, he thought. There were dark circles around her eyes that she'd obviously tried to cover up with make-up, but not well enough to convince those with keen sight.

'I was just saying, Peter, that when my grandmother died, about twenty people contacted my mother to say that she'd promised them all five thousand pounds in her will. She had, apparently, gone around to all her friends and neighbours and people in her whist club and even showed them her will to prove it. But she had three hundred pounds to her name and owed four hundred to a catalogue company. Batty as a box of bananas,' said Maurice. 'She was clearly insane, but they'd have taken it, if she'd had it.'

'Alas, people can move in and take advantage, preying on the goodwill and naivety of the bereaved,' said Molly.

'Des's brother said he'd been promised all sorts,' said Yvonne. 'I knew he hadn't because they hated each other, so I told him to waddle off, but in less polite terms.'

'I had a strange encounter the week after Alex's funeral,' began Laurie and then pulled her words up. No, she really couldn't tell that story. Coffee and cake and this teashop were loosening her tongue more than a bottle of Chenin Blanc would do. All eyes turned to her and she shook her hand, as if to wave attention away from her. 'Ignore me,' she said.

'You don't have to say anything you don't want to here, Laurie,' said Molly.

'Well I for one am intrigued now,' said Maurice.

Oh sod it, thought Laurie. It might be good to get some perspective on it. And other opinions rather than Bella's 'the wanker' one.

'Okay,' she began, '... Alex left his best friend, let's call him Mr X, his music and DVD collection in his will disbursements. I hadn't even had time or inclination to get them together before he called to pick them up.' She looked up to find she had a captive audience and really wished again she hadn't started this tale, but she could hardly stop now. 'I tried to fob him off and said I didn't have any boxes but he'd brought some. And I was a little disorientated, so we just started packing them up. Then Je— ... Mr X asked if I'd make him a coffee. So I made us one and we sat at the island in my kitchen and he asked me if I needed anything, anything at all. I thought that was very considerate of him ...' Laurie looked up to find she had them all in the palm of her hand. '... I said I couldn't think of anything, not put on the spot like that anyway. Then he asked me if I ...' she swallowed as she neared the crux of the story '... if I needed anything "servicing". I thought he meant Alex's car or the gas boiler and I knew neither of them were due. And then he ran his finger up my arm ... and I realised what he meant by *servicing.*'

Maurice gasped, Yvonne gasped, Mr Singh's jaw fell open. Sharon asked, 'What did you do, Laurie?'

'I couldn't move. I just sat there while he carried on doing that thing on my arm. Then something clicked in my head, and I threw my coffee all over him and told him to get out and he did just that without saying another word.'

At the sight of their shocked, frozen expressions, Laurie burst into laughter. She couldn't stop. She hiccupped through the rest of the story. 'He just dripped coffee all over the floor. I didn't know a mug could carry so much liquid.'

Sharon started laughing then, joined by Maurice, Mr Singh, the others. Laurie's sides started aching. 'And I haven't seen him since.' Tears were rolling down her face. Funny, daft tears as she remembered Jefferson's white polo shirt stained with coffee, drops clinging to his stupid goatee beard that consisted of about six hairs. The only other person she'd told about it was Bella, who hadn't seen any mirth in the story at all. Maybe if she had, it would have shattered the awful memory. Blasted it out of her system instead of keeping it sitting inside her like a festering egg.

Eventually the laughter subsided. 'Oh my goodness,' said Laurie. 'I'm not even sure if I should have told you that, but it felt good to share it. I kept wondering if I'd led him on in some way. I know I didn't really but you start to doubt yourself sometimes because you're so mixed up. He's the fiancé of Alex's sister as well as his best friend, which made things really awkward but luckily his family don't speak to me because they wanted me to sell our house and give them half.'

Blimey, talk about laying her soul bare. It was rolling out of her now like sewage down a pipe. The frivolity left her voice, dried up as if it had been hit by microwaves.

'I really liked his mum and dad so I can't get my head around all this. The same way they can't get their heads around how a joint mortgage works. They think that because the house was half Alex's, I should split the equity with them.'

'That is very bad form,' said Maurice. 'The point of a joint mortgage is to keep a partner in their home and gift them security. Did your partner write a will, Laurie?'

'Yes, Maurice. We both wrote wills to protect each other. His parents are well off. We, on the other hand, had a huge mortgage and no savings so we covered ourselves adequately.'

'Good that you were both so sensible,' Maurice said then, sounding more of a solicitor than she was.

'Greedy bastards,' said Yvonne. 'Des never bothered about insurance. Luckily I did, otherwise I'd be on my arse now. I've never been as comfortable.' And she grinned. Clearly the enormity of being a widow still hadn't impacted fully on her senses yet.

'Sorry, this is a bit of a confessional booth for me this week,' said Laurie. 'With multiple priests present. I didn't mean to take over.' She'd given away too much of herself, she wasn't used to it.

'You're in a secure arena. The first rule of Molly's Club is that you do not talk about Molly's Club.' Molly smiled at her and Laurie instantly felt that she hadn't overstepped any mark. She was safe, no one was judging her here.

'So, can anyone top that? Please,' asked Laurie then.

'I'll try,' said Pete. 'My wife's sister has been coming over to the house, which is fine and I make her welcome. But I'm pretty sure she has a hidden agenda. I don't want any of you to think I'm up myself and God's gift to women—'

'I wouldn't mind God gifting you to me,' Yvonne butted in with a snort of laughter which made Pete's words flow easier because he too had wished he hadn't started this story and could spool back half a minute and keep his mouth firmly shut.

'I think I told you that I gave a lot of Tara's things to her sisters because it was designer stuff, expensive. But one of the sisters, *Miss X*, wears my wife's clothes when she comes round, and her perfume and she's changed her hairstyle to the same as my wife's was and she's just getting a bit too close. It's not my imagination, I know it isn't, but I have no idea what to do about it. I understand that she's grieving too but it's a complication I don't want.'

'Wow,' said Maurice. 'That is a tough one.'

'Not fair that she's putting you in that position,' said Sharon. 'It's manipulation.'

'She may be grasping at keeping her sister alive by latching on to you,' said Molly. 'Were they very close?'

'Yeah, they were quite. Certainly closer than my wife was to her oldest sister. I get a totally different vibe from her. It's ... it's as it should be.'

'I'd trust your intuition and distance yourself,' advised Yvonne, which is exactly what Laurie would have said had she voiced her opinion.

'There was a bloke who lived near us who tried to get his daughter to take the place of his wife when she passed,' said Sharon. 'If you know what I mean.'

'That's not a normal response,' said Mr Singh. 'Sometimes people use situations to excuse warped behaviour.'

'He got locked up in the end,' Sharon went on.

'Good,' said Yvonne, not quite under her breath. Then she stood up abruptly and unlooped her bag off the back of the chair. 'I'm sorry, I'll have to go home.'

'Have we said something to upset you?' asked Maurice, concerned, also rising to his feet.

'No,' said Yvonne, 'I think I've left the iron on.'

'I'll run you home,' said Maurice, standing up to rifle in his pocket for his keys.

'I want to walk and get some fresh air.' Her tone was

insistent, with a snap in it. She realised this immediately and tempered her next words to him. 'Thank you though, Maurice. It's very kind of you, but I'll walk.'

She hurried out; Molly followed her. Through the glass in the door, Laurie could see them talking. Yvonne looked in a bit of a state. Something had really got to her.

Maurice took a step towards the door but Sharon placed a cautionary hand on his arm. 'Just let them be, Maurice,' she said gently. 'Let Molly handle it.'

'Anyone for another drink?' asked Mr Singh – a diversionary tactic.

'I suppose I could squeeze in another,' said Maurice, approaching the counter.

Just as Mr Singh had finished serving him, Molly came back and all eyes lifted to her. In her wake was Yvonne, not smiling for once. She looked smaller somehow, as if the mere action of going outside and returning had shrunk her. She sat down on the same seat she had recently vacated and looped the strap of her bag on the chair again, as if someone had hit a rewind button and put things back to how they were a few minutes ago. Maurice gave her a look that silently asked the question, *are you all right?* and she answered it with a stiff nod, no eye contact.

'It's very odd how little vocabulary we have when dealing with other people's grief,' said Molly, picking up the thread of the meeting once more. No one asked about Yvonne's iron because none of them believed she'd left it on anyway.

'Nobody knows what to say, do they?' This from Sharon. '"I'm sorry for your loss" doesn't cut it. Then again I knew what to say when the old bag down the road told me that she didn't know why I was so upset because Billy was only a dog. I had plenty of vocabulary for her, let me tell you.'

'I might get myself a pet,' said Yvonne. She was back in the room with them mentally again and that made Maurice smile.

'Plenty of rescue centres wanting good homes,' said Molly. 'That's how I ended up with my cat Queenie. She was fourteen when I got her six years ago and she'd been in the shelter for three years. No one wanted her because she had to be the only pet, no children, was terrified of men and is blind in one eye. She settled in a treat. And she's even taken to Pavitar.'

'Yes, she gets white hair all over my trousers,' he chuckled.

'I daren't have animals before. I always wanted a cat but I was frightened of Des kicking it.'

'I'll go with you if you want some help choosing, Yvonne,' offered Maurice.

Yvonne gave him another brief nod. Something had really touched a nerve for her. Laurie tried to think back to what they had been talking about when she'd dashed out, but it evaded her.

'Returning to what we were saying about inappropriate behaviour, a woman at my mother's funeral pulled me on one side to say Mum owed her five pounds from years ago and she thought my mother would rest in peace easier if I settled the debt,' said Maurice.

'Cheeky article,' said Sharon with a tut. 'Tell me you didn't pay her.'

'I felt I had to. I wouldn't have wanted Mother not to be at peace for such a paltry amount,' came the reply. 'Then the week after, an envelope was pushed through my letter box with five pounds in it, no note. Guilt must have got the better of her, I suppose. I thought at the time it was very odd my mother owing anyone money, she was most against borrowing or lending.' Maurice swivelled to address Laurie. 'I'm presuming your fiancé's friend didn't come back and apologise.'

'Not yet he hasn't,' she replied. 'I don't think he will now.'

Behind the counter, Mr Singh shook his head slowly from side to side.

'Taking advantage of the vulnerable has always been a cardinal sin in my eyes.'

Molly nodded sagely. Sadly it was too common an occurrence. At least now she was surrounded by people who were kind, but then being strong for others had always been her forte.

The meeting drew to a natural close about half an hour later and Yvonne relented into letting Maurice take her home. Laurie and Pete walked out to the car park together.

'Wonder what made Yvonne flip,' Pete said. 'I was trying to remember what we were talking about but I couldn't.'

'Me too,' said Laurie. 'I hope it wasn't something I said.'

'Wasn't I talking about my sister-in-law?' asked Pete. 'Maybe it wasn't either of us and she was just . . . ready to burst. Nothing seems to be happening in the right order for Yvonne, does it? She's not going through the stages of grief as it's written down: denial, anger, depression – or whatever it is.'

Laurie knew how she felt. She hadn't exactly gone through the stages in the right order either. She had been consumed by rage initially, then cried a lot, then she had willed Alex back into her life with all her strength and her heart, unable to get her head around the fact that he was gone forever, that she would never see him again with so many things unsaid between them. How could that be possible? Now she felt trapped as a fly in aspic with frustration and anger and confusion that he could have left her in the middle of a maze — as Pat Morrison put it. She was a long, long way off the acceptance stage.

'Everything all right?' asked Pete, noticing the cloud that passed over her features.

'Sorry, I'm okay,' said Laurie, snapping back to the here and now. 'Anyway have a good week and—'

'No you aren't okay,' said Pete.

Laurie was about to counter protest but what came out of her was a long slow weary outward breath.

'I was just thinking that I'm stuck like Yvonne. There are so many questions around Alex's death, so much that I don't understand ...' She trailed off, knowing that once she started talking about this, she wouldn't be able to stop. 'Ignore me. Have a—'

'Like what?' he asked, not allowing her to cut and run.

Laurie shook her head. 'Ohh ... It's too much to say in a car park. I really don't want to burden you anyway.'

'Do you want to go for a drink?' He held up his hands, splayed palms out towards her. 'I'm not coming on to you. Not that you're not coming-on-to material.' He muttered to himself then: 'Stop digging, dickhead.' Laurie smiled and that evoked a smile from him too. 'Whenever I do get back into the dating game, I need to refine my chat-up lines, don't I?'

'I'd love a drink,' said Laurie. 'There's a pub in Little Kipping. The Spouting Tap, I think it's called.'

If ever there was a more aptly named pub to discuss tonight's shenanigans, thought Pete. 'I'll follow you down there,' he said, zapping his car open.

Chapter 23

The Spouting Tap was a charming olde worlde village pub with low ceilings, beams, a fireplace and exposed brickwork. It hadn't followed the trend of transforming itself into a Prosecco or gin palace as it was quietly confident of pulling in trade with its array of craft beers. The car park was empty but the pub itself quite full, indicating that it was a bar frequented by mostly locals. A woman descended on Pete and Laurie as soon as they walked in.

'You 'ere for t'quiz?'

'Er . . .'

She didn't wait for an answer; instead she shoved a pencil and a piece of paper into Pete's hand and accosted someone else with the same question.

'Seems we are then,' Pete said and Laurie sniggered. 'What can I get you to drink?'

'Oh, just a J20 please. Any flavour. I'll go and grab that table in the corner.'

The table was at the side of the fireplace and would have been as cosy as apple pie on a dark night with logs burning in the grate, thought Laurie. She hoped Pete didn't think she'd picked it for its intimate position: she was scared stiff of giving out 'take me' vibes after what had happened with Jefferson.

She let her eyes drift over the activity around the room. The harassed woman giving out the quiz sheets was having a few choice words with the young man behind the bar, who didn't seem to be coping with the customers fast enough for her liking. There were a couple of old men sitting on stools chatting, drinking from dimpled glass tankards. They looked the type to have their own stored there, thought Laurie. There was a knot of young men in T-shirts that showed off their bulging muscles standing with their slim girlfriends, all from a similar mould of hair extensions, false eyelashes and shovelled-on make-up. Laurie loved places like this, but they were an anathema to Alex. He preferred trendy wine bars with noise and vivacity and prices as inflated as those girls' lips. Her eyes came to rest on Pete, waiting for his order. He looked extra tall standing under the low roof and she saw one of the muscle-boys at his side give him the once over, an envious look perhaps that they could bulk up but they were stuck with their medium height. His back was broad and his jeans showed off a good chunk of bum. She pulled her eyes away. She couldn't remember the last time she'd actually appraised another man. She hadn't needed to because she had Alex, and he was all she wanted.

'Sorry about that,' said Pete, eventually arriving at the table. 'There was a bit of a queue as the barman had just come in from his emergency vape-break. A modern-day catastrophe I think.'

Laurie smiled at that. 'Thank you,' she said. 'I'll get the next one.' Oh blimey, that was inferring they'd stay for another. 'If we . . . I mean . . .'

Pete cracked a smile. 'Don't worry about it.'

'Forgive me. Ever since the thing with Alex's best friend, I've been hypersensitive about what I say to the opposite sex.'

'You and me both,' said Pete and knocked his own J20 against Laurie's. 'Cheers. Here's to being two fish out of water, united in our gawkiness.'

'Cheers,' said Laurie and took a sip before speaking again. 'Funny lot aren't they at the group? But lovely. I feel quite at home with them. I'm so glad I gave it another go.'

'You've hit the nail on the head,' replied Pete. 'I still can't believe I actually signed up to something like this. It's not really my sort of thing. I'm more your *stop being a wuss* and getting on with it person. Until this year happened anyway.'

'What was it that made you join in the end? I think you said there had been an incident at work, have I remembered that right?'

'Yep. I lost it, simple as that, cutting someone out of a car. It was either get help or take sick leave. My boss has been brilliant. He's swapped my shifts around so I could come to the sessions; I'm lucky I'm so well supported. It was one of the other firefighters who gave me Molly's number. She's known her for years. Didn't you say that someone at the *Daily Trumpet* recommended her to you?'

'Yes, the editor. His recommendation is gold.'

'Really?' said Pete, incredulously.

'Alan Robertson is a man fighting a lion with a blade of grass. He wants the newspaper to succeed, but the only way it will is if it carries on as it is. The owner, Sir Basil Stamper, is on course for out-wealthing Richard Branson so Alan is forced to strive for damage limitation at best. And even if he is a journalist, he would never betray a confidence.'

'Funny how you can be surrounded by family and friends

and still feel that they're too close to talk to, don't you find?' Pete put his glass down on the table and Laurie noticed how large and square his hands were. She wondered how many individuals those hands had rescued, saved.

'I don't really have many people close to me,' Laurie admitted. 'I'm an only child and my mum's never been on the scene much. We're very different. Never knew my dad. Neither did my mum so there's a blank on my birth certificate. My best friend is great but she's quite forceful in that I should concentrate on the future and not on dissecting the past, but I can't help it. Until I can dissect the past and find answers, I won't be able to move forward.'

She toyed absently with her necklace as she spoke. Pete's attention was drawn to the small ring on the chain. The square diamond looked almost too big for it. Laurie traced his eyes to her neck.

'Alex died with this ring in his pocket. He was going to propose to me that night. He'd bought a celebratory meal to cook for us, very typical Alex-style, but my mind is fixated on small details that he wouldn't have missed.'

'Like what?' Pete asked.

'You'll think I'm mad.'

'Try me, I bet I don't.'

Laurie took a deep breath. 'There was no champagne.' She looked at Pete intently to gauge his reaction. She expected to see his eyes roll like Bella's had when she told her, but his gaze never faltered.

'You'd know him well enough to tell if that was unusual,' Pete replied, after deliberating what answer to give.

'I did.' She breathed a long sigh of relief that he hadn't dismissed the niggle as insubstantial, as something that didn't merit further investigation. It inspired her to go on.

'He'd chosen food I really liked. There was wine, because it was in the meal deal, but Alex would have bought champagne as well. And there would have been champagne in M and S. If, by any chance, they'd totally run out, which is highly unlikely, he would have bought something else special to toast us with. I know how he thought. And this . . .' – she pulled the chain away from her neck to show him the ring – '. . . it's too small. And much too small to be made larger and yet I know it's for me from the inscription on the inside of it. They are words that mean something to me. To us.'

Pete was listening to her. He didn't know Alex from Adam but he could understand why her brain would be caught up in a net of fine points that didn't make sense.

'I told you in the meeting that I'd fallen out with his parents – well, what I mean is they've fallen out with me – so it makes it difficult to ask them why a few months before Alex died, he started having his bank statements sent to their house. They posted them all through my letter box a couple of weeks ago. They show that every month, after all his direct debits had left his account, he drew out the balance in cash but I never saw him carry cash, so why would he do that? Unless he didn't want me to see what he was spending his money on. I mean I didn't go snooping, there was no need for him to hide his finances from me. I don't even know why they brought them round; I wish they hadn't.'

Yet as soon as Laurie had said this aloud, the answer came to her.

'Actually, scrap that, Alex's parents like to think they're doing things by the book. They will have given them to me because despite what they think of me, it would be the right thing to do in their eyes. And' – she might as well tell him everything – 'he took out a Visa advance of one thousand pounds while he was on a work thing in Scotland the month before he died. He never took Visa advances out.' She shook her head in annoyance at herself, realised she must sound half-deranged. 'I think if I found out that he had white toast at that conference, I'd be fixated on why he didn't have his usual brown. I've got everything out of perspective, trying to drill into these minutiae, but I know it's important somehow. I *know*. Or do I? Is my inner compass so damaged that it's leading me directly to Loonsville?'

She raised her eyes to his and he saw the anguish in them, dulling the light that usually sat there.

'Before he died, there was a change, just subtle, but he was different. Last September, October, November he was snappy with me, blamed it on working too many long hours because he was preparing to go into business by himself and was busy building up a client base, all perfectly feasible but I didn't quite believe it was just that. Then at Christmas he changed again, became extra-considerate, happier, bought me loads of beautiful presents and that should have made me feel better but it didn't. Whenever I tried to talk to him about it, he fobbed me off and so I didn't press it.'

Laurie glanced up, checked that Pete hadn't nodded off or was looking at his watch; he was doing neither. 'There was just something *wrong* and it scared me, he was holding me at arm's length, I know he was. And then he died. But then again, he was going to propose to me. And he was planning a holiday for us, maybe our honeymoon, somewhere I'd always wanted to go. I worried we were drifting apart and it was only when he died that I found out that he wanted us to stay together forever. Or have I got it all wrong? But I can't have, can I? I feel like I'm doing a jigsaw puzzle and all the pieces fit together but they don't look anything like the picture that's on the box.' She realised that the words were rolling out of her like an avalanche and in danger of engulfing the kind, listening man at the other side of the bar table, but she couldn't stop their flow. 'I went to see a psychic and she picked up on the proposal and the holiday. That's how screwed up I am. I'm so sorry, I don't think I'd have told a priest half of this.'

She sat back then, all scooped out of secrets. There was nothing left to tell.

'Don't be silly apologising,' Pete said. 'That's why we're here, having this drink. To talk. Kind of extra time to the main event.' He noted her guilt-ridden expression and he gave her what he hoped was a smile of encouragement. 'To nick your compass reference, this grief lark is like a wilderness with a spinning north, isn't it?'

Laurie nodded. 'The dreams are the worst. You think sleep would give you some respite but they dredge everything up.'

'You said you'd been to see a psychic?'

'Do you want her number?'

'Not for me, thanks. I'm not sure I believe in all that stuff. Not that I would judge anyone else who does,' he added hurriedly. 'My mum did and she told me that if she had something to tell me, then she'd find a way. Directly – not through a third person. So far ... nothing.' He might be more inclined to believe in the supernatural if a bowl of washing-up water suddenly threw itself over Cora, he thought to himself. 'So tell me, how accurate did she get?'

'Well, as I said, she saw the engagement, and the holiday and that I'd had a falling out with Alex's mother who, she said, had the answers I was looking for. She told me that someone I knew had suggested that I get some therapy – although I suppose that bit you could just attribute to common sense. And she seemed to know that I'd tried it but not gone back and she said I should. Some things she didn't quite get right: she thought Alex had died on an important birthday, which he didn't, but the stuff she did get right more than made up for the misses. I mean, how could she have possibly known he had an M and S meal in the car when he crashed?'

'How did you know he had?'

'The policewoman who gave me his effects told me that it looked as if I was in for a special night. I think she was trying to give me some comfort. I fixated on what was in the carrier bag, to see if it matched up to the receipt.' Laurie cringed visibly. 'There was an itemised bill but I asked her to check for champagne, it was all I could think about. I couldn't get it out of my head. I dread to think what she must have thought of me.'

'I'm pretty sure that she put it down to you being shocked to the core and grief-stricken. She'll have heard much stranger things,' said Pete.

'Thank you,' said Laurie. 'Thank you for making me feel less of a madwoman than I have for the past seven months.'

But Laurie wasn't the only one with unanswered questions; Pete's were butting against the inside of his head like angry bees.

'My wife shouldn't have been anywhere near where she was when she died. We spoke on the phone and she told me she was on the M1 coming back from Leeds, but she was miles away from there. I kept wondering if I'd misheard what she said, but I know I didn't. And I didn't know she was pregnant until after she died. I can't remember if the doctor told me first or I found the pregnancy test in her handbag, it's all muddled up.'

'I'm so sorry you had to learn that way, Pete,' said Laurie, seeing the shine of tears in his eyes before he turned his attention to his drink.

'No one mentioned that one of the stages of grief that we had to go through was insanity, did they? I think I bought a jigsaw puzzle from the same shop that you did,' he said and drained his glass.

'I'll get us a refill,' said Laurie, deciding that he might need a minute alone to recover.

'Thank you. I won't say no.'

Pete twisted in his seat to look at how full the pub was now because it was certainly much noisier than when they had walked in. His eyes snagged on Laurie at the bar and he tried not to think that he was appraising her, even though he was. She looked slender as a reed sandwiched in between the young group of muscle men and the portly duo of pensioners sitting on stools. Slim blue jeans, cropped above the ankle, the type that women wore to look smart rather than fit like a second skin. Pink pumps, the same colour as her shirt which wasn't tucked in and she unconsciously tugged it down as if to make sure it hadn't ridden up. But it was her hair that fascinated him mostly, the colour of silver and gold melted together. He figured it was natural, she didn't strike him as the sort of woman who would bleach her hair to within an inch of its life. He wondered what it would look like, released from the plait. He mentally replaced her with a picture of Tara at the bar, her long caramel and blonde-streaked hair loose, a statement. Her jeans would have been cinched in at the waist, tight, cut off at the perfect length to parade the ridiculous heels that she strutted around on as if she'd been born in them. Her shirt would have been unbuttoned just enough to give a tantalising glimpse of the boobs she'd bought herself for her twenty-fifth birthday. She would have been smiling in the sure and certain knowledge that eyes everywhere were raking up and down her, loving that they were.

No sooner had Laurie sat down than a man's voice came over a PA system.

'One-two, one-two. The quiz will be starting in a minute. And will consist of twenty questions. Please put all mobile phones away. Anyone seen using one or going to the toilet in order to look up answers will be immediately disqualified.'

Pete pulled a face. 'How will they be able to tell if someone looks something up in there?' he asked.

'CCTV?' Laurie answered.

'Or PPTV,' Pete replied, then wondered if that was a bit rude, but Laurie laughed.

'Shall we have a go? It's ages since I did a pub quiz,' he said.

Laurie didn't have anything to rush home for. 'Why not,' she replied. 'What do we call ourselves?' The quiz sheet called for a group name.

'Er . . . Double something . . . Mixed Doubles, that work?' said Pete, thinking quickly. It was better than a boring 'Pete and Laurie'. He scribbled it down, having taken charge of the pencil.

'Question one,' said the quizmaster and the pub fell into silence. 'In what film did George Lazenby play James Bond? Question two . . .'

'Hang on, slow down, bloody hell,' someone from around the corner shouted.

It was a question they both knew. After that, they became more and more obscure. Both Laurie and Pete reckoned they might have less than half of them right. At the end, they swapped their papers with the people at the next table.

'Answer to question one. George Lazenby was in *On Her Majesty's Secret Service*,' said the quizmaster. Cheers and groans filled the air.

'Answer to question two: on the periodic table La is the symbol for Lanthanum.'

'Blimey, we have two right,' said Pete. 'I'm impressed.' He felt a little guilty putting a cross next to the answer he was marking on The Four Horsemen of the Acropolis's sheet – Llandudnium.

'I have no idea where I remembered that from,' said Laurie. 'I hated chemistry at school.'

In the end they had twelve answers right, one more than the Four Horsemen. As soon as all the sheets were collected, people were permitted to go to the toilet.

'We need to stay for the results,' said Pete, getting up to go to the bar. 'Same again? Nightcap? We might have won.' He pulled a hopeful face and Laurie chortled.

'Okay then, thank you.'

There was a mad rush at the bar now and to the toilet, so much so that there was a queue outside the gents.

Laurie relaxed against the back rest and tried to remember the last time she had gone out socially with Alex. He'd been so ridiculously busy the last few months. They'd been out with Naomi and Jefferson and his parents but as far as going out for a quiet date-night drink together – just the two of them – she couldn't recall. Not that this was a date. She shuddered, thinking about the prospect of dating again one day. This drink with Pete was safe. Only a drink.

Pete had arrived back at the table just in time for the results to be announced.

'Very poor scoring this week, very poor,' said the quizmaster. 'In fifth place with twelve was Mixed Doubles, but they get nowt for that.'

Pete and Laurie looked in amazement at each other.

'What a result,' said Pete, placing his hand over his heart. 'I feel quite proud.'

'In fourth place with thirteen, Penelope Pitstop and Dick Dastardly, you get nowt either except a do better next time. In third place with fourteen: Last of the Summer Homebrew, you get a voucher for four pints. In second place with fifteen: Les and Sonia, you get a bottle of Prosecco and a box of chocolates; and the winners with sixteen . . .' People started to make drum-roll noises by tapping the table. '. . . The Three Amigos.' No one heard what they'd won because the cheer was so loud. The quizmaster called for order. 'Can a representative from the Three Amigos come up to try and answer the snowball question, the kitty of which currently stands at one hundred and sixty pounds,' he announced, which resulted in a loud chorus of oohs.

'I can't believe we came so close to winning the four pints,' said Pete, who appeared so genuinely crestfallen that Laurie let loose a hoot of laughter.

They sat without saying a single word for a few minutes, soaking in the convivial atmosphere, feeling inconspicuous and normal. Two people out of many, in a pub. No one here knew their history or anything about the muddle their heads were in.

'Thank you for this,' Laurie said then, suddenly overcome by a drench of appreciation.

Pete looked puzzled. 'What?'

'Sitting here while I offloaded stuff that I can't say to anyone else and not making me feel as if I'm unhinged.'

Pete's lips stretched into a smile. 'You're not unhinged. I've found it very difficult to talk to people and I have great mates, and a close family.'

'That's good ... well, you know what I mean,' replied Laurie. 'Your brother looks friendly.'

'He's brilliant and he'd be really cut up to find out that I'm holding things back from him. He and his wife are trying to have a baby and they're in the middle of all sorts of tests to find out what's wrong.'

'And you don't want to add to all that?' suggested Laurie.

'Yep. I don't want him worrying about me because stress won't help them. He knows that I'm nowhere near a hundred per cent, but I play it down. I've become a good liar. So ... talking to you has helped me too. I've felt recently as if all the goalposts in my life have been shifted and I can't trust my own judgement as much as I used to.'

'You mean the thing with your sister-in-law?' asked Laurie.

'Yes, that.' He shrugged his shoulders. 'I hope I've got it wrong and – or – I hope it goes away.'

'How's your brother getting on with his new car?'

'He's like a kid with a new toy. It's cheered him up no end.'

'Order, order,' called the quizmaster down the mike. 'The representative from the Three Amigos has not answered the snowball question correctly so next week the kitty will stand at one hundred and seventy pounds. The question was, which is the only place name in Britain to have an exclamation mark after its name.'

'Westward Ho!' whispered Laurie and Pete to each other.

'Westward Ho!' said the quizmaster.

'We would have smashed it,' said Pete.

'Totally,' said Laurie. She lifted her glass and drank a long throatful of juice. It was time to go, before she got too comfortable.

'Work in the morning?' Pete asked her, taking his cue from her.

'Yep, bright and early. You?'

'I'm on nights tomorrow.'

Laurie finished her drink then stood, Pete followed and they pushed through the people to the door. A grateful couple dived straight onto the seats they had vacated.

In the car park, standing by their respective cars, they turned to each other.

'See you next week,' said Pete. 'Unless you happen to have a Ferrari for sale going really cheap, in which case I may see you at the weekend.'

'Sadly not. I'll have a house for sale though if you're interested.'

'You're selling up?' He seemed shocked at that.

'It was always too big for two, it feels extra enormous for one.'

'It is pretty huge.'

'Alex wanted to fill it with children.' Laurie sighed, and smiled.

'Well if you get anybody coming to view and you want a man around . . . you know, for security purposes . . . if your friend with the red hair and the black belt can't be there, please give me a ring.'

'Thank you,' said Laurie. 'Have a good week.'

'You too.'

There was no awkwardness as they got into their cars, no *how do we end this evening?* because it wasn't a date. At the exit to the car park Pete turned left and Laurie turned right. Both of them were exactly half a mile down the road when they realised that even if Laurie had needed his help, he hadn't given her his contact details.

Chapter 24

19 September

Pete was just about to head off to work the next night when the house phone rang. Only his dad or his in-laws rang it, or scammers. He checked to see which number was displayed before he picked up.

'Hiya, Dad.'

'Hiya, son, you on your day off?'

'I'm on nights. Just setting off. Everything okay?' There was a tone he didn't like in his dad's voice, a weight of worry.

'I'm just giving you the heads up, lad. Griff and Lucy have had some bad news. They went up to the hospital to discuss their test results and it turns out that both of Lucy's fallopian tubes are blocked.'

'Can they unblock them?'

'They think they can. So that's bad news but not as bad news as it could have been. I thought you'd want to know.'

Poor Lucy, thought Pete. She had a feeling that the problem was with her and she'd been right. Intuition was a voice to listen to when it spoke loudly. As it was speaking to him also.

The night shift was quiet and after all their checks had been made, a few of Red Watch grabbed some shut-eye in bed. When the lights began to flash and the beep-beep alarm went off, even those in a deep sleep were up and dressing within seconds.

'Male reported up a tree,' said Andy Burlap once they were in the fire engine and underway, pulling up information on the onboard computer.

'Stag do?' asked Sal, driving.

'Doesn't go into that much detail,' said Andy. 'I've never really got why anyone who is your mate would tie you to a lamppost naked or that sort of thing.'

'My mates hired a stripper for mine,' said Jacko. 'She must have been thirty stone. She sat on my knee and it's never been the same since.'

'How very PC,' said Sal with a sarcastic tut.

It was a five-minute drive to the Red Rec, at least it was in the early hours of Friday morning with a dot of traffic on the roads. They could hear the distressed cries of a woman before they could see the man up the tree. As soon as the engine pulled up, she tore across the grass towards them. She was dressed in a grubby pink tracksuit and black wellies which must have been at least three sizes bigger than her feet.

'Now, take a deep breath and calm down, love, because I can't hear what you're saying,' said Andy gently, trying to steady her as she burbled at him. 'What's your name?'

'Martine Brightside and I've been worried sick about him,' said the woman. 'He's been clean for a couple of weeks and I thought he'd fallen off the wagon again. I've been out looking for him since midnight and I find him up there.'

'Hello lads,' called a familiar voice from up an autumn-stripped tree. 'I can't wave, my hands are tied.'

'Juice, is that you?' said Andy, recognising those dulcet tones.

'Hiya.'

'How the bloody hell did you get up there?'

'Can't remember. Likkle kids I think,' Juice replied.

'Here we go again,' said Jacko.

'Jacko, grab the short ex, that'll reach him,' commanded Andy, directing him to get the ladder from the vehicle.

'No, I remember, it was the mayor. All because I chucked those Vulcan sausage rolls at him,' yelled Juice.

'Bastard. I'm going down to the town hall soon as it opens to have a word with him. I'll hang him by his sodding chain,' shrieked Martine, pacing up and down on the grass as if she were a life-size toy full of fresh batteries.

'I think we can safely assume it wasn't the mayor,' Pete told her, hoping to appease her at least a little.

'Hurry up will you, I'm dying for a widdle,' Juice yelled at them.

Krish calmed down Martine who, it turns out, was Juice's girlfriend. He made her sit on a nearby bench while Jacko climbed up their ladder, cut the clothes line which was tethering Juice to the tree, and helped reunite him with terra firma. Once there, a sobbing Martine flew herself at her lover and hugged the breath out of him. 'I've been going daft fretting about you.'

'Don't squeeze me, I need the toilet,' he protested.

'Who's doing this stuff to you, Juice?' asked Pete.

'Well, I can't say, can I?' Juice said, the smile on his face still there but convincing no one. No doubt there would be some pictures circulating on Facebook of the town clown stuck up a tree, legs dangling. He looked small and fragile, like a man made out of matchsticks, thought Andy. It was as if the years had whipped them back to Ketherwood Junior school and he was the undernourished kid with the scruffy uniform and holey shoe soles that had come away from the uppers.

'You all right, Juice? You're not hurt are you?' said Andy.

'Bit stiff and cold, but I'm all right,' he replied.

Martine looked rough as a badger's arse but squashy and warm and caring and she stood with her large arms circling her man as if he was Leonardo DiCaprio.

'Let's get you home,' she said. 'Would you like some soup?'

'Don't mention liquid,' said Juice with a wince.

'Get home, Juice, it's freezing,' said Andy. 'Get back into bed with this lovely woman of yours and both of you have a nice restful sleep.'

'I'm straightening him out, you know,' said Martine. 'He's a good man. Kind. Best I've had anyway. I'll get him there. I'm taking him to live with me in Wakefield out of the way of all the bloody knobheads round here.'

'I like Wakefield,' said Juice with the same wistfulness that someone might use for Sorrento.

'You do that, love,' said Andy. 'Look after yourselves.' His voice faltered, he sounded choked with emotion.

Arms wrapped around each other, Juice and Martine wended their way across the grass in the direction of wherever they were residing.

'I hope he does get to Wakefield because if he stays here, he'll be dead at fifty,' said Andy with a loaded sigh. 'Come on then, girls and boys, let's get back to the station so I can do the paperwork.'

Pete lingered, watching Juice and Martine weave away. The concern in her face had touched him, as did the sight of her embracing him, glad to have him in her arms, relieved he was safe.

When he was back on the vehicle, it brought lots of other thoughts to the fore, like bubbles which had been trapped and then freed to rise to the surface and pop, releasing memories as fresh as the day they were made. He remembered when he and Tara had been at the stage when they couldn't keep their hands off each other, when they felt the need to be physically connected as much as possible, sitting close together on the sofa to watch TV, legs touching if they were out for a drink. She had been very physical from the get go, so much so that it had crossed his mind she was trying to blot out someone else, stamp him over a past lover. She'd told him that was a ridiculous notion and he'd bought it, because he wanted to believe it.

He met her four years ago and she proposed to him the following Valentine's Day. He knew the fierce initial blaze of passion couldn't last, but he was looking forward to the long-lasting warm glow of marriage. And for a while they had that. But the embers began to cool too quickly and that glow faded and he couldn't pinpoint how or when it started, or if their fire could be rekindled.

He hadn't even told Griff that he and Tara were having a few problems. He didn't even know if they were. There were no arguments, no post to nail suspicions or accusations onto. She said it was all in his imagination, that nothing was wrong, and yes, she had changed her mind about having a baby sooner rather than later but people were having them older, and that was sensible, when they had savings and had fixed up their houses. What was the rush?

In the months before the accident, they hadn't made love at all. He had been rebuffed so many times with a cornucopia of excuses that he'd stopped touching her; there might as well have been barbed wire down the middle of the mattress. Then on the night of their anniversary – January first – she had turned to him in bed and unexpectedly initiated sex and then afterwards, she'd pulled his arms around her and went to sleep like that and he'd felt this was a new dawn for them as well as a new year for all. She must have conceived that night: a baby born from flames fanned, a fire brought back to life.

Now he knew that the changes happening in her body were the reason why he felt her slipping from him again – hormonal surges, malaise, insomnia – he felt relieved, could reconcile this with her pregnancy not her rejection of him. They were righted, on course, they would have found their way to happiness again. They would have travelled the pregnancy together, he would have cherished his wife and his child.

He wanted someone to hold, to have a family with, to protect, to laugh with, cook for, wash up with and be there for. He wanted a woman to put her arms around him with love in her eyes and care in her voice. And what hit him that night was that he couldn't remember Tara – even in their early days – ever looking at him the way Martine had looked at Juice.

And why *was* she on the road from Sheffield when he was as certain as he could be she told him she was coming from Leeds?

Chapter 25

23 September

The following Monday, Griff and Lucy came round to Pete's with fish and chips to discuss plans for Nigel's sixty-fifth birthday. Pete was glad to find they were both positive about the medical news. The doctors were confident that they could unblock Lucy's fallopian tubes. And even if they couldn't, it would still be possible to have IVF if they did decide to go down that route – and they were softening to the idea. Pong sat on the edge of the table nonchalantly waiting for fish goodies. As usual, he got plenty.

Originally, they'd been hoping to put on a surprise party for Nigel but knew they hadn't a chance in hell of getting Cora on board with that.

'The worm in every one of our plan-apples,' muttered Griff. 'What the frig is he doing with that awful bitch? I can't stand her more every time I see her.'

'Griff had a bit of a do with her on Saturday,' said Lucy, dousing the remainder of her fish and chips liberally with vinegar.

'Did you?' asked Pete.

'I told you not to say,' said Griff.

'I think Pete should know,' she responded.

'What was it about, Griff?'

'The garden,' said Lucy, before Griff could answer. 'Griff found her cutting Mr and Mrs Moore.'

Pete's jaw tightened. Mr and Mrs Moore was a rose bush. Griff had had a rose named after his parents for their last anniversary. The roses were scarlet and scented and the bush had flourished from the moment it was planted.

'Cora was in the garden. Nigel was upstairs in the loo and Griff saw her hacking away at it through the window. So he charged out and told her to stop and she told him that it was taking over and needed cutting right back,' said Lucy.

'Luce, I can speak for myself,' Griff insisted.

'What happened then?' asked Pete.

Griff took over the narrative now. 'What you'd expect. She told me it wasn't my house. I told her it wasn't hers either, it was my father's and that rose bush was my mother's and my father's and she had no right to even touch it. I said that my mother was part of his life and she could not erase her from it however much she might try to.' Griff paused, took a bolstering breath and Pete knew that what was coming next was worse.

'Then she told me not to set foot in the house ever again and carried on pruning.'

Pete winced, anticipating more.

'. . . So I grabbed the cutters out of her hand and flung them over the fence—'

'—At which point, I stepped in hoping to be the voice of reason but it was so hard,' said Lucy. 'I told her that it was a special rose and Nigel would be very annoyed to know she was trying to destroy it. Then Nigel came down and she played all innocent that she didn't know, but of course she did. Griff was very upset. He told her that if she touched that rose again, he'd make sure she ended up where the cutters were ... only not as politely as that.'

'Oof. What did Dad say?'

'He surprised me, Pete,' said Lucy. 'You know what your dad is like, wanting everyone to get along, but on this occasion he backed up Griff, so you can imagine how well that went down. He wasn't happy at all; in fact he told Cora that she could do as she pleased in the garden but she wasn't to touch that rose bush. She was absolutely livid, she stormed off and that was the last we saw of her.'

'Unfortunately any row they had after we'd gone didn't result in her leaving him,' said Griff.

'Anyway,' continued Lucy, 'before all that happened, Nigel told us that he's decided to have the birthday party at his house. He's arranged it himself.'

'Don't tell me he's got Cora making sandwiches,' said Pete, incredulously.

'He's paying for caterers.'

'Wow – go Dad.'

'There's more, Pete. Tell him what you did yesterday, Griff,' urged Lucy with an elbow nudge.

'I bought Dad a snooker table,' said Griff. 'Well we did, because you're giving me half of the money for it.'

'What the actual fu—?'

'It's in our garage,' said Lucy.

'Impulse buy,' said Griff. 'The working men's club next to the gym has gone bust and they need to liquidate all the assets they can – and quickly. The steward came in, asked if anyone wanted a snooker table going really cheap.' He threw his hands up in the air. 'Perfect timing. How could I not take it?'

'But where the heck is he going to put it?' asked Pete.

'He can come round to ours to play. Or we can surprise him and dump it on his garden on the morning of his birthday and force Cora into putting it into her *parlour.*' He gave the word a prissiness he thought it deserved.

'Not fair on your father,' said Lucy.

'Not fair on my father having to give up a room he had built for a snooker table just so she can use it to entertain her cronies in,' said Griff, feeding Pong the tail end of his fish.

The doorbell sounded – two brisk *brum-brum*s. A Ria ring.

Lucy read the expression on Pete's face, guessed why his smile dropped like a plumb bob.

'Don't leave,' he warned them.

'We won't,' said Lucy, turning to Griff and saying quietly, 'Now I'll see if it's in his imagination or not.'

Pete went to the door, opened it and Ria gushed in with her layers of Tara scent. This time he didn't recognise the clothes as being Tara's but they were very much in her style: tight jeans, heels, top artfully unbuttoned to reveal a generosity of décolletage. Ria's shock at seeing Pete had guests was priceless, Griff and Lucy would later discuss this with each other in the car.

'Oh, you've got visitors,' Ria said, disappointment easily discernible despite her smile of greeting. 'Hi Griff, Lucy. How are you both?'

'Fine, yourself?' they chorused.

'As good as can be,' she replied. 'Look, I'll talk to you another time when you aren't busy,' she said to Pete; the meaning evident: *I'll come back when you are alone.*

'Don't be daft,' said Griff. 'Pull up a chair, have a chip.'

'I'll put the kettle on, unless you prefer a juice or something?' asked Pete.

'Oh er ... well, a coffee would be lovely, thank you,' replied Ria.

Pete clicked on the kettle and then slipped out to the loo. He'd had three coffees in the time that Griff and Lucy had been there.

'We're just planning Dad's birthday so we're here for the long haul,' said Griff. Lucy kicked him under the table. He was about as subtle as a morbidly obese bull in a very tiny china shop.

'Oh. Are you having a party?'

'Just close family,' Griff answered. 'And Cora.' Not making it at all obvious where she stood with him.

'It's nice he's found someone,' smiled Ria. 'He's far too young to be alone. Sixty-five is nothing, is it?'

Lucy hadn't said this, even to Griff, but out of the three sisters, she'd only really liked Alana. She was aloof, forthright but kind and genuine. Ria, she'd never quite trusted; she wasn't a woman's woman. As for Tara, Lucy had always thought she and Pete had rushed to the aisle. They hadn't been going out very long when Tara made a flashy proposal and from the next day on, the wedding plan machine had cranked up to max, almost as if she was desperate to become Mrs Moore – except weirdly then she hadn't taken his name, kept herself as Ms Tara Ollerton. The wedding seemed to be more important than the groom to her. She'd taken over Pete's life like an ivy plant, so much so that Lucy had wondered if she'd come to Pete on a serious rebound from another relationship and needed to plug up a wound in her heart with the first man that came along. She'd asked Pete this once, tried to phrase it so it sounded casual and not mean, and he'd assured her it wasn't the case. But there was something about Tara she couldn't quite warm to even though she wanted to. She and Ria were both still waters running deep whereas Alana was a fresh, clear brook with everything visible. Tara tended to keep people at a distance. Maybe the baby would have changed that. Sadly, they'd never know.

'Do you think they'll get married?' asked Ria.

'Doesn't do to rush new relationships after a bereavement,' said Lucy. 'That's when big mistakes get made.' Now it was Griff's turn to give her a warning kick under the table.

'Everyone's different. Some people need a crutch more than others. No point in being lonely when you don't have to be.'

Ria's tone was light, but there was an underlying bite of annoyance and Lucy was always up for a battle, especially when it was to protect one of her own.

'Unfortunately there are a lot of people who can sniff vulnerability at fifty paces—'

Griff cut her off. He knew he'd get earache for it later but they were guests in his brother's house and they should be respectful of that. It wasn't Lucy's place to turn into a Doberman Pinscher and start snarling and warning her off. 'How's your mum and dad, Ria?'

'Dad's taken Mum for a short break to the villa in Cyprus.'

'And Alana?'

'Oh I do like Alana,' piped up Lucy. 'Give her my love when you see her.'

'To be honest,' said Ria, addressing Griff, 'I don't see that much of her. Alana tends to do her own thing.'

Pete walked back into the room and Lucy noticed how Ria brightened instantly. Her pupils dilated to the size of satellite dishes and any minute they would start pumping out cartoon hearts. Pete hadn't got it wrong, Ria was waiting for him to ripen like an autumn fruit and drop into her waiting hands so she could make jam out of him.

'So, what sort of party are you planning for Nigel?' Ria asked Pete as he put a mug in front of her on the table.

'He's planned it himself,' said Pete. 'I'd have liked to have thrown him a surprise barbecue.'

'Oh, I love barbecues,' said Ria. 'The smell is always so delicious.'

Lucy tried to imagine Ria eating a flame-grilled steak oozing juices over her hands and couldn't.

'When is it?'

'Two weeks on Wednesday.'

'Two weeks,' repeated Ria and made a series of eye-blinks that indicated quite a lot of activity in her brain. She wrinkled up a disappointed nose. 'Awww. I'm on a hen do in Tenerife or I might have gatecrashed. What are you buying him?' she asked.

'No idea,' said Griff. He didn't want to tell the truth and risk the secret getting out and back to Cora. His father was having that snooker table whether she liked it or not. Nigel had wanted one for years and Griff had wanted him to have one for years.

'What was it you needed me for, Ria?' asked Pete. Ria looked blank, then remembered what she'd said about talking to him another time.

'It's fine, it'll wait. Really.'

'We can go out of the room for a couple of minutes if you two want a private word,' said Lucy with a pleasant smile.

All eyes were on Ria now and she knew she'd have to admit what pretext she'd used for turning up.

'It was nothing much, Pete, it was just that I wondered if you'd thought any more about going to see Jackie Crawford. You know, the business card I gave you.'

It took a few moments for the name to register with him. 'Oh, er no . . . I . . .' It nearly came out of his mouth that he was going to a support group, but he thought he'd keep that to himself. He didn't want to give Ria his whereabouts more than he had to. '. . . I . . . not yet.'

'What's this?' Lucy said, as Pong dropped from the table to settle into her lap.

'Ria very kindly gave me the number of a grief counsellor,' explained Pete.

'She's very good,' said Ria. 'Talking helps so much.'

'I agree,' said Lucy. 'Some poor souls don't have anyone to talk things through with. That's when being a twin comes in handy because while ever Griff is on this planet, I'd hope Pete would turn to him first.' She smiled again, but Pete and Griff, who knew her as well as she knew herself, could tell it was her *I'm riding a horse of impatience* smile.

Ria stood up, her drink untouched.

'I feel like I'm interrupting your birthday party plans. I'll call again another time.'

'No stay, finish your coffee,' said Pete, politely. Griff said something similar, Lucy stayed schtum.

'I insist,' said Ria. 'Lovely to see you both. Hope you have some good news soon. You know . . .'

'Thank you,' said Lucy and smiled – genuinely this time. 'That's sweet of you to say.'

Pete walked to the door to see Ria to her car and Griff gave his wife a hard stare.

'What?' she demanded.

'You,' he said, with a gritty whisper.

'Just making sure that she knows that I know,' she replied.

'Oh, you did that all right,' said Griff.

Pete walked back into the kitchen. There was a lipstick mark on his cheek.

'You've been branded,' said Lucy, pointing at him. 'Property of Ria Ollerton.' Pete turned to the mirrored tiles on the wall and grabbed a dishcloth to wipe it off.

'Oh and by the way, you aren't imagining it, she is after you,' she added. She gave Pong a stroke and Griff thought his wife, at that moment, looked not unlike a female Blofeld.

'I hope you know you *can* talk to me, bro,' said Griff. 'If you're considering therapy, you must feel you need some help. Whatever else is going on in our lives, we've got more than enough time for you.'

Lucy nodded, thumbed at her husband. 'What he said.'

Pete sat back down heavily on the chair.

'I don't want to see a therapist,' said Pete, 'but I have been going to a sort of support group.'

'Really?' said Griff. A gulp of hurt. 'You never told me.'

'He doesn't have to tell us, Griff,' said Lucy, before turning back to Pete. 'How long have you been going there then?'

'I've been three times so far. The woman you bought the car from, Griff, she goes too. That's where I met her, I lied when I said it was a function. Ria's right though. It does good to talk and oddly enough – and don't beat me up about this – it seems to help that they're all strangers. Don't ask me how that works but it just does.'

'I understand that totally,' said Lucy tenderly. 'But you know that we are here for you, don't you?'

'Of course I do, you daft woman,' said Pete.

'So this lady with the car . . .' she continued, her interest piqued. 'Griff said she'd recently lost her partner.'

'Yep,' said Pete. 'I ended up in the pub with her after the last session. We got drawn into doing a quiz.'

'She looked really nice,' said Griff. 'Young to have lost a partner. How did he die?'

'A car crash.'

'Be careful,' warned Lucy. 'I know I'm probably worrying too much but you are an incredibly good-looking man—'

'Aw cheers, love, because if he is, so am I,' butted in Griff and brought some levity to the conversation.

'Laurie is nice . . . and safe,' said Pete. 'She's easy to talk to and there's no awkwardness. It wasn't a date, it was just a drink. You don't need to worry at all.'

On the way home Lucy brought Laurie up in conversation.

'So what's she like then, old man?'

'Tall, slim . . . I thought she was Swedish when I saw her at first. She's very blonde, friendly, a little fragile-looking I thought, but that's only to be expected. The MR2 was her partner's pride and joy. I only hope he looked after her as much as he did his car. She had a massive house as well. I'd like to think our Pete has found someone he can really talk to, who can help him, and that he can help her. She was very different to Tara, if you're asking that.'

'Good,' said Lucy. 'It's not that I didn't like Tara—' her voice dropped as if she might be listening '—she was fun and spirited and gorgeous but I never thought they were a great match. It was as if as soon as they were married, she changed her mind about everything they'd got married for. I never felt they were as happy as they should have been. As happy as we are.'

Griff raised and dropped his shoulders. 'Not everyone is like a double act, Luce. We got lucky.'

'I know, but still ...' She shrugged. 'Just a woman's instinct that all wasn't as it seemed between them.'

Griff sighed. 'It cuts me up to think about Pete not being able to talk to me.'

'Don't,' said Lucy. 'Sometimes, as he says, it's easier to speak to people who don't know you. You should appreciate that, Griff, because as secrets go, we might be keeping the Mack Daddy of them all from him.'

Griff nodded. His wife was right – as always. Sometimes close was too close.

Chapter 26

25 September

Pete was more than aware that his heart gave a discernible thump of delight when Laurie rushed through the teashop door on the fourth session at Molly's Club. She was last to arrive and he could feel the anxiety creeping in his veins that she might not be coming. It was the opposite to how he felt on seeing Ria Ollerton and that kick of excitement worried him as much as it thrilled him.

Laurie gave him a small wave. She was aware how a warmth spread inside her when she pushed open the door to find him there. Her thoughts had strayed too much to Pete over the past few days and she really didn't need that sort of complication in her life. Luckily getting the house spick and span for an estate agent to come and photograph it had taken her mind off things it could happily dwell on. As she vacuumed and mopped, she wondered what Meredith and Brendan would say when they drove past and noticed the For Sale sign. The estate agent she'd chosen had been up that day – hence why she was running late – and said that they'd aim to get the basic details on their site by the morning.

'Come in, come in, Laurie,' Molly smiled in welcome.

'Sorry everyone for holding you up,' said Laurie, breathy after a sprint from the car park.

Mr Singh bounced back into position behind the counter, ready to serve.

'There's a butterscotch cake on today and I highly recommend it, Laurie,' said Maurice, mid-mouthful.

'Oh well in that case . . .' Laurie hadn't had time for lunch. She'd been caught up with the intricacies of a very acrimonious divorce case. Mr and Mrs Pullman were fighting over ownership of everything from curtains to their Koi carp. Coffee and cake would go down a treat.

'You sit down and I'll get it for you,' said Maurice. 'Go on.' He was insistent.

'Better do as he says,' whispered Sharon. 'He likes to be a gentleman.'

'I could get used to this service,' said Laurie. There was an obvious seat next to Pete and if she hadn't taken it, it would have looked like a deliberate snub, so she did. She felt instantly calmed in this space. What an odd little place it was with its lovely ambience and gentle people that she would probably never have come across if Alex had been alive. She liked all of them, without exception.

Maurice ferried over a huge piece of cake, serviette, fork and a coffee and set it down in front of her.

'I'll never eat all that,' she exclaimed. 'Mr Singh, what are you trying to do to me?'

'I bet you do,' said Pete. 'And if you don't, I'm happy to help out.'

He gave her a lop-sided smile and Laurie felt something

inside her akin to a light being turned on. A dangerous light.

'So our little band is here and complete. Have we had a good week?' Molly's eyes drifted over everyone but seemed to linger a beat longer in Yvonne's direction.

Mumbles from everyone in the affirmative; Maurice's 'yes' was the loudest.

'I don't think Yvonne will mind me saying that we went to the Roysley animal shelter, and not only did Yvonne adopt an aged cat but I did as well and I didn't expect that outcome, let me tell you. Mother was allergic to them but luckily I didn't inherit that defective gene.'

'How wonderful,' said Molly. 'And kind of you.'

'Yes, Felix has settled in right away. He's an indoor cat. He has no hair. And Yvonne's cat Conference has made himself most at home, so she informs me.'

'He sleeps on the bed. It wasn't the plan, but he kept scratching at the door and I couldn't get any bloody sleep, so I let him in,' Yvonne said with a soft smile. 'Takes up as much room as Des did but I don't mind it.'

'Conference?' asked Pete.

'He's enormous,' Maurice answered for Yvonne. 'He's got a tail the length of a washing line. And when he sits down he assumes the shape of a Conference pear. That's the name they gave him at the shelter when he was brought in as a stray.'

'Conference,' echoed Mr Singh with a chortle.

Yvonne nodded. She still looked as if a cloud of gloom was hanging over her head. Whatever had so obviously affected her last week had a tail as long as her new cat.

'I had an unexpected visitor this week,' said Sharon. 'A friend of mine heard about Billy and came to visit. I haven't seen her for a couple of years. We drifted apart over something and nothing and well . . . she got in touch. And we picked up where we left off. It's been lovely.'

'That's wonderful news too,' said Molly. 'Something positive coming out of a negative.'

'And a sign of true friendship that you feel as if you have never been apart,' said Mr Singh from his position behind the counter.

'I couldn't remember what we'd fallen out over,' continued Sharon. 'I think she can but she hasn't said. At least, she hasn't given me the right story because the one she told me doesn't ring true.'

'What does it matter, if you're back together being friends again?' said Maurice. 'Surely that's the important thing. Putting the past to bed.'

Something skimmed past the surface of Laurie's brain then zipped away, like a fly dodging a swatter.

'It's just niggling me, that's all,' Sharon went on. 'It would have had to be more than she said for us not to have been able to sort it out then. I think it had something to do with the fella I was going out with at the time but I suppose I should just forget it. Part of me's worried to bring it up in case it's something I don't want to hear.'

That fly again. Laurie nearly pinned it, then Pete scared it off by distracting her, asking the group the same question he and Laurie had talked about in the Spouting Tap last week.

'Did anyone feel as if they'd gone a bit insane after . . .?' He didn't finish, but everyone knew what he meant.

'Goodness me yes,' replied Maurice. 'I forgot when to eat for a few days, which sounds stupid now, but that's exactly what happened. Totally disorientated. As if I was in a snow globe and someone had shaken it vigorously.'

Sharon was nodding too. 'I caught a train to Sheffield and I forgot to get off. Ended up in Nottingham. I don't know how I managed to do that. I even remember pulling into Sheffield and it not registering that I'd landed.'

'What about you, Peter?' asked Molly. 'What happened to you that made you ask?'

'Sometimes I had dreams about my wife being alive that were so vivid, I thought they were real, and it was reality and the accident that were the lie,' he replied.

'That's so typical, Peter. Have you been feeling very disorientated, Laurie?' asked Molly.

Laurie swallowed, prepared to answer. 'My head is caught up on so many stupid details about the accident Alex was in and it won't let go of them. Conflicting facts that are like oil and water and they won't mix into one truth.'

'Like what, can you say?' asked Molly.

'Like—' Laurie started and then closed up immediately. She couldn't give details, not now. She'd felt fine telling Pete about it in the pub but when she got home, she'd begun to think about all that she'd said to him, and cringed in horror at such candour. 'Oh, just minutiae, too much of it.' A ring that didn't fit, yet inscribed with a message meant for her alone. A cruise for Mr and Mrs Wilder. Bank statements sent to his parents. No champagne. *Don't be late home, Laurie. There's something important I have to tell you.*

She had exhausted herself trying to remember how he sounded when he rang her and every time she came to a different conclusion. She'd been excited when she heard the message, presumed it was something special but since then, she'd wondered if she had overlaid her expectations onto his tone. She wished she still had it on her phone because then she could have listened to it reasonably and might have been able to decipher what sort of 'something important' his tenor intimated – serious, frivolous? But she'd deleted it as soon as she'd played it, as was her habit.

Yvonne's voice snapped her out of her reverie.

'I think you might have gathered that I didn't have a very happy marriage. I did all my crying when Des was alive so I didn't have any tears left when he died. There were times in my life when I've felt insane enough to do terrible things but now I feel as compos mentis as I could ever be. My snow globe's settled for the first time ever, I think.' Her voice was quiet but commanding as she continued. 'I'm sorry about losing it a bit last week. You were talking about that lass who was expected to take the place of her mother in her dad's bed and . . . and you might as well have been talking about me. That's why I flipped. I married Des to get away from a house of men who had no barriers. I thought Des would be my salvation and he was my sodding damnation – talk about falling from a frying pan into a fire. I got sick of telling people I'd walked into doors or fallen down the bloody stairs. I lost a child because of what he did to me but I couldn't leave because I had nowhere to go. And that's why I can't cry. Because I'm glad he's dead, I hated the horrible bastard.'

There was a momentary pin-drop silence then Molly came to sit beside her and Yvonne reached for her hand, for strength.

'I once cooked him toadstools from the garden in a chicken and mushroom pie hoping I'd kill him after he split my lip open, but it had absolutely no effect on him at all apart from curing his constipation,' said Yvonne, with a hiccupped hoot of laughter. 'I always thought the devil must be keeping him alive. But then he must have pissed him off as well because he went arse over tit down the stairs and broke his miserable neck. I used to dread hearing his feet walking up them stairs when he came from the pub but that night when I heard the bump bump bump bump, I prayed that he'd knocked himself out cold and he'd be in hospital for a few days and give me a rest. After five minutes of silence, I had to get up and check and I knew as soon as I saw him that he'd gone. And I'll never go to heaven because the first thought that came to my head was ... I've won the sodding lottery. That's insanity for you, love.'

Her head fell into her chest and she began sobbing hard. Maurice put his arm around her, Sharon supplied tissues, Molly carried on holding her hand.

Poor Yvonne, thought Laurie. During her time as a solicitor, she'd seen some horrific domestic abuse cases come through the doors of Butler and Jubb, read statements of how vile people could be to each other. It never failed to shock her and just when she thought she'd seen it all, something else came along to trump it.

No one minded that Yvonne poured out her soul, wept, expunged tales of how miserable her life had been living with Des. How she'd hidden as much as she could from her daughter, pretended things were her fault when they weren't so Lola could be protected from how much of a beast her father was.

'He never touched a hair on her head though, so he did have some control over how much of a rotten twat he was. I'd have knifed him dead if he'd as much as raised his hand towards her,' said Yvonne. 'But at the same time he couldn't be arsed making it nice for her at Christmas or her birthday – it was always me and he took the credit.'

'You need to tell her the truth,' said Maurice.

'I'd break her heart,' said Yvonne.

'You don't have to tell her every detail,' put in Mr Singh. 'But your own relationship with your daughter needs to be on the right footing. Don't live a lie any more. You have suffered more than enough, Yvonne.'

'Do you really think so?' croaked Yvonne.

'Children see more than you think they do. Don't be shocked if what you tell her doesn't come as a complete surprise,' this from Molly.

Yvonne sniffed. 'She loved him, though. I don't want to destroy her.'

'You won't,' said Molly, 'but you need to tell her a little more of the truth than you have done already or it will carry on destroying you.'

'Sorry, everyone,' said Yvonne. 'I've taken over this meeting tonight. I didn't mean to.'

'My goodness, Yvonne, that's what we are here for,' said Maurice. 'It's a support group. I for one feel so much better for it than I ever imagined I could. I loved my mother but she wasn't very kind to me and I was never really sure why I blighted her life so much. She used to say that I'd ruined everything and if it wasn't for me she'd be happy, but never gave me any reason why that should be, other than I was born. I am totally aware of how cold my mother was, yet I did love her. But I feel positive about this new phase of my life. I have a set of friends now—' he smiled at them all '—and my first cat.'

'Do any of you believe in the afterlife?' asked Yvonne. 'I'm worried that Des is up there waiting for me so he can thump me.'

'Yes, I believe in it, Yvonne,' said Molly. 'And I think it is a place of peace. When my husband died there was so much love in the room that I could almost touch it. It convinced me that he had gone on to somewhere full of goodness where hate and fear and pain do not exist.'

'Look at the time,' said Sharon. 'Where's it gone tonight?'

'I gobbled it up for you all,' said Yvonne.

'It was spent gladly, helping one of our own to get back on track,' countered Maurice. He held out his hand towards Yvonne. 'I'll give you a lift home, dear lady.'

'Thank you,' said Yvonne to Molly in the doorway. Her shoulders weren't sagged, her spine was straight and she had a smile in place. 'I feel better tonight than I have done for ages. Like a storm's cleared me up.'

'Long may that last,' said Mr Singh and waved goodnight to her.

'Well, that was intense,' said Sharon with a whistle when Maurice and Yvonne had gone. 'I'm glad for her. That husband of hers sounded a right prick.' She put on her thin jacket and picked up her bag.

'Yes,' said Molly with a nod. 'I think this marks the beginning of her journey to a new and kinder life on a proper footing.'

'Isn't it funny how none of us would ever have met normally. I mean this nicely—' Sharon looked at Laurie '—but you and me wouldn't mingle in the world. I'd think you were too posh for me and you—' she turned to Pete '—are just too handsome for me to have ever spoken to without melting into a pool of drool, but here . . . we all mix lovely, don't we?'

Pete chuckled. 'Yes we do, Sharon.'

Laurie was smiling too. She put on an affected posh voice to say, 'See you next week, Shar-onn.'

'Ha. See ya, love.'

'If you ever want to talk to me on a one-to-one basis,

Laurie – and Peter of course – you have my number,' said Molly when Sharon had exited. 'When someone has died and isn't around to answer questions only they can answer, it can send your life into a tailspin. If closure is impossible to find, sometimes it is necessary to make it for yourself. It's possible, with the help of guidance.'

'Thank you, Molly,' said Laurie. She had the sudden urge to hug the woman, but didn't.

''Night Molly, Mr Singh,' said Pete, falling into step with Laurie towards the door and out of it.

'Wow,' he said as they walked across the square to the car park. 'Didn't expect that tonight.'

'Poor Yvonne,' said Laurie. 'I hope she makes up for all the life she missed.' She zapped her car lock. 'Well, see you next week.' She found herself hoping he'd keep her talking, suggest the pub quiz again.

'Have a good week,' said Pete, zapping his own car. He really shouldn't mention the pub quiz. He shouldn't open up the door to familiarity.

'Bye.'

'Unless, you fancy a drink?' He hadn't meant to say it – really. The words came out of his voice box as if they'd bypassed his brain.

She should say no, he would understand a polite refusal.

'Oh why not,' she said. As if the words had left the blocks before her brain could halt them.

The *Daily Trumpet* would like to apologise to Eric Bradbury, the landlord of the Spouting Tap in Little Kipping, after wrongly reporting that he had been admitted to hospital with an enlarged prostitute. We did of course mean 'prostate'.

Chapter 27

'You 'ere for t'quiz?' said the same woman as last week, as soon as they had walked into the Spouting Tap. Again she looked harassed and again she didn't wait for an answer but stuffed a pencil and a piece of paper into Pete's hand.

'Groundhog Day,' said Pete, which made Laurie giggle.

She has a lovely smile, thought Pete. Sweet, natural. Tara had a toothy smile and a sexy gap between her two front teeth. Perfectly straight because she'd had blinding bright white veneers. A smile she could turn on to get what she wanted.

They sat in the same seats as last week and Pete went to the bar and again Laurie tried not to study his form, appraise his wide shoulders, imagine him in a firefighter's uniform. Imagine him out of a firefighter's uniform.

She hadn't had sex in ages. Maybe the night he died – the night Alex was going to propose – they would have made love. He hadn't touched her for weeks before then and she hadn't felt able to initiate intimacy, as if there had been an invisible barrier in place between them. The last time she remembered them getting close in bed was Christmas Eve but he hadn't been able to get an erection. He'd apologised and she'd said it was fine because she was just happy that he'd tried after such an arid period of nothing. He'd cuddled up to her and said, 'You do know that I love you, don't you?' and she tried not to think that she'd just been given a compensation prize.

Pete arrived at the table with the red wine that Laurie had asked for, a pint and two packets of crisps.

'Couldn't resist the highly recommended craft ale Old Buggerlugs,' he said. 'And I thought these might go down well with them, although we shouldn't crunch during the questions. Hope you like cheese and onion.'

'Thank you, but I'm allergic to potatoes,' said Laurie. 'I come out in big lumps if I'm anywhere near them.'

Pete looked horrified. 'Oh crap, I didn't know. I'll take them back.'

'I'm joking,' said Laurie.

'Ahh ... you had me there,' said Pete with a laughing growl. He smiled and Laurie thought again what a drop-dead gorgeous smile he had, set in a drop-dead gorgeous handsome face.

'Just got here in time by the look of it,' said Pete as a large group pushed into the pub, looking for vacant seats. He picked up the pencil. 'Mixed Doubles again?'

'I can't think of anything else,' said Laurie.

'How's the *Daily Trumpet*? You been there this week?' asked Pete.

'Oh yes. They've had a bumper crop of mistakes recently. Poor Alan. If he had a swear box in his office, he'd be able to buy Fleet Street.'

'You get on well with him, don't you? You know, just from how you speak about him, I can tell.'

'He's a great bloke. Very funny and kind.' She took a sip of her wine and then dived into the crisps. Pete noticed her nails, short, neat, practical. She filled him in on why she enjoyed working there so much and Pete sat open-mouthed as she told him about some of the cases. It sounded like a madhouse.

'Is this bloody mike working?' said the disembodied voice of the quizmaster who was sitting out of sight around the corner.

'Yes,' came a chorus.

'You'll all be glad to know that Eric is back home upstairs in bed,' the quizmaster went on and a cheer erupted. 'His enlarged prostitute has been dealt with.' More laughter, big *hurrays*. 'Are we all ready? Right, question one, it's a music one.'

Laurie gulped as the strains of 'Always on My Mind' came out of the speaker. Whenever she heard it, a cocktail of conflicting emotions bombarded her and their base ingredient was despair.

'It's a two-part question, who first released it and in what year? You get half a point for each correct answer.'

The tune prodded something deep in Pete's brain. It had been playing for his and Tara's first dance at their wedding reception. Her favourite love ballad, she'd once told him. She'd cried as he held her. He'd felt her tears soak through his shirt. He had found a single of the Elvis recording at an antiques fair and put it in a frame for their first anniversary. She had cried then too.

'B. J. Thomas. 1970,' whispered Laurie.

'Wow.' Pete was impressed. 'How does anyone know that?'

'I just do,' she said.

'Question two: what is a Chinese gooseberry?'

They both knew that, but it was the easiest of the questions. This week neither of them thought they had sailed anywhere near to the prizewinning top three.

At the end of the quiz, Laurie stood up to buy a round before they did their marking, but found she was jammed in.

'I'll get them,' said Pete, spotting a gap at the bar. 'What do you want?'

'A J20 please. Any flavour. Let me pay.' She reached into her bag but Pete had gone by the time she'd found her purse. He cut through the crowd with ease and she noted that there was only one man standing who was the same height. Pete had a few inches on Alex, but Alex's lean, long-legged build made him appear taller than he was. He had a body for suits, his mum said. He looked like a model in them, especially with a white shirt. A blink of sunlight and his skin tanned and his beautiful blue eyes popped like Paul Newman's. How could all that life and beauty and promise be gone, she thought again and swallowed down the hard lump of emotion that threatened to clog up her throat.

Pete returned to the table with drinks and more crisps. Chicken, this time.

'I'm starving,' he explained. 'And there's only about four crisps in a packet these days.'

'I haven't had chicken crisps for years,' said Laurie. 'I didn't even know they still made them. Reminds me of being a kid.'

'School tuck shop?' suggested Pete.

A pause. 'Er, yes,' said Laurie.

'That's a lie,' replied Pete. 'What's the memory?'

'I used to have to make my tea a lot when I got in from school. I was supposed to put something in the oven or the microwave but instead I'd have crisp sandwiches on that really thin-sliced bread that you don't seem to be able to buy any more.'

Pete ripped open both packets, invited Laurie to dive in.

'How come you had to make your own tea?'

'Mum was working.'

'I see.'

'Actually I'm lying again,' admitted Laurie, thinking that this man was too easy to talk to. 'Mum liked to play bingo. She was very lucky at it. She won so many times that it more or less constituted a wage. In the end she won a national prize jackpot which was enough to buy her a small house in Spain. She reinvented herself there. Married an ancient expat who wanted a companion more than he did a wife and he died and left her well provided for . . .' Laurie stopped then, before she got on to her mother's succession of expat lovers. 'Believe it or not the crisps do have happy memories. I enjoyed them far more than the boil-in-the-bag fish and oven chips.'

Pete didn't say what he'd been about to in case it came out as smug. His own mum was always at home when they got back from school. He and Griff would walk into the house and be greeted by the aroma of their dinner cooking which they took entirely for granted. Only later when he compared his warm, well-fed, loving, secure childhood to the lesser experiences of some of his peers did he really begin to value it properly. He had loved his mother so much. He had a framed black and white photograph hung on the wall of her bending down to him on his first day at school, holding his face in her hands, about to give him a kiss. If his mother was ever going to show herself to him, it would be doing that – holding his face so he could feel the warmth of her fingers on his skin, transmitting through her touch that he was going to be all right.

'Okay, the answers,' said the quizmaster.

Pete grabbed the pencil in readiness. This week they were marking the answers of the bearded trio on the next table: 'The Grandfather Cocks'.

'Number one, the year was 1970 and the singer was B. J. Thomas.' Groans around the room, fist-bumps on the Mixed Doubles table. 'Question two: a Chinese gooseberry is a kiwi fruit ...'

Pete carried on marking but 'Always on My Mind' was playing on low volume in his head like a soundtrack, a picture of him dancing with his bride, holding her close, feeling his shirt dampen. Tears of happiness, he'd always thought.

'Oh my, that's miserable,' said Laurie after all the answers had been given and the sheets were reunited with their teams. 'Thirteen points.'

'Four more than the Grandfather Cocks,' answered Pete quietly.

They handed in their sheets and then listened out for the results. Last of the Summer Homebrew were fifth with eight points, The Grandfather Cocks were fourth with nine points, The Three Amigos third with twelve and second, with thirteen points, Mixed Doubles.

'Very poor scoring this week,' said the quizmaster. 'And the winners, with pie and peas for four, are the Four Horsemen of the Acropolis. Please come up to the bar and collect your prizes and can a representative from the Four Horsemen come up for the snowball question, the kitty of which currently stands at one hundred and seventy pounds.'

'How the hell did we do that?' said Pete, with stunned

delight. 'I'll fetch our prize.' He returned a minute later with a monster-sized bottle of Prosecco and a box of Milk Tray.

'Here you go,' said Pete. 'You have them both.'

'No, don't be silly, we'll split them. Which do you want?'

'When we win the pie and peas, I'll have those.' Then Pete realised what he'd just said. He'd overstepped the mark, presumed they would be back. Went for damage limitation, played it down.

'But, seeing as winning in this most obscure of all quizzes is unlikely, it's not really worth trying. Here you take these, please and spare my figure.'

'I insist you take one,' said Laurie.

'You pick, then.'

'I'll take the Prosecco. Bella and I will obliterate it tomorrow. She's coming round for dinner.'

'You'll never get it in your fridge,' said Pete.

Laurie laughed. On the next table, one of the Grandfather Cocks was taking the others to task, fuming that they'd missed out on a prize. 'I told you it was a bloody kiwi fruit, not a lychee. And I said it wasn't P. J. Proby.'

'Some people take these quizzes very seriously, don't they?' said Pete in a low voice. 'I must confess I was well impressed with you knowing the answer to the first question about the song. I think we must have been the only ones to get that right.'

'It was a special song for us,' said Laurie. 'The year after Alex and I got together we split up. He met someone else. Don't know who, never wanted to put a face or a name to her because I knew I'd obsess about her. Then he came back to me. Said he'd made a big mistake and wanted to put things right. The song was playing on the car radio once when he was driving and he got quite emotional, so much so that we had to pull over. It was the only time I've ever seen him cry. He said the song reminded him of when we split up. He said that I'd always been on his mind. That's why—' *Oh God*, what was she telling him all this for? She hadn't even told Bella about it.

'That's why?' he prompted.

'That's why he had the song title inscribed on my engagement ring.'

She held it out for him to see, but the engraving was so tiny he could barely make it out.

'I expect it's a special song for a lot of people though,' she said and he nodded and wondered why anyone would go to the trouble of having a ring inscribed without choosing the right size first.

She mistook his moment of musing for boredom and apologised. 'Sorry for going on.'

'Hey, don't apologise,' he said. 'I'm flattered you can talk to me so openly.'

'Too openly,' said Laurie. 'I'll be telling you my PIN number next.'

Pete picked up the stubby quiz pencil and pretended to write on his hand. 'What is it, then?'

She smiled and he thought how beautifully that smile sat on her face.

The smile segued into a yawn and she clapped her hand over her mouth.

'I'm only impressed you lasted so long in my company before falling asleep,' Pete said.

'It's so not your company, it's just been a hard day,' replied Laurie. It was only in this relaxing, convivial setting that she realised how tired she was. There was so much torturing her mind that her sleep was made up of a mass of short fractured shallow naps.

Pete took that as a cue. He was too comfortable with this woman who shared the same world as him, one full of craters and confusion. He downed the rest of his drink and she took her lead from him and downed hers.

'You leaving, pal?' said a man with a neck full of tattoos, on the hunt for a seat.

'Be my guest,' said Pete, standing.

'Cheers, pal.' The man's girlfriend reminded him of Tara with her artfully made up look-at-me face and dress sense. Proud tumble of hair, glossy lips, brown eyes made so much larger by her skilful ways with kohl.

As they were walking out, they heard the quizmaster announce that the snowball question hadn't been won again and they both wondered if they'd be back next week.

'Well, hope you get a good sleep tonight,' said Pete, at their cars.

'I just might do,' Laurie answered, though she couldn't remember the last time she had a proper, restful, dreamless sleep.

'Don't fall asleep before you get home.'

'I'll try my best not to.'

Pete got in his car quickly, because it would have been too easy to lean over and kiss her cheek and bypass a boundary that he both did – and didn't – want to cross.

Chapter 28

February, earlier that year

They peeled apart, sticky and sweaty from sex. She flopped backwards, head sinking deep into the pillow, fat with its newness, heart drumming a satisfied tattoo.

'You are amazing in bed,' she said.

'You're not so bad yourself.'

She laughed, closed her eyes, relived the moment when the climax shuddered through her body at the same time as she felt his last thrust inside her. There was an odd but thrilling synchronicity between their bodies – and their minds. People said they had found their soulmates when they hadn't really, just the one who fitted the present requirements, but this, this was the real deal. They'd felt it from the first time they met each other; it rumbled through them like thunder and lightning, connecting them, binding them, with its energy. It had been all-encompassing, obsessional, a fire too hot to sustain and with the cooling came the guilt. It had parted them and they'd tried to move on, but everything was weaker by comparison, a watered-down version of what they'd had with each other.

He had picked up his life where he left it; she had thrown herself at anyone to stem the bleed from her heart that she thought would never stop. She'd met someone lovely, thought it could work – wanted it to work. Then she met him again. A chance encounter. More than that – a clear indicator that whatever direction they tried to go, all roads served to push them back together. So they gave up the fight and let themselves happen again. They were home to each other. Home and heaven.

He swung himself out of bed, strolled over to the scatter of clothes on the floor. It was part of their ritual, tearing them off each other. They both enjoyed the urgency, the chaos.

He lifted up his jacket, rifled in the pocket.

'Too late if you're looking for a condom,' she called.

'Good.' He grinned.

He was as confident naked as he was dressed, and she sensed there was purpose in the slow swagger towards her. But not even when he dropped to one knee and held up a box to her in a fluid beautiful movement did she believe what that purpose was.

She sat up quickly.

'No way.'

He smiled. 'Will you marry me?'

She gulped. 'Really? Are you serious?'

'I was going to give this to you tomorrow, but how can I wait now? This is our most special day,' he said. He jabbed the box at her, urging her to take it, open it.

Her hand fluttered as it reached out. She took the box. It opened with an old, satisfying creak. Inside the lid the words stamped on the silk, 'Van Cleef & Arpels' and a ring – platinum – and a central square diamond, simple and pure. She lifted it out, held it up to the bulb above her head, saw the words 'Always on my mind' inscribed on the inner side in tiny letters, because the circumference of the ring was so small. Their words. Nothing to do with Elvis or Dolly or Willie Nelson, there was no tune dancing at the side of them.

'Yes!' She threw herself at him. 'Yes, yes, yes – a million times yes.'

'Put it on. I want to see it.'

'You put it on for me.'

He took it from her, slid it onto her finger, which was trembling with anticipation. A perfect fit, of course it was, because he'd chosen it to be.

She tilted her hand, watched the bulb light sparkle in the diamond. Then she removed it, replaced it in the box, handed it to him.

'Keep it until tomorrow,' she said. 'Then I'll put it on and never take it off.'

They dressed, slowly and carefully, assumed their old identities for the last time.

'When did you do the test?' he asked.

'In a loo in Meadowhall. I wanted to tell you to your face but I had to call you. I was so excited.'

'We don't need any more time to think this through, it's for the best that our hand has been forced. What will you say to him?' he asked, brushing the creases out of his trousers with the flat of his palm.

'I'll be honest,' she replied. 'I'll tell him that I've met someone else and I think it's best that I leave.' She winced. 'We're supposed to be going away for the weekend. He's booked a hotel.'

'Go if you want. I can wait—'

'No, no more waiting. It'll only make things harder in the long run. What about you? What will you do?'

'I'm cooking us a meal tonight. I called in to the M and S Foodhall on the way here, picked up something nice. I just hope that we can work things out civilly,' he replied. 'I'll tell her the truth too. Well . . . sort of. None of the details that will hurt her more than I have to.' He came to sit on the bed at the side of her. 'I'll pack a case, come back here and fetch the rest later. We'll have to sort out the house and finances and all that crap at some point but I'll try and make it as painless as I can for her.'

'Will she cut up your suits?' she asked.

'She's not the type,' he said, without having to think about it. 'She's a lovely person. Even after what I've done to her, she won't do that.'

'Did you ever tell her who you had the affair with?'

'No. And she never asked.'

'Will you tell her who you're leaving her for?'

'If she asks the question, I will.' He sighed. He knew her so well and he still loved her and wanted the best for her, and the best wasn't him. The best was someone who would not rip her heart out and stamp on it, heal it and then repeat.

Her hand instinctively came to rest on her stomach. 'Will she be hurt about the baby?'

'It will shred her.' He rubbed his forehead with the tips of his fingers as if trying to alleviate a pain. 'We bought the house to fill it with kids. I pushed for that. I thought I could forget you and have everything with her but you were always on my mind, you never left it.' He reached for her hand, lifted it to his lips. 'The song came on the radio once when we were in the car and I had to pull up. I couldn't see. I had to tell her a total lie about why I was so upset. I just wanted you back so much. Then we . . .'

'. . . bumped into each other.' She finished the sentence for him, as she so often did.

'We were meant to be together. I knew it then and I know it now.'

'At least you don't have a divorce to arrange,' she said with a sigh. 'I worry he'll find out about the baby and make things awkward.'

'But surely when he finds out it can't possibly be his, that will make things easier?'

'Yes of course.' The one lie that she'd told him, that the baby couldn't possibly be her husband's, because it could be. She'd secretly come off the pill, hoping to get pregnant by her lover, knowing as soon as she did, it would be the catalyst for them to throw all caution to the wind, step out of their old lives like a snakeskin. She hadn't slept with her husband in that time. Not until their anniversary, when she didn't avoid it, but asking him to wear a condom, when he never had before, would have ruined the moment and she didn't want to ruin the moment so she risked it. Guilt had been instrumental in wanting to give him affection that night, this man who was pulling out all the stops to mend the hole in his marriage that she knew could not be repaired. If she could have forced her heart to love him instead, she would have.

'Life isn't a fairytale, darling,' he said. 'But I'm going to do my best to give us our happy ending. Tomorrow when we wake up here in our bed, it will be the first day of the rest of our lives together,' he said. 'The three of us. Nothing is going to ever part us again.'

WEST

Come scattering west wind and sow
Your seeds to quicken and to grow
When Autumn's fierce and cleansing breath
Has hounded out the old year's death

THE WEST WIND

ANON

Chapter 29

26 September

'I see your sign's up,' said Bella thumbing in the direction of the bottom of the drive when she walked into Laurie's house with a bottle of wine. 'That was quick.'

'I know. He only came to photograph everything yesterday,' said Laurie, giving her a welcoming hug. 'It was so odd but when I came home from work to find it there, I wanted to rip it out. I panicked.'

'Tell them you've changed your mind then,' said Bella. 'It's your call.'

'No, I'm doing the right thing, I know I am, but . . . I'll be saying goodbye to so many memories that we made here.'

'And hello to a fresh, new gaff that's easier to clean.' Bella took a long appraising sniff. 'Something smells lovely.'

'It's only lasagne. Lentil and mushroom, you don't miss the meat at all. I prefer it.'

'And it's the perfect clear-out for the system. Lentils go straight through me.'

'As classy as ever,' said Laurie with an affectionate tut.

'You have to admit that pulses are conducive to a great bowel movement.' Bella followed Laurie into the kitchen.

'Good job we aren't on a first date, isn't it?'

Bella laughed. 'Stu sends his love. And the wine. I can't tell you how much it's worth because you'd be afraid to open it. Prezzie from a buyer – ridiculously expensive. And I bet we won't be able to tell the difference between it and a good old Hardy's.'

Alex would have been able to tell the difference. He would have cooed and appreciated the wine's price tag. He would have pulled out the cork and smelled it, poured a few sips into the right-shaped glass, swirled it around, inhaled the aroma and then tasted and appraised.

Laurie opened up the fridge door. 'Prosecco to start with?'

'Jesus Christ, couldn't you have got a bigger bottle?' said Bella when Laurie took it out.

'Won it last night at a quiz. I won't be responsible for the quality.'

'Who were you at a quiz with and where?'

'Pete. The guy who goes to my support group thingy. And the Spouting Tap in Little Kipping.'

Bella's eyebrows rose to their physical limits. 'The fireman? Nice. Spouting Tap – very cosy.'

'Don't look at me like that. My brain isn't even thinking about romance.'

'It doesn't matter if it was, Laurie. You're thirty-three years old. You can't dress up in black and mourn for the rest of your life.'

Laurie poured out the Prosecco, with difficulty because it weighed a ton and was difficult to tip.

'Stu's got a new manager at work, single, gorgeous, tall,

dark and handsome. He's called Reid West-Hunt, he even oozes class out of his name,' said Bella.

'And?' There was a nip of suspicion in the word.

'He's fresh from a divorce, and asked Stu if he knew any single ladies who might enjoy being wined and dined as he doesn't want to negotiate the shark-filled waters of internet dating.'

'Please don't set me up with a blind date,' said Laurie.

'Don't be silly. But Stu did mention that he's a catch and if you ever – i.e. in the future – wanted an intro, we would be more than happy to fix up a meet. Dinner at mine and—'

'By the time I'm ready to date again, Reid will have celebrated his silver wedding and have a brood of seven children,' said Laurie, handing over a glass flute.

'Hmm, surprisingly pleasant for plonk. Oh . . . ah and I'm really sorry, I know I said I'd go with you to see the new *John Wick* film on Sunday night but I'm working away all weekend. Crisis at the Cedar Springs in Reading. It's too boring to even go into, but I'm needed.'

'It's fine,' said Laurie, hiding her disappointment. She was so looking forward to seeing it and it was the last weekend it would be at the cinema. 'We can go another time to see another film.'

''Course we will.' Bella drained her glass and filled it up again.

'Tough day?'

'Forest Hotels make the *Daily Trumpet* look competent by comparison,' Bella said. 'They don't pay me enough by half for what I have to do. They fry my brain.'

'My life is all the richer for the *Daily Trumpet*,' said Laurie, putting a stick of garlic bread into the oven.

'Mine isn't for Forest Hotels. No wonder I drink.'

'You must have fun parts though. Scandals,' said Laurie. 'Hellraisers. People checking in with someone they shouldn't.'

Bella froze, just for a beat, as if a pause button had been hit by accident then released.

'Like who?'

'Celebs, who did you think I meant? Meredith sneaking in for an afternoon with that neighbour of hers who cuts his bushes into animals? Didn't you once say your hotels always got the bookings when there were film shoots happening?' Laurie reminded her.

'Sorry, my mind went blank there,' Bella excused herself. 'Yeah, I once booked that actor from one of the soaps – Dom Donaldson. He came with a redhead from one of the other soaps. Then – blow me – she appeared in the Sunday paper that week in a feature about her idyllic married life to someone who was not Dom Donaldson.'

'He's gorgeous though, isn't he? I used to think Alex looked like him.'

'He was a prick,' said Bella, with venom. 'An arrogant shit.'

'Steady on there, lady,' Laurie chuckled at the level of vitriol in her friend's voice.

'He talked to me as if I was something that wouldn't flush away.' Bella tossed another mouthful of Prosecco into her mouth, and just for a second Laurie wondered if she was talking about Alex or Dom Donaldson.

Odd how alcohol clouded some parts of the brain while it sharpened others, thought Laurie as she cleared away the mains plates and began to dish up some banoffee pie. She suddenly recalled what had caused her ears to prick up in yesterday's session at the teashop: Sharon, relaying how she hadn't really believed her friend's explanation of why they'd stopped talking. Seeing Bella now as half-cut as she had been at Bertie and Anna's wedding had jogged her memory. There had been no fallings out that night; in fact Alex and Bella had been jiving just before the taxis arrived. Alex, sloshed, was funny and silly, far less sarcastic than he could be sober. Alex and Bella had not acted like people who'd had a verbal war. If they had, Bella would not have been able to carry on as normal with him because she would have been too annoyed and Alex would have avoided her totally. Bella had lied to her. The thought sobered Laurie up as surely as a jet of cold water sprayed in her face.

'Calamerized bananas as well, I am super-impressed,' said Bella, who was on her second glass of the expensive red wine by now and no, they couldn't tell it from Hardy's. 'So tell me more about the flyer . . . firelighter.'

'I don't know much about him other than he's in the same boat as I am.'

'He's very tall isn't it. Nice eyes. *Ding dong.*'

'Neither of us want to do any dinging or donging, thank you. We're just a similar age and I find him really easy to talk to. He doesn't want anything from me and I don't want anything from him.'

Bella smiled. 'Unlike Jeff the lech.'

'Please, you'll make me bring up my pasta.'

'Not heard anything else from that lot then – the Wilder Beasts?'

'Not a peep.'

'And not had any more daft ideas about giving them a slice of cash when you sell the house?'

'No,' said Laurie, although she hadn't dismissed it fully,

especially if that's what it would take to entice answers out of Meredith and give her peace of mind.

'Good.'

They sat for a few moments, then Laurie launched in.

'Did you like Alex, Bella?'

'Honestly?'

'Of course.'

'I thought you were a good match. I thought he could be a little arrogant, but what man can't. Better to be self-assured than a wimp.'

'But did you like him?'

'I did, but I don't think he liked me. You can be straight with me, Laurie, if he said that. I think we were both a bit too feisty to get on properly, but yes I used to like him.'

Bella had fancied the pants off Alex as soon as she'd laid eyes on him. They'd all been at a Forest Hotels charity function at Beechwood Hall, Laurie had gone as Bella's plus one.

'Look at that man over there, three o'clock,' Bella had said to her. 'He keeps staring at me.'

But she was wrong because it was Laurie who had caught his eye. Bella was gracious in defeat and they'd had laughs about it afterwards. Alex, as Laurie remembered it, had always been charming and flirtatious towards Bella, until he wasn't any more.

'Why didn't you talk to me though, when you and Alex had words at Anna's wedding? Why did you just cut yourself off from me, Bella?'

'Jesus, are you really bringing this up again?' said Bella, smiling wearily. 'I feel crap enough about it as it is. It wasn't a conscious thing to dump our friendship, it was just a casualty of complications. Please, Laurie, just forget it. It happened. It shouldn't have, but it did and it was all my fault so forgive me and let it lie. I can't talk about it any more.'

Laurie nodded resignedly and lifted the bottle to replenish Bella's glass, but she quickly placed her hand flat over the top.

'I think I've had enough to drink. Fancy putting on the kettle and knocking me up a decaf before I ring a taxi?'

Subject firmly closed. Laurie wouldn't prise anything more out of Bella tonight. But there was more, Laurie was sure of it. And she *would* get to it.

Chapter 30

27 September

'You look different,' said Sal, tilting her head one way and then the other at Pete as they were having a coffee in the station kitchen.

'Do I? In what way? Is it cos I 'as 'ad a bath?'

'Could be,' she leaned forward and sniffed the air between them. 'Very fragrant, but it's not that. You just look a little . . . happier. Bit more like the old Pete.'

'I'm getting there I think,' he replied to that.

'I'm not one to pry—' began Sal before Pete cut her off with a sarcastic hoot of laughter. 'Shut up, you. How's it going with Molly?' She waited expectantly for the answer as Pete formed some words in his mouth, dismissed them, shook his head and grinned. 'What's so funny?'

'Sal, if you'd told me a month ago that the highlight of my week would soon be having tea and cake with an abused wife, a bloke in a knitted tank top, a woman grieving for her dog, an old lady, a Sikh surgeon-turned-barista and a platinum-blonde solicitor, I'd have laughed you out of town.

But—' he shrugged two shouldersworth of acceptance '—it is.'

Sal gave an impressed nod to that. 'Sometimes circumstances push together people and the unlikeliest of friendships occur. Tell me about the platinum-blonde solicitor, she sounds the most interesting.'

'Why zone in on her?' asked Pete.

'Because of the way your face changed when you said those three words.'

'Bullshit.'

'Connection made?'

'Sort of.'

'Knew it, you bastard.'

Pete's turn to grin now. 'She's called Laurie and she's about the same age as I am, lost her fiancé in a crash so we have plenty of common ground, but neither of us are in a position to step over any barriers. She's a friend, I like her, no more than that.'

Sal listened patiently. *Laurie*. She thought it sounded a name that would belong to a gentle woman, a pretty one too.

'She's working some magic, I can tell,' she said eventually.

Pete prepared to divulge something. 'I'll have to be careful, Sal. The last two times after the sessions, we've gone to the pub and done the quiz and it's been . . . too . . . good. I feel as if I've known her far longer than I have.'

'What's wrong with that?' asked Sal, sweeping up Pete's mug and taking it with hers over to the kettle to make refills.

'It's only been seven months since Tara died.'

'Read the textbook on grief and how to behave,' said Sal.

Pete looked incredulous. 'What textbook?'

'Precisely. There isn't one. Just because you feel something for her, doesn't mean you're on course for the aisle,

Pete. There's nothing wrong with some companionship. You can feel love for friends too, you know. I'd even go as far as to say that I love you, in a non-bodily-fluids-swapping way, obviously.' Sal mock-shuddered and chuckled to herself. 'Your heart is lonely, mate, so it's reaching out. You're obviously both benefitting from being together, so don't chuck it up just because you're scared of what other people might think.'

'I've had a lonely heart for ages, Sal,' said Pete. The disclosure was out before he had a chance to haul it back. Sal was easy to talk to too, in a different way to Laurie. Sal felt like a sister, close, easy but without the family ties that clouded judgement, stirred up emotion.

Sal spooned the coffee granules into the cups, added milk and sugar, put the mugs down on the table and closed the kitchen door so they couldn't be overheard.

'Talk to me,' she said.

'I haven't told anyone this before,' Pete said. 'Tara and I were going through a rough patch for months before she died. We'd stopped sleeping together. Apart from once, on our anniversary so that's when she must have conceived, which makes sense now because her moods after that were all over the place. I don't know if you knew but she died the day before her thirtieth birthday. I'd booked a weekend away for us, as a surprise. I was going to give her the full works: best room in the hotel, trip to the theatre, champagne, roses, massage in the spa, everything to try and keep us together. I didn't know what was going on because something was, but she said it was all in my imagination. I didn't know if we were back on track or what was happening with us.'

'But you didn't realise she was pregnant. It does a lot of

things to a woman's body and mind. She was obviously going to tell you that night, wasn't she? It would have all been all right, mate. If life hadn't been so fucking cruel and thrown you that curve ball.'

Pete felt hard prickles behind his eyes, sharp as fragments of glass.

'What was she doing on that road, Sal, when she told me she was somewhere else completely?'

Something Sal had wondered herself a few times, not that she had ever said. Maybe Pete had misheard. They'd never know.

Sal reached across, kneaded Pete's shoulder affectionately.

'The here and now is all we have for certain, Pete. Life is for the living. How many times have we said that to each other when we've been to a job and found someone isn't going home again? Take comfort in your new friendship and just let it happen. Let life happen.'

Pete nodded, smiled. He couldn't think of a single person whose opinion he valued who wouldn't have said the same. But coming from Sal, it felt like a blessing.

Chapter 31

29 September

Laurie pulled up in the car park, killed the ignition and continued to sit for a few moments while she revved up her nerves to do what she had forced herself to. Some entity inside her had decided that if no one would go with her to see the film, she should go by herself. This was a test. If she passed, she would say to hell with it and book herself a holiday. Other single people went away and it wasn't such a stigma these days. The Canaries maybe, in spring, something to look forward to, to ease her into the world of singledom. But before she jumped over that particular hurdle, she needed to get her ass out of her car and into the cinema.

It was a late night showing and it was unlikely to be packed full of people totally ignoring what was on the screen in order to obsess about why a lone female was in their midst. Plus it would be dark, she wouldn't be noticed. Maurice had done it and said it wasn't half as bad as he'd imagined.

On the count of three she threw herself out of the car, refusing to give herself any more thinking time. She'd dressed in jeans and a casual top because she thought it made her look less likely to have been stood up than if she was tarted up to the nines. With every step towards the cinema, she could have sworn her mouth became drier. Totally ridiculous. She didn't get nervous standing up in courts, but here she was, heart thumping because she had to join a small queue to buy a ticket to see Keanu Reeves on a screen. She mentally rehearsed saying, 'One, please,' and then mentally saw the kiosk clerk flashing her a look of sympathy. This was a stupid idea. She wondered if she should take out her phone and pretend to ring someone, make sure people heard her saying, 'Oh, you're running late. Okay, I'll meet you inside.' Or maybe she'd just slink off back to the car – she wasn't sure which would draw less attention to her.

Pete hadn't been to the cinema by himself before and he wasn't sure why he was going there tonight by himself either. That there was nothing on the TV and he was sick of the four walls of the house was a reasonable explanation. He'd noticed in the *Chronicle* that the new *John Wick* film was showing and some persuasive voice in his head had decided it would be a good thing for him to go and see it. The more single stuff he did, the quicker he'd get used to it. It was a test, he told himself, as he parked up in the Courthouse car park in town.

It was no good, thought Laurie, standing in the queue for far longer than she'd anticipated because someone's card wasn't recognised by the machine. She felt sadder than sad among other couples, imagining them gossiping about the poor, friendless woman with the long, blonde plait. She'd try this another time, and would catch up with Keanu when he appeared on Netflix. She slipped away from the queue as if she was hanging around, waiting for someone to arrive before joining it again.

'Laurie.'

She heard her name and turned to see a familiar figure coming across the road from the direction of the car park. She felt her heartbeat respond with a flutter and silently cursed it. *We do not want this complication,* her brain sent down a stern message. She cringed, knowing she wasn't going to be able to avoid talking to him, not to mention explaining why she was loitering outside the cinema at this time of night.

'Well fancy meeting you,' he said. 'Are you here for *John Wick* as well?'

Oh God, thought Laurie. The humiliation.

'Erm . . . not sure.'

That was a ridiculous answer, said her brain. No wonder he gave her a puzzled look. He had a date, of course. He must have. He couldn't possibly be here like she was, flying solo, trying to be a brave and confident singleton.

'I mean, that . . .' *Oh, just tell him.* It couldn't get much more mortifying, unless a stunning woman turned up, linked his arm and drove him forwards to the end of the queue. 'Okay . . . I thought about coming here as a test, to see if I could. I convinced myself I needed to start and socialise, even if I am socialising by myself.' *Pathetic,* said the brain voice.

'Oh God, that is so sad,' said Pete, hands on hips, shaking his head slowly from side to side. He didn't expect his words to bring a flush to her cheeks quite so quickly. 'I'm joking,

Laurie. Guess what – I'm here doing the exact same thing. Ownsome lonesome.'

'It's somehow more acceptable if a man goes into the cinema by himself. Even in this day and age.'

'Well, I really wanted to see it so I figured ... I could see it or I could sit at home grumbling that I wish I'd seen it.'

Laurie smiled. 'I hope you enjoy it.'

'We could go in alone together if you like?'

Laurie's heart smiled. She could feel it growing warm inside her chest. *Idiot.*

'Oh ... okay, if you don't mind.'

'I don't mind at all. I'll even pay us in if you get the popcorn, then no one will talk about me letting the lady buy her own ticket.'

'Have you seen the price of the popcorn?' she answered him.

He took hold of her shoulder, twisted her forwards and gave her a small push towards the ticket kiosk. She felt the imprint of his hand all the way to their seats.

'When Mum used to bring us, we'd watch the trailers and stick our thumbs up if we fancied seeing the film, or down if we didn't, as if we were in the Colosseum watching gladiators. Or wiggle them from side to side if we weren't sure,' said Pete when they were seated with popcorn.

'Is that what I'm expected to do now?' asked Laurie.

'Er ... obviously, that's why I'm telling you.'

They both thumbed up the new Liam Neeson, thumbed down the big car-chase film, wavered over the horror, thumbed up the Tom Cruise sci-fi.

'Great minds think alike,' said Pete.

'Fools seldom differ,' replied Laurie, which made Pete laugh. He realised that when the laugh stopped, his lips still carried a smile. He seemed to smile a lot around Laurie, that wasn't lost on him.

The film started and Pete tried to think back to the last time he'd been to the cinema with a woman. He couldn't be any more specific than early on in his relationship with Tara. 'Thank God that's over,' she'd said at the end of it.

'Didn't you enjoy it?' he'd said, a little crestfallen, because he'd suggested it thinking she would.

'The cinema isn't really my thing if I'm honest,' she'd replied, linking his arm. 'I'm more a live band girl. But I enjoyed the company.' They'd gone to dinner then and the evening had been recovered, but though he'd accompanied her to watch live bands when it wasn't really his thing, she never suggested the cinema, knowing it was his.

Out of the corner of her eye, Laurie could see Pete's shoulder. He was even tall sitting down and she'd noticed the people in the seats behind had moved to get an unrestricted view. He was fast becoming a friend, she thought. Nothing more. So why was she so conscious of him at her side?

Neither of them moved when the credits started to roll at the end.

'I haven't fallen asleep, I just want to see the cast list,' Pete explained. 'I thought I spotted a basketball player.'

Laurie was in no rush to move either. She half-wished they'd put on another film.

'Yep, thought it was him. Okay, now we can go,' said Pete eventually, standing up, stretching.

Laurie noticed that he said goodnight and thank you to

the staff member at the door. He had nice manners, she liked that. Alex wouldn't have. He didn't give thank yous freely to people who 'served'.

'What did you think, then?' asked Pete when they strolled outside and the fresh night air greeted them.

'I thought it was great. I'd have been sad if I'd missed it,' said Laurie.

'I love going to the cinema,' said Pete, as they headed to the car park. She noted the small courtesy that he'd swapped places so he was on the road side of the pavement. 'My wife didn't like to go. Sometimes I've had to tag along with my brother and his wife like a great big gooseberry.'

Laurie smiled. 'I know what you mean. Alex preferred meals or bars ...' *the more people the merrier joining them, so he could hold court,* she didn't add. 'I usually went to see films with Bella. That's who I should have been going with tonight, but she had to cancel.'

'Well—' He pulled up the words he was about to say: *If you're ever at a loose end again, give me a call.* He couldn't say them, but he wanted to. He scrabbled around for an alternative end to the sentence he'd started. 'Well ... she missed out big time. She'll have to watch it on the TV next year.'

'Not the same though, is it? You don't get the atmosphere.'

'Nor the massive screen or the surround sound.'

'And the popcorn always tastes better in a cinema, don't you think?'

'So it should at that price. How can they charge so much for it?'

'Because they can.'

They arrived at Laurie's car, turned to face each other.

'Thank you for your unexpected company,' she said.

'And back atcha.' He cringed at himself. 'How old am I? Why would I say that?'

She laughed and Pete thought how sparkly her eyes looked. She was beautiful and he wondered if her fiancé had told her that enough.

'I mean it. You've made a lonely evening so much more pleasant. Although we still have to get that first solo cinema trip out of the way, so back to square one.' He gave a long drawn-out comedy sigh.

'Yep. Well, goodnight.' She didn't move and she didn't know why. What was she waiting for?

'Goodnight, Laurie.' His arms opened wide before he could even think about it. They closed around her and he felt the warm yielding press of her body against his chest, caught the faint scent of her perfume and he knew that he had feelings for this woman and he didn't know what to do about them.

He let go first. She left his arms slowly and it would have been too easy to bend down, kiss her. He had an inkling she would let him.

Laurie smiled, bashfully. He'd shaken her. She dropped her keys, but she didn't drop the smile.

'Drive safely,' he said, wagging a cautionary finger at her.

'You too,' she replied, hardly able to hear her own words because of the heartbeat thudding in her ears.

In the car, Laurie tried to compose herself. The bloke had only hugged her goodbye, so why was she as quivery as if he'd snogged the face off her? This was why bereaved people were so vulnerable, because a little affection went a long way. Especially when they had been denied it for so long.

The *Daily Trumpet* apologises for the error that appeared in the 'Top Tips' section of Saturday's edition, namely: 'To prevent your eyes watering when slicing up onions, dip them into boiling water for a few seconds'. We did of course mean dip the onions into boiling water and not your eyes.

Chapter 32

1 October

'I'm going to have either a heart attack or a stroke before I can have the joy of telling Sir Basil Stamper to stick this job up his entitled bumhole,' said Alan Robertson, putting a cup of coffee down in front of Laurie. 'I'm sure he gets some perverted kick out of giving me sleepless nights.'

Sometimes Laurie had thought exactly that too. She chuckled to herself.

'You all right, lass?' said Alan suddenly then. 'You seem different somehow.'

'Different?' Her expression and voice both registered puzzlement.

'If I was a fanciful man,' began Alan, 'which I'm not because the Stamper family have battered it out of me, I'd say you seemed *lighter*. Not the ideal word, but an aura reader might detect a hint of sunshine yellow dancing around you.'

Was it so obvious? thought Laurie. It wasn't something she wanted on show to the general public, that there was levity in her soul, because it wasn't right what she was feeling. She knew it was the 'fake news' of the emotional world, her empty heart scrabbling around for something to stave off its hunger and finding a fireman, a film and a carton of popcorn.

'I'm just getting on with things,' said Laurie.

'Are you off to your session tomorrow? With Molly?'

'Yes, I am.'

'Going okay?'

Laurie sighed before the 'Yes' and Alan was straight on it.

'That was a sigh full of meaning.'

'I've met someone at the group.' She sat back, waited for Alan to look disgusted, tell her she was a hideous human being, shudder with disbelief. Alan did none of those things.

'A man, you mean? And if so, what's wrong with that?'

'There's nothing going on—'

Alan cut her off. 'It's no business of anyone's but yours if there is, Laurie.'

'I don't want to feel the way I'm feeling and I'm fighting against it,' she said. 'I went to the pictures at the weekend – alone – intending to start fully feeding myself back into the real world as a single person and bumped into this man from Molly's group doing the same thing. If I didn't know any better, I'd wonder if something wasn't trying to push us together.'

Alan chuckled. 'Like those old gods you see on films playing chess with people's lives.'

'Just like that. So we went in together and I sat there trying to watch the film but all the time I was thinking, *I have feelings for this person and I don't know what to do with them.* And I think he might feel the same about me. I didn't go looking for it, Alan. My friend wants to set me up on a blind date and I can't think of anything worse. It really was the last thing on my mind. I'm not over Alex. Not by a long chalk.'

Someone knocked on Alan's door and he gave them the Vs through the glass – his way of saying, *Come back later, unless Armageddon is underway.*

'You're a living, breathing creature, Laurie. And our feelings aren't on reins. There's no sin in helping each other along, it might be a solid foundation to build on or just a helpful stepping stone. Don't presume it's a harmful thing, or wrong. As my dear old great gran, God rest her soul, used to say, "Life is here and now – live it or miss it." You see, she did say some things without F-words.'

'Thank you, Alan,' said Laurie, meaning it.

'What for?'

'Not making me feel like I'm not normal.'

'Normal isn't anything to aspire to,' said Alan, with a disapproving click of his tongue. 'The Stampers think they're normal. So did the bleeding Borgias.'

Chapter 33

2 October

Pete would have to shoot off straight after the fifth teashop session as he was working the night shift, which meant he'd miss going to the pub with Laurie, doing the quiz. Maybe that was a good thing, though, because he wasn't sure he could trust himself not to take Laurie's lovely face between his hands and kiss her as they said goodbye. She had been in his mind constantly since they'd been to the pictures together. He had no idea what was cranking up inside him, but he didn't want to stop it. Even if it wasn't reciprocated, it made him feel more alive than he had done for a long time. But then she walked into the teashop and smiled at him, and he knew that whatever was going on in his heart was also going on in hers.

'Hi,' she said after Mr Singh had served her up a coffee and a slice of strawberry drizzle. Pete noticed a faint blush had painted her pale cheeks.

'Hi,' he replied, savouring the bloom of warmth spreading in his chest. 'Okay?'

'Yep, and you?'

'Good, thanks.'

There was an awkwardness between them now that hadn't been there before, born from affection growing, born from the increase in caring what one thought about the other. It was a stage that fledgling lovers wanted to get past and yet when they had, they looked back at it with fondness and longing.

'How is everybody?' asked Molly, herding everyone's focus to her.

'Remarkably good,' said Maurice. 'Yvonne and I had a little jaunt out to the coast for an afternoon tea.'

'I'd never had one before,' said Yvonne.

'It was a feast and a half,' chuckled Maurice. 'It was a joy to watch Yvonne's face when the cake stand came out. Four tiers-worth of food. We could barely fit in the car on the way home.'

Molly took heart from the connection they'd made, the 'date' they'd had. It wasn't unheard of for people to meet outside the group, for friendships to flourish beyond the teashop walls as well as within them. And it was obviously doing Yvonne and Maurice good. He had a stripey shirt on today and looked years younger than he did in a tank top. And Yvonne had put some make-up on and her mouth had a default setting of an upward curve rather than the downward one she'd had for the last couple of meetings .

'Everything all right with you, Sharon?' asked Molly.

Sharon quickly cleared her mouth of caramel cake before speaking.

'Really good. I've been spending some time with my friend, you know, the one who got back in touch. It's been smashing.'

'And what about you two?' Molly's head swivelled round to Laurie and Pete.

'I'm certainly feeling better,' said Pete, running his fingers across the back of his neck – a nervous gesture. 'More positive. I'm back in the groove at work and . . . just had a lovely week.'

He wondered if Laurie would read into that that she had contributed to his lovely week.

'And me too,' Laurie said. 'I feel as if I'm fitting in more with . . . life and . . . that I'm making forward steps. I've had a really lovely week too. Full of nice things.' She was looking at Molly as she said it but her words were for Pete to hear.

'Excellent,' said Molly and beamed. *This group of people are good for each other*, she thought. Sometimes the dynamics worked better than others and it always surprised her that the more motley the crew, the better the connections made. She thought that maybe these people would be leaving her, not needing her support any more soon and that both saddened and heartened her because this might be her favourite group so far. They were all especially vulnerable and yet, at the same time, surprisingly resilient.

'It was Mother's birthday at the weekend,' said Maurice. 'I thought it would hit me hard and it did . . . but not quite the body blow I expected.'

'That's why I suggested going out,' put in Yvonne. 'I hoped it might cheer him up.'

'And it did, but I don't think I needed cheering that much,' Maurice went on. 'I was dreading the date and felt that I had to mark it in some way. I took flowers to her grave, of course, and said a few words to her but . . . I presumed I'd be felled by a wave of emotion and then guilt set in when I wasn't. Is that normal?'

'Dates are stamped on your memory and they trigger off alerts in your brain that in turn release emotions around people,' Molly explained. 'You don't need to beat yourself up because you didn't collapse into a sad heap. You are moving on, Maurice, out of your grief but that doesn't mean you have forgotten your mum or love her less. The unconscious mind remembers the dates even if the conscious mind has forgotten. The brain is a very complicated and clever computer, but it doesn't always have its host's best interests at heart.'

Maurice nodded, then said, 'Thank you, Molly. I'll always be grateful for this group and the sense and order it has brought to my life. And friendship and joy I never thought I'd find.' He gave her a smile of such tenderness that it brought a lump to Molly's throat. A picture flashed in her head of the first time he came to her group, unkempt, lost, confused and dangerously low in mood. He was a different man now and she hoped his life would be full of the contentment that had eluded him so far. Yes, these people were healing and she would miss them terribly but she would be proud to send them all into the world stronger and happier.

Sharon was thinking about adopting a dog because the woman a few doors away had to go into a home and she couldn't take her pet with her, and wanted to talk through if she would be disrespecting Billy's memory.

'I think you'd be honouring Billy's memory by giving the new dog the love you can't give to him,' said Mr Singh. 'Plus you can take the dog to see the old lady. She must be quite distraught to have to let her go.'

'She is. And I could, couldn't I?' said Sharon with a bright smile.

Yvonne and her daughter had had a good chat but it hadn't gone that well, she explained. Lola had stormed out, accused her mother of lying. Everyone had expressed regret at that.

'Then she came round to the house with a bunch of flowers yesterday.' Yvonne turned to Molly. 'You were right, a lot of it didn't come as a shock, she'd seen more than I thought she had but she'd buried it because she didn't want to see her dad in that light. I didn't tell her everything, she doesn't need to know it all, and I certainly didn't tell her about the toadstool pie.' This elicited a ripple of laughter. 'We'll get there or we won't,' she went on, 'but I'm glad I said my piece. I've cried a bit this week. I should have left Des years ago. I would have coped somehow.'

Molly smiled at her. Life didn't come with a rewind button but often she wished it did. She and Harvey could have had so many more happy years if only she could turn the clock back and they'd talked more; it would have changed their history. Words unsaid made bricks for big walls.

At the end of the session, Pete pulled Laurie to the side of the room where they couldn't be overheard.

'I can't go to the quiz tonight, Laurie, I've got to do an extra night shift. Pay a favour back that someone did for me by swapping shifts.' He saw the disappointment register fleetingly on her face before she overcame it.

'Oh, don't worry, I didn't expect it was a ritual. I have some work to do at home anyway.' An obvious lie.

'I would have really liked to go,' he added, in case she was in any doubt.

'Those quizzes hurt my brain. I'll be glad of the rest.'

'Can I take you to dinner?'

He'd blurted it out, made it sound as if it hadn't been on his mind when it had and he'd rehearsed asking it. It should have come out much better than that.

'Oh, er . . .' Her mouth was an 'O' of shock.

'Sunday. Firenze? If you haven't been, it's top-notch.'

Laurie had been and she knew it was.

'Well, that would be just lovely. Thank you.'

'I'll pick you up at seven? That work?'

'It does.'

'Okay, I have to dash off now but I'll see you then.'

'Yes, see you then.'

Laurie tried not to grin like a child who had just been told that Christmas was coming well ahead of schedule, but failed. She was in trouble.

She dawdled behind, looking at the lovely literary goods which filled the cabinets around the room, and waited for the others to go so she could have a private word with Molly.

'Can I ask you something, Molly?' said Laurie, quietly, away from the ears of Mr Singh who was busy doing the washing up.

'Of course you can, my dear.'

Laurie opened her mouth, couldn't find the starting point and so just leapt in. 'When is too soon to start . . . having feelings for someone else? Asking for a friend.' *That was convincing*, said the sarcastic voice inside her head.

'There's no right time, Laurie. Some people never want to, because the love of their life was enough and friendship adequately fills the lonely places; then again, for some people, that whole connection is an essential and they don't want to live without it, so the answer to your question is that it's different for everyone. Obviously people are vulnerable at the time of bereavement and feelings can run haywire; mistakes are made, but not always. Lovely, genuine people can come into our lives at any time and our hearts respond to them.'

Laurie nodded, absorbing the words.

'My husband left me and came back into my life many years later,' Molly went on. 'I wouldn't have missed having him for the world, even though I expected that world to disapprove of us being together again.'

'My friend ... she's in the same boat as I am but she honestly didn't think I'd ... er ... she'd be able to even consider going out with another man yet. She's worried people will think that her ... husband hasn't even been gone a year and his parents would hit the roof if they found out.'

Molly put a comforting hand on Laurie's shoulder. 'Tell your friend that this is her life, not anyone else's and she has to live it for herself.'

'She isn't over her husband. She misses him so much and she feels conflicted.'

'You know who Janus is, of course. A god with one face turning back to the old and one face turning forward to the new. Your friend is climbing out of the pit of grief, heading for acceptance that her old life has gone and a new one awaits and so there will be a period of inner struggle,' said Molly. 'Tell your friend not to turn away love because the timing isn't quite right. It has a tendency to ignore protocol.'

'Thank you, Molly, yet again,' said Laurie. 'You're so wise.'

'Most people are, who have learned from making a lot of mistakes,' replied Molly. 'I'll see you next week, dear.'

'Bye. Bye, Mr Singh.'

Pavitar waved. He did wish people would call him by his first name but it never seemed to happen.

As Laurie got into her car, she hoped she could have that conversation with the Wilders before they got wind that she'd been out on a date with another man. She would never get the answers she needed from them if that happened.

Chapter 34

Early October

The closer it got to Sunday, the more stupidly nervous Laurie became. Almost to the extent that she could have rung Pete and told him that she didn't want to go, except that she didn't have his number. She was looking forward to it and dreading it at the same time. She tried to talk some sense into herself, that this was dinner, he wasn't asking her to marry him. It might be their first and last proper date. But still, she could feel the portcullis over her heart begin to rattle, squeaking open a little as if someone had sprayed the cogs with WD40.

She also put her money where her mouth was and booked a holiday. She was working from home on Thursday and broke off from the murky details of Mr and Mrs Pullman's divorce to pull up holidays for singles on her iMac. There was a whole industry devoted to finding them which was both encouraging and daunting, because there was too much choice. She projected herself into a resort, dining alone, eating alone. Did people go on those sorts of holidays primarily to hook up with other singles? She didn't want that, she didn't want people to look at her and think that because she was alone she was lonely and they must remedy that. And who'd guard her handbag on the beach if she went for a swim in the sea? She knew she was drilling down into stupid minutiae, but it suddenly seemed like the worst idea. Then she went into Alex's office to take his atlas from the shelf to find out where Ikaria was in the world and discovered the oddest thing. There, spread on his desk and open at the page with 'Mr and Mrs Wilder' scribbled in the top corner, was the Figurehead Winter Cruises brochure. She must have put it there – who else? But she couldn't remember doing anything with it other than replacing it in the desk cupboard.

'You trying to tell me something, Alex?' she asked, lifting it up, listening hard for the slightest breath of air or noise, but there was nothing. She took it through to the lounge, looked at the cruise he had chosen for them. Twelve nights in Norway: February, four ports. It left the day after the anniversary of the crash. She wanted to be away from here at that time of year, as far away as possible.

A cruise would work for her as a solo passenger. Meredith had once told them, in one of her many post-sailing anecdotes, that it was an ideal way for a single person to travel. They'd be safe and secure and could mingle as much or as little as they liked. 'Put it this way, if Brendan snuffs it, it wouldn't stop me going back on board,' was what she'd actually said once.

Alex had been planning to make her dream come true to travel to the Arctic and see the Northern Lights, the huskies and reindeer, the hotel made out of ice, the mother-of-pearl clouds. He wasn't bothered about cruising or seeing them himself but he'd been intending to book it as a gift for her. She couldn't remember him ever choosing a holiday based on her likes alone before. It touched her deeply.

She rang the Figurehead Cruises booking line and was put immediately through to a sales agent.

'Hi there, I'm just enquiring about cruise number FH710,' Laurie said to 'Ruby'. 'It's a twelve-night one to Norway, in February.'

A sharp intake of breath. 'Ooh, they get booked up very quickly,' said Ruby. 'But let's have a look for you.'

Laurie heard a lot of taps and then a lot of silence.

'Well, that's surprised me. We do have a cabin, balcony, for two, is it?'

'No, just me.'

'There would be a hundred per cent surcharge on that cruise for single occupancy I'm afraid,' said Ruby. 'It's a very popular one. I'm absolutely stunned we have a cabin left. There must have been a very recent cancellation.'

Ruby gave her the price. It wasn't cheap.

'Can I think about it and ring you back?' said Laurie.

'You can but this cabin will have gone, trust me,' said Ruby.

What's stopping you? You can afford it and you'd be safe and not have to worry about who was looking after your handbag because you won't be dipping in any sea. The voice in her head sounded like Alex's now. She could imagine him standing there, egging her on, the way he used to when she couldn't quite decide whether or not to buy shoes or a handbag because they were indulgences she didn't need. *Just do it,* he'd say. And she had, every time and never regretted it.

'Hello? You still there?' prompted Ruby.

'Yes, I'll take it,' said Laurie.

'You can put a deposit of fifteen per cent down and the balance will be due—'

'I'll pay everything now,' said Laurie, reaching for her credit card. That way she wouldn't back out.

She put down the phone half-proud of herself, half-wondering if this was the most expensive mistake she would ever make in her life.

She rang Bella to tell her about the holiday and Bella had said 'good for you' and that it would give her something fabulous to look forward to and told her that of course she hadn't made a mistake at all. Why would she want to be in the UK at that time of year with all sorts of bad memories when she could be fulfilling a dream, stamping something lovely onto February instead? Then Bella had squealed with delight about the forthcoming date with Pete. She was flying off to Spain for a ten-day break the next day to celebrate Stu's thirty-fifth birthday but wanted all the details on her return. Bella sounded more excited about it all than Laurie did.

Laurie went to Meadowhall on Saturday morning to buy something new to wear for tomorrow. The last time she had been there was when she needed an outfit for Alex's funeral. It had been hell. Shopping for clothes for that purpose had knocked the stuffing out of her. She'd bought a wildly expensive dress, coat and shoes that she put in a charity bag the next week because she would never wear them again and didn't even want them in the house. She'd bought a hat too, to cast shade onto her face so people wouldn't see her crying and she cried a lot that day, quietly, her tears a constant stream that refused to stop. It had been Meredith and Brendan who insisted on a traditional dress code for the mourners. Alex's funeral had been very sombre and very black. *He wouldn't have wanted this*, she'd thought as she stared at his coffin in church. He would have wanted Blur blaring out of the speakers not 'Lead, Kindly Light', but Laurie had deferred to his parents' wishes for the service because she felt they needed to have some control more than she did. Organising their only son's funeral helped them survive it as bringing his ashes home, putting them at the side of her bed helped her.

She bought a blue flowery dress in House of Fraser with three-quarter sleeves, simple in style without being frumpy, and a matching pair of blue suede wedge sandals. As she waited in the queue to pay for them, she thought back to how she'd been in the run-up to her first date with Alex. Bella had gone shopping with her for something wow to wear and she'd been giddy as a kipper. She'd even bought new lingerie. It all felt like so long ago, another lifetime, one that lay behind a locked door with no key.

On the Sunday, she stood in front of the full-length mirror in the bathroom and checked her reflection. She'd had to reapply her lipstick because her hand was shaking so much that she'd gone over the lip line twice. She was wearing her hair loose tonight. It was so long, swishy and shiny that she'd once been asked by a teen in town where she got her extensions done.

Seven o'clock came and went. By five past seven Laurie's nerves were taut as harp strings, when she saw the arc of headlights swing into the drive.

'Oh crikey, he's here,' she said aloud to herself. She couldn't have been more jumpy if armed police had turned up.

She picked up her bag, her keys, said bye to Keith Richards and hoped that he'd wish her luck. Her new shoes felt too unfamiliar, too high; she had a vision of herself falling over, landing in a heap at Pete's feet. Pete – her *DATE*. The word screamed in her head as if Meredith had said it.

Pete was out of the car and was walking towards her. 'I'm so sorry I was late. There were roadworks at the end of the street and I thought the traffic light had broken, it took so long to change and I don't have your number, do I, otherwise I'd have rung to tell you.' He was waffling, flustered as she was. He wondered if he should kiss her hello, rejected that as an idea, felt it was too much. She looked even more beautiful with her hair down. He was right not to kiss her hello because he might not have let her go.

He opened the car door for her and she tried to get in gracefully, a simple act hampered by anxiety. She sat as prim and proper in the passenger seat as a teacher from *Little House on the Prairie*.

As he got in to his side of the car Pete knocked his head on the door frame.

'I have never done that in my life before today,' he said, mortally embarrassed by his clumsiness and she laughed then. The ridiculous bubble of tension that was enclosing them had popped.

'You look lovely,' he said.

'Thank you,' she said, overriding the stupid compulsion to bat away the compliment. 'So do you.'

He did too. Black trousers, jacket, pale grey open-necked shirt. A waft of his aftershave reached her nostrils. It wasn't one she recognised, but it suited him. Bergamot, lavender, fresh, light. Alex wore Rose Smoke by Atelier, heavy, spicy, exotic.

'Hungry?' he asked her.

'I've had nothing since breakfast,' she answered, not saying that she was too nervous to eat.

Pete grinned. 'So I'm in for an expensive night then.'

'I fully expect to pay my way,' said Laurie.

'Oh, shush. You can get the next one.' He'd meant it as a joke but began to worry that she'd think he was too pushy. What a minefield. He hadn't even felt this nervous on his first proper date with Tara. Then again, she'd been so self-assured and clear in her attraction to him that he knew exactly where he stood.

'Any fires since Wednesday?' asked Laurie.

'A small one in a wood. Homeless person decided to have a barbecued rabbit and ended up burning down his tent with all his worldly possessions in it, which admittedly weren't much.'

'Poor soul,' said Laurie. 'We don't realise how lucky we are, do we?'

'We had a whip-round for him. Got him a new tent and some bits. And yes, us people who live safe and secure in houses are lucky. I saw you had a For Sale notice up on yours. Any idea where you'll move to?'

'None,' said Laurie. 'The plan is to sell first and then maybe move into something rented until I decide. No point in getting in a chain or setting my heart on a property only to lose it because I can't get rid of mine. I'm not expecting it to go quickly. The Elms, two doors away took over four years to sell.'

'That's my next job,' said Pete. 'Tara wanted a new house but I prefer old ones. I like a project.'

'Handy, are you?'

'I am.' Pete puffed out his chest. 'Dad was a joiner and we learned at his knee. Griff drives his wife mad by constantly building things and knocking them down. She once came home from work to find her kitchen ripped out because he was bored.'

'Blimey.'

'The one he put in in its place more than made up for it but she was slightly aggrieved at the time.'

Silence fell between them, a companionable one though, like a thick, warm blanket as they drove on towards the quiet hamlet of Lower Hoodley where Firenze was situated, on the lip of a nice big splodge of Yorkshire countryside.

Once it had been a run-down establishment called 'Burgerov' until the chef there bought it and turned it into a fabulous eaterie which served Italian food that tasted so authentic, it was as if it had just been flown in from Puglia. Pete considered himself lucky that he'd managed to get a booking as it was always busy, but fortune had favoured the brave on this occasion.

'I was nervous about tonight,' admitted Pete, as they pulled up into the restaurant car park. 'I don't think I've been as nervous about going on a date since I was fourteen.'

'Me too,' said Laurie. 'But then I reasoned a first date after what we've been through was bound to be a toughie.'

She smiled at him and he felt his heart give a jaunty bounce inside him.

'I'm not any more though, I'm looking forward to it so much,' he said, then his stomach gave a well-timed keen of hunger which made them both hoot. 'Come on, Laurie, let's kill all the daft anxiety and stuff ourselves stupid.'

Laurie had eaten here once before, with Alex, though it wasn't quite grand enough for him. Not *expensive* enough, because Alex equated cost with quality, but Laurie had enjoyed it far more than many of the stupidly priced places

Alex had taken her to. The restaurant had undergone a total refurbishment since she had been there last: now it featured crumbly stucco walls, a blue ceiling with soft white clouds painted on it, pale warm lighting and a stunning central fountain which provided a backdrop of gentle water sounds and changing colours. They were inside a building in South Yorkshire in mid-autumn, but could have easily been outside on the seam of the Mediterranean on a balmy summer evening.

While they perused the menu, Pete sipped from a pint of Peroni and Laurie from a glass of Shiraz.

'Lovely, isn't it here?' she said.

'You'd think you were abroad, wouldn't you?' replied Pete. 'It wasn't like this the last time I came. They've done it all up.'

'I love Italy.'

'Me too. I've booked some time off work early next year. I don't really want to be around for ... you know ... the anniversary of ... so I might take myself off to Venice. There will be a carnival on.'

Laurie opened up her mouth to tell him that she had booked a holiday too, when the waiter arrived to take their order and they had to quickly turn their attention back to the menu to decide.

Later they would both try and remember what they had talked about and could only recall snatches, yet they filled almost three hours chattering about their jobs, the people they worked with, family, school, life. Conversation between them coasted on smooth, easy tracks. They shared a dessert, neither able to attempt a whole one. A tiramisu, two spoons. Talk waded to deeper water over coffee.

'When did Alex die?' asked Pete.

'The sixth of February,' Laurie replied. 'There was a crash on a dual carriageway. A lorry driver was texting, skidded on black ice, crossed the central reservation and thudded into a lot of cars. If Alex had been sitting in the passenger seat he would have survived because he took the impact on his side. The consolation, if there is any, is that the emergency services said it would have been so quick he wouldn't have known anything about it. I'm not sure if I believe it, but I hope it's true.'

Pete swallowed. He'd died on the same day as Tara, he hadn't realised that. A flash of the scene lit up in his head. There in the carnage, a black Mitsubishi crushed on one side, unscathed on the other. *That* was her fiancé's car? The same crash? It had to be. Something stopped him probing more; they would be swallowed up by the detail if he did. Their tentative steps forward would count for nothing as they would be dragged by the scruff of the neck backwards into that dark February night. That was a conversation for later, not now.

Laurie felt a gloom begin to lower itself onto her and she shimmied it away. 'Anyway . . .' she began, at the same time as Pete said, 'I'm sorry, my fault, I shouldn't have asked.'

'For another time,' said Laurie. It was inevitable that talk would stray to the thing that had brought them together.

'Eat your truffle,' said Pete, pushing the saucer of handmade chocolates towards Laurie. She picked one up and popped it into her mouth and her face registered delight, like a much younger girl having an illicit treat. He thought again how pretty she was, softer with her hair down; a few more dates along the line and he would reach over and thread his fingers through it. For a moment he had a brief insight into what his father must have felt when his mother had gone and he'd met Cora: that life had changed and a different hand of cards with a different queen had been dealt to him. Memories would not keep him warm at night and he had too much love banked inside him not to share it.

It reminded Pete to tell Laurie that he wouldn't be at Molly's Club on Wednesday.

'Dad's sixty-five. He's having a party in the garden. He's going to crank up the firepit for the cold and set up the drinks table under the pergola in case it rains.'

'Oh, how lovely. Fingers crossed that the weather holds.' Laurie bit into a dark truffle this time and a tumble of soft toffee dribbled down her chin. She laughed and wiped it away quickly, bashfully, and Pete pictured himself leaning over and kissing the caramel from her lips.

'Have you bought him something nice?' she asked.

'A snooker table,' he said, not opening up the can of worms by telling her how his father's partner would consider that a thrown-down gauntlet. *Cora* and *crash*, both C-words he'd avoid tonight. 'You'd be welcome to come.' He said it without thinking. 'I mean I know it's a bit early to start introducing you to the family. I mean – oh lord, that sounded a bit full on. If you're at a loose end . . .'

Laurie rescued him from his gabbling. 'That's very kind of you, but you concentrate on your dad, it's a family day. You can tell me all about it next time we see each other.'

'Yes, okay, I will.' The good bits anyway. Probably not about Cora's reaction to the surprise gift.

The bill came, which Pete snatched up. Laurie opened her mouth to protest.

'Save your breath. It's not happening,' he said.

'Do you ever watch *First Dates*?' said Laurie. 'When the woman lets the man pay and they get to the "do you want to see this person again?" line and she says no. I think that's so mean.'

'Would you say no?' asked Pete, suddenly emboldened.

Laurie took in a deep breath, suddenly emboldened. 'No.'

'No "no" or no *no*.'

Laurie smiled. She'd smiled a lot this evening. She smiled a lot around this man. 'I'd say yes, I would like to see this person again.'

'Good, because it's a really awkward figure to halve.' Pete pretended to wipe sweat from his brow. He had a sudden vision of the old TV advert where the man from Del Monte said 'YES!' Yes she wanted to see him again, in the context of a date. He didn't want to feel this thrilled but it was bulging dam walls within him.

He waved his Visa at the waiter who glided over with a card payment machine, thanked Pete, wished them both a good night.

'Let me at least pay the tip, Pete,' offered Laurie.

'It's done,' said Pete. More than ten per cent, she estimated as he put down some notes onto the bill plate.

They stood, he held out his arm and she took it, felt the firmness of the muscle through his jacket. They walked out into the cool October air. The sky was deep blue velvet and the moon a fingernail snip, edges crisp. A beautiful evening, a memorable evening. The start of something, they both sensed it.

Once again Pete opened the car door for her. Laurie thought he might be the type of man who would keep to this behaviour. This wasn't a veneer that would wear off; consideration was part of his DNA. She imagined he would be still opening doors and offering his arm to his wife after many years of marriage.

They turned into her drive. The real end of the date. Would he attempt to kiss her? she thought. *Should I attempt to kiss her?* he thought.

Laurie dashed away the awkward moment before it came, or rather delayed it.

'Would you like a coffee?' she asked him as he applied the handbrake.

He wanted to squeeze every second out of this evening, but played it cool. 'I could manage a quick one I suppose,' he replied.

She opened the door, switched on the light, invited him to follow her through to the kitchen where she put the kettle on.

'Thank you for the most wonderful evening, Laurie,' said Pete, sitting at the island. 'I have so enjoyed your company.'

'Thank *you*,' Laurie replied. 'I've had a lovely time too.' She brought the coffees over, sat on the stool next to him. She noticed how his large hands made the mug look much smaller than it was. They sipped their drinks in a silence that seemed to shimmer around them like a forcefield. It didn't matter that neither of them said anything, just being there together was enough, each wondering if the other felt it too, but at the same time knowing they did.

'Look ...' eventually Pete spoke, a nervous drag of his fingers around the back of his neck '... I don't know what this is between us. I don't know if we are bound by circumstance or if it's something stronger but I think you're great, Laurie, and this ... this feels so right, it sounds bonkers but it's true. I can't wait to see you again.'

Later she would remember that she moved to kiss him first. She would recall in glorious detail how his hands closed around her back and held her as if she was something precious. She would not remember how they got up the stairs but she knew she must have led him to the second bedroom, not hers, not in the room where Alex's ashes sat. They fell onto the bed there undressing each other urgently but tenderly too. She had never done this before, never slept with a man on the first date. Pete had slept with Tara on the first night he met her but it wasn't like this, two pieces of something drifting around in the orbit of life, chancing together, fitting as if they were whole a long time ago but had been smashed up, separated and together they became repaired. As if they had found each other. As if they were meant to be.

Chapter 35

7 October

A bee buzzing around the room woke Laurie up with a start, then she realised that it was the alarm on her phone with its insistent drone. She had to shift Pete's arm to roll towards it and the action woke him up too. His eyes told her that he'd been in as deep a sleep as she had.

Laurie pulled up the sheet to cover her nakedness.

'Morning,' she said meekly.

'I don't want it to be,' he said and pulled her back against his chest, savouring the tickle of her hair, the scent of her faded perfume, sleep and sex.

'I have never done that with anyone on the first date,' she said.

'I don't care if you have or not, it's not my business,' he said and placed a kiss on her neck that seemed to ripple through her whole body.

'I wish I had now, what have I been missing?' she said in a New York accent and it made him laugh.

She didn't want to move. She wanted to stay in this warm

circle of his arms and replay the last twelve hours over and over. She'd recognised a desire in him to touch and be touched, to give and be given to in their lovemaking. It was gentle, intense, generous all at the same time.

Then the alarm on Pete's phone, which was somewhere on the carpet, went off as well.

'Nooo,' he protested. 'Go away.'

'Day shift?'

'Yep, first of four.'

'I'll get a quick shower. Time for a coffee?' she asked him.

'Last time I said yes, look what happened. Yes yes yes yes.'

She laughed again, reluctantly prised herself from him and darted out of the room, naked and self-conscious now.

By the time she had showered and dressed and gone downstairs, he had a mug of coffee waiting for her.

'I didn't know if you wanted me to make some toast for you or fry you some eggs but I didn't want to go poking around in your cupboards,' he said.

'This is fine,' she said, wondering if her smile would ever close. The muscles were starting to ache in her face.

Laurie was preened and perfumed and Pete was creased and smelled of bed and she thought he was perfect.

'I didn't plan to do that,' he pointed upstairs.

'I could tell.'

His eyes rounded. 'Was my technique that bad?'

She threw back her head and laughed. 'It was great.'

In reality Laurie had always thought sex a little overrated. It was nice, exciting sometimes but what they'd had last night felt like nothing she'd ever experienced before, not even in the early days with Alex – or in the post-his-affair days when sex had been something she craved on a primal, heightened, desperate level to prove that he was all hers. But last night there had been more hungers satisfied than mere bodily need.

'I've written down my number for you, something which I should have done long before now,' said Pete. 'If you ring me, I'll store yours.' He handed her a page from the pad that sat by the telephone with his mobile written on it.

'I'll do that now.'

He heard the phone in his back pocket register her call. Even that refreshed his smile. 'So I will see you again?' He needed to ask once more, this time in the cold light of day.

'I'd like that.'

They walked to their cars together. He kissed her good-bye. Held the back of her neck, his lips falling softly onto hers.

'I'll ring you and arrange something, after ...' he said.

'... After your dad's party.' Laurie finished off his sentence. Pete's brain was already starting to suggest places that he would take her.

But he wouldn't. Because his dad's party would be the end of them. Before they had even begun.

Chapter 36

When Pete got home, Pong greeted him indignantly as if he knew his shift patterns and he wasn't at work last night, so where the hell was he? He butted his head insistently against Pete's hand as he ripped open a pouch of cat meat as if to hurry him along and then turned up his nose at it when it was in the bowl.

'You're sulking aren't you, Pong?'

Pong let loose a short, sharp meow which seemed to answer that he was.

Pete sat at the table, pulled out his phone, searched.

He hadn't ever read any of the press pieces about the accident before because he didn't want to be piqued by any skewed details. He typed in *crash, February, Tara Ollerton* and entries appeared: 'Horror Crash, Multi Vehicle Pile Up', 'Texting Driver Causes Deaths', 'Six Killed in Horror Smash'. He scrolled through the lead article in the *Yorkshire Post*, tried to avoid the accompanying photo of the half-crushed black car, but his eyes were too quick and registered it, transferred the image to his brain. The name in the main part of the article: *Alexander Wilder, 30*. Laurie's partner.

His name appeared on the list of the dead next to *Tara Ollerton, 30.* 'She wasn't thirty until the next day,' he growled at the screen. The details always mattered, the small things in life, the tiny considerations and kindnesses, short words such as please or thanks had a power much greater than their size. Tara died in her twenties, not her thirties; that one day's difference made it seem all the more poignant.

Alex, Tara, Laurie, Pete. The four of them joined by fate and bound together by a force he didn't understand but still, he felt the weight of its significance.

Griff rang when he was parking up at the fire station.

'Morning, bro,' said Pete. 'How's your bits for crabs?' A common greeting when they were in a playful mood.

'Quick one. Just ringing to firm up the plans for Wednesday,' said Griff. He sounded flat, not engaging in the joke.

'Everything all right?' Pete asked.

'Yep. Dad's invited a load of people. He and Cora had a bit of a bust-up about inviting Auntie Sue but she's on holiday anyway. All we have to do is turn up. He's ordered champagne, glasses, you name it and he's thought of it. Lucy's doing the cake so at least he's left it open for us to sort out one surprise for him.'

'Two if you count the table.'

'Oh yeah, forgot about that.' Griff sounded distracted. He sounded not like Griff.

'Candles and matches?' It was set in stone that Nigel had a cake. Julie-Anne had always made him one. Lucy had taken over that duty now. Cora wasn't the baking type unless it was for her ladies' group; then suddenly she remembered how to grease a tin and produce the best Victoria sponge in the county.

'Got them on the list,' said Griff. 'What time will you finish work?'

'Krish is jumping in for me so I'll be ready from about quarter to six.'

'Okay, we'll swing round for you then.'

'Let's just get a taxi then we can all have a drink.'

'I'll drive, I don't want to drink,' said Griff, his tone clipped.

'Griff. You okay? You sound . . . not okay.'

'Stop asking me, I've told you that I am fine. See you Wednesday,' said Griff. The line went dead.

Laurie came home just after lunch that day. There were builders in the offices above and she couldn't concentrate with all the drilling so brought some work back with her. As she turned into the small estate, she noticed Brendan and Meredith's Lexus parked on the road, unmanned. She sped up the drive in time to see Meredith about to put something through her letter box, no sign of Brendan. This, Laurie decided, was her chance to ask what she needed to.

Laurie's brakes squealed her arrival. Meredith turned quickly, hoping to avoid a confrontation; Laurie moved faster to force her into one.

'Meredith, how are you? It's lovely to see you.' Laurie smiled weakly, hopefully, making it as hard as possible for Meredith to be nasty to her, easier to engineer without Brendan there to bolster her.

Meredith's steps halted. Ingrained civility obliged her to answer, however curtly.

'I'm fine, thank you.'

'Are you coming in for a coffee?' asked Laurie. She needed this conversation so much she was suddenly anxious how far she would go to get it.

'No. No thank you. I just brought you something. Here.' Her hand shot out, holding a long envelope, her handwriting on the front, one word – *Laurie*. A letter probably, containing Meredith's thoughts about her.

'Meredith, please come in,' said Laurie, not taking it. She unlocked the door. 'Say what you have to me face to face. Please.'

Maybe it was because Laurie's obvious despair brooked no refusal that Meredith gave a slight nod, acceded, stepped into the house behind her.

'Please sit down. Tea or coffee?' asked Laurie in the kitchen, moving quickly to fill up the kettle before Meredith could change her mind.

'Tea please. Milk, no sugar.'

'I remember.'

Laurie lifted one of the two mugs that were on the draining board. She put coffee in the one that Pete had drunk from for herself. She dropped a teabag into a teapot because Meredith would not have drunk tea that had been brewed in a cup. At home she still used loose leaves. Laurie took out one of the bone china mugs which had now been jostled to the back of the cupboard.

Meredith sat stiffly on a bar-chair at the island. 'I see you've put Fairview up for sale.'

Laurie didn't want to get to a showdown about the house and the monies that would come from it before she had her answers. 'Yes, but I think it'll take years to sell. I may even change my mind and take it off the market.'

Laurie brought the teapot over to the island. Poured a

little milk in the bone china mug, Meredith had milk in first always and the tea had to be barely brewed. Total waste of a teabag, Alex used to joke.

'How are you?' she asked again, noting how unpreened Meredith was by her own standards: her face devoid of make-up, her hair not its usual perfect golden billow.

'We had some bad news,' said Meredith and slid the envelope across the island. 'We intended to give it to Naomi on her wedding day, so it's as you gave it to us. The cheque. Please open it so I know you have seen it.'

Laurie opened up the envelope and just as Meredith had said, the cheque she had written was in it, nothing else. No covering explanatory note.

'Oh my. What happened?' asked Laurie.

'Naomi called it off. Jefferson had been unfaithful to her and she found out. We are deeply disappointed in him,' replied Meredith, not holding eye contact, as if it was her shame as well as Jefferson's.

'I'm so sorry to hear that,' said Laurie.

'Alex would have been very angry. We thought of Jefferson almost as a son,' said Meredith, a tremble shaking her words. Another son lost to them. Now, close up, Laurie could see the dark circles under Meredith's eyes, further hollowing of her cheeks. The wedding had taken their focus away from their loss and now it had shifted back to it.

'Is there any chance they'll . . . make up?'

'Of course not. Naomi has pride and dignity,' said Meredith indignantly, the strength suddenly returning to her voice. 'Jefferson has made his bed and he is lying on it with another woman. Anyway, there it is. And I . . . owe you . . . an apology,' she added, as if the words had been squeezed out of her through a mangle.

'For what?' That confused Laurie, because it wouldn't have been easy for Meredith to admit she was wrong about anything.

'We consulted a solicitor about this house. He explained that when two people take out a mortgage like the one you and Alex had, the family of a deceased partner have no direct claim on the equity.'

Laurie pressed down on a rising vortex of anger. They had really been to see a solicitor about this? She drank some coffee, hoping it would drown the retort sitting in her mouth, said instead, 'Don't worry. You've been through a lot.'

Meredith sipped her tea, gave her head a little shake as if the tea was all wrong.

'Yes we have,' she agreed. She did not say, *and so have you.*

'Meredith . . .' *oh please don't get up and walk away* '. . . you posted some of Alex's bank statements last month through the letter box.' Laurie forced herself to appear casual, uncritical. 'Do . . . do you happen to know why they were sent to your house? Did Alex say?' A heartbeat began to thump in her head with a growing momentum.

Meredith considered the question before speaking. 'From what I recall, he said that he was planning something and he didn't want you to catch wind of it.'

Remember, she will put a spin on this, Laurie warned herself.

'Is that what he said exactly? It's important, Meredith, please,' she said, appealing to Meredith's decency, her sense of right which her chagrin would not eclipse.

Meredith thought again. 'He said he was planning a surprise and so it would be best if we didn't mention it, and just to keep them there and he'd pick them up when the coast was clear. He wouldn't be drawn on explaining. In fact he was a little irate with his father when he asked. Not that we believed Alex was into anything dodgy, but it seemed odd and he should not be keeping secrets from his parents, we thought. Then some time after Christmas Alex said not to expect any more as he was having them sent somewhere else.'

'Somewhere else?'

'Yes, that's what he said, but he wanted us to keep the statements there for now. So we did. I forgot about them, if I'm honest, until we found them when tidying out the understairs cupboard.'

What on earth did all this mean? Laurie was more bewildered than ever.

Meredith then put the mug on the island in the same way that someone would place down their cutlery on a plate to denote they were finished. She picked up her car keys and then surprised Laurie with a question of her own.

'Did Alex buy us a cruise?' she asked.

'Pardon?'

'We have a significant wedding anniversary next February and Alex asked us if we would like to go on one. He said he would arrange it as our present.'

Laurie's heart plummeted. That's why he had scribbled *Mr and Mrs Wilder* in the brochure. He was looking for his parents, not for them.

'I don't think so, Meredith, I'm sorry,' said Laurie. 'I haven't seen any paperwork for it. I just saw a scribble in a brochure and I presumed he was planning it for us.'

Meredith gave a brittle hic of laughter then. 'Alex wouldn't have gone anywhere on a ship, he thought they were ridiculous. We have even offered to pay for you two to come with us and he point blank refused. Did you know him at all, Laurie?' A point scored, offsetting her disappointment.

She stood up then. 'Thank you for the tea.' Laurie stood also; her legs felt unsteady and the heartbeat was booming in her brain now.

'I'm sorry to hear about Naomi. Please send her my warmest regards,' she said, fighting the crumble in her voice.

'I can see myself out,' said Meredith, stinging from Laurie's grace, but Laurie followed her out of the kitchen all the same, in the wake of her cold silence.

'Take care, all of you,' said Laurie. It wasn't returned. Then as Laurie was about to close the door on her, Meredith turned and said, 'I have to say, Laurie, that we find it very difficult to believe that Alex was going to propose to you on the night he died. We have thought long and hard on this and we know he would have told us first, out of respect. On that I have absolutely not one single doubt. I'm sorry.'

She didn't sound sorry at all.

Chapter 37

9 October

There was something not right with Griff and Lucy, Pete felt it as soon as he got into the car on the day of Nigel's party. It was as if they had been replaced by aliens who looked exactly the same, talked and walked like them but who couldn't replicate the souls within their skins.

'Of course I'm all right, stop asking will you,' snapped Griff.

Lucy turned in the passenger seat to address Pete. 'He's just stressed about being in Cora's company, as am I. But tonight it's about your dad and not her and not us, so let's put on our party faces.'

Pete sat quietly in the back next to the box containing the cake. A three-tier three-flavour extravaganza covered in 65s. Lucy had put a lot of work into it, but that was Lucy all over.

Two miles down the road, Pete noticed Lucy looking at him in the vanity mirror on the turned-down flap.

'What are you smiling at?' she asked.

'Nothing,' he fibbed. The truth was, he hadn't stopped smiling since Sunday night. Sal at work had asked him the same question and he'd given her the same lie, as if he didn't want to tempt fate by talking about it. About them. Laurie had been constantly on his mind – either as a presence hovering in the background when he was busy at work, or fully in the forefront when he was free to dwell on her. She had sent him a text that day hoping that his dad had a lovely party and she was glad the rain had stayed off. He'd replied immediately, like a teenager, telling her thank you and asking if she wouldn't mind giving Molly his apologies that he wouldn't be there, and to save up any stories of Maurice and Yvonne's outings and Sharon's new dog for the next time they met. His bed had felt extra lonely for the past two nights.

Griff's driving indicated his mood, snappy, with last-minute braking. Pete noticed Lucy's grip on her seat suggesting she had spotted it too but didn't want to mention it.

Ordinarily Griff would have been wearing something totally unsuitable and jolly; badges bearing the number 65, banners stapled across him as if he were in a beauty queen pageant, but today he just looked flat and angry. Pete was glad that Lucy was there, ready to pour oil on his troubled waters. He could feel disquiet emanating from his brother in waves, as he were a mini power station generating them on max.

There were more cars than usual on Northwood Avenue, which indicated they weren't the first to arrive by any means. It didn't help Griff's mood that everyone seemed to have left large gaps between cars which were still too small to parallel park his Passat into. The side gate was open for a change, which rescued them from the indignity of knocking and having to be admitted by Cora, after a delay long enough to prove a point.

Luck was on their side, weather-wise. There was no rain, no wind, only the still chill that often comes with October, but two giant fire pits in the garden – and ready supplies of blood-warming alcohol – were working hard to reduce guest-shivering to a minimum. The skies were dark and clear, the moon just a little fuller than it had been on Sunday night. *Sunday night.* All roads, for Pete, led back there. A new moon, a new phase.

The garden was bustling with friends, neighbours, old work mates. Young people in black and white livery were circulating with trays of drinks and canapés; the summer-house doors were thrown open and Pete could see a buffet set up in there. Nigel, it seemed, had catered for the five thousand. Lucy bobbed into the kitchen to put some presents and her cake down on the work surface. Pete stood with Griff, who was scanning the guests.

'I'm looking for Cora so I can avoid her,' said Griff. 'In case you're wondering.'

'I wasn't,' Pete pretended not to have noticed.

'My boys.' Nigel broke loose from a huddle of two couples and headed towards them, fizzing as much as the contents of the glass he was holding.

'Hellooo,' he said, enclosing them in a clumsy hug, sloshing his champagne all over Pete's arm in the process. 'Where's my gorgeous girl?'

'If you mean me I'm here, Nigel,' said Lucy, appearing on cue. Nigel abandoned his sons to cuddle her. 'Oh, I do love you three,' he said. 'You're my whole world.'

Pete expected Griff to say something on the lines of 'It's

a good job Elsa didn't overhear that', but he surprised him by saying nothing.

'Happy Birthday, Dad,' said Pete and handed over a bag of presents. A silver engraved snooker chalk holder, chocolates, a bottle of his favourite brandy and a book about being an old fart. The decoy presents. They'd tell him about the snooker table tomorrow.

'I've put ours in the kitchen,' said Lucy. 'Do you want to come and look at your cake?'

'I do,' said Nigel and took her arm. At Pete's side, Griff stiffened, assumed the stance of the human equivalent of a Pointer and Pete traced his eyes to Mr and Mrs Moore, the rose bush.

'She's fucking cut it back even further,' the words ground out between his teeth.

'Griff, have a drink, relax and forget about it for tonight,' said Pete. 'We can leave the car here and get a taxi home. You've both got tomorrow off, I've booked tomorrow off, so what's stopping you?'

'I'm not drinking, I'm driving.' Griff was resolute.

Pete whipped a glass of champagne and one of orange from a circulating waitress's tray and pressed the latter into his brother's fingers. He spotted Cora in the summer house talking to a couple. Her head rotated in their direction, as if she knew she was being discussed, but without the slightest acknowledgement of them.

'Nigel loves the cake,' said Lucy, newly returned. 'We'll bring it out later with the candles lit so everyone can sing Happy Birthday to him.'

Griff didn't respond, just strolled off to take a closer look at Mr and Mrs Moore.

'What's wrong with him, Lucy?' asked Pete. 'Because something is.'

'Just stuff, playing on his mind,' she answered. She sounded worn out and Pete was reminded that she had hospital appointments looming to sort out her fallopian tubes. Griff, he knew, would be worried sick about her.

'I'll go and talk to him,' said Pete and wandered over to his brother. Griff was facing away from everyone and when Pete got near to him, he realised the reason for that was because Griff was standing with tears falling from his eyes. The rose bush represented something else to Griff, that was clear, but Pete knew that his brother didn't respond to pushing.

'It'll grow back stronger than ever,' said Pete, clapping him on the shoulder. 'I'll sneak up in the middle of the night and water it with extra-strong Baby Bio.'

Despite himself, Griff gave an involuntary chuckle. 'You're a good bloke, Pete, have I ever told you?'

'No. You've told me I'm a bellend and a gonk on numerous occasions, but you have strangely bypassed the slop.'

'Does it hit you hard sometimes, Pete, about Tara, when you're not expecting it?' said Griff, giving his eye a surreptitious wipe, making it look like a scratch.

'Always when I'm not expecting it,' said Pete.

'I was thinking about Mum today making that cake for Dad's sixtieth, can you remember? The snooker table. It was a work of art. She *got* Dad. She put him first and he put her first, but *her* . . .' His lips pulled back over his teeth.

'It's his choice, not ours, mate,' said Pete. 'Mum's gone and none of us wants to see Dad lonely for the rest of his life.'

'I'm not sure I could move on if I lost Lucy,' said Griff. 'But I want you to. You deserve to find someone who really loves you, Pete.'

Griff was scaring him now. He was trapped in something dark, riddled with fear and frustration and pain. Tomorrow, he'd insist on taking him out for a pint and he'd get to the bottom of it, thrash it out, bash whatever was really troubling him into some perspective.

'Come on, Cora's moved out of the summer house, let's go and get some of those posh vol-au-vents that Dad's spent our inheritance on,' Pete said, driving his brother forwards.

The food offering was superb but Pete knew that if his mother had been alive, it would have been better and everything homemade, from the buns to the bunting hanging on the pergola. He loaded his plate with pastry, his hunger seemingly signalling a renewed appetite for life. Griff picked up a couple of things half-heartedly, Lucy nibbled on an egg triangle.

'I thought you'd dive in like Tom Daley,' said Pete. Griff usually stacked a buffet plate as if he was gearing up for a fortnight's siege.

'Give it a rest will you, babysitting me,' said Griff, moving away from his brother and mumbling something about going to the toilet. Lucy rubbed her forehead and sighed.

'Tomorrow, I'm taking him out and he's going to talk to me,' said Pete.

'He's okay, really,' said Lucy, her smile weak, which was not how Lucy usually smiled; tonight she was on dipped beam rather than full headlights.

Pete's eyes skimmed across the garden; everyone seemed to be enjoying themselves, chatting, eating, drinking. Cora and Nigel had their heads together and she was talking at him as if she was telling him off. He thought he ought to go over and say hello to her, disarm her.

As he wound his way over, he heard snatches of the exchange between them.

'I don't want them using the inside toilet, Nigel, there's a perfectly acceptable one outside. No one has any reason to go in the house.'

'Hello, Cora,' said Pete, sticking on a friendly smile. 'Really nice party for Dad.'

'Just having a domestic about the loo arrangements,' said Nigel with a tipsy grin on his face.

'There's already mud on the hall carpet and I'm not getting out the Vax,' continued Cora, ignoring Pete.

'Okay, I'll clean the carpet tomorrow but I am not asking guests to use an outside loo.' Nigel flapped his hand as if swatting the argument away, like a persistent fly.

'Yes you will. Or rather you can buy another because you will never get that carpet looking the way it was this morning. It's ingrained.'

Cora moved off and Nigel grimaced. 'I'm in proper bother,' he said with a giggle. 'But today, I don't care. You all right, son?' Nigel turned suddenly serious. 'I worry about you two boys. I know you're all grown up but you never stop worrying about your kids.'

Griff appeared from the house and crossed Cora's path, blanking her and she turned, eyes knives in his back. A smile appeared on his face as if triggered by a switch. He was pissing her off just by breathing the same air and he was glad about it. He waved over at Lucy to join them.

'Dad,' said Griff, putting his arm around his father. His voice was loud, meant to be overheard. 'We couldn't bring your real present. You can keep it at mine until you have a space for it but it's all yours.'

Lucy flashed a look at Pete. They'd arranged to say this tomorrow, in order not to inflame Cora.

'What do you mean?' said Nigel. 'You've given me my presents.'

Pete was aware of Cora hovering nearby. Griff wanted her to be inflamed.

Griff reached into his pocket, pulled out his phone, clicked on photos and found the one of him and Lucy sprawled on the table that they'd taken with a very long selfie stick.

'Here you go. Happy snookering.'

'As if,' said Nigel with a chuckle. His eyes zipped between the three of them and the picture. Shock settled on his features. 'No. You're joking. You are bloody joking.'

Pete shook his head slowly. There was nothing for it now but to go with the flow. 'We're not. Happy sixty-fifth, Dad.'

Nigel cheered, threw his hands up in the air. 'Yes,' he shrieked like a little boy, drawing the attention of everyone. 'They've only gone and bought me a snooker table.'

Claps and laughs broke out, but Cora's expression was murderous. She stomped towards the house, cutting through anyone in her path and Pete found himself hoping she'd stay there, let his dad enjoy himself for one night without her casting a fat, black cloud over the proceedings. He'd intended to take advantage of not being the designated driver and have a few beers but he changed his plan. He'd remain sober and keep his eye on things. There was an undercurrent to the evening that he wasn't happy with.

Lucy brought out the cake with the sparklers fizzing on top and everyone sang 'Happy Birthday' to Nigel and after he had blown out his candles, there was a chorus of 'Speech, speech.'

'Well thank you everyone,' began Nigel. 'I welcome you all to my . . . our house. Where is Cora?' He craned his neck, but she hadn't made a reappearance.

'Toilet,' someone yelled and chuckled.

'I'll shout then so she can hear me,' said Nigel. 'It wasn't so long ago that I didn't think I'd be here to cebrelate . . . er celebrate—' guffaws all round '—this birthday because I thought I'd have died of a broken heart. But I'm here with my family and my friends and I'm smiling again. You've just got to live life until you stop, haven't you?' People nodded, *hear hears* ensued, whistles and hails of agreement. 'We've had a lot of sadness in a short time in our family and I'd like you to raise your glasses, not to me but to loved ones. In the hope that sadness will never defeat them because we are nothing without love, and with love we can get through anything. To loved ones.' He lifted his glass and Pete noticed that Lucy was upset, fighting not to cry. He put his arm around her, pulled her into his side and wondered why the usually attentive Griff wasn't doing this instead of staring at his parents' rose bush.

After the cake had been carved up and people were tucking in to slices of it, Pete went into the kitchen to get some tap water. He opened the cupboard where the tumblers had always been kept and was startled by a voice from behind.

'What are you doing?'

He turned around. Cora.

'I'm just getting a glass of water.'

'There are glasses outside and a tap on the wall,' she said, a snap in her voice.

There were no pint glasses, he'd checked and no one was drinking water at this party, least of all out of a spidery hosepipe tap. 'Thanks.' He'd do without rather than annoy her further. He took a step towards the door but she barred his exit.

'Why have you bought your father a snooker table?'

Presented with a chance to take the heat out of the situation, he grabbed it with both hands.

'The honest answer? Because it was an offer that Griff couldn't refuse and he knew that Dad had always wanted one. You needn't worry, Griff will keep it in his garage for him.'

'It will not be coming into this house,' she said, pronouncing each word precisely.

Pete kept his tone level, calm. 'As I said—'

Cora didn't let him finish. 'You did this to cause trouble, didn't you?' She fixed him with her small bird-like black eyes that looked permanently cross.

'No, we didn't, really.' He couldn't let this continue. His dad loved the woman, they had to try and get on with her. He didn't want his dad suffering repercussions from this night. Pete sighed. 'Look, Cora, I have never treated you with anything but respect.'

'Huh.'

'I know it must have been hard for you coming into a close-knit family, but we have one thing in common and that is we all want Dad to be happy. And we want you to be part of the family thing, especially when children come along.'

'Close knit?' There was a smile dancing on the corner of her lip, twisting her face. 'You lot – close knit?'

She was dangling a hook full of bait and he couldn't resist rising to it. 'What do you mean?' he asked her.

'There aren't going to be any children. Hasn't anyone told you yet in this "close-knit" family of yours?'

Pete swallowed hard. She was trying to wound. She obviously had only half the facts about Lucy's condition but he wasn't going to discuss that with her now and put her right.

'I'm sure that there will be—'

She sliced off his words yet again. 'Your brother's tests came back. He can't have children.' As if in slow motion, he watched her tongue snake outwards to dampen her lips before disappearing again, as if she wanted to savour the words sliding from her mouth. 'And neither can you.'

Chapter 38

Laurie was all too aware that her attention kept drifting off in Molly's Club, picturing how Pete's dad's party was going. She thought how proud his dad must feel having two strapping sons who loved and cared for him so obviously and she wondered if one day that might be her.

At first it was Alex who had been the keener of them both to have children. Meredith and Brendan had been loving parents and Alex and Naomi had grown up with their support and the best they could give them. Laurie had been less keen to have them, because she hadn't had that family dynamic to use as a template. Neither had she ever felt the burning desire to carry a baby inside her, though she would have – for him, and fully embraced motherhood. But she'd always thought there were too many children out there already in need of a family to love them, look after them. If she and Alex hadn't, for whatever reason, been able to conceive, she would have pushed him to adopt a child, the way she wished she'd been adopted by a couple who would have painted a bedroom pink for her, taken her to the park on a shiny new bicycle, been there waiting for her to come home from school in a warm house that smelled of dinner cooking. She knew first hand that just because people could have children, didn't mean they should.

Laurie would probably have been taken into care if one of the neighbours had reported that she was so often in the house by herself overnight. Maybe if the curtains at their windows would have been dirty and they'd had a sofa rotting in the front garden, the De Veres might have slipped onto the social services radar but outwardly all looked respectable. Laurie was well fed because she fed herself well and beautifully turned out because she'd been using a washing machine and an iron since long before she became a teen. Laurie always handed her homework in and revised for her exams because she loved school and she knew what she needed to do to go to university and study law. And Paula De Vere, with her pretensions of being middle class, was always so friendly with everyone and glamorous, a product of self-funded elocution lessons and lucky tasteful bargains in charity shops. No one suspected that her daughter wasn't cared for because she was – but by herself.

Alex's dream of a houseful of mini-mes wore through Laurie's reservations and she knew that with him she could build the sort of family she'd never had, a second chance to have a happy home with the excitement of Father Christmas calling and hunting the Easter Bunny's eggs in the garden. Her children would never have to make themselves crisp sandwiches for tea or hunt around finding coins to put in the meter to fend off the dark and cold. She'd tortured herself in the weeks after he died that she might have altered the path of their fate if she'd thrown caution to the wind, come off the pill and let nature take its course; then perhaps she wouldn't have felt that slight shift in their relationship, like a ship testing the weight of its anchor. She'd told herself she was imagining things, Bella had told her she was imagining things, but she wasn't. There was a reason why he'd had his bank statements sent to his mother's house and though she knew Meredith had been trying to hurt her with her line about Alex not letting them in on the secret that he was going to propose, she was right – it was exactly what Alex would do, include his parents in the big decision. So what was he going to tell her, the 'something important', if not that? She had pinned all her hopes on it being the proposal, because if it wasn't, then it might have been something bad, a shock not a surprise. Why had he said *tell* and not *ask*? There was a hairline crack in their relationship that his passing had widened to a fissure, a canyon, taking him to the other side of something that couldn't be breached. Had he died not being hers? Had he died being someone else's?

'It'll be odd for Pete going to a party without his wife there,' said Maurice openly, but looking at Laurie as if he had unconsciously bracketed them together. 'I do hope he's all right.'

'I wish I were sixty-five again,' said Mr Singh, who was as much at home behind a teashop counter as he ever was in an operating theatre.

'I never liked birthdays,' said Yvonne. 'At least not my own. I always made sure my daughter had a nice day but no one ever bought me a cake with candles on it and I always wanted one.'

'What, never?' asked Sharon.

'Never.'

'Then we will certainly remedy that this year, dear Yvonne,' said Maurice, quite vociferously. 'When is your birthday?'

'April Fool's Day,' said Yvonne and gave a little laugh. 'You couldn't make it up.'

'I shall make a note in my diary and I'll take you to Betty's in York for afternoon tea, if you'll let me,' said Maurice. 'There will be cake coming out of your ears by the time we've finished.'

'What a treat,' said Laurie. She didn't ask Yvonne if she'd ever been to Betty's before because she could guess what the answer would be.

'Really?' said Yvonne. 'You would?'

'We should go before, give it a trial run, in case you don't like it, then we could pick somewhere else instead.' Maurice smiled at her and Yvonne beamed back at him in such a way that it was as if it was the first time she had properly smiled. Laurie felt overcome with a blast of emotion. Some people had seen such little kindness in life, it was pitiful.

She wished she had gone to the party with Pete, wished politeness hadn't stood in her way and to hell with it being too soon to meet his family. If anything, they both knew that you shouldn't sit around and wait, but take what was on offer when it was offered. She wondered if he would ring her that night on the pretext of telling her all about it. She had felt like a bottle of shaken champagne since Sunday, and that she was taking sure steps forward into something special and sweet and new, a landscape devoid of unanswerable questions and uncertainty. It was as if a giant hand had reached down and scooped her out of a dark pit at a speed that barely allowed her to catch her breath.

She couldn't wait to see him again.

Chapter 39

From behind Pete, Lucy seemed to fly forwards out of nowhere. A Lucy he didn't know.

'You fucking bitch,' she said, throwing herself at Cora, both hands locking into the older woman's hair. Cora began to shriek, slapping defensively, before Pete had a chance to dive forwards and drag the possessed Lucy away. Cora was staggering, her usually perfect lacquered iron-grey hair sticking out at angles like a befuddled scarecrow's, a scratch already rising on her cheek; Griff now striding towards them with a purpose that Pete didn't even want to guess at. Pete pushed Lucy at him, jammed himself between the warring factions.

'Look after your wife,' Pete yelled at his brother, his world a fast-growing blur of madness. Nigel came hurrying in, following his son.

'She told him,' said Lucy, face pushed into Griff's chest.

'What's going on here?' asked Nigel.

'Ask your poisonous bastard girlfriend,' boomed Griff, arms wrapped tight around a near-hysterical Lucy.

'That was assault,' said Cora, palm flat on her face. 'Nigel, ring the police.'

'Oh dear God, Cora, what have you done?' said Nigel, his voice weighted with distress.

'What have *I* done? Have you seen what—'

'Cora, shut up, just bloody shut up.' The words rang loud. Pete had never once heard his father shout at his mother, never mind swear. It was almost as if he hadn't spoken but was channelling someone else, someone much more angry than he could ever be.

'Dad, we're going home,' said Griff.

'I'll tell everyone to go home,' said Nigel, sobered instantly.

'No, you mustn't,' insisted Griff. 'You carry on, this is your big day and you don't want all this to be the residing memory of it. You must promise us that. Please. We'll talk tomorrow.'

'You've spoiled everything,' Cora spat at him.

Griff advanced, finger extended hard like a weapon. 'No, you have.' Nigel and Pete shifted positions to keep him apart from Cora, for his sake, not hers. 'Don't worry,' said Griff to them both. 'I'm not going to touch her. I wouldn't soil my hands.'

'Griff.' Lucy's tone was pleading, lost. He returned quickly to her, held out his hand to Pete.

'Pete, come with us,' he said.

'Son—'

'Dad, we'll talk tomorrow. I want to get Pete and Lucy away from here.'

'Dad, go and be with your guests like Griff says,' Pete insisted in a softer tenor. 'I'll ring you tomorrow.' He pushed back Nigel's protestations, turned his attention to his brother.

'Give me the keys, I'll drive,' he said. He had no idea what was happening but Griff was in no fit state to be in charge of a car.

Pete walked silently out behind his brother.

Not a word was said on the journey to Griff and Lucy's house. They sat in the back, holding each other, bound together by something awful. Pete felt as spaced as if his one glass of champagne had been spiked. His gut was twisted. He tried to concentrate on driving and not what Cora had said to him about not being able to have children. A cheap, bitter shot from a woman who couldn't take her drink? A perfectly aimed one, even if it was a lie, because the bullet had hit his head and screwed with it.

Pete parked, took the key from Lucy's hand, opened their house door. No one offered to put on the kettle when they filed into the kitchen, sat down on the chairs at the table there, emotionally beaten. Griff and Lucy looked like soft toys who'd had the stuffing pulled from them and then been pounded by a heavyweight boxer. Pete had never seen Griff like this, not even at their mother's funeral and he'd been battered by grief then.

'What's going on?' prompted Pete.

'We didn't know how to tell you,' said Griff. 'I was going to leave it until after Dad's birthday.'

'Tell me what?' said Pete. He was scared now. One of them was ill. His head prickled with anxiety at the words about to damage him.

Griff pinched the top of his nose hard, he left fingernail marks when he withdrew his hand.

'We went for test results. We can't have kids,' he said eventually.

A breath of relief. 'Dad told me,' said Pete. 'But he said that they might be able to operate and—'

Griff cut him off. 'Yes they can – on Lucy. But that won't help us because I've totally outdone her in the infertility stakes. *I* can't have kids. Not ever.'

'Is that what they said?'

'Oh yes.'

Pete swallowed. 'Are they sure?'

'I have something wrong with my Y chromosome, I can't remember the terminology for it. A deletion on it, a germline mutation I think they said. It's been present from birth. They've done extensive tests, they're quite certain of what's wrong. At first they thought I had a very low sperm count and I was building up to the deep joy of telling you that you might need to get checked out for that in future in case you had hopes of one day having a family the size of the Waltons, then this bomb landed. And . . . oh fuck . . .' he paused, took in a long ragged breath '. . . because we're identical twins, you have it too.'

'Well how can that be right?' said Pete with a hard laugh of incredulity, 'we know it isn't. Tara was preg—'

'You can't have kids, Pete. It's impossible. They're one hundred per cent sure of that.' Griff's voice was full of pain both for himself and equally for the brother he loved.

A silence followed that seemed to swallow Pete up; a black hole that allowed nothing in, nothing out until it had done with him and then spat him out again.

'That was my baby in Tara, don't you say it wasn't,' he said at last.

'It couldn't have been, mate.' Pete watched a tear slip down his brother's cheek, lodge in his beard and glisten. Another followed and another.

'They're wrong.'

'They're not, Pete.' This from Lucy, her face drawn, pale. 'I wish they were. For all our sakes.'

Pete stood up. He kissed the head of his brother and Lucy's cheek and headed for the door.

'Stay here with us,' said Griff. 'Don't go, I'll worry about you doing something daft.'

Pete turned. 'I swear I won't do anything like that. We've had enough misery but I need to be alone to think and you need to be alone with your wife.' He strode out. His world turned upside down for the second time. And this time he wondered if it could ever be righted.

*

Cora made a remarkable recovery after Pete and Griff had gone. She patted her hair back into place and applied a bag of frozen peas to her face to reduce the swelling, then took her compact out of the kitchen drawer, sat and dabbed some powder onto her cheek. She'd won, her smile said. A victory worth the price of a small injury. There could be no coming back from this for the brothers Moore. She then announced to Nigel that his family were not welcome in the house again or she would leave.

Nigel, who had sat at the kitchen table watching her five-minute repair transform her before his eyes, raised his head and spoke.

'Then leave.' His voice barely above a whisper, but heavy with repulsion.

Cora pulled her head back into her wrinkly neck.

'I beg your pardon, Nigel?' she said.

'Throw your tenants out of your house and move back to

where you came from. I don't want you in *my* house another night. Another hour, actually.'

She waved away his words with an impatient flick of her wrist.

'You're being ridiculous. You saw what happened there. How can you defend it? You have no idea what I've had to put up—'

Nigel slammed his hand on the table like a gavel and Cora jumped and tellingly, she also shut up.

'You know, Cora, I have never witnessed evil before today, but that was pure and simple evil what you did, and to a boy who didn't deserve it and has been through enough without hearing that – from *you*. My God . . .' Nigel threw himself from the chair then, paced to the far end of the kitchen '. . . I thought, I really thought we could overcome things with a bit of patience. I knew you were putting your stamp on the place, I defended you always until you cut down the rose bush because *I knew* you'd done that out of sheer callousness, to hurt my family. When we got together, you weren't *this* Cora. Was it an act to reel me in? I kept on hoping the Cora I first met would turn up again, the real Cora. But this . . .' he threw his open palm in her direction '. . . this is the real one isn't it, one capable of a level of malevolence I have never seen before and hope I never see again.'

Cora sat silently, letting him expunge. She clutched at the thin row of pearls around her neck, a present from Nigel. He loved buying presents, wanted to spoil someone the way he had spoiled Julie-Anne. But this woman wasn't Julie-Anne, and after what she'd done tonight, Nigel didn't know who or what she was. He felt nothing for her. Nothing. His feelings for her had been dashed away with one clean sweep.

'You would always pick blood over water, Nigel,' she said eventually.

'That's a cheap line you have used too much, Cora and it won't wash with me this time.'

She changed tactic because her usual get out of jail free card wouldn't help her any more.

'I will apologise,' she relented stiffly, driven into a corner.

'That'll undo everything, of course,' he said with a scoff.

From outside a raucous chorus of the Hokey Cokey reached them, reminding them of the context they were in. Cora jumped on it, knowing Nigel wouldn't want to cause a scene, would be quicker to forgive.

'It was an overreaction on my part, that's all.'

He saw her skin blotching underneath the pearls.

'Well, I'm not overreacting,' replied Nigel, calm, steady. He had said everything that he needed to, any more would be superfluous and would change nothing. 'Take a suitcase, get out of my house and I'll have everything else of yours packed up by the morning.'

Cora blinked heavily. She had expected the promise of an apology would blow it all away. She had mistaken Nigel's kind manner for weakness, not strength. She needed to play for some time and affected a wavery voice.

'I have nowhere to go that quickly, Nigel. I think we should sleep on it.'

He remained a brick wall to all of her shots. 'If you don't, I will get the police, who will escort you out in full view of everyone here, don't think I won't, because I don't give a bugger what the neighbours think. And, while we're on, if you so much as mention Lucy's name to the police, I'll make sure that every one of your sponge-eating ladies' group cronies hears exactly what you're capable of. Now, I'm done.

Your stuff will be in my drive at seven in the morning. Don't even bother thinking about knocking on my door because you won't get in.'

His mind clear, incisive, he strode out then towards the key rack in the hall, wrestled the front and back door keys from her keyring, pocketed them and returned to the kitchen.

'I'll give you one hour,' he said, and rejoined his party.

*

A text pinged on Pete's phone.

> **Hi, only me. Hope the party is going well and you're having a great time. Missed you tonight at the meeting. Wasn't quite the same. Yvonne and Maurice left the meeting arm in arm. My best – L xx**

More fool them, said Pete to himself. He didn't reply and switched off his phone.

Chapter 40

10 October

Pete barely slept. He felt both physically and mentally sick. Sick to the stomach of the situation he was in, because it was like being plunged back into a different pool of grief, a colder, harsher one. He needed to keep his thoughts herded, the job he had decided to do firmly in his sight or he would crumble and there would be nothing left of him to reconstitute. He set off for Bannen's Financial Holdings, asked to see Tara's old boss, laid on the importance. He said he'd wait. He wasn't in a mood to be sent away. Wendy McCulloch wasn't someone Tara had liked much and Pete got the feeling it was two-way traffic. He parked himself for twenty minutes in reception with a complimentary coffee and eventually Wendy McCulloch came out to greet him. She was much younger than he'd imagined, a whizz-kid probably. Tara was always rather disparaging about those. She'd not been very kind about Wendy.

'How can I help you, Mr Moore?' said Wendy, shutting the door of her office behind them.

Pete reached into the carrier bag he had brought and pulled out Tara's eighteen-month desk diary. It was one of the items he hadn't thrown or given away. He'd stored it in a box with the pregnancy test, photos, her bright red lipstick, the Burberry scarf he had bought her for Christmas. Her wedding ring.

'I need to know where my wife was on certain dates. It's important,' he said.

'I'm not really sure if we can do that, Mr Moore,' said Wendy with a sympathetic half-smile.

'Can't or won't? Sorry.' He apologised immediately for the snap in his voice. 'It's really important,' he stressed.

'Why do you need to know?'

'Insurance policies.' He'd thought of this in the car to give as an answer if asked, vague enough to be believable. 'They're asking me questions about where she was when she died. If she was working or not.'

Wendy drummed her fingers on the table, the equivalent of thinking dots on an open phone message. Then she stood. 'Can you bear with me?'

'Yes of course.'

Wendy left the office. He saw her through the glass windows approach an older woman with grey cropped hair sitting at a computer and talk to her. They both glanced at Pete. The older woman took out a large book and Wendy returned with it.

'Gilda arranges the client appointments, she prefers the old-fashioned approach of paper and pens,' said Wendy.

'The day she died, Tara was supposedly with a client in Leeds,' said Pete. 'It was the afternoon of February sixth.'

Wendy flicked through, found the date, checked the information on it. 'I can't . . . see . . . ' she began.

'What does it say? Please tell me,' said Pete.

'Tara wasn't working that day. She'd booked it off,' said Wendy.

It had to be a mistake. He said as much.

'No, Gilda is very reliable and she has recorded here that Tara asked for the time off the day before, for an emergency dental appointment that apparently was going to take up the whole day.' Her tone was slightly scathing.

Pete's brain began to spin. There had been nothing wrong with Tara's teeth.

'I don't understand this at all,' said Pete, hand raked in his hair. 'We walked out of the house together that morning. She was dressed for work and she was carrying files. She said she had a full day of appointments. I'd told her to drive carefully between them because snow had been forecast and she said that she would.' That was what happened; he had no doubts about it. 'Are you sure?'

'Gilda doesn't make mistakes.' Wendy said it in such a way that indicated Gilda's word was reliably gospel.

She looked at the man sitting in front of her, his brow creased as he tried to make sense of the information she had just given him. She wasn't a fool, he wasn't asking for insurance purposes. For a moment she was poised on the horns of a dilemma, but the truth would always carry a greater weight for her. He should know, she decided.

'Were you aware that Tara had a verbal and a written warning because of false appointments?'

'What do you mean?' asked Pete.

'Tara was very good at her job, well respected and a brilliant deal-closer. She brought us in a lot of clients who wanted to invest in us. She earned the firm a lot of money, which is why we were patient with her. She went AWOL quite a lot in the months before her death. She'd miss turning up for some appointments and tell us she was in places that she wasn't. Gilda made a follow-up call to one of them to find that Tara had lied. So Gilda went on a detective trail because once she gets her teeth into something, she doesn't let up. She uncovered a few of these transgressions. Between you and me, Gilda has a form of OCD that makes her quite invaluable where accountability is concerned, but maybe doesn't endear her to her workmates that much.'

'Did my wife have close friends here?' Pete asked, but he doubted it. Tara didn't make women friends easily. Not close friends, not friends she'd ever confide in. Not outside her family.

'Not really. Someone mentioned, the other day in fact, that they'd worked with her and known her for years but didn't *know* her at all. She didn't let people in very easily, did she? Always played her cards close to her chest.'

What hand was she playing that she needed to do that? came the thought.

Pete opened up Tara's diary. He'd marked a couple of dates, ones where he could remember she'd been late home, moaning about clients. *July twenty-sixth, James Brecht, Buckmans.* November fifth had stuck in his mind. It was the only day that *A. Bakewell – Paragon Holdings* could do so he'd gone alone to Jacko's bonfire party. *January fifteenth – Edinburgh.*

'Could you cross-check these for me, please?'

'Paragon Holdings? I've never heard of them and I'd know about them if they were potential clients,' said Wendy, opening Gilda's book again, flicking through the pages.

'Yes to Brecht, yes to Edinburgh, that was a one-day financial course with an overnight stay booked for her. No to the mysterious Paragon Holdings, as I thought. Tara rang in with a migraine that day.'

She didn't get migraines. And she'd been in Edinburgh for four days. She had definitely been there because she'd sent him photos of the city and texts saying how boring all the presentations were. He'd dropped her off at the railway station and picked her up there four days later.

Pete stood up, stuffed the diary back in the bag. 'Thank you, Miss McCulloch.'

Wendy McCulloch stood up and held out her hand. She'd made the right call telling him the truth but she gained no joy from it. Her disclosure did not extend to the office gossip that Tara must have been having an affair though. It was a conclusion that others apart from her had reached but she hoped for the sake of this man, who looked bewildered and *felled,* that they were wrong on that.

'I'm sorry, Mr Moore. I don't feel as if I've helped you at all.' She held on to his hand and he felt the warmth and sympathy in it. Wendy seemed nothing at all like Tara had described. When she let go she said, 'I'm sorry for your loss, Mr Moore. I can't imagine what you must be going through.'

'No, you really can't,' he said and left.

Pete checked his phone in the car to find a flood of messages and voicemails. From Griff, from his father, from Laurie.

Laurie here. Everything okay? X

Pete, ring me, I'm worried about you lad. It's your dad. I'm driving over.

Dad's chucked that bitch out. G. Ring me

P where are you, ring me. G

P will you ring Dad, he's worried sick. Then ring me because we are as well. G

Pete I'm here at your house. I need to know you're all right. Dad

When he got home, it was to find his dad parked outside, having a snooze in the front seat. Pete rapped on the window and Nigel woke up with a start.

'Where the bloody hell have you been?' said Nigel. 'I've driven all over the place looking for you. Let me ring Griff and tell him you're still alive. He's worried daft.'

Pete unlocked his front door while his father and brother communicated. Nigel then went inside, opened up his arms and closed them around his son. His father was inches smaller than Pete was now but Pete remembered being a boy, looking up at him, feeling his dad's arms enfold him like a papa bear's.

'Put the bloody kettle on,' said Nigel, letting go and sitting down at the kitchen table. 'What a day already and it's not even lunchtime.'

'How did your party go after we left?' asked Pete.

'I went through the motions, lad. I couldn't wait for it to end. I was sick of holding up a smile I didn't feel. I should have gone with my first instinct and chucked everyone out.'

'You couldn't. Let people think you had a great time. You didn't want loads of questions coming back at you to spoil it after all the trouble you'd gone to.'

'There was nobody at that party more special to me than you three.'

'We insisted and we meant it.'

'I know, I know. But today couldn't have come soon enough.'

Pete put a mug of strong black coffee down in front of his dad and Nigel held it in his hands, as if he was drawing strength as well as warmth from it.

'I was so upset when Griff told me what was wrong and what it meant for you. I had to talk to someone and so I told Cora. I never imagined in a million years she would have done what she did.' Nigel looked distraught. His eyes said he hadn't slept much.

'She's your partner, of course you'd have told her.'

'Was,' amended Nigel. 'I couldn't forgive what she's done. And I certainly could never forget it.'

'I need to find out whose baby Tara was carrying,' said Pete, his voice hard. A coat of armour was growing around him, toughening by the second.

'Why, Pete? Why would—'

'I didn't want to think that she was seeing someone else and so I kept believing other reasons why we weren't right.' His voice broke as the anger inside him landslid into despair. He'd lost his baby all over again, the baby that never was his. He'd rather not have known, imagined a future that he could have had, not one that he never would have.

Nigel put his arms around his son once more, as far as they would go, laid his head on Pete's, felt the wetness of his boy's tears dropping. The little lad he took fishing and whose knee he stuck plasters on. He could see him now in the fireman's outfit Julie-Anne had stitched because she couldn't find one to buy that looked good enough, sitting in the crate he'd converted into a fire engine for him, scrapping with his brother about who was driving. His tears hurt him more now than they ever did when he was a child.

'Let it out, lad. Your dad's here.' And Pete did.

Eventually they subsided; Nigel sat back down, kept his hand over his son's as if he needed to take from the contact as much as he had to give.

'What happened to Cora, then?' Pete asked.

Pong jumped up onto the table, butted his head against Nigel's cheek. Pong was always assured of a warm welcome with 'grandad'.

'I'd tried to make it work, even kidded myself that it was ... but it wasn't. I haven't dated a woman since I met your mother and that was so easy, because it was right. I knew I'd never find that sort of love again, but I always considered myself lucky that I'd had it once. I'd have been content with a lesser love, companionship – on both sides. Whatever Cora and I had it was certainly lesser, but it wasn't love. It was too much hard work for it to have been that.' He made a huff sound, devoid of amusement. 'I told her to pack a bag, be out within the hour and come back for the rest of her stuff this morning. I was up at the crack of dawn getting her things together and I put them on the drive. I even dragged that bloody dressing table of hers down the stairs. Rage doesn't half give you wings, never mind that Red Bull stuff. It'd all gone by half-seven when I looked out of the window to check and that's the end of that.' He gave a groan of anguish. 'Your mother will be spinning in her grave. This is down to me, you getting hurt like this,' he said.

'No it's not you, Dad,' said Pete firmly. 'It really isn't. Don't you be thinking that. Griff would probably have told me today anyway. It's done now and I would always have had to be told the truth.'

'I'd never see you upset like this, lad, never. Let it go and move on. You deserved better. Swear to me you will.'

'Okay, I will,' said Pete. 'I swear.' He was lying, but he didn't think a great big hand would come out of the sky and smite him down for doing so. He didn't even care if it did. Oblivion would be preferable to this state of hell his mind was in.

Chapter 41

When his father had left, Pete took out Tara's diary, sat at
the table and studied it with a microscopic eye. He wished
there was a key to all her scribbles and initials because it was
a hopeless task really. Lots of entries for nails, hair, pedicure,
Botox – he didn't even know she'd had any of that. There
were flowers next to a date in March and the letter R – but
he recognised it as Ria's birthday. Same for Alana's but with
an A. Next to his own birthday in November only a 'P &
G', no drawing. There were red drops in some of the corners – a record of her periods, presumably. He counted
forwards from when the last set of drops ended – she was
three weeks late when she died, if her diary was to be
believed. Feb 5th: 'Buy T'. *Buy test?* He was grabbing at
straws, it could have been turmeric, tapioca, tangas . . . anything, but 'test' made sense. Their anniversary wasn't even
noted and that stung. Her card to him had been a 'Dear
Husband' one; she'd chosen one without a verse, signed it
'All my Love, Tara xxxx'. He knew now why it had been
dutiful and not emotional. He'd cooked for them, the full
works, they'd made love that night at her instigation – but

why wouldn't she have marked that the day had any special significance for her? Periodically there was an image of what looked like a flat pie. *Lunch? If so who with?* None of these before July last year. July 24 marked with a large asterisk ... *why?* Other mad doodles, he couldn't decipher. Why was she even writing in code? They didn't have the sort of marriage where they checked up on each other. They had no need to, there was trust.

His brain ached. There was nothing of note in the diary, he would have found it. As he leaned back in his chair and stretched, his phone pinged. A message from Laurie.

Hello. Sorry to pester but is everything all right? X

Lovely Laurie. He'd ignored her previous texts because he'd been on lockdown. He replied.

Apologies. I've just been really busy with something. All okay. See you soon. Pete x

He hit send and within a minute there was a reply of a smiley face, the antithesis of what he felt. Why couldn't he excise the last couple of days from his memory like a tumour, he thought? On Monday morning he was walking around as if he had springs on the soles of his feet and now he had on boots of cement.

Wendy McCulloch's words revisited him. *She didn't let people in very easily did she?*

She didn't, but she did let her family in. If Tara was going to confide in anyone, it would one of her sisters. It would be Ria.

*

The sound of the doorbell. That all-too-familiar Ria *brum-brum*. Pete had texted her, asked if she was free that evening after work for a chat, could she come over? Of course she could. For once, he was ready to open the door and invite her in.

She looked super-tanned and was wearing a white shirt, white jumper thrown over her shoulders and white jeans to set it off.

'Wow, you look amazing,' he said, aware that he had resorted to the kind of rhetoric that would appeal to her. He would use her tonight, for once. People used him so it was payback.

She primped her hair, smiled, handed over a glittery gift bag with number 65s all over it. 'It's for Nigel. I forgot to drop it off before I left for the hen do – idiot.'

'I'm sure he'll be delighted.' He bent to kiss her cheek and was enveloped by her scent – Tara's scent – and it made him feel sick. 'Coffee?'

'Love one. Been dashing about trying to catch up ever since I flew in this morning. Had to go in to work straight from the airport. That's the problem with having time off from your own business. And staff always miss something in your absence that you have to sort out as soon as you get back.'

He boiled the kettle, prepared two mugs.

'How was Tenerife?' he asked.

'Hot.' She fanned her face as if the sun had followed her home.

'I can tell.'

She beamed. 'How did the party go? Did Nigel have everything he should have for his special day?'

Dear God.

'Well, he had cake, a crowd, champagne . . . fireworks.' He couldn't resist.

'Oh I love fireworks. Eek.' She shrieked as Pong leapt up on the table, seeking attention. 'Go away, Pong. Go on, shoo.'

Pete lifted the protesting Siamese and put him in the lounge and closed the door. He never would have done this usually, but he could be forgiven once. He didn't want Pong ruining Ria's expensive jumper, he needed her on side.

'Here you go,' he said, passing a mug to her while trying to ignore Pong's pitiful yowling and glowering at them through the glass panel of the door.

'Thank you,' said Ria. Her teeth looked ultraviolet against her tan.

Pete tried to dredge up some small talk even though he wanted to lean over the table and bawl in her face, 'WHO WAS MY WIFE SCREWING BEHIND MY BACK, RIA?' He needed to keep his powder dry, shock her into revealing what she knew. Tara would have been desperate to show off to someone, share the salacious details with them.

'It was lovely of you to invite me over,' said Ria.

'Well I always seem to be too busy or knackered to talk so I thought I'd remedy that,' he replied. 'I've been having some counselling.'

'Jackie Crawford?'

'No, I didn't go to her. I was told about a group, quite informal and that sounded more up my street.'

'Oh, how many of you go there?' She lifted her mug, sipped daintily.

'Five of us. Three older people and a woman my age who lost her partner at the same time as I lost . . . Tara.' Her name came out in a near-spit.

'Oh.'

He'd poked her jealousy button, which was easily

depressed and he would keep his finger on it for a touch longer. Play with her, like a cat tormenting a mouse.

'We have a lot of common ground, being younger than the rest. It's helped me a lot talking to her. She's a solicitor.'

He smiled wistfully, saw Ria's mouth contract as much as her enhanced lips would allow.

'Oh I see. And have you got . . . close to this woman?'

'God no,' said Pete, 'that would be a disaster. I'm not looking for anything like that. Not outside my familiar circle anyway.'

He watched relief break through her clouded expression, saw her eyes blink as her brain tried to decipher what he meant by the phrase 'familiar circle'.

'So she didn't go with you to Nigel's party?'

'No, I went alone. Well, with Lucy and Griff.'

'Ah, Lucy and Griff, how are they? It was lovely to see them the last time I was here.'

He couldn't hold off any longer. Pete felt his foot step on the travelator that would take him to the conversation he wanted to have. Needed to have.

'Not great, if I'm honest.'

'Oh, why's that?'

'They had some really bad news recently. Griff can't have children.'

Ria put down her mug, her face creased in sympathy. 'I'm so sorry to hear that. Tara told me last year that they were going to be checked out because they were having problems. We both hoped they'd find a simple fix.'

Pete felt his jaw tighten, his mouth dry up as if all his salivary glands had suddenly pulled down their hatches and closed their doors like townsfolk in a cowboy film did before a gunfight.

'Yes, he has a birth defect. Tests have shown it up so there is nothing they can do about it.'

'Oh my, that's awful. The poor loves.'

Now.

'And the thing is, because we are identical twins, I can't have children either.'

'Oh Pete, I'm so sor—'

He watched the realisation dawn on her face. Saw the sympathy segue to confusion, then something akin to horror. Even her tan seemed to pale. He held her gaze, defied her large doe eyes to leave his.

'So, Ria. The big question is – who was the father of my wife's baby?'

Chapter 42

Pete thought it would be much harder work to winkle something out of his sister-in-law than it was. She wouldn't have held up well in a serious interrogation. He watched Ria's mouth move over words unformed and when she eventually said, 'I don't know what you mean,' the denial came far too late to be credible.

'Ria,' his voice soft, pleading now, 'it might make no difference to anyone else, but it does to me. I can't live not knowing.' He reached across the table, took both of Ria's hands in his, felt her jerk a little at the contact and he hated himself for having to manipulate her like this. 'I know she was seeing someone else. She'd been in trouble at work for not being where she should; in fact she told me she was in Leeds on the day she died and she wasn't and that's been playing on my mind since the accident. She lied for a reason. Did you know she was having an affair?'

Again that denial after a telling pause. 'No, I didn't.' Then she added. 'Not really,' and he wanted to shake her and ask what 'not really' meant, because it could only mean that she did know but didn't want to tell him.

'Ria, who was he?'

'I don't know, I honestly don't.'

'So there was someone?'

'Yes . . . no . . . I mean no . . .'

Pete let go of her hands, pushed himself to his feet, leaned against the kitchen work surface, turned from her, tried another way into this maze, a brave one.

'I'm sorry, Ria, but I think you should go. And I don't want you to ever come back here.'

'Oh Pete, don't say that.'

'You have no idea how much my heart is breaking about this. Just go.'

He was lying. His heart was strong and pounding with anger. It would break when he stopped being angry so he needed to keep the fire inside him stoked.

He turned back to her when he heard a hiccup of a sob. Ria's hands were shielding her face from his view.

'I'm so sorry. I told her she was being stupid and cruel and an idiot.' Her shoulders were shaking but no teardrops were landing on the table top. Fake tears, but he wouldn't call her out on them now because the dam had burst on her words if not her eyes.

'Ria, tell me, for God's sake please tell me,' pleaded Pete. He broke off a piece of kitchen roll, handed it to her to wipe away her 'tears'. 'Don't get upset, love. None of this is your fault.'

'Thank you, Pete.'

Ria dabbed at the corners of her eyes with it. Her eyeliner was smudged. Real tears were making an appearance.

'I don't know who he was, I swear. All I know is that she said you and she were in trouble and she needed to get away from you to think. So she'd taken out a rental on a house. A cottage.'

'Where?' His tone insistent.

'Bakewell.'

'Bakewell in Derbyshire?'

Ria nodded. 'I asked her if she was seeing someone else and she told me not to ask that.'

'And what did you say?'

'I told her she was a fool and that she couldn't get better than you and what was she playing at. And she said that she knew that but she still couldn't stop it . . . she said . . .' Ria tapped her head, as if it would bring the thought to the surface. Pete waited impatiently.

'I can't quite remember the exact words but something like . . . she'd never stopped thinking about him. I got the feeling it was a man she'd been in a relationship with before.'

'Who?'

'That could be any number of people with Tara,' said Ria with a huh. 'But there was one man she was very much in love with. He was with someone when they met and he ended up leaving his partner for her. Then he went back to her and Tara was in a really bad place. She met you not long after and she seemed happy again. I presumed she was totally over him.'

'Where exactly is the cottage, Ria? Do you have an address?'

'I don't know it. I could take you there though.'

'You went there?'

She looked at him sheepishly. 'Just the once, but I didn't know—'

'Take me then.'

Ria's eyebrows attempted to bypass the Botox and ride up her forehead. 'What, now?'

'Yes, now.'

Ria opened her mouth to say something on the lines of 'don't be silly' but then realised that she had the opportunity to be in Pete's company for hours more.

'Okay,' she said. 'My car or yours?'

Pete drove. He needed something to concentrate on even though his mind was sifting through evidence in the background. Were the 'pies' in her diary Bakewell puddings? It was a ridiculous conclusion to come to but then again it made some sense. Were those the dates of her assignations with the man whom she'd 'never stopped thinking about'?

You were always on my mind.

The words crashed into his head like a wrecking ball. Is that why she cried when she heard that record? Was it *his* and Tara's anthem? Was that why it meant so much to her?

'When did you go to this place?' asked Pete, as they exited Hathersage village.

'I think it was three weeks before she died,' Ria answered. Now the secret was out, she was singing like a canary. 'We went out for lunch, she suggested a pub in Ashford in the Water which I thought was a bit out of the way, but she said she had something to show me afterwards. She wouldn't tell me what until we got there. I thought it was a holiday cottage for the both of you; she couldn't wait to show it off. When we went inside, it was then that she told me you were having problems and she needed somewhere to go and sort her head out. She said she wanted to be alone but there were men's things dotted around: trainers, shaving stuff. She never did think I was the brightest button and she tried to make out that they had been left by the last tenant. I told her that I wasn't stupid and asked what the hell she was doing and she said she couldn't help it. She was very emotional and you know that Tara wasn't like that.'

That was true. Thinking back, on her wedding day dancing with him, and then on their first anniversary when he'd given her the framed Elvis single were the only times he'd ever seen her cry openly.

'She said . . .' Ria's voice faltered, fearing she was saying too much, being disloyal to her flesh and blood, speaking ill of the dead.

Pete encouraged her to go on. 'Please, Ria, you might as well tell me everything now.'

'Tara said that she'd never been able to forget him and . . . oh yes . . .' More came back to her as the memory unravelled '. . . that she wasn't going to lose him again. She was getting a little angry by then that I'd uncovered her secret so easily and wasn't telling her what she wanted to hear. She could be quite hurtful when she felt criticised. I told her that she wouldn't find better than you and she said that—' Ria shook her head, not wanting to go on.

'You can't stop there. Just say it, Ria. It can't get any worse.'

'Okay, she said that I could have you soon enough. I felt so bad for you, Pete, when she said that. She sounded as if she was throwing you away.'

He could imagine Tara saying this. They'd hardly ever argued but that was because Pete hated rows, avoided them but they'd had a couple and he'd been surprised at how cutting she could be, spitting and spiteful, though she curled up around him like a cat afterwards. She was the youngest daughter and spoilt, used to getting her own way, but it didn't excuse anything. Hurt seeped through his anger and he fought it back. He needed to be strong now, strong and focused.

Eventually they came to Bakewell and Ria told Pete to slow down while she got her bearings, which was harder in the dark. They took a couple of false turns but then Ria recognised a postbox set in a wall and knew the cottage was at the end of the next narrow lane.

They parked up in the turning circle at the end and got out of the car. There was a rose arch over the gate and an overgrown wooden sign bearing the cottage's name, 'Crumbledown'. The gate opened with a quaint creak, the path was overgrown, the garden sad and neglected, unknowing of the circumstances of its occupants.

The cottage was detached, small, with weather-worn wooden windows. Its white frontage had seen better days; Crumbledown seemed an apt name, but he could guess at how much a rental in this area would cost and he had no idea how Tara could have afforded it on her salary – not alone, anyway. Pete peered in through a window: he couldn't see anything through the net curtains but he certainly wasn't going to come all this way and not gain entry. He'd take the rap if someone saw him breaking in, but Ria was searching for something over by a small garden pond covered in powdery green lichen. A stone, hollowed out, bearing a rusting silver key with a long shaft that wouldn't have looked out of place on a jailer's ring.

'I remembered her replacing it here,' Ria said, handing it over.

Pete knocked on the door, not surprised that no one answered. He put the key in the lock, had to exert some force to turn it and then put his shoulder to the door because the wood had swollen. There was a drift of post stacked behind it, adverts and brochures, free newspapers mainly. The odour of damp rushed at them as if eager to escape.

They stepped into a stone-flagged kitchen with an iron range and a small sofa set in front of it. He flicked the light switch and the low-wattage bulb gave off a glow that made the room look old-fashioned and wartime quaint. There was a table with a plastic cloth on it bearing a salt grinder and a pot full of cutlery that spiders had spun webs around.

'That's just a pantry,' said Ria as Pete took a step towards a door. 'The stairs are this way.'

He followed her forwards, poking his head into the next room. It was empty apart from a vacuum cleaner and a box with cleaning equipment and cloths in it, small yellow Marigold gloves. They walked up the steep carpeted stairs; to the right was a tiny white bathroom, to the left the only bedroom. Pete pushed open the door and saw that this was where all the occupants' energies had been concentrated. The bed wore top quality smooth white sheets, fat pillows. There were reed diffusers placed on various surfaces, Tara's go-to choice, Jo Malone, though the scent had long since dried up. An old wooden dressing table with a hair brush, a glass bowl full of cotton wool balls; Pete recognised the Mac lipstick, her brand of make-up remover. A man's toiletry bag snuggled up to hers, bearing an almost empty black and gold bottle of Atelier Rose Smoke cologne. He lifted it to his nose and the expensive scent punched his brain. *This* was what the father of her baby smelled like. On a long trestle table near the window was a record player, modern but fashioned to look vintage, a stack of vinyls. A record sat on the turntable, the cover propped up against the wall. Elvis, *Hits of the 70s*. The fourth track: 'Always on My Mind'.

He snatched open the door of the mirrored wardrobe and saw familiar sweaters folded up on the shelves, scraps of underwear, packs of tights and stockings. Her tiny Jeremy Scott Angel Wing trainers that he hadn't been able to find at home. On the bottom shelf, men's underwear: white Hugo Boss trunks, socks, green Adidas trainers, a beautiful pair of Valentino Garavani calfskin derbys. Hanging up: a grey suit, shirts, sweaters, the black Vivienne Westwood dress he had bought her for their last anniversary.

Ria was rifling through the drawer in the bedside cabinet. A charger, a packet of menthol cigarettes, a lighter. There was a clutch of pictures taken with an instant print camera, also there. Selfies of a laughing Ria with a man. The same man in all the photos. In the last he was naked, asleep, a white sheet draped around him like a toga.

'Who is this?' asked Pete snatching it from her. His hand was shaking with fury and shock and pain as he held the photo.

'I have no idea,' said Ria. 'I swear, I have no idea.'

This was *him*. Lean and handsome. He wore classy clothes and smelled expensive. The man who had been *always on the mind* of his wife. Where was he now? It looked as if no one had been here for months.

No, it couldn't be. Pieces of a puzzle started to push together in his head, looking to fit. Fitting.

'Do you want to take her stuff, Pete?' asked Ria, but he had left the room to head back downstairs. In the kitchen he scooped up the pile of post, deposited it on the table, picked through the junk, ripped some open. *Tara Ollerton* – a Visa statement. She'd started having her post delivered here then. *Tara Ollerton* – an invitation to a fashion show in Derby. *Tara Ollerton* – a receipt for a delivered case of champagne. Then the name he had been searching for on one of the envelopes. He slit it open to find a rental agreement on this cottage. Paid a year in advance, cash. *Mr Alexander Wilder.* The man who had died in the same crash as his wife; Laurie's partner.

Chapter 43

Pete drove home. He held on to the steering wheel as if it prevented him from slipping off the side of the earth. His head was a horrible merry-go-round of details blaring out a distorted tune. Laurie's partner was his wife's lover, the father of the baby he thought was his own. He'd find a photo of Alex Wilder to be sure, but he knew it would match. His name had meant nothing to Ria and he wasn't going to enlighten her on what it meant to him. He took a corner too fast and Ria shrieked and he forced his thoughts back onto getting home safely and nothing else.

Ria had gathered two carrier bags full of Tara's possessions and set them down on the kitchen floor in his house. He didn't want them. Pete thought of the ring that Laurie wore around her neck, the ring that would have fitted his wife's slim finger. *Always on my mind.* Poor Laurie. He had all the answers to the questions that were torturing her, but no answers to the load he had just inherited. He didn't want to be the one to tell her. He didn't want her heart to feel like the punchbag his did.

'I'll put the kettle on,' said Ria. Pete didn't resist. From the back Ria looked just like her younger sister and for a moment Pete let himself believe it was Tara, standing there, her belly swelling with another man's child and he felt hate and sadness crash together inside him like rival seas meeting.

'I don't know what to say,' said Ria, delivering the coffees to the table and sitting on the chair next to his. 'I wish I hadn't guessed what she was up to.'

But you did, he said inside, anger swirling within him like a slow-moving whirlpool. Ria had known his wife was sleeping with another man. He wondered if Tara was intending to leave him or lead a double life. *I've got something I want to tell you.* She didn't know he couldn't have children, so was she intending to let him bring up another man's child? Did she know Alex Wilder had a ring in his pocket for her? Was Bakewell where they were both driving back from when the lorry hit them? Did *he* get to know on their last day that he was going to be a father?

Pete felt the stirrings of a painful pulse in his temple.

Ria's hand slid across to his, her small, Tara-like fingers fell on his wrist, pressing warmth into his flesh. He looked up, saw her brown doe eyes shining. He reached over, threaded his hand into her hair, drew her face towards his, felt her gasp as his lips found hers, felt her yield as he gathered her into his arms. Tara's scent assaulted his nostrils. He pulled away, saw the desire in her eyes.

'Come on then, Ria, let's go upstairs,' he said.

She jerked, unsure if she had heard him correctly, gave a nervous laugh.

'This is what you want, isn't it? Come on, let's do it.'

'Pete?'

'Your sister's gone, I'm all yours. You both should have told me sooner. You and I could have been fucking for months.'

The F-word felt good in his mouth, cleansing and hateful, bitter and sweet at the same time. Rage let you act without conscience.

'I think I ought to go,' Ria said, crushed, disappointed.

'Oh come on, Ria. Now's your big chance to get your sister's leftovers to go with her clothes and the perfume.'

Ria's face was flushing crimson before his eyes, she looked as if she had been slapped. She picked up her bag and looped it around her shoulder.

'I'll call you tomorrow,' she said.

'Don't bother,' snarled Pete. 'And take your sister's shit with you.'

Pete kicked the carrier bags. They spilled out their contents: his dead wife's make-up, shoes, clothes, the thongs she had worn for another man – or not worn. Ria pushed them back into the bags, and scurried out with them. Pete slammed the front door hard behind her and the wonder was that the glass didn't break. The reverberations of that car crash had rippled far further than the accident scene, crossing timelines to buckle lives as surely as it had buckled metal. The destruction had to end and it had to end now.

He took his phone out of his pocket, threw himself back down at the kitchen table. Without letting thought get in the way, he scrolled through his text messages, found the last one from Laurie and started to compose a reply.

Sorry Laurie. Made a mistake. Won't see you again. Don't want to mess you around. Good luck.

No kiss. He blocked her number, then deleted it. No door left slightly ajar. No way back. He couldn't have kids. How could he drop yet another bombshell like that on her when she'd bought a massive house to fill with children? He had to forget her, she had to forget him. And it was better that one of them was protected from knowing the whole truth about their respective partners. Eventually she'd accept that she wouldn't get answers and she'd make her closure. She'd get over Pete far more than she would ever get over finding out what Alex Wilder was planning to do to her.

Chapter 44

14 October

Laurie knew this was insanity, coming back to see Pat Morrison again and throwing down the toilet – as Bella would put it – another hundred and fifty pounds. But her world was a mad whirl and she didn't have anyone to talk to as Bella was still on holiday with Stu. She'd been tempted to ring Pete so many times and ask if he was all right, hear something that would indicate he hadn't meant to drop her so swiftly and absolutely, give him a way back in, but she daren't – in case she discovered instead that he'd acted with cold deliberation.

She was devastated by this sea change in him and worn out with trying to get into his head. Had they moved too quickly? Was he feeling overwhelmed with guilt? Or maybe they were creatures who had just learned to float and, filled with bravado, had decided to swim the Atlantic. Too much, too soon, scrambling in panic back to hide on the shore. She had to put him out of her mind, let him find his peace. He had lost so much more than she had. But still, she hurt.

She'd pinned up her hair, with a raspberry beret to cover it, put on her reading glasses, wore bright red lipstick in an attempt to look totally different from the last time she had been to Pat Morrison's pink palace. She'd even given a false name and was going to assume a Welsh accent. Pat opened the door to 'Linda Parks' and told her to sit for five minutes in the small front room holding a crystal and choosing from a bowl of objects. This time Laurie avoided the match and chose a small elaborate key.

Fifteen minutes later, Pat Morrison led Linda through to the room that smelled of cherries with a chirpy apology about overrunning.

'So,' said Pat, taking the crystal, closing her eyes as she concentrated on the forces emanating from it. Then her eyes sprang open. 'Have I seen you before?' she asked. 'Your energy is quite familiar.'

'Ages ago,' Laurie lied in a Welsh accent that kept sliding into Indian. 'Years in fact. I was a redhead then. And my face was fatter.'

Pat chortled. 'Goodness me, lovey, I see hundreds of new people every month. Apart from a few regulars, I wouldn't recognise someone's face, only their vibe.' Which was a total lie because Pat Morrison had excellent facial recognition skills. There was definitely something familiar about the young woman in front of her, but she couldn't recall any detail about her.

'If you've been before, you'll know how I work,' said Pat.

'Yes I do,' said Laurie, sounding more Kashmir than Cardiff.

Pat took in a deep breath and closed her eyes.

'You've lost someone,' she said eventually. 'A man. He's passed. He's sending you a lot of love.'

Comforting but limp, thought Laurie. She needed a lot more for her one hundred and fifty pounds.

'I can see a maze, clear as day,' said Pat. 'You're walking around it and you're looking for something. Answers to questions. Somebody has these answers, someone close to you. A woman.'

She said that last time, thought Laurie, admiration and cynicism balanced on her internal set of scales. Pat was either consistent or she told everyone the same thing.

'She doesn't want to tell you, but you need to know because this will help you move on. Ooh – déjà vu—' Pat gave a start '—I told you this before, didn't I? I remember this image of a maze. There was a break in your relationship with this person. Female, for sure.'

Laurie did her best to remain impassive, hoped she wasn't blinking too much or a facial tic had been set off.

'She's still hoping you'll not ask. She's frightened of what she knows, upset.'

That sounded nothing like Meredith, thought Laurie. She couldn't wait to tell Laurie what she knew, savoured her disclosure in fact. Plus, she'd already said it all, hadn't she?

'And I see a man, I see new love growing,' said Pat, concentrating hard. 'I'm hearing very strongly that you have to give him a chance. He's the right one for you. My spirit guide is very clear about this, *Give him a chance* is what he's saying over and over.'

There had been a new love but he was now old news. Pat was clearly viewing her life on TVCatchup.

Pat noticed that the Welsh woman didn't look as thrilled as everyone else did when she told them that love was just around the corner. She should, though: the feeling was very intense. The trouble was that when her newly encountered spirit guide came on the scene, he used up all the energy in the crystal and it went dead in Pat's hand very quickly. She thought she'd throw in a little of her own philosophy to bulk up the session; after all, the woman was paying over the odds for her time.

'Never give up hope where love is concerned. It's like a butterfly. It flits here and there, settles, buggers off and just when you think you've seen the last of it, blow me, it comes flying towards you again.'

Yes it came flying towards me, it hit me full on, it smashed up my heart and left forever, thought Laurie. Not exactly a great advert for hope.

'And the ball has gone cold.' Pat opened her eyes and put the crystal down on the table at her side. 'Ah you've chosen a key,' she said, holding out her hand for Laurie's object of choice. 'You're searching for something,' she went on, rolling it around in her hand, absorbing Laurie through it. 'You will find it, but what we discover isn't always what we've been looking for. I think this is to do with the woman again.'

Laurie tried to hang on to her deadpan expression.

'The key is very warm. I see a lot of heat, I see happiness.' *Eventually.* She didn't say so but felt the woman had a big hurdle to get past. A few wrong turnings in that maze before she found her way out of it. Sometimes Pat only saw images of blackness and experienced a feeling of dread, but she would never say as much. There was a large blot of darkness in her thoughts regarding this young woman, she didn't like the look of it at all. It wasn't an illness blot; it denoted danger. She had to be careful what she said now, as scaring someone was more likely to lead to them being jittery and setting off a self-fulfilling prophecy. She really did see happiness for this young woman; after the blot had cleared. She decided to leave well alone and not mention it. She turned her full attention back to the key.

'I can see ... I can see a sky lit up with colour. Could it be fireworks? And that man standing with you, looking at it.' She smiled at Laurie and had the urge to stick her hand up like a child in class so she went with it, first finger extended. 'Does this mean anything to you?' she asked.

Laurie shook her head. Pat Morrison, with her arm pointing north, looked not unlike John Travolta about to launch into 'Night Fever'.

'It will. Look out for it,' said Pat. One of her convenient get-out phrases usually, but here it was genuine, even if she didn't have a clue what it meant.

At the door, Pat shook the young woman's hand. If she was Welsh, Pat was a Spice Girl.

'All I'll say to you as a parting shot – and I'm feeling this very strongly – is that someone from the spirit world wants you to be happy,' said Pat Morrison, who was suddenly filled with a sensation of love, as if injected with it. It lasted as long as a finger click but it was strong and powerful – and lovely.

'Is ... this person happy in the spirit world?' asked Laurie, with a gulp.

'He's in paradise,' said Pat.

Chapter 45

15 October

Alan Robertson had told her once that his great gran, God rest her soul, had taught him that sometimes saying nothing said far more than saying something, so Laurie beat back every burning desire to text or ring Pete, hoping he'd wonder why she hadn't answered his last message. She wished hard that her silence would move him to contact her, but it hadn't. Five days had now passed since she received it. If the text message had been a letter, it would have worn thin for the amount of times she had opened it up, looked at it, tried to read some meaning into it that left her with possibility. Every time she failed, saw only dismissal and end.

The night after she saw Pat, she drove straight from work over to the Blue Duck, a new gastropub which had opened in Maltstone, where she'd agreed to meet Bella although she didn't feel in the slightest bit hungry, and hadn't since Pete's text landed on her phone. At the traffic lights a red fire engine pulled up in the next lane and her heart left its post and jumped into her mouth. She kept her head forward but the temptation to turn it to the side was hard to resist. She felt the sting of tears behind her eyes and was cross that she'd opened her heart a little to let someone in who ransacked what was left of it and then ran out.

Bella had already arrived and was chewing some complimentary bread when she walked in to the pub.

'Starving,' she explained, spluttering through a mouthful of seeded plait, getting up to give Laurie a hug of greeting. Bella grinned expectantly. 'So? I was waiting for you to send me texts full of lurid details about your date and I got zilch.'

'I didn't want to butt into your holiday.'

As Laurie sat down opposite to her, Bella took in her friend's thin frame and her unsmiling demeanour and her grin faded.

'How was your holiday?' asked Laurie. 'You look tanned.'

'Surprisingly hot for the time of year,' said Bella. 'How are you?'

'Oh, I'm fine.'

'Let's choose then chat,' suggested Bella. 'Although I've chosen. I'm having the Chicken Milanese with parmesan and truffle chips.'

'I'll have the fish cake I think,' said Laurie, scanning the menu for something that sounded small. They gave the waiter their order for food and drink and then Bella asked, 'Okay, so what's happened because something has. Please don't tell me that Meredith and—'

'It's nothing to do with them,' replied Laurie. 'I've been dumped.'

Bella blinked rapidly. 'What do you mean, dumped? Not by the fireman . . .?'

'Yep,' said Laurie.

'What the actual fu—'

'He sent me a text saying that he'd made a mistake and that he didn't want to see me again.'

'Eh?' Bella didn't know whether to be angry or gobsmacked first. Her features formed a hybrid of both. 'Start from the beginning.'

'We went to Firenze. I can't tell you how wonderful it was, lovely, romantic, perfect. He drove me home . . .' She left a pause that spoke volumes and Bella's eyes rounded. 'It just happened and it all felt so right. He said he couldn't wait to see me again, after his dad's birthday last Wednesday and then I got this text message on Thursday.' She pulled it up on her phone and handed it to Bella to read. Bella studied it, handed the phone back.

'Nothing since?'

'No,' said Laurie. 'I didn't reply. I didn't know if I should or not.'

'Absolutely not. He doesn't deserve one. I have no words,' said Bella, despite then digging up plenty. 'The wanker. The absolute tosspot. How bloody dare he! I can't get my head around it. Screwed-up arsehole.'

'C'est la vie,' said Laurie flatly.

'Well better you found out now before you'd got in any deeper, is the only positive thing I can say.'

'Maybe he thinks I'm a slag because I slept with him on the first date.'

'He slept with you on the first date too don't forget. If he thinks you're a slag but he's not, then he's a sexist pig and you're better off without him.'

But Laurie knew it wasn't that. It had meant something to them both. She'd felt it; he said he had too.

'My compass is obviously off,' she said, then had a sudden

flashback to Pat Morrison standing with her hand pointing north. She'd got it mixed up with south.

Their drinks arrived, then the food straight after.

'We decided on holiday that Stu would move in with me – we more or less live together anyway.'

'That's nice, I'm happy for you,' said Laurie. And she was. Bella had had her fair share of bad relationships and Stu was steady and kind.

'We thought that we'd have a party to christen the new phase. Bonfire night. I was hoping to invite you both – you and *him* – but you come by yourself. We'll pick you up and you can get a taxi home, or stay the night. But you *are* coming. You're going to have a few wines and some good food with us. No buts, it's happening. The bastard. How could he do that to you after all you've been through?'

'He's been through it too. Maybe he's still screwed up and scared.'

'It's not an excuse. You're screwed up and scared. Would you have done that to him?'

That put it in horrible perspective. Laurie didn't want to talk about him any more. She had to put him out of her mind. Checking her phone every ten minutes to see if he had texted had done her no good at all over the past few days. She changed the subject.

'Meredith came round to the house while you were away. She stayed for a cup of tea.'

'You invited her into your house?' said Bella, incredulously. 'Please tell me you're joking. You never invite witches over your threshold.'

'She came to bring me back the cheque that I'd given to her for Naomi's wedding present.'

'Bloody hell,' said Bella. 'There is a decent bone in her body then.'

'She told me she'd been to see a solicitor about suing me for half the house.'

'I take it back, there isn't a decent bone in her body, the . . .' Bella seemed to have run out of fresh expletives.

'She did apologise when she found out that it wasn't the done thing to contest your son's water-tight will.'

'Whoop-di-doo.' Bella tutted. 'Did she say why she'd brought you the cheque back?'

'Naomi called off the wedding. She found out Jefferson had been cheating.'

'Twat,' was Bella's only comment about that.

'And I went to see Pat Morrison again yesterday.'

Bella's fork fell out of her hand and clattered down onto her plate. 'Oh for God's sake, Laurie. Why didn't you just give me the fifty quid and I could have made up some shit for you to believe.'

'A hundred and fifty.'

'A hund—? Are you out of your tiny mind? What else haven't you told me?'

'What else haven't *you* told me?'

The words came out of Laurie from a deep place well below conscious thought. Something behind the scenes, trying to make sense of unsolid, ever-changing puzzle pieces, put them together in the only way that made sense. Secrets. A woman. A maze. Meredith was not this woman because Meredith couldn't wait to give up her secrets; so who was she? There was no one else other than the red-haired woman sitting opposite her, doing her best to look as if she had no idea what Laurie was talking about. And failing.

'I don't know what you mean,' Bella said, attempting to pull nonchalance out of the bag, but it was too late.

'Pat Morrison said that a woman wasn't telling me something that would help me move on. So if that's you, Bella, you'd better tell me because I'm tired, worn out with trying to work out what is going on while people think it's in my best interests to mess with my head. I would rather just have everything out in the open so I can deal with it. And if it is you and I find out that you're keeping things from me then we are done, because what I'm not being told is so much worse than being told and I will not stop asking and prying and going to psychics until I *know*.' Laurie's face creased. It took all her effort not to rest her arms on the table and sink forwards into them.

A beat. Bella continued to chew. 'Pat thingy is talking bollocks, Laurie. This is why you should never go to these people, they prey on the vulnerable.' But her voice had suddenly lost its fire. If anything, it had gone too quiet.

They didn't have dessert, they didn't have their customary coffee following the strained main course. They went their separate ways with Bella telling Laurie that she'd be in touch about her bonfire party and then fifteen minutes after Laurie had arrived home, she was surprised to find Bella on her doorstep. A Bella that was whey-faced and contrite.

'I do have something to tell you, Laurie, can I come in?' she asked. Laurie moved aside to let her pass. She noted the slump in Bella's shoulders as she followed her into the lounge. It sent out a clear message that whatever her friend was about to tell her wasn't good.

'I'm sorry I kept this from you, but I didn't know what to do for the best.' Bella dropped down heavily onto the sofa, her hands weaving together as if one was taking comfort from the other. Laurie sat in the armchair, waited for Bella to find a starting place.

'Remember when we ... when I told you that Alex and I had a bit of a row about how he'd spoken to you,' began Bella.

'Yes,' replied Laurie.

'It was a lie.'

Laurie nodded because she'd worked that out already. Her compass hadn't been that far off, then. Despite everything, her intuition was still managing to point to the holes in people's stories. It was doggedly trying to guide her to the truth, sticking to its course, not letting the magnets of lies steer her elsewhere.

'I'm sorry, I'm so sorry,' Bella shook her head. 'Stu said I should have told you before this but I didn't want to, I thought I was protecting you,' Bella went on. 'And you have to believe me when I say to you that the only reason I started avoiding you was because I didn't want to hurt you.'

'Why? Protecting me from what? Just say—'

'Alex was having an affair, Laurie,' blurted out Bella. 'And I caught him out.'

Chapter 46

People sometimes said that time stood still – a cliché – but that's exactly what it felt like at that moment for Laurie. She couldn't move, and yet her brain exploded with activity. An affair. She'd known all along, she'd been right. Here she was, staring the unsavoury truth in the eye and the victory was Pyrrhic.

Bella sat hunched, folded into herself, as if her admission had robbed her blood of its warmth. 'It was not long after Anna's wedding. I'd just had my promotion so I was covering the whole country, not just Yorkshire. I was in the office at the new hotel, the Little Acorns in Derby. The door was open and I saw Alex at reception. I went out to say hello, I presumed he'd been on a work thing but his face fell when he saw me. He was checking out. It was a double room. A woman was standing with him.'

'What did she look like?' asked Laurie, her voice a dry croak.

'She wasn't all that,' said Bella wrinkling up her lip like an angry Elvis.

'Tell me honestly, Bell.'

Bella's shoulders gave a small ruffle. 'Slim, false tits, long browny-blondey hair, gap in her top teeth, well-dressed, loads of make-up. The sort who are good-looking and know it.'

'What was her name?'

'They'd booked under Mr and Mrs Dankworth, he paid cash.'

Dankworth – Meredith's maiden name. She had a sudden recollection of Meredith's proud claim that it was on the list of the rarest surnames in England.

'What happened then?' demanded Laurie.

'He just stood there like a deer in the headlights, as you can imagine. I had to walk back into the office before I said or did something I regretted because I was so angry. I expected him to try and contact me, ask me what I was going to do with the information, but he didn't. I really liked Alex, and I'd forgiven him for cheating on you the first time because . . . if *you* could, it wasn't up to me to bear the bigger grudge. But to find out that he was doing it again . . .'

Bella's voice faltered. Laurie sat rigid, waiting for her to continue.

'I checked the records. Mr and Mrs Dankworth had stayed before, a couple of times, always in the same room, always paid cash for it. It has a small private terrace with a hot tub. Surprisingly enough, they never did again though. And as I say, he didn't contact me, but he'd put me in an awful predicament that I shouldn't have been in, all that responsibility, so I lobbied him at work the week after. I said if he didn't get in my car to talk, I'd scream at him in the atrium. He got in the car and I tore a right strip off him and he said that he was going to tell you but was waiting for the right time.'

'That he was having an affair?'

'Oh God . . .' A pause. A terrible pause. '. . . That he was leaving you, Laurie.'

Laurie gulped. She couldn't have forgiven another affair and would have had to end their relationship, but to hear that he had been planning to leave her for months was like a stab in her heart. Going through the motions of being a couple, lying in bed with her while thinking of another woman. No wonder he couldn't manage to make love to her.

'He said he'd do it in the new year. He didn't want to ruin Christmas for you.'

A picture landed with a bump in Laurie's mind of all the lovely things he had bought her for Christmas. He was always generous with presents but he'd surpassed himself. Pity gifts, wrapped up in guilt and trimmed with deception.

'He broke down,' Bella continued. 'Had I not hated him so much right then, I'd have felt sorry for him. I asked who she was and he wouldn't tell me, only that he wasn't in the habit of screwing behind your back. He said that she was the woman he'd left you for before, as if that made it any better. He said that his conscience had forced him back to you, he couldn't bear what he'd done to you, and he'd *really* wanted to make it work with you but that the other woman was . . . always on his mind and had never left it.'

Always on his mind.

'Did he say that? Did he use those exact words, Bella, that she was *always on his mind*?' Laurie asked and waited for the answer she knew would come.

'Yes. Like the song. Like the inscription on . . .' Bella's voice faded as she nodded towards Laurie's necklace.

'I see.'

Laurie reached behind her neck and undid the fastening,

slid the ring from the chain, rolled it in her fingers. It explained so much: why it was so small – because it wasn't meant for her. Was he going to tell her that night he died? *Don't be late home, Laurie. There's something important I have to tell you.* That's why there was no champagne, because he wasn't going to propose to her. He was going to end it. Over a civilised dinner. So where was this woman now? Why hadn't she made an appearance? Had she turned up in church for his funeral, sat at the back and privately grieved for the man in whose mind she permanently resided?

'I was damned if I told you and damned if I didn't,' said Bella, crying now, tears dragging her mascara down her cheeks. 'He said he loved you so much and the last thing he ever wanted to do was hurt you. You can imagine what I said to that.'

'You have no idea what she was called?' asked Laurie.

'They'd arrived at the hotel by separate cars. I wrote down her registration plate; there was no way I could trace her by it but I kept it, just in case. I went through all the hotel records – the whole chain – hoping to throw something up on her but nothing. God forgive me, Laurie, but I couldn't face you. I had to distance myself, hoped it would all blow over and he'd see sense because if I stayed around, I was terrified I'd give his game away. I was in a proper state. I'd have been there for you if he did leave, I'd have made it up to you, I was waiting for your call to say he'd gone and it didn't come and I just hoped that was because it had ended and you were happy. I played it so wrong, I know I did but at the time that seemed to be all I could do. Then the crash happened and I was worried sick she'd come into your life and cause trouble, so one of Stu's mates in the police did something that would have got him fired if anyone had found out and gave us the name and address of the car owner – and she'd died. And I thought that would close it up, that you would never need to know any of it.'

Laurie's brow furrowed. 'She died? Who was she?'

Bella groaned. The words were injuring her to say, as if they had barbs that stuck in her throat on the way out, because they didn't want to be said.

'She died in the same crash as Alex. Her name was Tara Ollerton.'

Laurie sat back in the armchair as if her spine had collapsed. Every part of her body felt tired.

'Thank you,' she said, her voice a weary croak.

Bella threw herself at Laurie, sobbing hard into her shoulder and it was Laurie comforting her now, because it was the right thing to do. She remembered the strain of not saying anything to Alex's family about Jefferson and she wasn't half as close to them as she was to Bella. Poor Bella, who loved her and was terrified to see her wounded again, trying to protect her, ending their friendship in the hope of saving her relationship.

'Don't worry, Bells, I understand.'

Bella pulled away. 'When you told me about the engagement ring in Alex's pocket, I was delighted, I thought "it did end, everything would have been all right". Then you told me it was too small and about the inscription and all the other things that didn't add up and I knew it must have been still been going on. I didn't want you to go digging and find the truth. I wanted you to be safe with the lies.'

Laurie made Bella a hot drink and wouldn't let her drive off until she was calm. Their friendship remained intact. Bella had been so afraid it wouldn't be, but there was nothing

Laurie had to forgive her for. Even if she had known earlier, it wouldn't have changed things. She would still have lost Alex; and who knows if he would now be alive. Maybe he would have died even sooner. Was life an indelible blueprint or a free-willed journey through a maze of many possibilities? They'd never know. All she had was the truth of what had happened.

When Bella had gone, Laurie went upstairs into her office, switched on her iMac and looked up the reportage of the crash on the internet. She had never done this before; she didn't want to read any details – salacious or otherwise. She knew everything she needed to about that day and that was that her fiancé had been killed; everything else was immaterial. Except he wasn't her fiancé, on that Meredith had been right; but Meredith couldn't have known about the other woman, for Alex would never have confided in his parents that he'd been conducting an affair and risk tarnishing his perfect-son image. Meredith didn't even know about the first time and Laurie knew this because when they got back together, Meredith had said something to her on the lines of, 'Now you must ensure you make time for each other', as if it had been their careers that had caused the split and not a woman called Tara Ollerton.

Tara. The same name as Pete's wife.

His voice: *'My wife shouldn't have been anywhere near where she was when she died.'*

Laurie felt cold, as if all the blood had suddenly drained from her system. A moment of recalibration – then she clicked on the first of the articles that her search brought up.

There was a photograph of the six victims on the *Daily Mirror* site: David Tinker, Gerald Seymour, Eleanor Stafford, Rashida Khan, Alex Wilder . . . Tara Ollerton, their names together on the list in death as they were in life. Tara Ollerton had long, tousled hair, large brown eyes and a wide, worldly smile and she had died the day before her thirtieth birthday. 'Six Dead in Tragic Crash' said the *Guardian*. 'Texting Lorry Driver Caused Death of Six' in the *Express*, alongside a picture of Kent Birchill, the forty-two-year-old driver who sustained no more than a broken arm and bruising. With mounting trepidation, Laurie googled Tara Ollerton. The lead result, a death notice: *Tara Ollerton. Beloved wife of Peter (Moore), dearly loved daughter of Pam and Bob Ollerton, sister of Alana and Ria. Tragically taken from us, aged 29, February 6th . . .*

Not every married woman took her husband's name. Alex had asked her once if she would and she'd say yes without hesitation. She wondered if Tara would have given Alex the same answer.

If only Laurie had taken direction from Bella, buried all her questions with Alex, she wouldn't have had to lose him all over again. If only she hadn't fixated on why there was no bloody champagne in that Meal for Two. In her heart she'd known there was some significance in that. The heart that was presently ripped in two, ravaged. She wasn't sure it could ever be put back together again. Not now.

Her thoughts drifted to Pete. Did he know what she now knew? She tried to herd her thoughts into order. No, at least not in the beginning. Had he found out somewhere along the line that they were chained together by this tragedy — and far more than merely by the coincidence of their partners dying on the same night, on the same road? Is this why he had suddenly cut and run? Because he would not be able to look at her without thinking of Alex, the man who was planning to take his wife from him. *Pete's wife had been pregnant when she died. Was that Alex's baby inside her?* The questions got too much for her brain to handle. She dropped her head into her hands and cried as she had never cried before in her whole life.

When her well had run dry, she tried to gather herself into a semblance of a whole person again. She needed to think. Crying wouldn't wash away any of this chaos, it would only blur her vision, blind her from finding the way out of this pit. She picked up her phone, pulled up Pete's contact details, stalled. What if he didn't know any of it? What if the reason he had finished it was only because he was still too raw to move forward out of his grief? If so, she wielded a power that could destroy him with only a handful of careless words and it would be too big for her to keep from him if they remained close.

He, like she, was a crushed mess, growing his shell, pretending he was stronger than he was, cracking at the first tap. But he would heal. First on the outside, then on the inside. Given time. Given distance from someone like her who could take away comforting lies in his past, replace them with cold, brutal truths. Maybe it was as well they had ended before they had even started. This way she could make sure that he was spared more pain. He'd had enough.

She deleted his messages, blocked his number and then erased the contact details. Closed the door she had kept ajar.

Chapter 47

5 November

Laurie viewed herself in the mirror and wondered why the hell she had agreed to go to Bella and Stu's bonfire night party where she knew without any doubt that her friend would try and set her up with Reid double-barrelled surname which she couldn't quite recall. 'Just give him a chance,' Bella had pleaded and those words had resounded in her head. Pat Morrison's spirit guide had said there would be a new love growing. A new love associated with fireworks, Pat had also implied. *You have to give him a chance. He's the right one for you.* But she really didn't want to go through all this again because she wasn't ready to trust love, anything or anyone. Trust was a five-letter four-letter word.

She looked thin and pale and people were starting to comment on it. Even Maurice at the last meeting had asked Mr Singh to cut Laurie an extra large piece of the strawberry and cream cake. The dynamic had changed in the group now that Pete no longer attended. He'd abandoned them all. Sharon, Yvonne and Maurice had all floundered through the deep lake of their loss, felt solid ground beneath their feet as they headed for their far shore, and Laurie pretended she was steps behind them and was following close, but she was drowning not waving.

A chirpy beep outside announced the arrival of Bella's car. Laurie picked up her handbag and keys, said a *see you later* to Keith Richards, who was feasting on a worm so he didn't reply, and walked out.

'Hello mate, you all right?' said Bella, greeting her with a tentative smile. The last three weeks, since she'd told Laurie about Alex, had taken their toll on her too. It was hurting her seeing her friend fading; she felt duty-bound to help Laurie find the happiness she deserved.

'Reid West-Hunt arrived just before I came to fetch you,' she said.

'Please don't push us together, Bella,' pleaded Laurie.

'I promised I wouldn't and I won't. Besides—' Bella grinned '—I think you'll naturally gravitate to each other. I won't need to do any pushing. He really is a dish and I can't wait for him to meet you.'

Bella didn't say that Reid seemed very keen to meet Laurie too. She couldn't understand how a catch like him was single. Maybe, she hoped, fate was keeping him single for tonight.

Stu, carrying a long barbecue fork, greeted Laurie warmly with such a bone-crushing hug of affection that Laurie felt shamed she had even considered he might have been the catalyst for the breakdown in hers and Bella's friendship. He had never been anything but a peach to her. 'My dear Laurie,' he said. What can I get you to drink?'

'Oh er . . .'

'She's having fizz. I'll sort it, you get back to your arson, darling,' said Bella, dragging Laurie over to the drinks table. She lifted a bottle of Prosecco out of an ice barrel and filled up two flutes. 'Here's to a bright and bubbly future,' she said. 'And giving new people a chance,' she tagged on the end, loosely quoting Pat Morrison. Laurie gave her an admonishing glare and Bella feigned innocence. They wandered over to where a small bonfire was raging and said hello to Mike, Stu's brother, who was in charge of the fireworks, and Bella's lovely neighbours who were wrapped up for Arctic conditions in his and hers puffa coats.

'Where's Reid?' Bella asked Mike.

'He was here a minute ago,' came the reply.

Laurie was getting more nervous by the minute. She wanted the introductions to be over and done with just to get Bella off her back and then she could friend-zone Reid – if she wasn't friend-zoned first – and everyone could get on with their lives.

Reid West-Hunt was a man that one could sense before he actually arrived, is how Laurie would most remember him. She turned towards the French doors that led from Bella's kitchen at the same moment as he emerged from them. She swallowed. At a distance and silhouetted, he looked remarkably like Alex with his tall, lean build, then he walked into the light and Laurie saw that he didn't look anything like him really, a different sort of handsome. Sharp cheekbones, mouth not as generous as Alex's but curved up into a killer smile, dark-chocolate eyes, almond-shaped. He was dressed casually, for a bonfire party, and yet he still managed to outgarb every single male gathered here. Bella waved, called his name.

'Reid, this is Laurie,' she said, beaming like a clown on happy pills.

'How lovely to meet you. I've heard so much about you,' Reid said in a voice that was as smooth and rich as molasses, holding out his hand, squeezing Laurie's at the right pressure to transmit strength and politeness. He bent, kissed her cheek and when she took in his aftershave, her senses purred. The scent of summer Mediterranean nights, the more fanciful part of her brain suggested.

'Anyone want a steak? I have rare ones,' called Stu. A loud crack preceded a firework burst that lit up the sky with a pink and green chrysanthemum.

Bella's sister Sacha appeared at their side with a plate of hot dogs in buns and both Laurie and Reid reached for the same one at the same time. They laughed.

Maybe, thought Laurie, she wouldn't friend-zone him just yet.

Chapter 48

February, earlier that year

'I thought Bella would have told her, I really did,' he said. 'It would have made my life much easier if Laurie had thrown me out. I know it sounds like a coward's way, but I wanted her to guess rather than me come at her from cold. I even left out the cufflinks you bought me, the Viv Westwood ones with the hearts. She would have asked me about them if she'd noticed them.'

'She will survive this.'

'I know,' he said. 'But I'm glad I don't have to live this lie any more.'

He sat down on the newly made bed next to her and smiled, took her small hand in his. Her small beautiful hand that tomorrow would be wearing his ring.

'Well, we have this place for another eleven months. I'm hoping my nesting instinct comes into its own soon. I might even bake apple pies and make soup,' she said.

He laughed. 'It's bad enough getting my head around seeing you make a bed, never mind knead pastry.'

'I love you so much. When we split up the first time I went a *little crazy I think. I stemmed the pain with Pete, used him like a bandage. I hated you more than I loved him. I wanted you to arrive at the church and stop the ceremony.'*

'What sort of bastard would I have been if I'd done that?' he replied. *'I thought you'd moved on. I couldn't blame you. I was happy for you. Sort of.'* He sighed heavily, passed her the wedding ring that was at the side of the bed. She slipped it on. She would take it off for the last time tonight, leave it behind with her marriage.

He hoisted her to her feet.

'Come on, let's do what we have to. Just a few hours and then we can properly be a couple.'

'Forever,' she said.

NORTH

Blow solar winds
Suffuse my soul with colour
Dazzling as the skies
And guide me home
To you
. . . My one true north

THE NORTHERN LIGHTS
ANON

Chapter 49

18 December

The week before Christmas marked the last of their Wednesday sessions together at Molly's Club, but far from being a sad affair, it was a jolly card-swapping and mince-pie-filled one. For most of them at least. Sharon had changed jobs, found herself training to be a dog groomer. She had adopted the old lady's lurcher and was allowed to take her to work. 'Jinny' had settled into her new surroundings beautifully and Sharon, in her own words, felt like a big hole inside her had been stuffed with sweets. Laurie envied her that: what must it feel like not to have that gaping emptiness inside you, to feel fulfilled and *whole*. Yvonne and Maurice were officially an item and he was intent on cooking Christmas dinner for her at his house and then she was going to her daughter's for Boxing Day. Molly was overjoyed to see how two people such as Yvonne and Maurice flourished in a climate of love and kindness. Yvonne had even taken Maurice clothes shopping and out went the frumpy slacks and knits and in came polos and his first ever pair of jeans.

Laurie concerned Molly though and she hoped she wasn't preparing to leave with the others, hoped she would stay on and continue to be supported. She hadn't been the same since Peter had left and Molly suspected there was a link between that and the dullness of Laurie's beautiful grey-blue eyes.

At the end of the session, Maurice pulled out of his pocket two small boxes. At either side of him Yvonne and Sharon were beaming with anticipation.

'Dear Mr Singh and Molly,' he began, as confident a man as ever there was. 'We've all bought you a little something to say thank you for helping us, for bringing us together and in my case certainly, giving me much happiness. I can't say I've ever had true friends before, but I have now.'

Yvonne, Sharon and Laurie clapped as Maurice handed one box to Mr Singh and one to Molly, urging them to open them. Inside was a rhinestone-encrusted brooch for Molly, a gold tie-pin for Mr Singh. Each one featured a ship.

'We know you both like travelling,' explained Sharon, 'but we thought as well that it was a symbol of how you have helped us all to cross our own sea.'

'We are very grateful to you,' said Yvonne, wiping her eyes. From years of having to hide her emotions, she was more than happy to show them now. 'You've not changed my life, you've given me one.'

'Thank you, dear Mr Singh and Molly,' added Laurie.

'I don't know what to say,' said Molly. She loved brooches so much that she had a collection of them, but this one would sit special among them. 'I'm so touched. I'm only glad I could help you, you're all wonderful people and we hope you are very happy. You are welcome to carry on coming' – she looked at Laurie as she said this – 'and you know where we are if you ever need help in the future.'

Hugs and handshakes, goodbyes and good lucks later, Yvonne, Maurice and Sharon left. Laurie was about to follow when Molly called her back.

'Laurie, you don't have to leave because the others have,' said Molly.

'I know, but it feels like a natural end,' replied Laurie. 'I think you've helped me as much as you could.' It was partly true. But at the same time Laurie wished she had never come here, never met Pete Moore who lingered in her head and refused to leave. As Tara Ollerton had probably lodged steadfastly in Alex's.

'Our policy has always been that people can come or go without pressure, but I have to ask you, what happened to Peter? Can you shed any light on why he stopped coming?'

Molly saw the small swallow Laurie's throat performed before she spoke.

'I think it was more that he didn't want to see me again, rather than you.'

'You got close to each other, didn't you?' Molly asked gently.

'Yes, but I've moved on now.'

Laurie reached over, squeezed Molly's arm affectionately.

'Thank you for everything you do. You and Mr Singh,' she said and opened the door quickly, hoping Molly wouldn't see the crippling sadness in her eyes. But Molly had. And in her measured and expert opinion, Laurie looked anything but a woman who had moved on.

Chapter 50

6 January

Laurie had been totally charmed by Reid at the bonfire party. He had been witty and attentive and she had fancied him a little – how could she not? So when he had suggested they meet up for dinner, she'd said yes. Pat Morrison's suggestion that she give a chance to the person connected with fireworks couldn't have sounded a louder klaxon, so she had heeded it. Reid had been a total gentleman, took her to a Michelin-starred restaurant, insisted on paying for her, opened doors, helped her on and off with her coat, kissed her hand when he dropped her off home and the next morning, a very beautiful bouquet of flowers had arrived with a card that said 'Thank you for a glorious evening and can I see you again' tucked among them.

She was wowed off her feet and she did see him again. And again. Except . . . all the pieces fitted but something still wasn't quite right. Bella's explanation was that Laurie had been messed about so much that her compass was wrong; she had trusted people she shouldn't, she wasn't trusting people she should. She did have a point, thought Laurie; however, she didn't dismiss her own misgivings outright. So far, her compass had helped her negotiate a whole mine-field of lies and crap.

She and Bella met up at the Blue Duck after work on the first Monday of the new year. Laurie hated January with a passion. There was always such a long build-up to Christmas and yet the festive season ended like a rug whipped from under the feet, leaving a feeling of drabness and depression. A comedian had made her laugh once talking about January:

Thirty days hath September, April, June and November.
All except February which has twenty-eight days clear and
twenty-nine in leap year.
And January which has a hundred and ninety-seven.

At least that's what it had always felt like to her. She took her Christmas decorations down on 2 January. It hadn't taken her long; there was just a tree, as opposed to filling her house with a Santa's grotto's-worth of sparkle and glitz as she had done before. Meredith and Brendan had sent her a card almost as if protocol demanded. A very ordinary charity-supporting one signed only with their names, Meredith, Brendan, Naomi, curt and cold. Laurie hadn't written any. Not this year.

'Well? How was your Christmas and *New Year?*' said Bella, with emphasis, hungrier for details than she was for food.

'It was—'

'It's what you deserve,' enthused Bella, not letting her finish. 'After what Alex did to you, and that bloody fireman.'

Reid was polished and sophisticated, generous and

affectionate. Masterful, Bella called him. She was already looking at hats for the wedding.

They'd swapped Christmas presents after making a pact to keep them small. Laurie had given him a scarf; Reid had presented her with an envelope containing details of an evening for two: dinner at the Ritz in London, a pair of theatre tickets and then back to the Ritz for an overnight stay there. It must have cost a fortune.

'How was the Ritz?' Bella grinned. 'Well, actually I mean how was your first shag together in the Ritz? How smooth is that – buying you a luxury night away?'

'It was certainly a surprise.' She'd been slightly put out and a lot embarrassed that he'd ignored the arrangement and he'd laughed and told her to enjoy and not even think about it. Bella had said the same. 'I'm not sure it's going to work with Reid, though,' said Laurie.

'Eh?' shrieked Bella. 'How can it not?'

Because Laurie couldn't forget Pete Moore, that's why. She didn't say it because Bella would have told her to get a grip of herself and Bella would probably have been right. On paper Reid was perfect for her. Then again, on paper she had been perfect for Alex.

'He wants to move too fast,' said Laurie. 'I'm not ready for it.'

'Tell him to slow down, then,' said Bella.

She already had. Then Reid had presented her with that Christmas present and she'd felt railroaded into spending the night with him. She'd even found herself hoping to catch the winter virus bug that everyone at work had, but she'd managed to dodge it – annoyingly.

She'd presumed she was just being stupidly nervous about sleeping with someone again after being dumped straight after last time. Bella told her not to judge everyone by Alex's and Pete's very low standards and just go, relish being spoiled. So she had eaten a fantastic dinner, seen an amazing show and then returned to the hotel. She suggested a drink in the bar – Fabian tactics, delaying the inevitable like a frigid virgin bride – but Reid said he wanted her stone cold sober for the rest of the night. And she had gone to bed with him. He had been attentive to her body but she had faked because she wished she were home alone instead, watching TV in a fluffy robe with a bowl of nachos and getting horribly drunk on red wine. Outside she could hear London cheering, the deep clang of twelve horrible bells that sounded more like a death knell than a celebration, sealing up a year that had been the worst ever ... but which had also brought someone into it who had given her a tantalising glimpse into a new chapter, a happier one, a love that made her soul sing. When she had finally got back into her house the next day, she'd shut the door on the world and had fought very hard against shedding a single tear over the hungry Pete Moore-shaped hole in her heart.

'The trouble with you,' said Bella, 'is that you've been steamrollered so much that you couldn't spot a decent man if he had a written testimonial from God. These are just tiny teething problems, Laurie, they'll sort themselves out. Reid is such a catch. He's absolutely minted as well. One day you'll come home and there will be a gift-wrapped Maserati on your drive.'

'Money isn't everything, I have enough of that myself,' said Laurie, with a rare snap in her voice.

'I know,' replied Bella, with a small smile of apology for overstepping the crass mark. 'I only want you to have someone who looks after you. You're scared, Laurie. And who could blame you? Just give him a chance. Isn't that what Pat Morrison said?'

'The fortune teller woman you said was rubbish?'

'Well, that was before she started talking sense. Please don't do anything rash like finish with Reid. Your heart doesn't know what to do with someone like him, that's the problem, someone strong and romantic who knows how to treat a woman. Listen to your head for a change, Laurie and *give him a chance.*'

Bella, she supposed, had a point. Her heart had made some incredibly dodgy choices in the past. Maybe it was the turn of her brain to take the wheel.

Chapter 51

7 January

The call came in during the night: house fire on the Ketherwood Estate. Both pumping appliances needed. Pete and the others launched themselves out of their beds as soon as the persistent beep-beep of the alarm and the pulsing light combo began, adrenaline streaming through their veins almost before their eyes had opened. Down the pole, out of the door, stepping into their trousers and boots. Onto the vehicle, donning their protective gear and breathing apparatus en route, ready to storm in, douse fires, pull people out, whatever they needed to do when they got there. When the two crews reached the building, there was already a crescent of spectators in pyjamas – but then around here that was all-day garb for a lot of them. A man was sitting on the grass holding his head, rocking back and forth, a woman with flying arms was bouncing with rage and distress at the side of him but was being held back by others.

'You fucking arsehole,' she was screaming at him.

A younger, stocky man was trying to get in through the front door.

'Her kid's in there,' he explained when Andy Burlap tried to move him back.

'She's in a cot in the bedroom above the kitchen,' sobbed the woman.

'Front or back, love?'

'Front. That fucking arsehole, pissed and making chips. Don't let my baby die, *pleeease*.'

Andy quickly assessed, directed.

Sal was first in with the hose. The fire had taken hold of the kitchen units, the curtains and had already burned through to the upper floor. The smoke was thick, rolling freely through the house. Pete and Krish, working as a pair, hurried up the stairs, following the sound of the wailing baby and their inner satnav sense of the house's layout. She was standing up in her cot, coughing, crying pitifully. Pete lifted her up, held her as close to his mask as possible, straight down the stairs and out. The ambulance had just turned up.

'*My baby,*' the distraught woman was screaming.

'Let me just check her over,' said the paramedic, calm and controlled, taking the child from Pete's arms.

'Where's my dog? Where's Barney?' The woman broke out into fresh hysteria.

'Did you say there's a dog, love?' Krish asked her.

'German shepherd.' She ran back to the man on the grass, kicked him hard on the thigh. 'Where's Barney, you fucker?'

'I shut it in the bathroom,' slurred the drunk. 'Bastard thing bit me.'

'Not hard enough, you're still alive, you waste of fucking space.'

Pete and Krish rushed back in, up the stairs. There was a

door at the end of the landing with a ragged punch hole in it pulling in smoke. They could see a dark shape on the floor through it and when Pete went inside, he found it was the dog unconscious, lying in its own urine.

'Come on, lad, I've got you,' he said. The dog was wet, large and limp, a dead weight. Pete stumbled over something on the floor, a rug he thought, but managed to stay upright. Outside Pete put the dog on the grass, felt its chest; there was a heartbeat. A young, strong one at that.

The woman was in bits.

'Oh Christ, my dog,' she said. 'He's like me second kid.'

Jacko raced over with the pet oxygen mask. Pete held it firmly over the dog's face, stroked the dog's fur, willed the dog to start breathing in that fresh clean oxygen and clear its airways. He'd done this before to dogs, cats, even a rabbit once. It was always a glorious moment when their lungs chugged into life, but it hadn't always happened. Pete concentrated, cut out the background noise of shouting and chattering. *Come on, lad, breathe.*

As if responding to the strangled cry of the woman behind him calling, 'Barneeeee', the dog's tail gave a dull thud; then it seemed to come to life from the back to the front.

'He's with us again,' Pete called to her.

When the dog's paws came out to push off the mask and it staggered to its feet, a woman with no teeth in a pink dressing gown and slippers like tiger paws appeared at his side with a piece of rope.

'I'll take him for you, Emma love. You see to your babby,' she said and hooped the makeshift lead around Barney's neck, then explained to Pete, 'We live next door but one. I sometimes go in and feed him when she's working.' In a surprisingly gentle voice she spoke to the dog, stroked his muzzle. 'Come on, lad, you'll be all right with your Auntie Christine and Uncle Dennis.'

Pete turned around and saw phones levelled at him. There was always someone ready to film someone else's distress these days and upload it to YouTube. He turned away, caught up with Andy Burlap.

'I thought everyone knew you don't throw a jug of water on a chip pan,' Andy said. 'I didn't even know people used them any more. They're bloody dangerous when you're sober, never mind when you're ratted. That could have been so much worse. Looks like you're going to be an internet sensation.'

'I hope not.'

The fire took fifteen minutes to put out; the real hard work was making the building safe, stripping back the plaster and the burnt timbers. Then, when all that was done, they returned to base to restock the trauma packs, change the compressed air cylinders, making sure all the equipment was ready for the next incident. Then and only then did they have what was called their well-deserved 'fire brew'. That cup of tea plus snacks was always extra sweet.

'One of the neighbours was telling me that she only took him back last night after he'd finished an alcohol de-toxing programme,' said Sal, talking about the house-dweller.

'She seemed as upset over the dog as the kid,' said Andy. 'I've never really understood that.'

'I can,' put in Pete.

'So can I,' said Sal. 'Some humans are shit to each other.' She looked pointedly at Pete as she spoke. 'There's a lot to be said for the unconditional love of an animal.'

'You've been watching too much *Lassie*,' scoffed Andy. 'Anyway, nice work, Pete.'

Sal led the applause and one by one the others drifted off, leaving just those two sitting at the table.

'No idea why I clapped you after what you did to Karen after our Christmas party,' said Sal.

'Karen who?'

Sal shook her head slowly, amazed – and not in a good way. 'Natasha's sister. Can't you remember her name? Did you even ask her what it was?'

'I haven't done anything to Natasha's sister,' said Pete.

'Ghosting is what twats do, Pete. She was devastated. There's me telling my girlfriend what a brilliant bloke you are and then you go and do that to her little sister.'

'I don't know what you want me to say, Sal. We got together, had a nice evening, or so I thought, and that was that. What else should have I done – said thank you for the fuck?'

Sal studied him, her brow furrowed. 'What's happened to you in the last couple of months? Because something has.'

'Don't know what you're talking about,' said Pete and slurped the last of his tea.

'That, for instance. When did you slurp your tea like a scruff? Use words like "fuck" in that context? Your whole attitude stinks. You're back in the job but you've lost your soul somewhere along the line.'

'What are you, my mother?'

'You're not a son I'd be proud of.'

That stung. 'Fuck off, Sal.'

'A mate would tell you that you've been acting like a wanker.'

'You a mate, are you, Sal?' Pete sneered.

'Yes, Pete, I am. And you're acting like a wanker,' said Sal, drained her cup and left.

*

No, he couldn't even remember Natasha's sister's name. He didn't want to. He'd just wanted to screw her and then walk out on her the next morning without a word. He would have done it to Ria if she'd ever come back, but she'd stayed away, not even sent him a Christmas card. He wished he'd felt shamed by what Sal had just said to him but he didn't, it bounced off the impenetrable wall of his hate and anger. He'd never trust another woman again. He'd even flirted with Lucy, wondering if she'd respond, but all she had said was, 'Are you drunk?' and laughed it off and he'd felt relief much more than the burn of rejection.

He thought he'd seen Laurie the previous week in the supermarket across the till aisles, a woman with a long blonde plait. As soon as she turned and he saw her profile, he knew it wasn't her, but his reactions were telling. He felt his heart thump hard as if it was trying to jump out of him and bound towards her, then a nuclear heat of fury overcame him that he'd had to let her go because of what Tara had done to him – and to her, fucking her man, getting pregnant by him even though Laurie didn't know that. *Please God don't let her ever find out.*

It frightened him how much bitterness had filled him. Recently it felt as if he was made up of it and nothing else.

Chapter 52

9 January

People were free to leave Molly's Club without explanation or excuses, which is why she had never chased Pete the firefighter to find out why he had stopped attending the sessions last year. But then something had happened to make her change her mind on that and break her own ruling. She'd fallen asleep in front of the TV in her rocking chair when she was rudely awoken by her sister Margaret and brother-in-law Bernard, both in their dressing gowns and slippers, bursting into her front room.

'Oh thank goodness you're alive, Molly,' said Margaret, collapsing onto the sofa. 'We've just sprinted across the lawn like a pair of greyhounds.'

Molly's small cottage was built in the grounds of her sister and brother-in-law's much larger house. It felt much further away when running from one to the other at midnight in nightclothes.

Molly, not fully emerged from her deep sleep, initially thought she was dreaming, especially when her twin sister said, 'I've just seen Harvey Hoyland sitting at the end of my bed. I thought he'd come for you.'

Molly went to move the weight of her old cat from her knee then, and realised that she was lifeless. She had slipped away in her sleep.

'Oh dear girl,' said Bernard. 'Well that makes it clear. That's why Harvey came. To take Queenie.'

'Oh darling,' said Molly and stroked the cat's still-warm fur, feeling the hard pang of loss. She'd miss the creaky-boned Queenie, who had settled with her so easily and gratefully. Pavitar would be upset, she knew. But if Harvey had come for her, she'd be looked after. Molly wished so much that she had her sister's gift to see those who had moved on. She would have given anything to see her beloved Harvey again, just a glimpse.

'Bloody old fool, giving me a scare like that,' growled Margaret angrily, patting her chest. She raised her head and addressed her remark to a place far beyond the ceiling. 'Wait till I see you again, Harvey Hoyland, I'll give you what for.'

Bernard lifted Queenie gently into her basket in the corner, tucked her blanket snugly around her. 'There you go, lass. We'll see to you in the morning.' Then he poured out three glasses of sherry from Molly's drinks cabinet, handed them around. 'I think we need these for our nerves,' he said.

'Clear as day he was,' said Margaret. 'Smiling at me, in that way of his, hoping to charm me. Nobody charms me at that time of night, especially not him coming a-visiting and scaring me enough to go back with him.'

'Dear Harvey,' said Bernard, nudging his glass upwards. 'I'm so glad he came back into our lives. For a short but blessed time.'

And that incident set Molly off thinking. Laurie and Peter were *right* together. She couldn't explain it, but there was an energy surrounding them, a positive, loving force. She might not have had her sister's unwonted abilities, but she did have a strong sense that persisted and would not go away that she needed to speak to Peter Moore. He needed help, he had lost his direction. Of that she had no doubt at all.

Molly drove to the address Pete had given her when he enlisted into her club. She parked up and knocked on the door and when he answered she saw the shock in his eyes. Not unlike a child opening the door to the truanting officer.

'Molly. Hello.'

'Peter. I wonder if I could have a word.'

'Er . . . yeah, come in. Excuse the mess. I'm just sorting things out. I've sold my house.'

The mess that Molly walked into was not moving house mess, she thought. It was 'my head is a mess' mess.

'I don't usually call unannounced on people who leave the group,' she said, following him into his lounge, 'but I'm making an exception in your case.'

'Sorry I—' *ghosted you too* '—I . . . I should have phoned and told you I wouldn't be back.'

Molly moved an empty burger box aside and sat down on the sofa.

'Is everything all right, Peter? You don't look it.'

He wondered what she meant. He looked the same as always from the outside, it was on the inside he was different. If she could see into his soul, she might have grounds for saying that.

'I'm fine,' he said, a slight bark of annoyance in his voice that she wouldn't have associated with him.

'We've started another group. Fresh people. Very nice bunch, if you wanted to rejoin. There's no one who has been before.'

'I'm all right, thanks, really.'

Pong jumped up on the sofa, made a comical 'Meow' at Molly and tried out her knee for size. Molly chuckled.

'Sorry,' said Pete and reached over to move him.

'No, leave him, he's fine. I lost mine very recently. I miss the warmth.'

So did Pete. He missed the warmth of a woman in his life. He missed the warmth of Laurie pressed against his chest. She was never far from his thoughts, however much he tried to hold her back; she was the sea and he was Canute. He slumped into the armchair. For such a big man, he suddenly looked much smaller than he should, thought Molly.

'I'm not all right, Molly. I don't know what I'm doing.'

'Ah, that's a shame,' said Molly. 'I had hoped my instincts were wrong. Is this anything to do with Laurie?'

'No,' said Pete. 'Yes.'

'Sometimes when you're in a vulnerable place people get too close too quickly—'

He cut her off. 'It's not that. I wanted to get close to her, I didn't want to stop getting close to her. But I . . .' His hand rubbed the back of his neck. 'I can't tell you what it was. I can't risk it getting out.'

'It won't,' said Molly, 'you can trust me.'

And he knew he could, so he told her.

'So you see why I can't be with her,' said Pete. 'To be honest, Molly, I think she deserves better anyway. I don't know what I've become.' He sniffed hard, embarrassed at the show of emotion. 'Since I found out that Tara was having an affair with Alex Wilder, I think my genetic make-up has changed. I've become – and you'll excuse my language – a knob. I've treated women badly, I even came on to my sister-in-law. I've been so full of bile, I couldn't keep it in. I don't recognise myself any more.'

'Oh Peter, as humans, when we can't rail against the true culprits, we use ourselves as the target instead,' said Molly. 'I think you – perhaps – were expecting your brother to take you to task about coming on to his wife and give you a thump because you want to punish yourself. And you're alienating your friends and denying yourself a relationship with Laurie because you don't think you deserve it. You're carrying on where your wife left off, because you don't feel worthy of love, and you are, Peter. You're a good man.'

'I would destroy Laurie's memories of Alex if I let it slip that he was planning to leave her, not marry her. I couldn't do it to her. I really couldn't. I wish I'd been left with lies. Look what the truth has done to me.'

'Can I give you a piece of advice from someone who knows?' asked Molly. He nodded, she began. 'Once upon a time, I kept something from the man I loved because I was frightened that revealing it would kill us, but not telling it killed us even more. What you think might cause damage could actually bring you closer together, more than you can ever imagine. We wasted so much precious time.'

Molly stood to go then. There was a fine line between advising and lecturing and she didn't want to cross it.

'Make amends to the people you hurt, Peter, that's your starting point. Return to the man you were, but trust me on this most of all – take the first step with Laurie.'

Pete let her words sink in, she was right, he knew she was and he felt a speck of light enter the darkness of his present world, a Molly-shaped lantern to guide him back to himself. 'I will, Molly, I promise you,' he said.

*

Laurie had started to wonder about the words and phrases that Bella used in conjunction with Reid West-Hunt: 'strong-willed', 'sweep you off your feet', 'masterful'. She'd sigh with regret like a Disney Princess that Stu was more of an 'I don't mind if you don't mind' sort of guy. It hadn't got past Laurie that it always seemed to be Reid's way or the highway, though parcelled in a generous loop of pretty ribbon. 'Which restaurant would you prefer, X or Y? X? But Y is so much better – I'll book us a table at Y.' Y was always a wonderful restaurant, how could she complain?

The changes were subtle when they came, blowing into the relationship like asbestos dust: 'Why do you plait your hair like that? I mean it's your choice and I understand it's practical, but it looks a little childish when it's so beautiful and womanly loose.' 'Why do you never pick up your phone? You can't always be in meetings?' He'd laugh, like someone fondly infuriated, but somewhere deep within Laurie De Vere, an alarm bell was softly tinkling.

Chapter 53

12 January

Karen Linfield snatched open her front door at speed, ready to see off the salesman or market researcher who had the nerve to knock on a Sunday afternoon, registered the man standing on her doorstep with the enormous bouquet and proceeded to shut it again.

'Please don't. Give me a minute of your time and I'm out of here,' said Pete. He didn't recognise her, remembered her as having red hair like her sister. That told him everything he needed to know about himself. His mother would have been ashamed to have seen him treat this woman no better than trash. Sal was right – he had been a wanker. A temporary wanker, he hoped.

'What the fuck would I have to say to you?' said Karen, scowling so much her eyeballs were in danger of popping out and rolling down her cheeks.

'You don't have to say anything to me, but I have something to say to you, Karen,' said Pete, emphasising her name as if to prove he'd had the decency to commit it to memory.

'I have behaved appallingly. It is not an excuse but I have been in a bad place and I have used people and I'm so very sorry that you were one of them. I hate myself more than you ever can, trust me on that.'

Karen Linfield's lips relaxed a little. She had really fancied Pete when she met him at Sal and Natasha's Christmas party, dragged him – willingly – back to hers and enjoyed the one-night stand enough with him to allow herself to hope for more. It wasn't the first time she'd been ghosted by a bloke, but he'd tricked her emotions, made her think he really fancied her back.

'You're a lovely young lady, Karen, and deserve better than some prick dicking you about. Please accept these as a token of my sincerest apologies. It won't wind time back, but hopefully it will make you feel that you are a person of value who deserves flowers. I hope you meet someone who brings you lots of them and treats you so much better than I did. Don't settle for anything less.'

Pete thought she'd tell him to stick his bouquet, Karen thought she'd tell him to stick his bouquet, but she did know what he'd been through, which was partly why she had been drawn to him at Sal's party, that air of vulnerability. Her hands came out to receive the flowers. She wished he'd now say, 'So, can we start again – when can I see you?' but he didn't, so it was up to her to dictate the closure terms.

'Good luck,' she said. 'I hope you get your head sorted out.'

Then she shut the door in his face.

Pete knocked on the door to Sal's cottage hoping she'd answer and not Natasha. Natasha answered, and gave him a look of disapproval that sent the one her sister had given him just twenty minutes ago far into the shade.

'Hi, Natasha, is Sal in?'

Natasha's eyes dropped to the bouquet and bottle bag in Pete's hands, looked back at his face again then turned her head to shout into the house.

'Sal, there's a little boy at the door who'd like a word with you.' She made it sound like the worst insult she could give.

Sal bounced to the door. 'Pete,' she said, slightly confused. She'd been expecting the boy scout from two doors down asking her to sponsor him or something.

'These are for you,' said Pete. 'An apology.'

'It's not me—'

Pete cut her off. 'I've just been to Karen's. Hopefully I've made my peace with her.'

'Oh.' Sal nodded, a few beats, and then stepped towards him, pulled him into a strong embrace that half-crushed the flowers. 'You pillock.'

'I am. A pillock, a tosser, an arsehole, a *little boy*. All of those things and more.'

'You're not,' said Sal. 'Come in and have a cuppa.'

'Thanks, but I've got more of these to deliver.'

'Serial tosser,' mused Sal. They both broke into laughter. She took the bouquet and the bag, peeped inside. 'Ooh, Grand Marnier, my favourite.'

'I know. I'm sorry. You're my best girl mate and I never want to be on the wrong side of you again.'

Sal was lost for words for a moment, which was unheard of for her. She loved this man standing with stooped shoulders in front of her. He'd been through so much, and probably extra stuff that she didn't know about if his recent blip was anything to go by. She figured that he wasn't seeing the platinum-blonde solicitor who'd made his face light up any more because he'd shut her right down once when she'd asked. Shame. He was a lovely, kind man who deserved a break. Their friendship had never been really threatened, she knew he'd sort himself out eventually.

'Welcome home, Pete Moore,' she said.

Pete sat parked around the corner from Ria's small detached house. It was his turn to stalk her this time, waiting until her blue Golf pulled up onto the drive. He gave it five minutes before ringing the bell and heard the strains of 'Für Elise' playing in the belly of the house. He saw, out of the corner of his eye, the blind at the window flutter and then a long minute passed before the front door flew open with the same alacrity as it had done at Karen Linfield's house. It did not begin to close on him this time though.

Ria stood before him with freshly applied lipstick and a shirt customarily unbuttoned down to mid-breast level. A fresh spray of scent drifted out to him. Not Tara's this time.

'Ria. I came to apologise. My behaviour, the last time we met, was appalling. I think you know me well enough to realise it was out of character.'

'I suppose you'd better come in,' she said, mouth gathered into a tight moue.

'Thank you.'

He stepped inside, kicked off his shoes in order to walk on her pale blue carpet, even though she was treading on it in high pin-heels.

'Come through.'

He followed her into her lounge. It was very Ria – black, white, pinks and golds. A huge black and white photo of her naked in a Christine Keeler pose astride an Arne Jacobsen chair took up one wall. The pink cushion covers on the sofa had her photo printed on them: the room screamed 'me, me, me'.

Pete sat down on the sofa at her invitation, pushing one of the cushions out of the way as he didn't feel comfortable sitting on her face. Ria sat down on the adjacent armchair, crossing her shapely legs.

'You were saying,' she said, in a tone that said she was going to make him work for this.

'I'm sorry. You have been so thoughtful and generous and you didn't deserve what I said to you. I acted bullishly – like a prick in other words – and I came to say that I am really, really sorry about that.'

'And you think a bunch of flowers is going to make everything all right?'

'No. I wish I could unsay the words I used, but I can't do that. This doesn't even begin to cut it, I know.'

The bouquet was full of pink scented flowers, clearly chosen with care.

'Yes, well, it was an emotional day. I can sort of understand why you flipped. But you really did hurt me, Pete,' she said, which was the understatement of the year. He'd smashed her heart into pieces actually, because she'd realised that day that he was totally aware that she fancied him and that's why he'd been keeping her at arm's length. She had been as cross at herself, for not taking him up on his offer. Maybe in bed he would have realised that he desired her as much as she desired him.

'Then please, accept these from me even though I wouldn't blame you if you threw them straight in the bin,' he said.

She took the spray of flowers from him. 'They're lovely, thank you. Can I get you a drink?' He was forgiven, because she still wanted him, even after he'd insulted her in such a horrible way. He'd rather she hit him in the face with them.

'No thank you. That's kind, but I—'*don't want to get sucked back into this* '—I don't want to keep you. I hope you'll not hold it against me.'

She smiled and for an atom of time he wondered if he should keep her, accept the drink, let her in. She was besotted, pretty, caring. Is this what Tara had asked herself about him: that Pete was a good man who adored her so why couldn't she settle for him, why couldn't she let Alex Wilder go?

'I wouldn't ever hold it against you, Pete. I'll call and see you sometime, shall I?'

He cringed inwardly. No, it would be cruel to give her false hope.

'I don't think that would be a good idea, Ria.' He said it as gently as he could, hoping she would realise he was being kind, not callous.

'Right.' Her clipped tone told him that he'd disappointed her again. She'd read hope and possibility as well as apology in those beautiful flowers.

He stood, smiled at her and said, 'Goodbye, Ria.'

'Just before you go,' she said, taking a paper bag out of a drawer. 'These are for you. They were in the bags of things that I took from the cottage. They're letters.'

His hand came out to accept them.

'I think you should read them all,' she said.

Later, when he did read them, he realised that if Ria had wanted to deal him a punishing blow for rejecting her, she couldn't have picked a more brutal method.

The *Daily Trumpet* apologises to 'Brown-eyed Girl' last week for the entry in our weekly WLTM column which should have read, 'Sue, brown eyes, ginger long hair WLTM man for power walking and fine dining' and not 'Sue, brown eyes, minger, long hair WLTM man for power wanking and fine dining.' If you are genuinely interested in the light of this amendment, please write again as Sue cannot possibly sift through all the responses she had first time round.

Chapter 54

14 January

When Laurie next went in to the offices of the *Daily Trumpet*, it was to find Alan Robertson banging his head against the wall. Not figuratively, literally.

'I'm doing this because all I can feel is pain,' he said. 'So my brain doesn't have to deal with those tosspots out there who aren't fit to run a tap, never mind a newspaper.'

'Alan sit down, for goodness sake,' said Laurie. 'I'll make us both a coffee.'

'We've gone online. Sir Basil's latest brainwave, even though he doesn't know one end of a computer from a witch's tit. It was a leap of faith and I've ended up missing the ledge and falling so far down my nuts are in hell,' he groaned.

'Giving yourself concussion is not going to help,' Laurie admonished him.

'No, but it feels so good when I stop,' said Alan. He sat down and twisted his iMac around so Laurie could see it. 'Story number one. Lovely story. German shepherd brought back to life by a fireman, but because they used the caption *Auf Wiedersehn, Pet,* people thought we'd put up a video of a dog dying . . .'

Laurie didn't hear any more. Her brain was totally taken up with processing the footage of the firefighter stroking the dog's fur, holding the mask over the creature's muzzle. Then the German shepherd's tail twitched and cheers erupted in the background. It was *him.* She knew it was, even before Alan Robertson's voice broke through to her, reading out the rest of the copy. *'Firefighter Roger Moore, who rescued the baby then went back into the building for Barmy the German shepherd who had been locked in the upstairs bathroom, said that the pet masks had saved many lives. He had once revived a rabbi with one.'*

'It's Peter Moore, not Roger,' she said.

'Know him, do you?' asked Alan. 'I did wonder if they'd got the name right. I usually have two hopes where stuff like this is concerned: one is "no" and the other is "Bob". I'm figuring he isn't ninety-three either.'

'Thirty-three,' said Laurie.

'Peter Moore?' The name registered with Alan. He made a finger-click of recognition. 'He's the . . . no, he isn't, forget that.' A sharp U-turn as his head slipped into gear. In the same crash that killed Laurie's partner, Peter Moore had turned up in one of the attending fire engines and discovered his pregnant wife dying in her car. Alan had smothered those details because he knew the nationals would have swooped on the poor bugger like carrion crows. He could have plastered a sensationalist headline on the front page, but instead he'd given a nod to it on page six, done his duty and no more – partly for Laurie, to let the press interest drain away more quickly, partly for that young fireman's sake. A one-off in his career, turning his back on a juicy bone of news. And people thought he was heartless. But then the Labour councillors thought he was a fascist and the general public thought he was left of Stalin. None of them knew him at all and he preferred to keep it like that.

They moved on to the next case but Laurie held on to that image of Pete stroking the dog tenderly. He was proving impossible to shift from her heart. She'd fallen hard and fast in love with him and it had felt easy and right but it couldn't happen, because the past would never let them have a future. *He's gone,* said a voice inside her. *Gone as much as Alex has. For his sake, let him go.*

Reid was preparing vegetables in Laurie's kitchen when the doorbell went and he opened the door to a man holding an enormous bouquet of flowers. Both men seemed as shocked as each other.

'I was looking for Laurie,' said Pete. 'Does she still live here?'

'She's not back from work yet, can I help you?' Reid said, coldly polite.

'These are for her,' said Pete.

'Oh. Whom shall I say they're from?'

'Er . . . Pete. There's a card. I'm a . . . er . . . client.'

'I'll see she gets them. Thank you.'

The man closed the door then, the exchange over and Pete swore to himself all the way back to his car. He'd hoped she'd be in, allow him to face her. He knew she spent Tuesdays in the *Daily Trumpet* offices and was usually home early. Hers was the most important bouquet, he'd needed a couple of extra days to build up to delivering it, rehearsing over and over what he would say, even though he knew it would go off-script, his brain would disengage and then his feelings would take over. If she let him into the house, he would have told her everything, blown the secret to smithereens and when she fell, he would have caught her and they'd work this out between them. Somehow.

The card said much less. Apologised, asked her to call him and he'd explain, but why should she? He hadn't factored into the occasion that she might have moved on and he'd be standing there stuttering like an idiot, spouting bollocks at her new partner. Of course she'd found someone new, she was gorgeous and the man in her kitchen was handsome, refined and presumably owned the Porsche on the drive that he thought might have been a new car for her. Pete had blown his chance. He wished Laurie well, hoped she'd at least forgive him, in the future if not now.

Reid took the flowers and shut the door. He wasn't in a great mood as it was, and now this. He carried the flowers to the kitchen island, and took the small envelope from the plastic holder, ripped the card out.

Dear Laurie, Forgive me. I would love to talk to you and explain if you will please give me the chance. All I ask is five minutes of your time. My number, as you'll probably have erased it, is on the back of this card. Pete x

Reid tore up the card into tiny pieces and stuffed them right down to the bottom of the kitchen bin.

*

Laurie turned on her phone when she got out of the *Daily Trumpet* HQ. There were six missed calls from Reid and three voicemails.

One: 'Laurie, can you please ring me back when you get a moment.'

Two: 'Laurie, what is going on? Why aren't you ringing me back?'

Three: 'You can't possibly still be in a meeting. Ring me now.'

She rang.

'Hello, is there something wrong?'

'Where are you?'

'I'm just coming out of the *Daily Trumpet* offices. What's the matter?'

'Why haven't you been returning my calls?'

'Reid, I always turn my phone off when I'm working.'

'And you've been working all day there have you, without a break?'

'We stopped for lunch. There were no missed calls on my phone then because I looked at it. I told you I'd be home about six.'

'And I told you I'd be making dinner for us.'

Laurie looked at her watch. It was ten to six. She didn't think he'd have it waiting for her to ladle out as soon as she walked in through the door. She liked to unwind first, not kick off her shoes and immediately pick up the cutlery, but she wasn't in the mood to remonstrate.

'I'm only about a ten-minute drive away.' Impatience creeping into her tone now.

'Send me a picture of where you are.'

She laughed, presuming he was joking, then he asked again.

'Why would you want me to do that?'

'Because I don't believe you are where you say you are. You shouldn't have a problem with it if you're telling the truth.'

'All right then.'

She pressed end call with as much annoyance as her index finger could muster, raised the phone, took a photo of *Trumpet* HQ and sent it to him, the good mood which usually followed her out of her meetings there now crushed.

Chapter 55

Laurie got caught up in a traffic snarl roadworks and a small collision between a car and a minibus on the way home which held her up. She was all too aware of her anxiety levels rising and wondered when this had become a normal state of affairs, to be so jittery. Reid rang her at half past six.

'Dinner is going to be ruined,' he huffed tetchily. 'Where are you now?'

'I'm stuck in a jam.'

'Send me a photo,' he snapped and ended the call abruptly.

She sent it and then took a mental freeze frame of her life as she sat in a dead snake of cars. What the hell was she doing kowtowing to this sort of behaviour? They might be in the early days of a relationship but were these teething problems, as Bella had called them, or dangerous seeds which would grow wild and high and choke her if she let them?

Seeing Pete on the video that day had reinforced what she already knew deep down, that a heart beat in a singular way for someone it loved. It was not beating like that for Reid West-Hunt. She wasn't sure it ever would.

Reid greeted her at the door in a rush.

'I know what you're going to say,' he said. 'I'm an idiot, a demanding boor. The trouble with us perfectionists is that we can be the worst sort of intolerant prats. I bought these for you earlier, but hopefully now they will double up as an apology.' From behind his back he produced a beautiful bouquet of flowers. 'Come eat and let's relax, you must be shattered and frustrated sitting in traffic for all that time.'

She was. And she was also temporarily disarmed.

Charming Reid came out to play. She found herself rationalising his temper tantrum as she ate his delicious meal. He'd wanted to cook for her and for it all to be perfect. She'd arrived much later than he'd planned for – she had to take some responsibility in nearly spoiling it.

'I need your help on something,' he said matter-of-factly, as he poured them another two glasses of wine. That would put him over the limit, he was intending to stay over, so it seemed. She really didn't want that, not tonight. She braced herself to tell him so. Everything felt a battle with Reid, she'd noticed. As with Meredith, when things were playing to their tune, all went smoothly; but neither took too kindly to being challenged.

'What?' She presumed it was her legal expertise he needed. It wasn't.

'I can't seem to book myself into your cruise cabin. I was hoping to surprise you and come with you but irritatingly, I need your permission.'

She hadn't told him about her forthcoming trip. She should have, if they were in a relationship, but every time a suitable moment had come up for it to be dropped into conversation, she'd stopped herself. To avoid the scenario she was about to have, she knew.

'How did you know about that?' She forced herself to keep it light.

He threw her a question of his own. 'Was it a secret?'

'No. I just hadn't mentioned it.'

'Why wouldn't you tell me?'

'Because I made a mistake,' she answered honestly. 'It was meant to be a fulfilment of Alex's wish for me but I'd got it wrong. I'm not going to throw all that money away so I'll just go and get it over with. I leave the day after the year's anniversary of the crash and I want to be alone.'

'All the more reason for me to come with you, because being alone is the last thing you should be. Anyway, I spoke to a ridiculous woman on the line who said it was fine to add another passenger but she would need to speak to you first. So I'll transfer the cash and you ring tomorrow. Want a coffee or will it keep you up? I'm hoping it will keep me up.' He smiled at her, a lop-sided smile with sexual meaning that would have had Bella swooning, but all Laurie felt was irritation that he thought he could ride roughshod over her wishes as if she were a bimbo who didn't know her own mind.

'No coffee for me, thank you,' she said, clearly vexed.

'I can't say I've ever considered a cruise before. But, for you, I'll go. I'll make us both a coffee.'

He even thinks he knows better than I do where a simple drink is concerned, she thought. Either that or he hadn't even bothered to listen to her answer because he had already decided what it should be.

She watched him cross the kitchen to the kettle, fill up the cafetière with ground coffee. She pictured Pete there instead, his strong back and big firefighter shoulders and felt her heart lighten at the thought of him.

'No point in paying for an empty place,' Reid said,

swiping his glass of wine up from the island. 'I usually go skiing in February, so I always take the first three weeks off anyway.'

Mentally she dug her heels in further. 'As I said, I want to go by myself.'

'Do you now?' he said, accusation in his words.

'Yes.' A very definite yes at that.

'We'd have a great time together. Why would you want to be alone for Valentine's Day? Oh come on.' He flashed a warm smile.

'That date wasn't why I booked it, it's incidental,' said Laurie.

'Why did you ask for a double cabin?'

Where had he got this information from? The only person she could think of was Stu – via Bella. It was such a Bella thing to do, contriving to put them together for Valentine's Day and doing everything to make sure Laurie wasn't alone and wallowing in a resurgence of grief that the anniversary of Alex's death was bound to throw up. Her heart was in the right place, even if her brain wasn't always.

'I booked late, it's all they had left.'

'Expensive.'

'It was. But I had no choice.'

'Not sharing it with *Pete* then?' The warm smile was still in place but the words were glacial.

'Pete?' She'd never mentioned Pete to him. Where had he conjured that name from? It *had* to be Stu via Bella, which made her seriously cross and she'd have words.

Reid tossed the contents of the wine glass down his neck, replaced it on the island none too gently.

'Hard day tomorrow, think I'll get an early night,' he said. 'Thanks for allowing me to cook you dinner and buy you flowers but as you have so much money to throw around, you can buy your own from now on.'

'Reid?' she said, confused, as he swept up his car keys from the work surface, picked up his jacket from where he had draped it over one of the bar chairs and left the house at speed. She heard his car fire up on the drive, the wheels squeal as if making a further statement of displeasure.

Laurie locked the door, poured herself another glass of wine. His exit was meant to punish her but it hadn't. If anything, he'd relieved her of the sticky task of saying she didn't want him to stay that night. A two-minute YouTube video of a firefighter rescuing a dog would linger in her head for longer, and mean much more to her, than his hissy fit could.

Chapter 56

15 January

When Laurie picked up her Norwegian krone the next day, she called in to the nearby Forest Hotel where Bella was working. She'd been too hacked off to ring her after Reid had gone, decided to let herself simmer down and speak to her friend face to face instead.

'What's up, you look narked,' said Bella, sitting down at one of the tables in the coffee bar. 'Everything all right with you and Reid?'

'Not really,' said Laurie, curtly. 'He stormed out of my house yesterday, because I wouldn't book him into my cabin on the cruise.'

'Wouldn't you like that?' asked Bella.

Her reaction told Laurie that she'd been right to suspect Bella of interfering in her holiday plans. Her infuriation cranked up a few notches.

'No, I wouldn't. And then he asked me if that was because I was going with Pete.'

Bella's eyebrows almost crashed together in confusion. 'Pete? Why would he say that?'

'You tell me.' Laurie answered her in a voice she usually saved for court.

'What do you mean?'

'It can only have come from Stu. Please stop feeding him so much detail about my life so he can pass it on to Reid, Bella.'

Bella slowly shook her head. 'Laurie, I haven't said anything to Stu about your cruise or mentioned Pete to him and even if I had, he's not a gossipy sort of bloke. Wherever Reid's getting his information from, it certainly isn't him. I swear to you. I can keep my gob shut sometimes, you know.'

Laurie's brow furrowed. *Well that was odd.* She had to admit, Stu never had come across as a man who indulged in small talk about other people's business, but how else could Reid know so much about her and her plans?

'... Although he told me not to say anything, but I'm going to tell you because I'm a bit worried,' Bella went on. 'Stu's off work at the moment with stress. I've never seen him like this before. He's always been a bit sniffy about people who go off work with those sorts of conditions, says they must be either wimps or swinging the lead, and then he has to swallow his own words and trot to the docs because he can't sleep and keeps on getting the most awful cold sores.' Bella sighed. 'He won't talk to me about what's wrong, just shuts me down as soon as I ask.'

'I'm sorry to hear that,' said Laurie. 'I hope he opens up to you. What do you think it might be? Has his job changed?'

'No, it's exactly the same. The only difference is Reid joining the team, and he and Stu get on fine, so it can't be that. What were you saying about him? That you'd had a lovers' tiff about the holiday?' asked Bella, cheering up slightly at the subject matter. 'I've bought a hat.'

'I hope you've kept your receipt then,' replied Laurie.

Sharp intake of breath from Bella. 'Why?'

'I don't think we're a match.'

'But he's gorgeous, Laurie. And clever – he's got a first from Oxford – and a Porsche and he's witty and ambitious and masterful and romantic . . .'

Bella's list went on and on and he was most of those things. But he wasn't masterful, he was controlling and he wasn't romantic, he was manipulative and his rich, attractive veneer was serving to mask it. Laurie had spent most of the evening after he'd gone thinking about her relationship with him and the recurring weave in the pattern: sulk, confrontation, profuse apologies, presents. Up until yesterday it had all been low-level stuff and that was the first time he'd shown his disapproval by stomping out, but somehow it signalled a cranking up of pressure. She'd taken a long hard look at them as a couple, recognised the changes he'd imposed on her own self: how she found herself bending more and more to his choices, his will, heard the alarm bells alerting her to the discreet chipping away at her confidence, how he turned the full beam of his attention onto her, then switched it off without notice, intending to disorientate.

She was right to think she'd been coerced into sleeping with him that first time in the Ritz. He'd wanted it and had wrapped up his intentions in a fancy-dancing Christmas present. She'd seen it often enough in the divorce cases she handled, how calculating some partners could be, how they slipped a choke chain on your neck when you least expected it, ready to be pulled tight when they felt it necessary to bring you to heel. She never thought she'd be the sort to fall prey to someone like this, but she had. She'd wandered into a spider's web where the danger signs had been rendered invisible by the blinding light of shiny good looks and gallantry. She'd even realised that she had blamed herself for bringing out the flipside of his personality. Being stuck in traffic did not cause a rational person to demand photographs to prove where she was. Emotional abuse was all so much easier to spot from the outside than from in.

She told Bella about what had happened with Reid yesterday and didn't leave her any space to comment.

'If he doesn't contact me again, that would be the ideal scenario,' said Laurie. 'If he does, then I will end it, but as far as I'm concerned, it's over.'

Bella opened up her mouth then to protest, but shut it. The old Laurie was on her way back, the one who knew her own mind and her worth. The one who knew herself better than anyone else could.

Chapter 57

5 February

Two nights before the cruise, Laurie turned into her drive after her last day at work until after her trip to find Reid's Porsche parked there. She hadn't heard a single word from him in three whole weeks and that, to her, sent out a clear enough message. But the lights were on in her house, and he was inside.

That morning she had been looking for the spare front door key to drop off at the estate agents. Someone had been to view the house, loved it and wanted to arrange a second viewing when she would be in Norway. It was only then she realised that Reid must still have it; he'd borrowed it from her so he could make dinner for them the last time he'd been there. She'd rung up a locksmith and arranged to have the front door lock changed in the morning, cursing herself that she could have been so lax to have missed such a thing.

Did he honestly presume they could carry on as normal after three weeks of silence, she wondered, parking up, taking her time to get out of the car. He must have gotten too used to volatile relationships with their dramatic leavings and fervid reconciliations. Some people thrived on those stormy, knife-edge affairs, falsely classifying them as 'passionate'. Not her. Love to her was a steady ship sailing on gentle waters. The sort of love she and Pete would have had, she thought with a gulp of wistful sadness.

She wondered if she should call someone, Bella perhaps, or even the police, then dismissed it as cracking a nut with a sledgehammer. She willed steel into her spine as she walked towards the house. She would be dignified and courteous, that was the way to 'consciously uncouple' as Gwyneth Paltrow so eloquently put it. Maybe that's what Alex had had in mind for them, a dinner and a kind, but definite, ending.

Reid greeted her as if they had only parted – and amicably so – that morning. He had a comedy apron on, was mixing salad in a bowl. Laurie felt as if she was walking onto a film set and hadn't been told her lines.

'Laurie, there you are. I thought I'd surprise you with dinner. Greek salad – my salads are legendary. I'm so sorry I haven't been in touch, it's been stupidly busy and idiots off with stress so everyone else has to absorb their workload. Come on, take your coat off, sit, here's a glass of wine. And I bought you a little something, to apologise for being an oaf.' He slid over an instantly recognisable blue gift bag: Tiffany. Then he kissed her cheek and she tried not to recoil. It was time for the full beam of attention to swing onto her, but she knew the rules of his game now and he wasn't aware that she did. She felt nothing for him, but she'd extricate herself from him as cleanly and quickly as possible and then she would spend a long time single.

'Open it up then,' he said, pointing to the bag, sounding

slightly hurt that she didn't pounce on it with unbridled glee. She reached inside, found a box; inside the box there was a pouch – like a posh 'pass the parcel' – and inside that a bracelet. It was beautiful, but she wouldn't accept it. She'd pretend, for now, to be grateful and then give it back. This time her defences stayed up and armed.

He transferred scoopfuls of salad to the plates. There were warm pitta breads in a basket that he must have found at the back of a cupboard, white butter, stuffed olives, falafels. They sat opposite each other at the kitchen island and ate. Laurie's appetite was non-existent. This wasn't normal, however much the flow of conversation was trying to be. *How was your day? Had any people to view the house? Are you feeling all right because you're not eating much?* Did he really think that she could be bought and manipulated so easily? Maybe this was the model he was accustomed to because other women accepted it.

'So, tell me about your holiday then,' he asked. 'What ports will you be visiting?'

'How *did* you know I was going, by the way?' She tried to ask the question as nonchalantly as possible.

'You mentioned it. Either that or I'm psychic.' He smiled and she smiled back, although she had never felt less like smiling. She hadn't mentioned it, and he wasn't psychic.

'So, the ports?' he asked again.

'I can't remember, if I'm honest.'

He laughed, a mirthless flat sound which she didn't grace with an acknowledgement.

'You're very frosty this evening, Miss De Vere. What's the matter?'

He was trying to unsettle her. She wouldn't let him see that he was.

'Nothing. Nothing at all.'

Her scalp began to tingle with the onset of anxiety.

'So, the ports. Let me remind you: Åndalsnes, Tromsø, Alta and then Stav-an-ger.'

The air was thickening with something nasty.

'You need a good memory when you're a liar, Laurie.' He carried on loading his fork with salad then pushing it into his mouth, chewing hard.

'Not sure what you mean, Reid.'

He waggled his fork at her, his smile odd now, as if it had been painted on his lips.

'What are you up to?' he said.

'I have no idea what you're talking about.' She put down her fork. Another mouthful and she'd throw up.

'No one books a double cabin for one.'

'They do. Reid . . .' No more, she'd meant to keep it polite but she couldn't stand it any longer. Let them just cut to the point where he stormed out, for that was surely coming next. The words fired out of her like a bullet: 'I think you should go.'

'What?' A chortle of disbelief from him. 'You're throwing me out?' He carried on eating.

'I'd like you to leave. Now.'

'Don't be inhospitable, Laurie, I'm not going anywhere.' He tipped wine down his throat, then refilled his glass so much that it spilt over the rim, flowed onto the island.

She knew then that she'd given him too much benefit of the doubt. She needed to get him out of her house, out of her life. He was no less scary for being handsome, clever and wearing a Fendi jumper. She should have gone with her initial response and phoned someone.

He raised the glass. 'Bon voyage,' he toasted her, took a slug and then tossed the rest in her face.

Laurie froze mid-gasp, paralysed by shock.

'Totally unbelievable,' said Reid. 'Give a woman everything and it's still not enough.' He picked up the bracelet, stuffed it in his pocket, got off the stool. She flinched as he stepped towards her, pushed his face into hers and said in a fierce whisper, '*Bitch.*' The lack of volume carried more threat than a shout.

'Get out now before I call the police,' said Laurie and her hand shot out for the fork next to her plate. His eyes travelled from it to her face and his eyebrow quirked as if she was insane.

'Have a great holiday, Laurie,' he said and strolled casually out of the door. She thought he'd slam it, but he closed it carefully, as if to defy her expectation. She leapt from her seat, locked it, dead-bolted it behind her and only then did she realise how much she was shaking.

She cleaned the island, cleared the dishes, went upstairs to shower the wine from her, loaded her wet clothes into the washing machine, leaving no trace that Reid West-Hunt had ever been there that night. It was, at least, over. And she was safe, it could have been so much worse. Given time, she was sure it would have been so much worse.

Sleep evaded her. Every tiny creak the house made as it settled startled her back to full consciousness. She lay in bed, glad that in just over twenty-four hours she was going away now, glad she'd booked the holiday, glad that Reid West-Hunt hadn't managed to inveigle himself onto the ship with her. She thought of his weird smile as he ate, the disparity of the comedy apron and the way he had called her a bitch, the convivial food and the air of threat, the bread basket which he had searched for in the kitchen cupboards. She sat bolt upright. She knew then how he'd found out about the cruise. She'd put all the documentation in a drawer in the lounge. She hurried downstairs to find her cruise ticket, luggage labels and passport cut up into confetti.

Chapter 58

6 February

The day before Nigel's cruise, Pete, Griff and Lucy were at his house. It was a year ago today that Pete had become a widower and not a day that anyone wanted him to be by himself.

The snooker table had been in the middle of the conservatory since the week after the disastrous birthday party and looked like a jewel set in a perfect mount. Nigel was whupping Pete's backside at the game which only added to his holiday excitement.

'So you've sold your house then, bro?' said Griff.

'Asking price, first-time buyers,' replied Pete.

'You jammy git.'

'If all goes to plan, Pong and I will be moving in with Dad when we come back until I find a place,' said Pete.

'Ah, not so jammy git then,' said Griff to that.

'Oy, cheeky,' said Nigel.

'You might not get Pong back. He's settled in too quickly for my liking,' said Griff. 'He was between us in bed last night, snoring.'

'Oh, we're going to have such a great time in Norway, lad,' said Nigel, laying on the eagerness for his son.

'I should be on my way to Venice and culture now,' said Pete with a sad sigh. 'Instead I'm going to have my nuts frozen off in the Arctic Circle.'

'No point in wasting a double cabin,' said Nigel, who'd persuaded him that accompanying his old dad would be a much better option than Italy. He wanted Pete to have something else to think about at this time of year, to stamp good memories onto future February anniversaries. Memories full of snow and Northern Lights, cheerful company and good food. He thudded the black ball into the top right pocket and fist-pumped. 'That's how you do it,' he said. 'Griff, your turn.'

While Griff was also getting beaten by their father, Pete pulled Lucy out into the garden under the pretext of checking up on how Mr and Mrs Moore was faring in the February frost.

'I owe you a massive belated apology,' he said.

'What for?' she asked.

'Coming on to you at the end of last year.' He knocked on his head with his fist. 'I can't even believe I did that.'

'Why, because I'm so ugly?' chortled Lucy.

'No, because you're like my own sister, which makes it extra gross.'

'You were having a screw-up moment. After what you found out, who could blame you. I imagine you went into a temporary fugue state of all women are bitches, which is why I didn't knee you in the gonads.' She rubbed his arm, a comforting gesture.

'If it makes you feel any better, I also tried it on with Ria and Sal's girlfriend's sister.'

'Wow – you went into full-on wanker mode,' gasped Lucy.

'That's what Sal called me. It's cost me a fortune in sorry flowers.'

They both chuckled, then Lucy dared to ask, 'What happened to the lady with the car, Pete? Laurie wasn't it?' Both she and Griff had wondered, presumed the worst, not wanted to pry.

'It didn't work out – on both sides,' was all he replied. The mere sound of her name stirred everything up inside him.

Sadly Laurie hadn't contacted him. Who could blame her? She had moved on and he was consigned to the history dump. No more than he deserved. He wondered if the good-looking man was taking her mind off things today, caring for her, loving her.

'So where are my flowers?' asked Lucy. 'How come they get flowers and I don't?'

'You get this,' he said and pulled an envelope out of his pocket. 'Go on, open it, it won't bite you.'

Inside was a voucher for a weekend stay at a cottage in Whitby.

'It's got a hot tub and a sauna,' said Pete. 'And a welcome basket of champagne and posh stuff to eat.'

'This for you and me or me and Griff,' said Lucy, pretending to be serious, then she laughed when Pete started choking.

'You had a hard year too,' said Pete, after almost coughing a lung out. 'I thought a little break might be in order for you both.'

'We're going to try and adopt a child,' said Lucy. 'No more prodding and poking, we're done.'

Pete smiled. One door might have closed, but there were plenty of adoption doors to open, leading to rooms full of children who needed a mother and father like Griff and Lucy. Maybe even one day he and a partner would open that door too.

'How come Ria didn't take you up on the offer?' Lucy continued.

'I didn't exactly come on to her romantically,' said Pete, cringing. 'She got her own back, she gave me a clutch of letters that she found in the cottage and they made for hard reading. I didn't want to at first, but the temptation proved too much and I went in.'

'What did they say?'

'That Tara felt more for Alex than she ever thought it was possible to feel for someone. That she didn't want to hurt me but he was her "one true north" and try as she might she couldn't forget him. His said similar, that he loved her beyond anything he could imagine and how sad he was that they had to damage people in order to be together. I never thought Tara was the sort to write letters, but they were beautiful. It was like . . . a different level of love between them. We didn't have that.'

Lucy put her arms around her brother-in-law and hugged him tightly. 'You'll find someone to love again, Pete. Your heart will point you to your own true north.'

It already did and I blew it, he didn't say.

*

'By the way, the estate agent has a set of keys so he can accompany anyone round who wants to view. Mr and Mrs Archer are coming on Friday morning for their second viewing, so fingers crossed there. I've had both the front and back door locks changed ... Right, back to Keith. Just a little sprinkle of flakes,' Laurie instructed Bella, giving her a Keith Richards refresher course demonstration. Keith swam to the top and expertly caught one, gobbled it down in an instant.

'Sorry, just run that past me again,' said Bella. She had something on her mind, obviously, her eyes looked as far away as her thoughts.

'What's up, Bells?'

'Nothing.'

'Liar.'

'Laurie, I know this is a rough day for you and so I'm not loading any more onto you.'

'Bells, you and I know that I lost Alex a long time before the sixth of February last year.'

Laurie's brain, like the worst kind of electronic diary, had woken her up especially to remind her that today was the anniversary of the crash, as if she could forget it. She had cried a brief flurry of automatic tears, then she had lain in bed and remembered how it was between her and Alex when it had been good and she had smiled. Then she imagined packing him away in a treasure box, carefully, in the best kind of tissue paper, shifting him to a different place in her heart. A part of her would always love him, just as a part of him would have always loved her, but they had ended. She had let him go, with the complete wheel-turn of the year.

'Really, I'm fine, Bells. Please tell me what's wrong.'

Bella puffed out her cheeks before answering. 'Reid West-Hunt has been a total dick to Stu at work.'

Laurie felt a cold worm wriggle down her spine at that

name. The locksmith had been that morning and while he was there, she'd had deliveries of fifty red roses and a bottle of Dom Perignon pink champagne. She'd refused both consignments. Her work files were full of women befuddled by emotional apologies, silky excuses and promises, their good natures convincing them to give their partners another chance because it 'wasn't all bad'. But the roundabout got increasingly wild and scary and they became too fearful to jump off it. She had leapt and would not be guilt-tripped or seduced into rejoining it. She had sent Reid West-Hunt a clinical text to tell him not to contact her again, they were over – those words needed to be seen by him and understood. She had threatened him with the full force of the law if he persisted, then blocked his number.

'That's why Stu's been on the sick,' Bella continued. 'He broke down yesterday, vomited out all the detail. Reid West-Hunt has been undermining him, belittling him. New brooms sweep clean and all that; turns out he isn't the great person we thought he was.'

Laurie gave her a potted history of what had passed between her and Reid West-Hunt last night and Bella listened with her mouth agape.

'Tell Stu to report him, Bella,' said Laurie at the end, without any compunction. 'He's an unstable bully and luckily the workplace is becoming much more aware of the damage those sorts of tyrants can do to people's health – mental and otherwise. No one should have to put up with it. If he's doing it to Stu, he'll be doing it to others too. Plus, I dread to think about the poor woman he'll target next.'

'I think you had a lucky escape,' said Bella. 'I've been a crap friend, haven't I? And on top of everything, I try and hook you up with a psychopath.'

Laurie put her arm around her friend, pulled her close. 'You're a great mate, you prawn. Let's just look forward and not back, eh?'

'You seem ... okay,' said Bella, as Laurie handed her a shiny new set of house keys.

'I am, Bells. I think I understand what happened with Alex and me. It wasn't his fault. I know he wanted to do the right thing, but you can't put love where it doesn't want to go. And that's why, when I come home from Norway, I'm going to put Alex's ashes and the ring wherever Tara is resting now. I think they belong together. The three of them.'

Bella nodded, fought back the desire to say something sarcastic, because Laurie was a bigger person than she could be, given the same set of circumstances.

'I'm also going to pay for Brendan and Meredith to go on their wedding anniversary cruise. It's what Alex was planning for them and he never got around to it, so I will.'

Bella, again, bit her lip. 'Will you tell them about ... *her*?'

'Why? It would only upset them. There's no need for them to know.'

'You're a good woman, Laurie. I only wish they knew how much.'

'It's better they think worse of me than of their son. They've suffered enough.'

Bella smiled at her friend. Her wonderful, sweet, best friend who deserved a big fat lump of kind karma. 'I hope you have a fantastic holiday and I'll look after Keith for you and check up on the house. Any funny business at all and I'm calling the feds.'

'Reid ripped up my eticket and my passport,' said Laurie.

Bella's jaw dropped. 'Oh my God. How will you be able to go then?'

'He must have been snooping around the house. I'm sorry I accused Stu of telling him my business, because it obviously wasn't the case. Reid found all the travel documentation in my drawer and then decided to sabotage my holiday. That drawer . . .' Laurie pointed to the said drawer, waited for the penny to drop.

'The stupid drawer?' said Bella eventually as a grin dawned on her face.

'Alex used to laugh at me, he said it wouldn't fool anyone, but it seems it really did.'

'It couldn't happen to a bigger twat,' Bella said, hooting with laughter.

'I've downloaded more luggage labels and another eticket from the Figurehead website. My proper passport and euros are in the house safe. The drawer might be stupid, but I'm not.' Laurie would enjoy her holiday a little more knowing she'd soured his revenge.

'That's my girl,' whispered Bella, which shocked her, because she had no idea where that had come from. It wasn't an expression she had ever used before in her life.

Chapter 59

7 February

Pete set off to drive to Southampton at stupid o'clock.

'I could have been in Venice now,' he said.

'I wish I had a pound for every time you've said that since I asked you to come with me,' replied his father. 'You didn't have to say yes, you know.'

That was true. And Pete had no idea what had changed his mind other than everywhere he looked, there seemed to be a mention of the Northern Lights as if he was being subliminally hijacked by them. TV programmes, cruise brochures advertising for next year dropping through his letter box, even that old song from the 1970s by Renaissance, 'Northern Lights' playing on the car radio, as it was doing again now and Nigel was warbling along to it, annoyingly singing all the wrong words.

'It's getting me right in the mood,' he broke off to say.

'Please tell me I haven't got a five-hour singalong to look forward to,' Pete groaned.

'Oh shut up moaning and drive, miseryguts,' said Nigel, giddy as a schoolboy. He gasped then. 'Oh heck, I hope Cora doesn't turn up at the dock still expecting to come,' he said and chuckled.

'Haven't you heard anything from her at all?' asked Pete.

'Not even a Christmas card. Ask me if I'm bothered.'

'Are you bothered, Dad?'

'No.' He mused for a moment or two. 'Looking back, she wasn't very smiley, was she?'

'She was a cheerless old crow, Dad. But it was your choice, not ours.'

'You get lonely when you've had the company of a good woman for so many years, son. But being with the wrong partner is worse than being lonely, I've learned that if nothing else.'

Pete knew that already. He'd been lonely in his marriage; he and Tara would never have worked and were limping along towards a finish line, that he could easily see now with the vantage point of time. She'd been a whirlwind, blasting into his life, not giving him a chance to draw breath, needing him to stem her pain. Then he'd met Laurie, who had gently breathed hope and warmth into his aching heart. She was broken, like him, but somehow in that night they spent together, they had made each other complete. He wished her all the happiness in the world, wherever she was, whoever she was with. He also wished he'd had that conversation with Molly so much sooner, heard her sage advice about what he should have done instead of what he did do. He thought he was being kind to Laurie, but he hadn't been. Not at all and it was no wonder she didn't respond to an apology on a small card stuffed into a bunch of flowers.

'The Northern Lights, la la la la. They will guide me back towards you,' trilled Nigel at full volume.

If only they would, thought Pete.

*

Laurie sat on the bus listening to the driver talking down his microphone about all the safety features for the benefit of the new passengers who'd joined them at Leicester but she couldn't concentrate. All she could think about was that she was the only person on here heading for Southampton who was not in a couple. Still that was preferable to being in a couple if the other half was Reid West-Hunt. She had a lot of time to think on that bus journey about the edge of the slippery slope she had been on with him, dissect how their relationship had evolved and – God forbid – what would have followed if she hadn't got out when she had. She shuddered at the thought of him snooping through the drawers in her house, wondered what he'd been expecting to find, but she'd never been able to work out where he'd dredged up Pete's name from. Anyway, she was on her way to Norway, away from him, she should think of him no more. She would let the cold, Arctic air sweep through her and tear out horrible memories and old sadnesses. *Alex.*

She hadn't even told Bella that she never felt as if she was enough for Alex. He was a force of nature all of his own, as if imbued with more than his fair share of life, a walking flare of energy. He burned bright and quick, like a beautiful firework. He did love her, she knew, but not enough.

She wondered where Pete was, hoped he was happy, hoped he had found someone to love. Someone to love enough.

Chapter 60

'I told you you'd be impressed,' said Nigel, beaming as Pete took in the beautiful atrium of the *Mermaidia* en route to their port side cabin.

He was. It was bonkers how big this ship was and Pete was slightly bewildered how something this massive could actually float. It was more like a town than a boat. There was a welcoming bottle of champagne cooling in an ice bucket in their cabin when they got to it.

'I ordered that to share with Cora, but I didn't bother cancelling it,' said Nigel, tearing the foil from the top, unscrewing the wire and popping the cork like a seasoned sommelier. He poured and handed a full flute to his son.

'Here's to the Aurora Borealis bringing us some luck. We are going to toast a new dawn,' he said. 'That's what the Aurora means, you know – dawn.'

Pete clinked his glass against his father's.

'You don't half talk a load of Borealis, Dad,' he said.

*

When Laurie reached her starboard side cabin, her suitcase had already arrived and so she had started to unpack. As she hung up her long black dress, she decided that she wasn't going to be a shrinking violet on this cruise, hiding in corners with a book or sitting in her cabin because she daren't venture out. By the time the coach had pulled alongside the ship terminal, she'd already had a nice conversation with the people sitting behind her. If she met them on board, at least she'd have someone to say hello to. Judging from the size of the ship, though, she wondered what the likelihood was of bumping into them again. It was enormous. And beautiful. And she had a cabin steward called Paul who would make her bed, leave chocolates on her pillow and give her fresh towels every day. She was going to enjoy every one of those pounds this holiday had cost, she decided.

There was a ship's newspaper, *Mermaidia Today*, waiting on her bed with details of all the events happening on board tonight and tomorrow. A theatre show might be nice, she could be anonymous there. She'd booked to have dinner every night at 6.30 p.m., on a table of eight: hopefully, nice friendly people, because that's what Alan Robertson had advised her to do. He went cruising with his wife because he liked the fact there was no internet or signal in the middle of the sea and so very little chance to get hold of him when things went wrong back at *Trumpet* HQ. He wouldn't have picked that way of travelling otherwise, he said. He might have been tempted to throw himself off the top deck as soon as his phone rang.

She had just finished unpacking when a tannoy call alerted her to attend a life-jacket meeting at her allocated muster station. Alan told her that he and his wife offset the monotony of those by 'watching out for the knobheads who disobeyed all the instructions and thought they knew better than the crew'. She bet a cruise with the grumpy old sod would have been fun.

After the meeting, Laurie went out on deck to watch the sailaway. She exchanged the voucher that had been left in her welcome pack for a glass of fizz from a waiter circulating with a tray of them, and stood in the freezing February air with lots of wrapped-up fellow passengers already in holiday mode. The engines rumbled and the water below began to churn and to cheers and whistles and to the music of a band playing outside the terminal building, the ship began to push away from the dockside. They were off, nosing into the chilled dark; she felt a hit of excitement and trepidation, and then a slap of sadness that came at speed from left field. She thought she was going to be making this trip as a new bride, not a dumpee. *Now stop that*, said a stern voice inside. *You are holidaying as an independent woman, a lone passenger free to go where you want and do what you want.* It was the sort of thing she could imagine Alex saying to her, if they'd split up and remained friends. Would they have been able to do that, she wondered, before shaking him away, letting him drift back to England on the current. She wouldn't take him with her any more.

'Are we supposed to dress for dinner?' asked Pete, holding up a suit in one hand and a polo shirt in the other.

'Nope. Not according to Chippy from the club, just casual on the first night,' said Nigel, again quoting from the Chippy Guide to Cruising. Pete had heard a lot of Chippy Craddock's wisdom on the drive down. Chippy and his wife had notched up over twenty cruises. What he didn't know about holidays on ships wasn't worth talking about, said Nigel.

'Ooh look, captain's got the same name as me,' said Nigel, showing Pete the front cover of the *Mermaidia Today*. 'Captain Nigel O'Shaughnessy. All the best-looking men are called Nigel. Nigel Havers, Nigel Mansell, Nigel Benn . . .'

'Dream on, Dad,' said Pete, laughing at him. 'When do we eat, I'm starving?'

'We're booked on a table at eight-thirty for eight,' said Nigel.

Pete looked at his watch. 'Eight-thirty? That's two and a half hours away.'

'Let's go and get a drink and have a wander,' said Nigel. 'Do you think they'll have a snooker table on board?'

Laurie put on a dark green satin cocktail dress for the first night's dinner, then seeing everyone else was in casual clothes she turned abruptly and went back to change into trousers and a top. *Lesson one*, she thought.

She went down to the restaurant not feeling half as confident as she looked, smiling at a line of waiters who smiled first and said good evening to her. Already seated on her table were four middle-aged women and an elderly couple looking at menus. They looked a cheery bunch and welcomed her warmly. A waiter pulled a chair out for her, tucked her under the table and flapped a serviette open to place on her knee.

'I could get used to this,' she said, breaking the conversational ice.

'Cruising by yourself are you?' asked the older woman who had a lilting West Country accent.

'Yes,' replied Laurie, expecting everyone to burst into laughter at that and point their fingers.

'First time?' asked her husband.

'Yep.'

'I'm Don and this is my husband Bunty,' she said.

'No, you aren't,' said Don. 'And that's before she's had a wine.'

That triggered off a tinkle of laughter and more introductions. The four women were Ven, Roz, Olive and Frankie and they were also from Yorkshire, although Olive said she lived in Cephalonia now, Frankie had moved to Cornwall and Ven had moved to a village in Hampshire because her husband was the captain of the ship. 'He'll be joining us,' she said. 'But not tonight.'

The four Yorkshire women were old school friends who were on the ship to celebrate their fiftieth birthdays. 'We don't get together much in person these days, as you can imagine with us living so far apart,' Ven went on to explain to Laurie.

'You'll love cruising,' said Frankie.

'I'll be honest, I'm pretty nervous about being a solo passenger,' replied Laurie.

'There are loads of them around. You can either hook up with them or do your own thing. You can always come and say hello to us of course,' Ven went on. 'We're either doing a quiz in one of the downstairs bars, shopping or having a cocktail.'

'Mostly the last one,' chirped up Olive.

'Have you booked any trips?' asked Frankie.

'I've booked everything,' replied Laurie. 'Visiting an Ice Hotel, a reindeer ride, a husky ride and an evening hunting the Northern Lights.'

'We've been up to Norway two years running now and we've haven't seen them once,' said Don, cutting into his steak as if it was directly responsible for causing the non-sighting. 'Then blow me, my neighbour went up to Scotland and saw them just before Christmas in Aberdeen.'

'Our neighbour's a bloody liar,' said Bunty. 'He said that just to annoy you.'

'He had pictures,' said Don.

'He'll have photographed other people's photos, the lying hound,' said Bunty. 'He's one of those that has to have done what you've never managed to do.'

'I've seen them every time I've come up here,' said Ven.

'You're our lucky charm then, are you?' said Don.

'She is,' said Frankie and winked at the captain's wife. 'Don't you worry. We'll see the lights if Ven is on board.'

'This is my lovely wife Doreen and I am Vernon Turbot, of Turbot fish and chip establishments. If you're from our part of Yorkshire, you'll have heard of me,' said the elderly gentleman, introducing himself to Pete and Nigel at their dining table.

'I have heard of them of course,' said Nigel, shaking his hand. 'My, it's a small world.'

'There seem to be a lot of Yorkshire people on this ship,' said Gerry from Herefordshire – he wouldn't narrow it down any further where he came from, in case one of the Yorkshire people traced his house and arranged to have it burgled while he was away, Nigel would say later. Gerry was on the ship with his wife Sylvia and their daughter Susan who – Nigel would also say later – looked like a hamster.

'Is this your first cruise?' said Gerry to Vernon.

'No, it's our forty-eighth,' said Vernon, closing down Gerry's chance to brag about his thirty-two. 'We're late starters, Doreen and I, so we thought *Caveat Emptor,* as the Romans used to say. *You're only here once.*'

He's got that wrong, thought Pete, but Vernon said it with such conviction that Pete wondered if it was actually the Romans who'd had it wrong all this time.

'Must be a lot of money in fish and chips,' said Sylvia with a haughty trill of laughter.

'And peas,' said Vernon. 'Best mushy peas in the country.'

Pete liked Vernon and Doreen from the off. Not so much the Gerry trio.

'And what do you do for a living?' asked Sylvia, shifting her attention to Pete and Nigel.

'I'm a retired joiner,' said Nigel, answering for them. 'Pete's a fireman.'

Nigel would swear later that it was at this point he heard Susan's pants hitting the floor. She looked like a woman who had never been kissed, never even seen a pair of lips puckered in her direction but who dreamed every night of being carried off and ravaged by Jason Momoa.

'Very noble profession, fighting fire,' said Gerry, chest puffing in anticipation of delivering his next words. 'I was a tax investigative officer and so was Sylvia.'

'Ah, snoops, you mean,' said Vernon, enjoying goading this fleshy toad of a man. This particular comment set Gerry's trio of chins wobbling for all they were worth.

'Fraud costs the decent taxpayers a lot of money,' said Gerry. 'My beautiful daughter has followed firmly in my footsteps.'

'How many daughters have you got?' asked Vernon, looking confused.

'Just the one,' said Gerry.

'Oh, I see,' said Vernon. 'You mean this daughter then?'

The waiter rescued the situation by arriving to take their order.

'So did you catch a lot of people dodging taxes?' asked Doreen.

'Gerry holds the record for most prosecutions,' said Sylvia proudly. 'Quite a few from Yorkshire.'

This seemed to tickle her husband and daughter.

'Loads of cash sales in fish and chips,' said Vernon, giving Pete a sly wink. 'You wouldn't have caught any of us. We're like the Scarlet Pimpernels to your Maurice Chevaliers I bet.'

Gerry, Sylvia and Susan didn't engage in any conversation with anyone else at the table after that and mumbled a goodnight after the main course.

'We'll not see them again,' announced Vernon. '*Ars longa, vita brevis.*' He tapped the side of his nose and smiled fondly at his wife.

'What does that phrase mean?' asked Nigel.

'Bloody arseholes,' replied Vernon.

Pete thought that he just might have made the right call changing his holiday plans after all.

Chapter 61

9 February

Laurie had read a poem about cruising once which began, *On the third day out I get it.* And she had. She'd felt like a spare sandwich at a picnic the first full day of her holiday, mooching around the ship not quite sure what to do with herself, killing time until dinner when at least she could hook up with the friendly people on the dinner table. But on the third day, it was as if she fell into the rhythm of the ship, of the passengers, of the sea. She strolled around the perimeter of the outside deck taking in the bracing wind, until it became too much and icicles started forming on her lungs, then snuggled into one of the padded armchairs in the coffee lounge with her book and had a hot chocolate which came with an Alp of marshmallows piled on top of it. The man on the next table laughed when it arrived.

'I don't know whether to drink it or climb it,' she commented.

'I think you've tempted me to have one of those,' he said and waved a waiter over. 'This your first cruise?' he asked her, because it seemed to be obligatory to ask this to anyone with whom one fell into conversation.

'Yes,' she replied. 'You?'

'Yep. I'm taking a trip with my lad. He's having a nap at the moment. The sea air has knocked him out.'

'And why not if he's on holiday,' said Laurie, thinking how lovely it must be to have a parent you would enjoy a trip like this with. She would never dream of holidaying with her mother, who would have instantly gone on the prowl for either a rich, old male passenger with a dodgy ticker or a young one with a pulse.

'What about you? Are you travelling with husband? Family?'

'No, just me.'

'I was going to come alone too,' said Nigel. 'It wouldn't have bothered me but my son decided to grace me with his presence. Anyway, I'll not disturb your reading.' He held up his Jack Reacher tome. 'I'm just at a good bit myself.'

Later in the cabin, Nigel Moore would tell his son, 'I've seen a lovely young blonde woman in that bar downstairs who's travelling alone. You should nip down and see if she's still there.'

Pete replied that he was okay, thanks. He was on a cruise to get away from life's complications, not to sail into them.

On the dinner table that night, Doreen and Vernon had them creased up with laughter about all the people they'd met on their many cruises and the nicknames they'd attributed to them. The Maurice Chevaliers had been added to their long list.

'Now Camper Van was a particular favourite of ours,' said Vernon. 'Doreen and I used to take bets on how many times he would say the words "camper van" through dinner. The nearest to it paid for the ice-creams at the next port. I knew every inch of that camper van by the end of the cruise. I could have changed all four of its wheels in my sleep.'

'What about Hair and Mouth?' said Doreen, lifting up her glasses to wipe the tears from her eyes. Nigel and Pete never did get to find out what was so funny about Hair and Mouth because the Turbots couldn't stop giggling for long enough to tell them.

'Are you getting off at Åndalsnes tomorrow?' asked Doreen when she had eventually got a grip of herself. 'We're on the Scenic Train trip looking for trolls.' She grinned excitedly at the thought.

'*Romani ite domum*,' said Vernon, with absolute certainty in his terrible Latin. 'When in Rome, do as the Romans do.'

'We're going on a bus up some mountains,' said Nigel. 'Lots of hairpin bends on the roads, I hear.' He rubbed his hands together with glee. 'I've become a bit of a thrill-seeker in my old age,' he said. 'I even went to bingo this afternoon.'

Pete looked around the room at all the people in couples and felt suddenly very alone. Not that it wasn't great here with his dad, but it would have been good to share this wonderful camaraderie and food with a loved one. There was nothing like being surrounded by an ocean of happiness to make you feel like a lost island in the middle of it all.

Chapter 62

11 February

On the fifth day Laurie was hit with the full slam of sea-sickness. The ship had entered the Arctic Circle and the winds were recorded as force eleven. She had had no idea that it could be so bad, there seemed to be no escape from it. She'd been given a tip – again from Alan – to look at the horizon if she felt nauseous, so she hauled herself over to the window, but seeing the ten-metre swells, *feeling* the ten-metre swells, and watching all the spray hitting the glass, she thought that, on this occasion, his best advice fell short. Up until that day, travelling on board the *Mermaidia* had felt like being in a giant cradle and she'd slept like a baby. Today, it was like being strapped into a white-knuckle ride at a theme park – something which she hated. Especially one that seemed interminable. She thought a walk around the ship might help, but it didn't. She barely had the strength to talk to Olive whom she met near the shops so she made her way back to the sanctuary of her cabin and face-planted onto the bed. She hadn't slept as much for years. She needed it, her body told her. She needed to let go of everything and rest and let the sea and the Nordic air work its magic.

In their cabin at the other side of the ship, Pete was experiencing much of the same.

'You'll feel much better if you venture out and come and sit in the coffee place,' said Nigel, who was remarkably unaffected by the sea swells.

'Don't even say the C-word,' said Pete, mumbling into his pillow. 'Or the sea word. In fact don't say any words, Dad. Just go and do your afternoon quiz with the Turbots, leave me in peace and remind me never ever to come on a cruise with you again.'

'This is just a momentary blip. The comforting thought is that if the ship sinks, the sea is so cold, we wouldn't suffer long.'

'And that's your idea of making me feel better is it?' groaned Pete.

'Trust me, you'll be thanking me in no time at all.'

'I'd put my life savings on that not being the case,' said Pete.

It was a good job that his father never took him up on the bet.

*

Ven O'Shaughnessy, the captain's wife, knocked gently on Laurie's door and stood patiently outside waiting for her to answer.

'Oh my life, you look like death not warmed up one little bit,' she said when Laurie opened up looking creased, and as pale as her complimentary bathrobe. 'I thought as a first timer you just might be feeling a bit off, especially as Olive said you didn't look that bright earlier on. It's quite rough out there today so I came to see if you wanted me to take you down to the medical bay for an injection. They really do work. You'll sleep and then you spring awake, eat lots of bread and feel great. That's what happened to me anyway.'

Laurie, too ill to even feel embarrassed that she was lumbering alongside Ven like a half-dead monster from a horror film, allowed herself to be directed to the onboard doctor. Ven stayed with her and after the painless injection in her buttock, she saw her safely returned to her cabin.

'This is so kind of you, Ven,' said Laurie, flopping back into bed.

'I'll see you for dinner,' came the reply. 'You'll be fine now, honestly. I'll put the card in your door saying you aren't to be disturbed.' Laurie was already half-asleep by the time she exited softly.

The ship continued to rock and roll but at six-thirty Laurie sauntered into the restaurant as if she cared not a jot, and ate a lot of bread.

'Well, you look better than you did earlier,' said Olive.

'Told you it would work,' said Ven.

'Has the euphoria side effect hit you yet?' said Roz.

Laurie smiled. She couldn't remember feeling this free and relaxed in a long time. Adrift in the middle of the sea, away from the usually horrible world news, away from even knowing or caring what day it was, free from the dictates of clocks and calendars with gentle, kind company on tap. She'd have to leave this fabulous bubble in a week but for now, she would relish every moment.

'Do you know, I think it has, Roz,' she replied.

*

'Doreen and I never get seasick,' said Vernon at the dinner table that night. 'If we feel the slightest bit nauseous, we retire to our cabins and make the ship rock a little more, if you know what I mean.' He winked at his male dinner companions. '*Vice versa*. Never be averse to vice.'

'Vernon Turbot, you'll have me blushing,' said Doreen with a hoot of laughter.

Both Nigel and Pete smiled. The Turbots were not only the funniest couple they'd met in years, but gave them hope that love was a butterfly that could settle on any age of flower.

Pete thought he'd seen Laurie that day. He'd been persuaded by his father to leave the confines of the cabin and line his stomach and he saw a slim, blonde woman rising up in one of the glass lifts. She was in his eyesight for two seconds at most and yet his eyes had scooped her up and sent his mind into a tailspin.

Even though he knew she was with someone else, it hadn't stopped his heart from wanting her. Like a spoilt child it continued to yearn. And, like a worn-down parent, he had run out of words to convince it why it couldn't have what it desired most.

Chapter 63

13 February

The ship was now cruising in calm, sheltered waters towards Alta. Today Laurie hadn't done much at all and it had been marvellous, because she never did nothing and she realised she needed to do it a lot more. Yesterday she'd been husky sledding in Tromsø, and had shrieked with delight as she bumped over the snow at top speed although she'd realised why so many seasoned passengers had brought a cushion with them, as the ride was rather rough on the bottom. Then she'd stroked the dogs who were licky and giddy and loved affection and played with the baby pups before thawing out around a fire, drinking hot chocolate and eating the cake that Norwegians seemed to be so fond of and baked so fabulously. She didn't mind the cold at all though. Nor did she mind not recognising anyone who was on the trip, because she didn't feel the least bit lonely or sad, just happy and bright that she was here in this glorious place where the air felt pure and clean in her lungs.

Today she'd rested, read her book, had her customary hot

chocolate in the coffee bar. She'd waved over at the man whom she'd met there the other day who said he was travelling with his son. He pointed to his own hot chocolate, piled high with marshmallows and then gave her a thumbs up and she laughed. She was so glad that she'd booked this cruise, paid the full amount, not given herself the chance to back out. It was like an ice-pack on her soul. She'd felt herself healing with every roll of the waves. Felt she was coming back to herself.

It was a formal dress code that night so Laurie put on her new dark blue velvet dress studded with tiny rhinestones, reminiscent of a starry night sky, a matching velvet stole draped over her shoulders. She put her hair up, decided it made her look too starchy, let it down again.

'Oh my, you look pretty tonight,' said Bunty, as Laurie took her place at the dinner table. 'Like a Nordic princess.'

Laurie blushed. She'd never liked being the centre of attention.

'More importantly, you look ... serene,' said Frankie, searching for the right word. 'Yep, that's it. Totally relaxed.'

'I've had the most wonderful day,' Laurie replied.

'Ooh, what have you done?' asked Don.

'Absolutely nothing,' replied Laurie which made them all laugh.

The captain was dining with them that evening. He was such an attractive, friendly man with an Irish accent to die for.

'I'll be honest,' Ven confided to Laurie, 'I thought I was done with fellas and destined for a life of singledom. But life is full of magic and surprises. If you'd seen us lot eleven years ago, we were all living such different lives; smaller, unhappier lives.' She smiled at Laurie. The smile of a woman who was both contented and loved. 'I shall pray tonight that you see the lights tomorrow, Laurie and that they bring some magic for you.'

'Me too,' said Laurie. Like so many things in life, seeing the lights would be a privilege, not a right, so she was prepared for them being a no-show. All she could do was hope.

'So, are you two ready for tomorrow then?' Doreen asked, as she ripped into her second bread roll and dunked it into her cullen skink.

'I'm very excited,' Nigel answered, running his finger around the inside of his collar because his new shirt was rubbing his neck. Not that he minded. He thought he could quite get used to strutting around in a tuxedo and was definitely booking another cruise before he got off this one. 'But I've resigned myself to the fact that if I don't see the lights, I don't see the lights.'

'*Morituri te salutant,*' said Vernon, nodding wisely. '*If it's meant to be, it's meant to be.*' Vernon was wearing a bow tie that had a fish and chip design on it. He'd had it made especially, he'd told them. He was very proud of the business that had made his money for him and revered it openly at every opportunity.

'You'll have a lovely time anyway, whether you see them or not,' said Doreen mid-soup. 'Just make sure you leave room in your stomach for the cake and hot chocolate. The Norwegians love to serve plenty up.'

'I think I'm going to move here,' said Nigel.

'Good,' said Pete. 'Because if I hear one more rendition of that "Northern Lights" song I'll scream enough to cause an avalanche.'

'There's an annoying amount of cloud cover,' said

Vernon, looking through the restaurant window. 'Sometimes you can see them from the ship, you know, as there isn't a lot of light pollution around these parts. Go and take a gander on the top deck later, luck just might be on your side.'

'We might well do that,' said Nigel. 'Although there's a tribute to the Rat Pack on in the theatre and then a late night film, *John Wick*. I've heard it's very good.'

It was as if something had grabbed Pete by the scruff of his wing collar and propelled him backwards through a wormhole to the cinema in Barnsley town centre, seeing Laurie there and his heartbeat quickening in response. Then sitting in the seat beside her, both of them dipping into their cartons of popcorn, eyes turned to the screen, but constantly aware that she was at his side, close. Why didn't life have a rewind button? He would have pressed it, never sent that goodbye and good luck text, never let her go.

'Your mother would have loved this,' said Nigel, as all four of them filed off together towards the theatre after dinner, the men in their tuxedos and bow ties, Doreen in a shimmering turquoise frock that gave her the look of a portly mermaid. 'But I shouldn't be scared of coming by myself in the future. In a way, I feel like she's here with me.'

'If life has taught me and Vernon anything,' said Doreen, who turned, having heard him, 'it's that you shouldn't waste time being frightened. You should embrace life and take chances. That's why we're going snowmobiling tomorrow morning. For what the extra insurance has cost us, we could have bought a Norwegian hotel, but we fancied it, so we're doing it.'

'*Carpe diem*,' said Vernon. '*Seize the day*, my friend.'

For once, he'd hit it right on the mark.

*

Laurie had been to see the lady violinist perform, a lovely restful way to end a lazy day, and was just on her way to her cabin when she noticed that *John Wick* was playing in the onboard cinema and her mind sparked into activity. She thought of that wonderful evening back in Barnsley, feeling the current of electricity that arced between herself and Pete as they sat in a comfortable silence watching the film, eating popcorn, and she knew he had felt it too.

In the lift she should have pressed the number of her floor, but something instead made her choose the number for the top of the ship. It was understandably deserted when she pushed open the door and walked out on deck. It was nearly twelve o'clock and of those who hadn't gone to bed, none of them wanted to be frozen, especially not in their best attire.

What had surprised her about this holiday was how the simple sight of the sea acted like a soothing medicine on her brain. It was so vast, so large and deep, full of secrets and treasures and it was as if it was allowing them to bear witness to how great a force it was in return for their respect. She could stare at it for ages, letting it work its alchemy on her, flowing into her mind, ripping out thoughts she didn't want to be there in its long ebb, casting them far away.

'Why did you lead me here, Alex?' she said quietly into the pure Norwegian evening air. 'Because I know you did.'

Her eyes framed a beautiful nightscape: the shine of the moon, cast on the waves in handfuls of sprinkles and in the distance, the mountains were darker presses of shadow frosted with snow that appeared blue in this midnight world. Laurie felt truly at peace with herself. After everything she had been through, she was here, still standing. She pulled her stole tighter around her shoulders as a shiver rippled through her.

It was then that she heard a voice that seemed to come from nowhere.

'Laurie?'

She thought she had imagined it, until she turned and saw him there, walking towards her. Pete Moore.

Chapter 64

February, the previous year

'My sister is infatuated with my husband,' she said, as she put on her coat. 'If I thought they were a good match, I'd encourage them to get together after all this. But it's not love. She's like me. And he's too good for another one of me.'

He smiled, but his heart was heavy. He wanted this woman standing in front of him so desperately that he was throwing away so much for her. A beautiful girl, a kind, sweet, gentle person. He didn't want to cause her pain, he loved her. He wished she was enough, wished he could atone for what he was about to do to her.

As if she read his thoughts, she said, 'I've always been a selfish cow, not stopping to get what I want, but I will do my damnedest to make Pete happier without me than with me. If you changed your mind and said that you wanted to stay with Laurie, I'd let you go. That's how much I love you.'

Alex opened the door, saw the first snow drops drift down. A cold eel snaked down his spine and he shuddered. A sense of fore-boding or anticipation, he couldn't tell which. He turned to her, held her, kissed her softly. 'Don't let me go, ever. But yes, let's both make sure that Laurie and Pete are okay. Whatever we have to do, let's make that happen.'

'Drive safely, darling,' said Tara, and she climbed into her car.

Chapter 65

13 February

Pete couldn't believe his eyes. He *really* couldn't. This was *Twilight Zone* stuff. He had gone up on deck, marvelling at how on a ship with over two thousand passengers, there was no one else around but him, letting himself absorb the quiet of the night, the peace.

There were no lights dancing in the skies, no stars; the clouds had snuffed them out, wisps drifting across the slim moon. He thought back to leaving Firenze that night in October and of looking up to see the same crescent of moon, feeling different, feeling shoots of hope and joy begin to quicken inside him, new life. All roads led back to her and how he felt about her, how she had made him feel about himself: a man reconstituted.

He had walked around to the other side of the ship, had seen the twinkle of lights on her dress before he noticed the wearer. Before he saw *her*. An illusion. It couldn't be her but neither could it be anyone else, not from the way his heart seemed to stop, then start again, its rhythm growing apace. *Laurie.*

*

She'd drunk too much wine at dinner, it was the only explanation. Except that it wasn't an explanation at all because he *was* standing there, in a black tuxedo, white shirt, black bow tie.

They both opened their mouths at the same time. They both apologised, both starting speaking again.

'Laurie, it's so good to see you,' said Pete, his voice filled with disbelief and genuine delight. She was so beautiful, the breeze fluttering her silver-gold hair, moonlight shining in her lovely eyes. His hands came out to touch her, dropped back to his sides, failing in bravery.

'And you. My, this is . . . madness,' she said, shock reducing her voice to a mere breath.

'What are you doing here? . . . Sorry, that's a stupid question,' he said. 'The same as everyone else on the ship.'

'Yep, just one of many hoping to see the Northern Lights.'

He was keeping his distance, she noticed and she took her cue from him on that. A distance that was full of something she didn't know or understand but she felt it as clearly as if it was a brick wall standing between them.

'When I was a kid once, we all went to this little village in Spain that no one had heard of as a break from the neighbours and lo and behold they were in the same hotel,' Pete said. *She must be here with the man he had handed the flowers to.* It was a Valentine's cruise, of course she was.

'I've heard stories like that too,' said Laurie.

'How are you, Laurie?' He wanted to close his arms around her, but the moment when he could have, even in platonic greeting, had passed.

'I'm okay. Are you?'

'I am. Are you? Sorry, you've just said . . . you're okay, you said.'

They both smiled. They both wanted to cross the divide, but neither dared.

'Did you drive down to Southampton?' she asked. A banal question, because her brain had frozen and it was all she could come up with. He looked so ridiculously handsome. The sort of handsome that the eyes register and then pass on to every other part of the body for it to appreciate too. He'd dressed for someone, made himself smart for a woman.

'Yeah, we drove down. You?'

We, he said *we*. Something nipped her heart hard. Something that felt worse than the seasickness she had endured the other day.

'Bus.' Her throat felt suddenly dry.

'We didn't think of that until it was too late. Next time.'

That *we* again. She should go. It was easy to miss bumping into people on a ship. They tended to move in orbits, she'd noticed. He hadn't been in hers, until then. She didn't want to see him again. She didn't want to see him with someone. Someone who wasn't her.

'Amazing how we're the only two people out here, isn't it?' he said.

Alone together, but not together.

'Yes. Though it is very cold tonight.'

'Not much of a moon.'

They were talking like Russian spies conversing in code, he thought. *The Norwegian sky is dark is it not, Pyotr Muratov?*

'Well, I hope you enjoy the rest of your cruise,' she said. She had to go. She couldn't bear to be this close to him, and yet so far away. She wondered again if he knew about Tara and Alex. Wondered if this was what had torn them apart, put them on different roads, to meet other people with less complicated backgrounds.

'And you.'

He bent, he had to, he needed to touch her, this woman he wanted so much, who belonged to someone else. He kissed her cheek. The lovely scent of her hair, her skin, her perfume entered his nostrils and found a part of his brain that both sighed and felt desperately sad at the same time.

Chapter 66

14 February

Laurie attended a theatre presentation the next afternoon explaining the phenomenon and folklore of the Northern Lights. The Norwegian head of the tour, who looked exactly like Ranulph Fiennes, warned that they all had to respect the lights if they made an appearance. They weren't to be whistled at or mocked because this could make them reach down and carry you off, he said with relish, making everyone laugh. Everyone but Laurie. Some people believed the lights were party beacons of gods celebrating, or reflections from the shields of the Valkyries. Some, that they were a bridge connecting the afterlife to the realm of mortals, a place where the membrane between this world and the next was at its thinnest, where the souls gathered in the colours of the skies hoping to see their loved ones again.

Laurie tried not to scan the room for Pete. The theatre was huge, however, and she didn't see him, but she was convinced he must be in there somewhere. She hadn't been able to shake him from her mind since meeting him again on the top deck and it had taken her ages to get to sleep afterwards. She replayed his kiss on her cheek over and over like a stuck record, but there was no meaning to read into it. It was a kiss of politeness, a kiss that said hello and goodbye at the same time. But still she thought of it over and over, tried to pause the moment when his lips made contact with her skin.

Knowing he was here on board had killed her enjoyment of the holiday. She wished she could fly home. She was on edge now, waiting for him to turn up around any corner holding hands, laughing with a woman. If Alex had led her here for that purpose, it was a cruel joke. She gave herself a mental shake, *What was she thinking?* He wouldn't have. In any case, Alex was gone, this was coincidence, pure and simple. She needed to pull herself together and not let it spoil what she had paid an arm and a leg to see.

There were four buses full of people going on 'the hunt'. Laurie sat with Olive, who was delightful company. She hadn't been away from her little boy and girl before and, although they were in superb hands with her husband and his huge Greek family in Cephalonia, she was missing them and told Laurie all about them.

'That big love, if you know what I mean, was the kind of thing that happened to other people, not me. Until it did,' said Olive. 'I always believed in some magic in life after that. It couldn't have been coincidence. If anything it made me believe less in coincidence and more in magic,' and she laughed.

'I met someone I know on the ship late last night, some-one from home,' Laurie burst out, even though she'd sworn to herself that she wasn't going to talk about him, think about him. She might as well have sworn that she wasn't going to breathe.

'Someone?' Olive angled for more details.

'Someone that I once really liked.' *Someone I fell in love with.*

'Happens all the time, Ven says. She saw my ex-mother-in-law on board once. She isn't a woman to easily mistake.' Olive smiled softly. 'I'd quite like to run into her, which sounds odd. Not sure she'd recognise me though, I'm a different person to how I was then. Funny isn't it how one lifetime can encompass so many phases and changes. It's like a book full of short stories, except now I'm quite happy being in a long romantic novel.' Olive pulled out her phone, showed Laurie her family: her twins, her good-looking stepson, her very good-looking husband. 'Once upon a time I was Mrs Olive Hardcastle, cleaner, slave and wilted weed. Now I'm a flourishing olive tree, I own land, property, I'm blissfully happy and my life is flooded with sunshine. Trust me, Laurie, if it can happen to me, it can happen to anyone.'

Norwegian Ranulph Fiennes had decided that the best place to find the lights would be in a camp two hours drive away. Laurie enjoyed looking out of the bus window, snatching fleeting glimpses of the cosy interiors of Norwegian houses dotted on slopes and in settlement clusters. She imagined being inside one of them, in a toasty warm lounge with fat squashy sofas and furry rugs, viewing the vast expanse of ink-dark sky through the window like a framed oil painting.

The Norwegian bus driver was well used to the snowy roads that cut through the mountains. But then snow was part and parcel of life here; no one's life fell to pieces for a few inches of it.

Finally the coach deposited them outside a field with a big log cabin, three teepee-style tents, large burning camp fires and benches covered with thick furry pelts set around them. There were two white husky dogs with coats as dense as sheepskin rugs, one lying in the snow, the other plodding around enjoying the petting and fuss. An oasis of civilisation and comfort in a deserted landscape of snow, mountains and sky.

The clouds had started to thin, a perfect smile of moon visible now.

Laurie followed Frankie and Roz into the log cabin where they sat near a crackling fire, helping themselves to the most delicious sweet hot chocolate and moist lemon sponge. It was seductively inviting in there, but she didn't want to miss the lights if they made an appearance.

'I think I'll have a wander outside,' she told the others.

'We'll be out as soon as we've finished,' said Roz, who was on her third piece of cake – chocolate this time. The Norwegians really knew how to bake, everyone was in full agreement on that one.

The camp was full of happy, expectant people of all ages though the smiles they wore were like the smiles of children waiting excitedly outside Santa's grotto. There was an sparkly anticipation that filled the air like the run up to Christmas aided and abetted by the vast expanse of soft, powdery snow that extended far beyond what the eye could see, and was so much different to the slushy stuff they were all used to.

On her way out of the cabin, Laurie's path crossed with the man she'd seen in the coffee shop a couple of times.

'Well hello again,' he said. 'I might have known you'd gravitate to the hot chocolate. That's where I'm heading now.'

'It's very nice,' said Laurie and held up her cup. 'This is my second. Just the thing to keep you warm. And probably fat.'

The man chuckled. 'I think hot chocolate counts as medicine to keep you alive in these temperatures. It's minus twenty degrees tonight, my son tells me. He's sitting on that bench over there.'

He pointed towards a figure sitting on a thick pelt on a bench, gazing up at the sky.

'That's your son?' she asked. Even with a furry trooper hat on and a huge coat, she could recognise his beloved shape.

We, he'd said. She'd presumed it was a woman.

'You're here with him?' Laurie asked, swallowing.

'Aye. That's my son Pete. We're taking a father and son trip. If we don't see these Northern Lights, he's going to give me some proper earache for convincing him that this would be a better option than going to Italy on his tod. I'm just going in for supplies and then I'll introduce you if you like. I've spoken enough about you to him. He'll murder me for telling you that he's single . . .' Laurie didn't hear any more. Her heart was swelling in her breast, its beat drowning out his words, drowning out the world.

There were twenty-eight steps to the bench exactly. Laurie knew this because she counted every one.

He saw her when she was ten steps away from him. Something shifted his attention from the skies to his side.

'Laurie.'

'Hello Pete.'

'Hello.'

'You came here with your dad?' Her voice was as shaky as the rest of her.

'Yes. How . . .'

'I keep meeting him in the coffee shop.'

'You're the ... the hot chocolate woman. The one travelling by herself?'

'Yes. That's me. The lone traveller. The hot chocolate woman.'

Laurie sat down on the bench beside him before she fell. Their arms were touching, just like that night in the cinema. She'd sat too close, but she couldn't move, didn't want to move.

Pete felt a low current tremble through his whole body, and it was nothing to do with the cold. *God in heaven, where to begin?* There was no gentle slope down into the pool of words. He just had to dive headfirst into them. Say everything without censor or cut.

'I'm so sorry. I'm sorry for everything. I'm sorry for just running away from you like that, I'm sorry for behaving like a selfish, cowardly idiot. I'm making no excuses. I ... I found out that my wife was in love with someone else when she died. I think she was going to tell me she was leaving me for him ... that night.'

Tell her everything. Give her the chance to run – or stay.

'The baby couldn't have been mine. I found out I can't have kids, Laurie.'

He steeled himself for her reaction, felt her press ever so slightly closer to him and a honeyed warmth flooded his chest.

So he knew, thought Laurie. But did he know it all? What the hell did it matter? She wasn't going to lose him again. They'd work it out somehow. As Alan Robertson's dear old great gran, God rest her soul, used to say, among her other adages, *Life is here and now – live it or miss it.* And she wasn't going to miss any more.

'I found out that Alex was going to leave me too. That

night,' said Laurie. 'The engagement ring wasn't for me. It was for someone he'd found who made him happier than I ever could.'

So she knew, thought Pete. His arm shifted position, moved behind her so that she felt the wonderful weight of his gloved hand as it came to rest on her shoulder. He turned to her and that word came to his mind: *apricity*. His mother's word. This was what apricity was, then. It was minus twenty degrees, the moon was out and yet he felt as if his face were lit with sunshine.

'My beautiful Laurie.' Her lips were dusted with chocolate and cake. She tasted how home felt. He would never let her go again.

A sudden rush, shouts, shrieks as people spilled out of the tents and the log cabin, heads tilted to the skies where grey wisps were billowing to greens, deepening to pinks. The Northern Lights spread like arms, embracing the earth, reflected for a moment or two in all their shimmering wonder. The solar winds had brought them here, or something else that defied reason and science. They suffused the sky with colour and then faded as suddenly as they had appeared. A glimpse into a world beyond where two souls, among many, were smiling down. Their job done.

One True North

Pilgrims for love, they had travelled alone
On separate journeys, crossing foreign seas,
No compass to guide, no magnetic stone,
Just the stars' chilly glimmer in the dark skies.
Hearts were at low ebb, there were many storms,
Searching the unknown with a taper light,
Nothing to hang their hopes upon, only dreams,
Adrift and shaken in an endless night.
Then the sight of warmth in another's eyes
Was their landfall; the promise of a home,
A miracle of finding, no disguise.
The breath of new love, and no longer alone.
Pilgrims for love, finding the beauty and worth
Of becoming each other's one true north.

JAMES NASH

Acknowledgements

As always thank you to a brilliantly supportive cast behind the scenes who do so much to guide, promote, make me look as if I know what I'm doing. Ian, Suzanne, SJ, Hayley, Gill, Joe, Jess, Rich, Louise, Alice, Maddie, Dom, Clare. You have grown around me like a family and I'm so very fond of you all. This does not mean I'm up for donating any organs.

Thank you to the title queen Jo Dickinson who brought out the best in me, a wonderful lady to work alongside and bounce ideas off. A springboard in human form – you have given me many a seed to grow into a book. No longer my editor but always my friend.

To my fabulous agent Lizzy Kremer who consistently has my back. I consider myself very lucky to have you. And thank you to the team back at David Higham HQ – calm ducks on the pond, legs paddling furiously under the water line.

To my copyeditor Sally Partington. I say this every time because it's true, I LOVE working with you, though I know I drive you bats. You're a writer's must-have and I hope everyone who writes has the equivalent of a Sally. If I could bottle you and sell you, I'd make more money than I do writing books.

Thank you to Emma, Annabelle and everyone else at ED PR. You've made such a difference to my writing life, please can I keep you. And Annabelle always makes sure I've been to the loo before I leave a venue, you can't buy that level of care and consideration.

Once upon a time a little dot of a girl went to school with my son and now she is studying Medical Genetics at university in Sheffield so she helped me enormously with the details of writing this. Dear Lucy Frost, thank you so much. I hope you are so very successful in your chosen career because you deserve to be. My best wishes and my love to you.

Thank you to James Lock who also helped me too with all the complicated genetic stuff. As authors we always have to know far more than we use to give us an overall picture; fascinating stuff that I needed to get spot on. All mistakes are mine.

Thank you to David Camp of Barnsley fire service, Ms Helena Rooke of Penistone fire service and Mr Robin Giles. All firefighters who were essential for the details in the book. They were so very kind in giving me their time and help. Here's hoping I listened hard enough to replicate everything you told me correctly.

Thank you to Andrew Harrod the editor at the Barnsley Chronicle for his help and guidance in matters journalistic. The *Daily Trumpet* is not based on them, even though I did use Andrew's expert knowledge of the newspaper industry and Andrew's Great Gran (God rest her soul) was very helpful in supplying philosophies.

Thank you to Stu my website designer who must dread the words, 'Stuuuu … I've got a new book out, can you redesign everything again please?' He's a marvel – I highly recommend his services. Tell him I sent you if you contact him. He won't give you a discount, he'll run off screaming. I'm joking. Really, he's the best. You can find him at www.nm4s.com.

To my new friend, fellow novelist, politician and the best raconteur (give or take Peter Ustinov) Alan Johnson for introducing me to that lovely word 'apricity'. Also 'unbepissed' which I was desperate to use, but I'll save that for another novel.

To my legal eagle Mr David Gordon of BCG Business Plus and the Robin to his Batman Mrs Mary Smith. Thank you as always for your keen insight into matters about which I know bugger all.

Thank you to my wonderful friend and incredibly talented poet James Nash who blows me away with his beautiful writing and I *needed* him to write me the closing poem for this book – it was a total no-brainer. You can find out more about James and his workshops at www.jamesnash. co.uk. Read his poetry. His books are on Amazon.

I am a proud patron of Yorkshire Cat Rescue (https:// yorkshirecatrescue.org) hence why there is a rehoming thread in this story. I've also written a book of poetry called *A Cat-Shaped Space*, available from my website (shipping worldwide) or on Kindle on Amazon and the charity receives all the profits. Having just adopted an ancient Siamese cat, let me tell you that the old boys and girls are as cute and loving as the kittens. Roysley Animal Shelter is based on our local Royston Animal Welfare (roystonanimalwelfare.org) who rehome other animals as well as cats.

Do remember that your local animal shelters are always on the look-out for raffle prizes, old towels and sheets as well as the obvious monetary donations.

I could have written this book without going on a cruise to Norway, but it wouldn't have been the same. And I did need my characters to have a week on board ship before the Hunt for the Northern Lights night as I wanted to write about it with authority. And what a trip it was. I fell in love with cruising when the kids were little and I've been on many since and had quite a few adventures aboard. I was lucky enough to see the Northern Lights and really, we all sat on the bus back to the ship feeling quite euphoric. Go in winter on a ship, it'll be rough and cold but my goodness it's fabulous (and the Norwegian cake and hot chocolate is a fabulous combo!). The sea is an untamed beast but it's a beautiful one and sailing to Norway, for me, is the only way to do it. And yes, the snow really is different up there and the air is premier cru. I'd like to thank Michele Andjel of P & O Cruises for her friendship and her support and help and warm onboard welcomes. I love the Britishness of P & O ships, I feel at home, just enough going on to entertain me but they also let my head rest in quiet corners with gigantic hot chocolates. If that sounds like a sales pitch, it's probably because it is – an unashamed one. I never endorse things I don't wholeheartedly believe in and their ships are little pieces of heaven on earth for me and that's what I tell everyone.

Thank you to my mates – the writing ones and the non-writing ones who keep me sane and insane in equal measures (personally I think insanity has far more going for it). Especially the inimitable Debbie Johnson who has got me through some proper storms this year.

Thank you to all my lovely readers who write me letters and spread the word and keep me in the game for writers are nothing without readers. You are my in-breath and I'm so grateful to each and every one of you.

And last but by no means least, a huge thank you to my family, who give me half my flipping material. I could not exist without them, nor would I want to. Especially Pete, my own true north who works like a mad behind-the-scenes director to make sure our home life runs smoothly whilst I'm trying to bash out a bestseller. Never did a man make as many coffees for a woman in the history of mankind.

During the writing of this book my father passed away and I find myself with the unenviable task of having to negotiate the path of grief that my characters in this book tread, which is a surreal experience and I know I'm in for a force twelve ride. I am indebted to him for so many things, too many and personal to list. But life really is here and now. Deliver those outstanding thank yous, see old friends and savour those you value. I feel blessed to have had such a smashing dad and that I could say 'I love you' to him and he could say it to me before he left us, even though we didn't do slop and it felt bloody daft at the time. We all need to say it and hear it more in life.

booksandthecity.co.uk
the home of female fiction

BOOKS | NEWS & EVENTS | FEATURES | AUTHOR PODCASTS | COMPETITIONS

Follow us online to be the first to hear from your favourite authors

booksandthecity.co.uk

books and the city

@TeamBATC

Join our mailing list for the latest news, events and exclusive competitions

Sign up at
booksandthecity.co.uk